I0819573

WHAT WE ARE SEEKING

ALSO BY
CAMERON REED

NOVEL

The Fortunate Fall

SHORT FICTION

The Girl That My Mother Is Leaving Me For

'Congenital Agenesis of Gender Ideation' by K.N. Sirsi and Sandra Botkin

WHAT WE ARE SEEKING

CAMERON REED

TOR PUBLISHING GROUP
NEW YORK

This is a work of fiction. All of the names, characters, organizations, places, and events portrayed in this work are either products of the author's imagination or used fictitiously.

WHAT WE ARE SEEKING

A Tor Book
Published by Tom Doherty Associates / Tor Publishing Group
120 Broadway
New York, NY 10271

www.torpublishinggroup.com

Tor® is a registered trademark of Macmillan Publishing Group, LLC.

EU Representative: Macmillan Publishers Ireland Ltd, 1st Floor, The Liffey Trust Centre, 117–126 Sheriff Street Upper, Dublin 1, D01 YC43

The Library of Congress Cataloging-in-Publication Data is available upon request.

ISBN 978-1-250-36473-9 (hardcover)
ISBN 978-1-250-36474-6 (ebook)

First Edition: 2026

Printed in the United States of America

10 9 8 7 6 5 4 3 2 1

For Pamela, who held me fast

I would indeed that love were longer-lived,
And vows were not so brittle as they are,
But so it is, and nature has contrived
To struggle on without a break thus far,—
Whether or not we find what we are seeking
Is idle, biologically speaking.

—Edna St. Vincent Millay, *A Few Figs from Thistles*

CHAPTER ONE

On the Free Ship *Edgar's Folly*, traveling away from Essius at ninety-nine one hundredths of the speed of light, it was the last day of summer.

Tomorrow the ship's engines would begin to sing, and everything that floated now would fall. The aft walls would become floors. Corridors would be converted back to elevator shafts, and where now the ship-folk glided freely *back* and *forward* through the air, they would be carried *down* and *up* in closed chambers. The informality of summer would give way to rank and hierarchy, bright clothes would be exchanged for uniforms; and on the old bridge, after the harvest feast, the summer captain would be laid to rest beneath the stars.

Winter was coming early, and it would be a hard one: brief days at the gravity of lost Earth, long nights at twice as much. A message had come in, that was what everyone said; the ship would slow down just enough to send rescue. It was, they said, unprecedented. But if the sudden change of seasons had unsettled them, they were too busy to let it show. In one day the life of the ship, which had expanded into three dimensions in the summer, had to be compressed back into two. The toolbox fastened by a thin strip of elastic to a wall, the winter cookware webbed into a forward corner, the fish tank held by magnets to what soon would be a ceiling, each had to find a place where winter's gravity would let it rest. And, from all the hidden spaces of the ship where they were kept, the parts of beds were being brought out: beams of metal and planks of wood, and what the ship called mattresses—which did not mean cloth made fat with moss or windweed silk, but great deflated bladders to be filled with water as a cushion against gravity. The comfort of beds was an intense preoccupation with them, for those who stayed awake in summer felt the winter in their bones.

John Maraintha, who had been summoned to attend the captain and did not know why, kept to the edges and moved slowly. He had thought the ship's ventral corridor, being widest, would be his easiest way to the old bridge, but now he realized his mistake: this was tomorrow's cargo elevator, and everything unwieldy had to come through here. Up and down the shaft as far as he could see, ship-folk guiding or towing their burdens launched themselves on long diagonals, missing each other by instinct and the imperceptible communication of the space-born. They could all see each other's next move in the set of a hand on a guide track, the tension in a leg or shoulder. John, not fluent in that language, could only try to make his path predictable. He clutched his bag tight, wondering if he should have left it behind. Nothing could make it practical in summer—it would not hang from his shoulder properly, and he had to bind it to him with a piece of borrowed netting, making a cumbersome mass above his hip. But he might need the medicines contained in it, and anyway he liked to keep it with him, the only thing he had from home that mattered. The bag's body was only waxed canvas, but the strap was a length of his great-uncle's soul.

At the corridor's end the traffic thinned, and through the fore-most door he came into the last mess—which meant, the dining hall where everybody either ate or wished to eat. This level was not subdivided into rooms, so he could see how the outer wall curved in a full circle, as if the whole ship were a series of hollows carved into the trunk of some ancient tree. A ring of dim lights picked out tables and chairs snapped together in stacks and bolted to the floor, and the glass cases in which plants were reared, piled up in staggered courses like a brick wall.

A round hole in tomorrow's ceiling opened onto the old bridge: another undivided level, slightly smaller, capped by a glass dome that had once been full of stars. Over the winter the star field had contracted to a crowded circle at the center, and in summer it remained that way; this was a custom, but the purpose of it was obscure. Before the disc, like a long dark shadow, the captain floated. He was facing the dome, looking outward.

"Captain, you wanted to see me? Is it your knees again, sir?"

"Dr. Maraintha, you made it in one piece. No, this isn't a medical appointment. Come join me."

The captain turned, still hanging unconnected in the air, without needing to touch the dome behind him. John could reorient himself without a handhold if he had to, awkwardly, bending his legs and throwing out his arms, but he could never have turned like *that*—as neatly as a bird-worm, hanging from a single thread of silk, twists to wrap itself up in another. The captain in his native season had a perfect grace. He had been conceived at the beginning of a long summer, carried and borne in weightlessness. Such infants made their landfall into air looking the same as any, but their hearts could not bear winter and their bones would break in it.

As a boy the captain had rebelled against the painful therapies and poisons that might have let him walk on worlds. As a man he was exceptionally slender of both leg and arm, since his muscles never had to fight against the pull of gravity, only to nudge and guide and to adjust his course. He had the kind of skin so pale the blood shows through and gives a pinkish cast, and that too seemed a kind of frailty—though one would never have thought such a thing of his sister, in whom the same complexion suggested instead the endurance of bone. Nothing else distinguished him. He wore plain clothing in the clear bright dyes that everybody wore in summer, kept his hair in the usual short summer cut; he spoke as they did. And when he came into a room where ship-folk hung at every angle, all of them aligned to point their heads the same direction as his—like sleepwell flowers rising up to greet the sun.

John hung back, holding the edge of the aperture. He knew he shouldn't keep the captain waiting, but the dome of night deterred him. It was only an illusion, like a television screen; he couldn't really break through and be lost among the stars. But the smooth glass afforded no handholds. If he launched himself toward it he would undoubtedly bounce off.

The captain looked impatient for a moment; then understanding the problem, he beckoned. "Sail on over. I'll catch you."

John thought he should arrive in parallel with the captain, not hurtle headfirst toward him, so he lined himself up carefully and pushed off with both hands. The captain watched his slow approach and then moved with unhurried precision. One hand pressed flat against John's center—just below the navel and a little to the right, because the bag made his mass asymmetrical. The other touched the dome behind the captain's back to cancel his momentum. A brush of fingertips against his thigh and then his collarbone corrected a barely perceptible spin. John was left becalmed a little closer to the captain than he would have put himself, assuming the conversation to be only about daytime matters. Maybe, he thought, the captain just wanted to ask for a visit before his long sleep. He had thought he saw an interest on the captain's face before—when he first came to the ship, in that hybrid season when winter went down to the world and summer reigned above. His clumsiness in free fall at that time could not have been appealing, especially to one as delicate as the captain, and awe had rendered him too shy to make an approach himself. The moment had passed and nothing had come of it. But maybe the captain had only been throwing back the little fish till it had grown. Suspended at this intimate distance, and still aware of all the places that the captain's hand had touched, John would certainly not have refused.

"Have you been here before?" the captain asked.

"A few times, yes. In winter."

"Oh, well you'll excuse me if I don't remember."

He had first come up with several of the younger crew from Medical, who invited him, he thought, because to him their stories were new and the exaggerations in them undetectable. In that season the floor had been filled in with soil and carpeted with little hairlike leaves, pleasant to sit on; the stars above were still flung wide. Matthew Bray, who had lured them out in nighttime gravity by brandishing two bottles of a ship-made liquor known as reflux, led them to the dorsal side, where the summer captain lay in a long vat of steel. This device, essential to cold-sleep, was known as a coffin, in reference to the custom of putting the dead in close prisons and hiding them under the ground; thankfully, having no soil deep enough for a burial, the ship-folk themselves did not practice this horror. As the others settled in a ragged ring nearby, Bray poured a little of the reflux out into a cup and set it on top of the coffin. Nothing was said about this. When the drink and the stories were used up, and one by one they were all levering themselves up off the ground to go, he took back the glass and drained it with a quick apologetic shrug.

Now, in summer, the captain glanced down at the floor where his body would soon lie again. "My great-great-grandfather thought captains would like to hold a kind of court up here all day. Receive petitions, give commands . . . tell everyone their jobs, as if they don't already know them. Sounds tedious, don't you think? It's better as a park. But I still use it for its original purpose now and then."

John began to be seriously alarmed. Since he lacked a shipboard education and was not one of the crew, his responsibilities were limited. The captain had once hoped that Essian medicine might hold an answer to his chronic aches—the legacy of the attempt to make him able to stand gravity—and that had put them in each other's company for a time. Now John treated routine injuries and illnesses among the crew, helped with awakenings from cold-sleep when the seasons turned, sometimes advised the *Folly*'s scientists on the uses of Essian herbs they were testing for possible ship use. None of that should come to the attention of the captain unless something had gone very wrong. John tried to think of what he might have done. But the captain was speaking again.

"You've probably heard, we've unfrozen a translator."

"The Dharanendran? I heard of the awakening. I hadn't realized his profession."

"What, is the rumor mill out of service? You must at least know why I've called down winter—that colonists on Scythia have found some animal they're afraid may be intelligent."

"That much, yes. Though I had not heard of that world."

"No one has, it's new. Making new colonies has become a popular hobby for some of the Free Ships lately—which is to say, in the last ninety years or so. And for most of that time, Dharanendra has been sending out translators, frozen in storage on any ship that would allow them coffin-space. They're friendly with the aliens on their world, and it's given them a mania for finding more species to talk to. Ours might be the first to have a chance at it. But to the point: these Dharanendrans have developed an unusual technique for learning languages. It's arduous and can be fatal if something goes wrong. So Mr. Jain needs assurance of medical support when he arrives. And, it happens, Scythia tells us in their message that they're dangerously short of doctors: down to one, in fact."

"One? For how many people?"

"Around four hundred, when they called to us. No doubt it's more by now."

It was disquieting. If life was safe on Scythia and the soil bore nothing poisonous, then possibly one doctor could maintain the health of hundreds, but the colonists' security would be balanced on a knife's edge: all practical knowledge of medicine could be ended by the silence of a single heart.

"So naturally," the captain said, "I thought of you."

"Of me? But any other doctor on the ship would be more qualified."

"For maladies of summer and of winter, sure. None of them has been a doctor on the ground."

That was true but it could hardly help him, on a new world, to know that chainflower counteracted the effects of post-hole gnarl, or that the root of fretting marisol was sovereign for hepatitis. He supposed that to the captain, whose infirmities made him unable to descend to them, planets were no more than hazily imagined wells from which resources were drawn up in buckets. They must merge in his mind into one floating raft of world-stuff, all conjoined at the equators, likely to share the same cuisine and a single flora.

In any case, it was impossible. When the captain offered him the chance to travel with the ship, he had accepted knowing he would not return home for a century or more. That was a small price to pay for the solution to an otherwise inexorable problem: that a man without sisters or ancestors could hope for little out of life. He had expected to come back only twenty or thirty years older—because the engines, through their labors, compressed time; a week at home could slip past in a single summer day. If he used cold-sleep, he might age as little as a decade. And then it wouldn't matter anymore that his family was gone, his name burned and his ancestors lost. As one of the few Essians to go to space, he would be eagerly adopted by some venerable house. Everyone that he had ever known would then be dead. And yet stonebirds would still dive for fish, springbacks leap for flies. Fringeflower would still shiver in the spring. The Umber River and the Boy would laugh their different laughs, and all the proper ways would be observed. He could endure the strangeness of the ship and its sterility because he knew he would someday return to a world that made sense. But if he let the captain send him down to Scythia, then there would be no coming back.

None of this was speakable. To the captain his insistence on returning home, if rooted only in the longing of his heart, would seem both petulant and trivial. The ship-folk thought in terms of loyalties and duties, which were never to a family but to something larger, if not altogether abstract. In order to refuse politely he would have to cite a countervailing loyalty of his own. And so he said, choosing his words carefully:

"I am honored that you thought of me. But I came here to benefit Essius as well as the ship. My people expect me to return to share the knowledge that I gain here—"

"We will make good their losses."

John understood that he was no more to the captain than an entry on a balance sheet. The ship-folk had been friendly to him for the most part; he liked many of them casually and cared for some quite tenderly. Yet he saw in them, at times, this cold and animal calculation—as if the stalked eyes of a lock-spider flicked back and forth at you out of the mouth of its burrow.

"The people are Ischnuran and Zandahean," the captain said. "They won't understand each other, so the official language is ships' English—you'll have no trouble there."

A chill spread out along his spine. "But—those are marrying people."

"Well, yes." The captain's voice was gentle and amused. "Every world has marriage except yours. We have it too, in case you hadn't noticed."

He knew that, of course; it disturbed him and he tried not to think about it. But there was no comparison. "You keep some of the forms of marriage, yes, but many of you never marry. You divorce easily and often. Even those who are in marriages often don't consider themselves bound to strict monogamy—at least that is my experience."

"From anybody else I'd take that as an insult." John wanted to protest that it was meant as praise, but the captain's raised hand stopped him. "Yes, all right, I see your point, they're more intense about it on the ground. But—look—you can't take what people claim they do or what is in some holy book too seriously. On every world there is, a man has opportunities. I don't think you'll be left shooting it into a drink bag."

That was not the point at all. But ship-folk never understood.

The captain frowned, struck by a thought. "Homophobic, the Zandaheans. Ischnurans too in their way, I suppose. But you're adaptable, you'll be all right.—You know, when I give someone an assignment, this isn't how the conversation usually goes."

John understood that he was not being given a choice.

"It's a beautiful world," the captain said, and now his voice was kind. "A little eccentric in its flora and fauna, otherwise it's the most Earthlike ever found. Green like Earth, too . . . Earth as it was. That's the color our eyes were made for, so they say."

John thought if he refused outright the captain would insist. His only hope was to get out of this room without agreeing and then find somebody who could intercede for him. The captain liked to have control, but disliked being seen to use it; he wanted to be everybody's friend. He would probably accept delay if he thought it would lead to consent. And he listened to his favorites. Elodie perhaps—she was still smiled on as far as John knew. He could not like the idea of asking a lover for help; it would damage a connection that he valued and taint some pleasant memories with the odor of an exchange. But she was his best chance, so he would do it.

"This is so sudden, I hardly know what to say. May I take some time?"

"Yes, of course." The captain sounded surprised, and for a moment John hoped he had misunderstood and could, after all, simply say no. But the captain continued: "Just because I'll go into cold-sleep as soon as I can doesn't mean you have to. Take a few days, or a month if you want, build up some winter muscle first—that's wise." He cupped John's shoulder briefly. "Good!

Then you'll dine at my table tomorrow night. That's tradition, when someone is leaving us. I'm giving a speech, but it's short, and the food is worth it."

"Yes, I will be there." John didn't trust himself to say more. He could still try to find help. There might still be a chance.

The captain studied his face, looking disappointed. He had not quite gotten what he wanted from the conversation, John thought; but no matter, it hardly troubled him. "Tomorrow, then." He laid his hand against John's center and pushed.

As John fell slowly toward the last mess, the captain moved again. His elegance was still breathtaking. He was turning back to the stars.

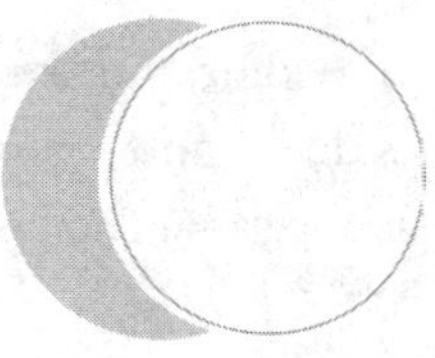

CHAPTER TWO

The dome of the old bridge was blue and bright, and clouds moved through it swiftly, suggesting a wind that was not felt below. Long tables in rows filled the round floor, each one garnished with a centerpiece of living plants. The ship-folk liked to surround themselves with flowers at the beginning and the end of winter, but there had been no time to bring valerian or aster into bloom. They were making do with a display of greenery, alleviated by the sweet yellow of squash blossoms and the sharp yellow of mustard flowers.

One table stood alone, raised on a dais. The way up was eight shallow steps, provided with a handrail that John leaned on heavily. He found his name marked on a little card that had been folded down the middle so it stood up on its edges, and settled into his chair with relief. Ships' medicine could help his body readapt to winter, but no pill existed that could make his brain remember how to set his foot down in the right place on the floor. Then, too, he had overtired his weakened muscles by going about the ship, trying in vain to find help, even when winter had settled down onto his shoulders. He would have saved himself considerable trouble if he had listened to Elodie, who had gently made it clear that neither she nor anybody else could intercede for him. The summer captain had made his decision, he would never change his mind, and not being a member of the crew, John had no right to refuse. She had been sad, but not outraged. It was just how the ship worked.

Stately and pale, the captain ascended the stairs to the dais. There was winter in her step and in the straightness of her spine and in her gaze too, the deep blue of a winter sky. She wore a long black dress, embroidered with silver at neckline and shoulders and wrists. The vine-and-moons motif showed that the work was Essian and of an earlier era, though surely no

Essian foremother had chosen a color and cut so severe: it had been made for her. Her iron-gray hair was down and she was smiling.

"Dr. Maraintha," she said as she sat at the head of the table. "How is your packing coming along?"

Her tone was warm and bright, as if she thought that he was leaving on some long-awaited trip and must be counting down the days. There was no use in contradicting this unspoken lie. So he answered her, honestly, that he would do it all the night before he went into his coffin; he had little to pack, just his bag and a few clothes. She told him he should get a winter coat out of the landing supply room; also a pair of good boots, since a new world might not have a cobbler yet; and he must tell the clerk she said he could choose what he wanted, so that they wouldn't try to give him the worst they had. She continued at some length about what supplies he ought to take, where on the ship he could obtain them, which items would weather the trip best if frozen in the coffin with him and which ones should be kept out of it—all useful knowledge that deserved his full attention and did not receive it. He was too exhausted, and he didn't see that it would make much difference to his future to be exiled with one warm coat more or less.

As she was speaking, the lieutenants who were chiefs of the two watches of her night arrived and took their places at her sides. As befitted their positions, both were strong and solid women, but Lieutenant Noor was also very tall, a striking figure even by the standards of winter-night. In his first months on the ship he had been taken by the way her muscles filled out her black uniform, by the bare nape of her neck and the curve of her skull under shorn hair, and had wondered if she might welcome a visit, but been warned off on the grounds that "both of the chiefs only like their own kind." It was not clear whether this meant women or night-watchers, but since neither answer held out any hope for him, he had not pursued the question.

A man came up to the table and walked around it, looking for his designated seat. He was young—no older than John, perhaps not even quite as old. His movements were graceful and gave an impression of great calm. His skin was of a brown as rich as finished camberwood, as golden in its highlights; his hair and eyebrows were deep black and full. Undoubtedly this was the translator. He couldn't be one of the crew; John would not have failed to notice a man who looked like that aboard the ship.

John had scarcely known what to imagine a Dharanendran translator doing with his time—whether pushing through pathless forests to discover uncontacted cities, poring over ancient documents in curious scripts, or conveying offers and demands in some interminable meeting. This man's appearance suggested the scholar more than the adventurer; though there was some promise of strength in his shoulders and arms, his face and his hands were not weathered, but looked very soft. Perhaps his clothes favored the diplomat: they were close-fitting and had a carefully tailored look, and the fabric was fine and smooth, in the color of a milk-nut lightly toasted. The standing collar, high but deeply cleft, revealed the perfect hollow of his throat.

He found his place, at John's right. He sat down and his eyes—deep brown and large—met John's, just for a moment. He might have been about to speak. Then the winter captain greeted him, and so he had to look at her. John stole a glance at the card in front of him to see his name: Sudharma Jain.

"Maybe you can explain something I've often wondered about," the captain said. "Half the planets we visit speak languages that were once English, but some of them are mostly comprehensible, and some might as well be Mandarin. Why would English deteriorate faster on some worlds than others?"

"That is a very complicated question, and if there were two linguists here instead of one, you might have started a fight by asking it. In some places innovation simply runs faster than others, for no reason we can work out. One of the factors we do know about is relativity: time moves slower on the ships, and so from our perspective on the ground, your language changes more slowly too. But language is always changing, even on the *Folly*. The silent *n* in words like 'dance' and 'intense' used to be pronounced, and on Essius, for example, it still is."

"Now that you mention it, I remember my grandfather saying 'sense' that way when I was a child. I believe I thought his mouth was too old to work properly."

The captain looked down toward the middle of the room, and John followed her gaze. The round platform by which people came to the old bridge in winter was rising up into the floor, and the summer captain was rising with it, seated in a wooden chair borne by a man of winter-night. It was no wonder that the captain was no burden for a man who worked in double gravity: he looked painfully thin, as if winter had withered him. His fingers curled around the ends of the armrests, his spine hunched forward, his legs and feet hung limply. He must have been in pain, but his face revealed it only slightly; he was either medicated, or else by sheer determination refusing to let anguish show.

The night-watcher climbed up the steps to the dais and set him down, chair and all, in the last empty place at the foot of the table. He said a collective good-evening to all those assembled, giving no special regard to his sister. She looked only at him, and there was a vast disapproval in her eyes.

A girl in winter uniform came to stand at his side, holding a metal capsule on a stalk—a microphone. "Are we ready?" he asked. The girl nodded, so he put his palms on the edge of the table and pushed himself up from his chair. John held his breath. He had listened to a speech like this from a lower mess when the ship left Essius, and he had heard the strain in summer's voice, but he had never imagined him standing. It was by no means advisable, and he must have fortified himself with powerful drugs to make it even possible. He was leaning heavily on one hand; his back was still painfully curved, and the blood-tint was gone from his face. With a sharp intake of breath, he managed to turn toward the crowd. When the girl holding the microphone had moved it near his mouth, he began.

"We meet under the sky our ancestors saw—and in the gravity that they endured—to mark another change of seasons. . . ."

John didn't listen, just waited and hoped the ordeal would be over quickly. This custom of the speech was sordid; it had an air of ritual humiliation, as if, to justify the change in government, winter had to prove that summer was unable to survive her season. The cruelty of it bothered him, even now that he had every reason to wish the man harm. It was strange, he thought, how empathy continued even when the need for it had passed. His heart flinched from the spectacle of pain by a mechanical reflex, as the mouth of a bud-corer still tries to chew when its head has been pulled off.

"Now once I have digested this feast, I am going to the comfort of my coffin and you are all going to become my little sister's problem. If I can leave you fat and sleepy you'll be easier to manage. So my last order to you is to eat well—drink deep—and take heart: this winter will be short, and we will have three years of summer when I see you all again."

The room rang with applause as he sat down. Then young men and women in night's uniform, who had been standing at the edges of the dome bearing lidded vessels, approached the tables. One leaned forward at winter's elbow and uncovered his dish. She served herself from it, then took it in her hands and passed it down the table; in this way the feast flowed from her.

John could smell that the dish was of rat. He would have guessed that, even if his nose had not informed him; the crew considered rat the greatest consolation of the season. You needed meat for strength in winter, that was their opinion, so they sectioned up a disused elevator shaft into long cages and let the rats breed to fill them all summer long. When the season changed they ate their way through the increase, starting with those that were injured or killed by the first shock of gravity. They called this the fall harvest, and had forgotten that it was a joke.

When the meat reached him he could see that it was cooked with mushrooms in a sauce of its own juices, and smell that it had mustard as the chief spice. John considered it with unease. He had seen living rats—even held one in his hand; they were so manifestly relatives of humankind that to eat them seemed the nearest thing to cannibalism. They were soft to the touch, and covered in fur like the hair on an old man's head. Their faces were not rigid masks, but flexible enough to form expressions. Their blood, like his, was warm. Yet this also was the food that humans had been made for. Throughout its history on Earth, the human species had fed on creatures that were near kin to itself. Though the tradition had been interrupted for his ancestors on Essius—who had no meat but the flesh of alien insects and of fish spawned from a very different sea—his body still remembered, and responded as nature had taught it to. Thus the aroma was an unanswerable argument. He spooned a moderate amount onto his plate and passed the rest along to the translator. Then without misgivings, but equally without enthusiasm, he took of brussels sprouts roasted together with potatoes; though they might look promising, he knew that any vegetable served on the ship would be underseasoned and lacking in complexity.

"These rats have been with us from the beginning," the winter captain said. "Not as food, at first. On our very first voyage, when our mission was to found a colony rather than to help those that have already been founded, they were brought along for experiments—testing native foods to find out which are edible, that sort of thing. But they've proven themselves the spaceworthiest of animals. You remember, don't you, brother, when our father thought we might have chickens? What a fiasco that turned out to be. They couldn't even swallow water without gravity. Some things ought to be left down on the worlds where they belong, no matter how tasty they might seem to us."

Summer said nothing to this, and if his face showed a reaction, John didn't see; he was busy serving himself from a vessel of cabbage and carrots. Then he passed it and, in doing so, saw that the translator's plate was empty. He had taken no food at all. John froze in shock, but the translator only took the dish from him and held it in his hands until the woman next to him was ready to receive it, as if this were the most ordinary behavior in the world.

What could be the meaning of it? If there was poison in the food, then everybody at the table was at risk. Yet the translator sat there with every appearance of calm, warning no one and accusing no one. The ship-folk kept filling their plates, taking no notice of the insult. If a guest had behaved this way on Essius, knives would have been drawn by now. No doubt on the ship poison was less common—people here couldn't just harvest death from the weeds on the roadside as they walked home from a lover's cabin—so they would be less on their guard. Still, John could not imagine that a guest's refusal of all hospitality would be a matter of indifference anywhere.

There was something here he didn't understand. But the next dish had come to him, and so he had to make a choice. It was small slices of wheat bread topped with oil and garlic, which would have to be picked up with the fingers. He disliked the thought of touching it until he knew exactly what the translator was up to, but the man's equanimity still said that there was no danger. Reluctantly, he took a slice, then passed the platter, trying to signify by his expression that he was alarmed.

"Dr. Maraintha," the translator said. "I'm told you are Essian. What part of the world are you from?"

The man's speech was more baffling than his silence. He spoke casually, as if nothing unusual was happening, and the purpose of his question was obscure. At least it didn't seem to be a question you would ask of somebody about to die of poisoning.

"From Faivai," he said. "That's in Ryvet, it's the city where the ship-folk come."

"And somewhere else, before that?"

"Yes, in fact—I'm inland born. My home village was called Riadstryn, but no one has heard of it even on Essius."

"When they say 'quite' in Riadstryn, do they pronounce it like 'bait' or like 'bay'?"

John had to shape his mouth to an almost forgotten habit of speech to be sure. "Like 'bay.'"

"The Clear Lakes region, then—unless my information is too out-of-date."

"That's right. It's just south of Croh Lake. How did you know that?"

"*Wia ir auyar ersians du aunohm*," he said—'Your radio plays are heard even on my homeworld.' Which must mean that some ship, leaving Essius before the introduction of television, had carried recordings to scatter among the stars, and some had come to Dharanendra, where the translator had listened to them for what must have been innumerable hours. The sentence he had spoken was idiomatic, pronounced accurately and even in a reasonable imitation of a Clear Lakes accent, though there was some tinge of the southern coast about his vowels. He had pronounced Maraintha, too, as in Essian, with the soft *th* of 'than,' not the sharp one of 'thin.'

"But why would you go to the trouble to learn that? The chance of meeting an Essian in space must be incredibly remote."

"Learning Essian was a pleasure, not a trouble. Also, once you know a ships' language and one or two of its descendants, the rest go very quickly. But yes, meeting you is a great stroke of luck."

A risotto, fragrant with onions, had come down the table and John received it with irritation. Having the captain pass every dish was an inefficient way of getting food to plates, and the rat was bound to be ice-cold before anyone could eat. He could see no point to the custom except to illustrate by tedious allegory that food springs from women, a fact every infant already knew. He still wasn't quite sure if the food was safe to eat, but not knowing what else to do, he spooned out a dab.

Once the risotto had finished its circuit, the uniformed youths returned with trays supporting glasses of some urine-colored beverage, no doubt alcoholic. One was allotted to each person; the ship would not be helping summer crew get drunk enough to kill themselves trying to walk in gravity, though in light of the captain's command to "drink deep" it was likely some would do it on their own.

The arrival of drink was a signal to eat; everyone took up forks and began. John looked at the translator to see how he would react, but his face gave no sign that the moment held any significance. He only smiled and asked, "Will you indulge me in trying out my Essian on you at greater length?"

"Certainly, yes."

"Good," he said in English, and then in soft and rapid Essian: "I think if we spoke in a thick accent, and didn't use too many words that are the same in flying-boat talk, no one here would understand us—do you agree?"

John thought this over carefully before he nodded. Some of the winter crew might speak a little Essian, but he had never heard of any ship-folk being fluent, certainly not in Clear Lakes dialect. He would just have to watch his vocabulary when he touched upon sensitive matters. Besides those terms borrowed from ships' English, such as 'English' itself, he had often noticed words and even phrases that had come down through the centuries unchanged—as you might find a scrap, brittle and black at the edges, of a letter burned in a fire.

"Then, be at peace. I don't suspect any poison. There are a number of foodstuffs Dharanendrans avoid, especially meat. If I can help it, I don't eat anything at all from a kitchen where meat has been cooked. You might say it is a matter of leaving a good soul."

You left a good soul by right conduct in visiting; by being kind, especially to your own family; by avoiding burns and injuries; by anointing the body with oil. None of those seemed relevant, so probably Sudharma was replacing the ships'-English word 'religious': he meant his diet was prescribed for him by some belief. This sort of self-denial was to be expected. Marrying peoples sought to bind desire of all varieties, not only sexual; on their worlds no human impulse could flow in the channels it carved for itself. But if he only meant he was observing a restriction that the human mind had placed on its own nature, why didn't he say so in English, and reassure the shipfolk at the table? John replayed the man's words in his mind and came up with no answer—but he did realize, with a tingle of amusement, that the translator was *not* speaking a slightly flawed version of Clear Lakes dialect; he was doing a perfect imitation of Clear Lakes dialect as pronounced by actors from the coast. Once, the falseness of this brackish accent would have irritated him, but at this distance even a muddied reflection of home felt like comfort.

There was no poison, and so he could eat. The rat was not as cold as he had feared. It was tasty, though he thought the richness of the meat ought to be lightened with some sweet and fragrant leaf like catch-my-ribbons. But all Essian herbs were lost to him forever, swept away by the wind of the ship's passage; he would never again have a meal that tasted like home. At this thought his appetite for the feast left him, yet he persevered in eating. No human problem was ever improved by an empty stomach; regardless of emotion, the body must be fed.

"Forgive me if the observation is intrusive, but you have the look of a man mourning a death," the translator said, still in Essian. "Do you regret agreeing to go to a new land?"

John considered saying he was happy to be sent to Scythia. But he knew he couldn't hide the way he felt forever. However he tried, it would come out, if only as a tone of voice or an arrangement of the face in some unguarded moment. It was better to admit the reason for these leaks of feeling than to let them be put down to natural surliness.

"I can't regret that," he said. "I never agreed."

"Then how does it come about that you are leaving?"

"On the ship if you're not crew you're cargo. The—" John hesitated, realizing that Essian *sumar* was pronounced the same as 'summer,' and that *kaptan*, borrowed from ships' English to describe a starship captain and used only for that purpose, was recognizable even when Clear Lakes dialect shortened it to *kapta'*. "The man at the foot of the table can send me anywhere he likes."

"I am sorry. When I mentioned a need for medical support I never expected this to happen."

"It's not your fault."

"Even so, I feel responsible. If you like, I will go to the ashen siblings and object to their treatment of you. Either of them, or both if you think it will help."

"I think they would tell you it's their business how they dispose of their passengers."

"In that case . . . excuse me, I don't mean to give offense, but I could say I object to the practice of visiting, and on searching my conscience I find I can't work with someone from your world."

"Is that true? That you object to it."

"No. I look after my own soul and take others as I find them. I must do that even more now that I am going to live among offworlders, who, I'm sure you've noticed, never know how to behave right."

John thought this meant he did object to Essian ways for some religious reason, and merely refrained from applying his own standards to others. In all likelihood, then, he would never want to be visited. If the problem was ideological then there might be hope, but it would never do for John to act as if he hoped.

"In fact," Sudharma added, "lying to the captains would not be good care of my soul, but in this case that is the lesser harm, so I will do it if you like."

"It won't make any difference. I'm not being sent to Scythia because I'm needed there. It's—" He stopped himself from saying 'politics,' because he thought the word's Essian disguise was too thin, and anyone hearing it would listen more closely. 'Corruption,' too, might be recognizable. And rather than search further for a euphemism, he found himself telling the translator what he had found out in his useless search for help. "This flying boat only supports so many people waking. There are long waiting lists to have a child. By announcing my departure in his own season, the . . . the man of a warm time gained control of it. They say he's given it to some man who is visiting him."

John took a bite of bread as an excuse not to look at the translator's face, and waited for Sudharma to reply. He didn't know what he was afraid to see. He had time to finish the bread and a remnant of cabbage and carrots. At the head of the table the winter captain was saying something about table manners on Vraha.

"I am appalled to have gained your help in this way," the translator said—and 'appalled' was ships' English, so maybe he had stopped caring whether anybody understood. "But I will be grateful for your help, if you do give it. I hope we can be friends despite the evil that brings us together."

"I see no reason we should not be," John said. What he really felt was much less tentative—a greater fondness than could possibly be justified by a brief conversation. Surely he would not have taken such a rapid liking to the translator if the man had not been quite so beautiful. It was foolish, no doubt, to be influenced by appearance when the chances of a visit were so poor. Yet the fact remained that he did like him. In this matter too, nature would have its say.

"We will discover a new world together, then."

John found the thought was not altogether unpleasant.

"But how am I to help you?"

The translator hesitated; there was a reserve in his eyes that had not been there before. "I may need some assistance in changing my mind."

John shivered, because the word the translator had used for 'mind' was *sheek*, which meant the soul when it has been extracted from the body after death. He didn't know what to make of that, except that it might be the only word for 'mind' or 'brain' Sudharma knew.

The winter captain was describing something called a shadow temple she had visited on Vraha. From the outside it looked like a tangle of steel, as if rods of metal had been planted in a circle, and grown up into a hedge, and curved together as they grew so that they closed into a dome. The only way in was a little square hole you could barely get through on all fours. You squeezed inside and sat against the tangled wall—your back breaking because of the curve of it—and waited for the maze of shadows on the floor to resolve into a god, a human, an entire battle, all rendered in such detail that you thought these things must really be there, though if you looked up you would see nothing but a maze of steel against the sky. Then they distorted and dissolved, and you waited again for the next image—or, if you weren't getting any younger and your joints were unused to the discipline, probably you fled before it became clear. The oldest of these wonders had been made before the ships came to that world, without computers, often by a single craftsman working his whole life to build a temple that might tell its story perfectly only on one day a year, and only if that day was fair, and that would gradually rust out of focus until it collapsed.

It was remarkable, she said, taking a forkful of rat. Still one couldn't help wondering what the builders would have achieved if they'd applied their skills to something more productive.

John thought that after all it would be worth being sent to Scythia, just to get away from this place and these people. He needed to be elsewhere, needed it with his whole body, as in a burning heat he would need to plunge into cool water. He might drown, but he needed it just the same.

"When will you be frozen?" he asked.

"At once after the feast." The vowels of *y'* and *fias'* no longer had that echo of the seacoast; the translator had perfected his accent. "It's an advantage of not having eaten."

John couldn't sleep as soon as that. He would have to wait eight hours after eating before he let the anesthetic take hold of him. Also he needed to pack, and to pick up his boots and coat. And a month or so of exercise in gravity would make him more functional when he arrived. But after that he would go to the long silver pod that would take him to Scythia. He would lie in his coffin and sleep, to wake on a strange world and learn what his new life would be.

CHAPTER THREE

He dreamed that a bird-tracker stung him on the arm. He tried to slap at it and woke.

The sun hung, large and yellow, above his coffin; even when he blocked it with a hand, the light still dazzled him. He squeezed his eyes shut, then opened them a crack, trying to acclimate himself to brightness by small doses, as you might build up a tolerance to a poison. Life on the ship was dim and it had left him soft; the air and sun would have to toughen him again.

A man leaned over the coffin to look down at him. He was fairer even than the captains; his hair was the watered gold of shedleaf stamens, and a little windblown. The sun, shining from behind him, made every flyaway strand into a filament of blinding light.

"Dr. Maraintha, do you know where you are?"

"Scythia," he croaked. His mouth and throat were dry; he licked his lips. "I hope."

This drew out the hint of a smile. "Don't worry, you've been delivered to the right address. How do you feel?"

"Nausea. Some headache."

"The usual. You'll survive. Did you come here straight out of weightlessness?"

"No. I had a month in winter—I mean, in gravity—with graduated exercise and fifty milligrams a day of myotrine."

"Rushed it a bit, didn't you? But I guess you'll be able to walk without falling over. The gravity's point eight six of Earth standard, so you'll feel a little off—don't try any athletics till you're used to it. Go ahead, climb out of the coffin."

John got one leg over the side and, with the pale man supporting his arm, made it ungracefully to the ground. Bracing one arm against the coffin's side, he straightened up as best he could, wobbly because of the long sleep or the anesthesia or the faint, uncanny lightness of his limbs. He glanced at the pod and away—in the harsh sun its metal was too bright to look at for long. Putting his back to it, he looked over the landscape he would have to live in. *Green like Earth*, the captain had said. He had imagined Scythia as a green field, a stream with emerald grasses bent beneath the braided current, a forest with jade boughs against the sky; in short, he had imagined Essius, as colored by a child with only half a set of paints. He had come down in a world of gravel and brown sand. There was no water anywhere, and by the look of it there hadn't been for a long time. Little shrubs no higher than his waist gave a patchy covering to the ground, gathering in denser drifts against the bases of the hills, as if the wind had blown them there. The green of their foliage was grayish and dull. Scattered among them, and spaced out as if they didn't like each other's company, were thick and waxy objects shaped like balls, like blades of oars, like long drums thrust into the ground. These were also green, but some were stained with purple at their bases and between the deep pleats in their sides. A few were giants—fluted columns that must have been six times John's height, and towering over even those, one huge cone with a blunted tip. The cone had a circular hole neatly bored near the top, and from the hole a foam of tiny leaves spilled out.

He would die in this arid land, John thought. Probably he would be buried whole in it—that grim custom was widespread on the settled worlds. His soul would be given over to the roots and ground-worms to stitch through with their long bodies, and would never be of use to anyone.

He remembered that his bag was in the coffin, and anxiously turned back to find it. He had been afraid to let the length of soul freeze with him, but more afraid to leave it alone in the pod for years with both its physical and spiritual needs untended to; it might have dried and cracked, or worse, become embittered. Gently he lifted the bag out, pulled it on over his head, and laid his palm over the strap. It was still soft and he still felt his great-uncle's presence, as warm and strong as if the soul had been conditioned and remembered yesterday. Immediately he felt better armored against disappointment.

John turned around again and realized the doctor had been watching him. He hoped his gentleness with the soul and his relief at reconnecting with it, when viewed from behind, would pass for disorientation and sluggishness, such as anybody might experience when just awakened from cold-sleep. In the future he would have to avoid touching the soul when

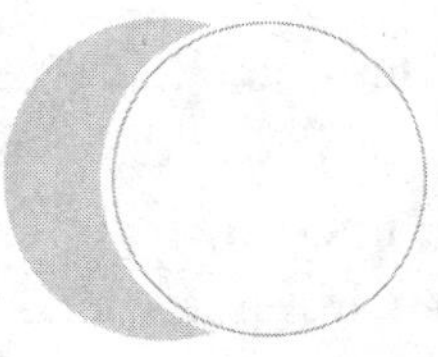

CHAPTER THREE

He dreamed that a bird-tracker stung him on the arm. He tried to slap at it and woke.

The sun hung, large and yellow, above his coffin; even when he blocked it with a hand, the light still dazzled him. He squeezed his eyes shut, then opened them a crack, trying to acclimate himself to brightness by small doses, as you might build up a tolerance to a poison. Life on the ship was dim and it had left him soft; the air and sun would have to toughen him again.

A man leaned over the coffin to look down at him. He was fairer even than the captains; his hair was the watered gold of shedleaf stamens, and a little windblown. The sun, shining from behind him, made every flyaway strand into a filament of blinding light.

"Dr. Maraintha, do you know where you are?"

"Scythia," he croaked. His mouth and throat were dry; he licked his lips. "I hope."

This drew out the hint of a smile. "Don't worry, you've been delivered to the right address. How do you feel?"

"Nausea. Some headache."

"The usual. You'll survive. Did you come here straight out of weightlessness?"

"No. I had a month in winter—I mean, in gravity—with graduated exercise and fifty milligrams a day of myotrine."

"Rushed it a bit, didn't you? But I guess you'll be able to walk without falling over. The gravity's point eight six of Earth standard, so you'll feel a little off—don't try any athletics till you're used to it. Go ahead, climb out of the coffin."

John got one leg over the side and, with the pale man supporting his arm, made it ungracefully to the ground. Bracing one arm against the coffin's side, he straightened up as best he could, wobbly because of the long sleep or the anesthesia or the faint, uncanny lightness of his limbs. He glanced at the pod and away—in the harsh sun its metal was too bright to look at for long. Putting his back to it, he looked over the landscape he would have to live in. *Green like Earth*, the captain had said. He had imagined Scythia as a green field, a stream with emerald grasses bent beneath the braided current, a forest with jade boughs against the sky; in short, he had imagined Essius, as colored by a child with only half a set of paints. He had come down in a world of gravel and brown sand. There was no water anywhere, and by the look of it there hadn't been for a long time. Little shrubs no higher than his waist gave a patchy covering to the ground, gathering in denser drifts against the bases of the hills, as if the wind had blown them there. The green of their foliage was grayish and dull. Scattered among them, and spaced out as if they didn't like each other's company, were thick and waxy objects shaped like balls, like blades of oars, like long drums thrust into the ground. These were also green, but some were stained with purple at their bases and between the deep pleats in their sides. A few were giants—fluted columns that must have been six times John's height, and towering over even those, one huge cone with a blunted tip. The cone had a circular hole neatly bored near the top, and from the hole a foam of tiny leaves spilled out.

He would die in this arid land, John thought. Probably he would be buried whole in it—that grim custom was widespread on the settled worlds. His soul would be given over to the roots and ground-worms to stitch through with their long bodies, and would never be of use to anyone.

He remembered that his bag was in the coffin, and anxiously turned back to find it. He had been afraid to let the length of soul freeze with him, but more afraid to leave it alone in the pod for years with both its physical and spiritual needs untended to; it might have dried and cracked, or worse, become embittered. Gently he lifted the bag out, pulled it on over his head, and laid his palm over the strap. It was still soft and he still felt his great-uncle's presence, as warm and strong as if the soul had been conditioned and remembered yesterday. Immediately he felt better armored against disappointment.

John turned around again and realized the doctor had been watching him. He hoped his gentleness with the soul and his relief at reconnecting with it, when viewed from behind, would pass for disorientation and sluggishness, such as anybody might experience when just awakened from cold-sleep. In the future he would have to avoid touching the soul when anyone could see, so as not to draw attention to its importance. It was possible that no one on this world except Sudharma knew what a soul was, and it would be best if they didn't find out.

The doctor didn't ask any awkward questions, just handed John a canteen. "You'll be dehydrated. Drink this." Then he held out a white pill. "And you should take this. It's sunscreen."

"Is that really necessary?"

"Obviously you're not susceptible like I am, but the sun here is fierce."

"Won't I have trouble with vitamin D deficiency?"

"No, the vitamin is in there too. Are you stalling because you don't swallow pills well?"

"No." John washed down the pill with water, pocketed a bottle of them, and nodded when he was urged to take one every day before he went outside. Privately he wondered whether the brightness of Scythia's star really required such vigilance, or whether the doctor's own pallor led him to an exaggerated caution. But it would not do to introduce himself to a senior physician by refusing treatment.

"I'm Marnevas—Marne for short. You've figured out I'm a doctor, and Ischnuran. And this is Piro Torres, a biologist."

He indicated a tall man who had been leaning against a large black vehicle nearby, but came forward on hearing his name. He was stout and his hair was graying from the temples, both to a very pleasing degree. Where his hair wasn't gray it was a glossy black, and his skin was the soft deep brown of wood-moths' wings. His smile was friendly. He put out his hand to shake—that awkward custom of ship's winter; it was strong and noticeably callused. Probably he did much of his work outdoors and had been roughened and kept vigorous by that. But his work sharpened his mind too, and you could see that in his eyes.

"Call me Piro, if you can stand it. We're all on a first-name basis here—the Ischnurans won that one by not having surnames."

"John Maraintha. By all means, call me John." He glanced back and forth between the two men, realizing that each of them came from a different one of the two worlds that had sent colonists to Scythia. Ischnura was cold, he thought, and the people there came in three sexes instead of two, so that his mind gave him the picture of an androgynous figure embedded in ice. Zandahe, as everybody knew, was fortunate to be a world where Terran plants grew easily—and he imagined endless fields and laden tables. Then John's heart sank as he realized the importance of a detail: Marne had a ring on his left hand. That was the sign of marriage. Piro wore one too, and that was even worse; Zandaheans practiced marriage in a particularly brutal and repressive form.

"I came along mostly to help drag your coffins out of the pod," Piro said, "but as long as I'm here, I can tell you a few things about this world that you'll need to know sooner than later. We'll leave that until your friend wakes up, so I don't have to do it twice."

"He should be ready by now," Marne said, and started toward the second coffin. When he had gone, Piro spoke in a low tone.

"You could sit down in the van a minute, if you like."

Though the suggestion was kindly meant, something made John hesitate to show that he was tired. Instead he used the time to look around. A bright animal caught his eye. It was shaped like a stretched rat, but hairless, its skin covered in little beads of green and gold. It was resting upside down on the side of a column, with its head raised so its nose pointed forward. Its tail—if 'tail' was even the right word—was nothing like the thin appendages on cows or rats; it was as if the body continued beyond the hips, tapering gradually, and finally, after a length far greater than seemed plausible, coming to a point. The head was like a wedge you might split wood with, and the mouth was a deep crack in it, running well beyond the eye—it must gape very wide when it was opened. The bent throat was sharp like the keel of a ship.

The animal's eye swiveled; it had noticed John watching it. Its belly tensed, then relaxed. Then it lashed its tail and was gone. The column remained, even more improbable than the creature that had clung to it.

"What are these . . . artifacts?" John asked.

Piro looked blank. Then he pointed to one of the small metal posts that marked the corners of the clearing where the pod stood. "Those? They're just beacons to tell you where to land. I'm surprised you don't recognize them—they're ships' tech."

"No, I mean these green things, all around us. The ones that look like they are made of wax."

"Oh." Piro broke into a grin. "Those are called candles. They're a kind of dryad. But seeing as you're fresh out of your coffin and still blinking in the sunlight, I'll simplify and say they're plants."

John found a nearer one to look at: a pleated cylinder no higher than his knee, crowned with a ring of white ovoids. It seemed nothing like a plant to him, unless a plant could be liquefied and poured into a mold to harden—or rather, he thought when he crouched to examine it, made into a paste and squeezed out of a piping bag. The surface was so waxy that it looked like it would melt on the first hot day.

"I wouldn't recommend touching that," Piro said.

John suppressed his irritation at the warning. Of course he wouldn't touch an unfamiliar plant; he was not a child. But Piro was only trying to keep him safe.

He heard two sets of steps behind him. He listened, still from a crouch, as introductions were repeated and he heard the name Sudharma spoken for the first time. He knew he wouldn't be able to say it right; the consonant represented by *dh* was like, but not the same as, *d*, and he had no idea what contortion of the mouth might be necessary to produce it. Then Sudharma was standing beside him, looking down at the little cylinder. If he felt sick or achy or unstable or half-blinded by the light, he gave no sign of it. He might have just alighted from a two-hour train ride.

"That looks oddly familiar. If it had spines, I'd wonder how you brought it here from Dharanendra."

"Desert plants are like that," Piro said. "It's an extreme environment, so they converge on the designs that work. In this case, the fleshy stem stores water and the ribs let it expand to hold more after rain. The waxy coating keeps the water in. No leaves, because a leaf is just more surface area for moisture to escape through. A lot of plants that look like this have spines or thorns or prickles for defense, but these don't need them. If you walk over this way, I'll show you why."

He led them to a shrub of tangled twigs studded with small oval leaves. All over the top of it red-purple buds stood upright, their petals smooth and shiny as an insect carapace.

"John, come closer and pick a bud. The big one, here."

The bud was connected to its twig by a short stem, and there was a seam at the point where they joined. He grasped just above this and twisted. There was a cracking sound, and the bud bloomed in his hand, opening like a red mouth. The center of it had eyes, was moving; it hissed at him like a teakettle. Then with a snap it broke free of the flower, shooting past him in a flutter of red wings.

He turned to see it flailing on the ground. Terrified, it tried to fly, but he had broken something inside it; it could only manage little buzzing hops that left it upside down on the sand, frantically trying to right itself.

When it was ten paces or so away, it stopped and looked back at him. It folded its wings down onto its back, hiding the red, so it was drab all over. It leaped into the air and flew off easily in a straight line.

"You were acting like a predator, so it tried to lead you away from the others. Since it couldn't, it'll go and feed and live its life. They can reach sexual maturity on or off the plant, so when the others swarm, if all goes well, it'll be ready."

"Is it some kind of parasite?"

"That's what this world has instead of flowers. All these things you see around you that look like plants—or maybe don't, if you're not used to deserts—are a stage in the life cycle of a dryad. Just like a plant, they grow in the ground and get energy from the sun. To reproduce, they bud off a cell without a cell wall that divides, develops, and becomes like an animal. Eventually it breeds and plants its seeds, and the cycle starts over.

"The problem is, they don't just plant them anywhere at random and then walk away. When Zandaheans first came to Scythia, we settled in a wooded area. We'd clear a patch of forest and it would get invaded by dryads who'd been waiting for a sunny patch to plant their seeds in. Some of them would stick around to help their young by digging up our seeds, or killing our plants when they came up. It was war. But we thought we had a handle on it. We were doing well enough for the ship that brought us, *My Grandfather's Axe,* to leave us on our own. Seven years in, we were overrun by a little dryad that pissed arsenate all over everything because its seedlings were immune."

"Can you subsist on indigenous foods here?"

"No. We can get some calories from fats, but the proteins and carbohydrates aren't digestible."

"It's remarkable that you survived."

"Some of us didn't. We made small garden plots scattered around, hid and protected them as best we could, but we'd lose half every year—not always to the same pests, there were a whole series of outbreaks. We were synthesizing food to fill in the gaps, until a gang of dryads called tumblers broke in and wrecked the machines. It was like all of nature had turned against us at once. We were in a bad state by the time *Rose of the Winds* showed up with its load of Ischnurans. Bad enough that when the *Rose* said to abandon our first settlement and come here, we weren't hard to convince.

"So that's why you're not in the lush green landscape you might have expected—it's safer here. Lack of rainfall keeps the dryad biomass down, and removing a few shrubs and candles from a field doesn't attract the kind of attention that clearing a forest does. Between the river and groundwater, we've got enough for at least a century of irrigation. By then we'll know how to live on this world a lot better and can spread anywhere we want. At least, that's the idea."

Sudharma, who had been silent during all this explanation, asked, "And are the people I came here to communicate with also dryads?"

"They're dryads, all right. As to whether they're people, I'm taking a wait-and-see attitude. You won't get to meet one for at least a month, probably longer—we only see basket-men when one decides to visit us, which is never until mid-spring, and they don't come every year. We've got a meeting set up tonight to tell you more about them, but it might be taken over by more urgent problems." He looked back and forth between John and Sudharma and sighed. "I'm sorry to tell you this so soon after you woke up, but Earth is here."

His manner suggested this was a grave development. John was not sure what he should think. The ships feared Earth and saw it as an enemy, albeit one too powerful to strike against; they said the people there mingled their minds with aiyi and so ceased to be human. It was in virtue of refusing this connection that the ships called themselves free. But the ships had no proper concept of freedom, so their judgment on that subject, even more than any other, had to be treated as suspect.

Sudharma did not seem alarmed. He only asked, quietly, "When did they arrive?"

"No idea—they didn't bother to announce themselves. Six years ago a trap set for invertebrates caught something that looked like a dryad but wasn't. That was after we'd already signaled for help, by the way—we didn't lure you into this mess on purpose. The last couple of years we've been seeing more of the spies, or scouts or whatever they are. Then a few days ago something huge with a lot of legs plopped itself down on our main street, said it didn't want to talk—in English—then apparently went to sleep."

"Did you evacuate?"

"No. The governor said stand our ground and most of us did."

"That took some nerve. And did the creature leave after our pod had landed?"

"Yeah, as a matter of fact, it did. It only moved a ways upriver and then stopped, but at least it's not squatting between us and church anymore."

"Interesting. I look forward to talking to your governor."

"You will, at the meeting. That's in four hours, so you'll have time to clean up. Even take a nap, if your circadian rhythms are off. Come on, I'll drive you into town."

John started to follow, then hesitated. "We should get our bags out of the pod."

"Already in the van, along with the rest of your podmates. Speaking of which, maybe you can help me understand something. Are the rats some kind of joke?"

"Ah. You said you had lost your livestock, and I am afraid that rats are all the *Folly* had. Their size and adaptability make them practical in a ship. But you will find them tasty, I think." John didn't know why he was defending the ship. Possibly he was defending the rats. "To be honest, it is strange food to me too, but I came to appreciate it."

"Strange how?" Marne said. "Didn't you grow up eating it?"

"No, I am not ship-born. I am from Essius."

Marne looked as if his boat had struck a hidden rock and was about to sink.

"But I trained on the ship, nearly four years," John hastened to add. "I assisted them in studying Essian medicines. For a time, I was personal physician to one of the captains."

Marne didn't look as if this reassured him; if anything, he was even more stricken. Then he made an effort and controlled his face, but John had seen the truth clearly: he was a disappointment. Livestock and a doctor.

They piled into the van, Piro driving with Marne beside him, John and Sudharma sharing the second row of seats.

"We had a house vacant, so we've set that up for you for now," Piro called over his shoulder. "If you'd prefer some other living situation, I'm sure we can work it out."

"John, you might prefer to board with a family," Sudharma said. "My dietary restrictions will be tedious in a housemate, and I spend a great deal of time in either ritual or meditation."

"Is that very loud?"

"No. Some is silent and some is speech at an ordinary volume."

"Then I don't see why I should mind. Diet can be worked out, I'm sure."

"Well, keep your options open. I won't be offended if you flee at any time. But we will be working together, so if you can stand sharing a house, it will be convenient."

They crested a hill and the town came into view below. It stretched out alongside a river as a Clear Lakes village might, but though the river's bed was deep, no more than a trickle of water could be seen at its bottom. The buildings were earthen, unpainted, and rounded at edges and corners, so that if their doors and windows had not shown them to be dwellings built by humans, one might have thought they were spontaneous extrusions of the ground. The town itself was dry and barren, only a few of the waxy plants having been suffered to remain; but past its edge, and on the far side of the river, the land was sectioned into fields, and some of these were vivid green.

The van stopped in front of a building, earthen like the others, with a plant shaped like a pleated bottle by the door. It was small for a house, but large for only two; indeed John could have wished it a bit smaller, to reduce the time needed for cleaning. Still he thought they would be very comfortable. The kitchen was adequate in size, with one side bounded by a counter rather than a wall; beyond that stood a small table and chairs. Though no Essian house would have so little separation between the places of cooking and eating, the arrangement would well suit the needs of a motherless pair. Most remarkably, the kitchen boasted a refrigerator and a sleek stove. It was hard to believe these appliances had been manufactured on a colony of well under a thousand people, yet if they had been brought here, then the *Rose* and the *Axe* were far more generous with their cargo space than the *Folly*.

Piro, on his way back from delivering luggage to the bedrooms, stopped by the kitchen door. "There's food in there, if your stomachs have settled. It should be enough to last a few days until you get on your feet. And the governor's planning on feeding you dinner tonight."

"Thank you," John said. "You've been very kind."

"I didn't do anything but drive. The tamales in the fridge are my wife's, though. Try those first."

John had begun to feel some warmth toward Piro, but at the word 'wife' a blanket of snow was laid over it. He must expect this; everyone he met on Scythia, or nearly so, would be involved in marriage, and he would be reminded of that frequently. Yet somehow he must learn to coexist with them. Scythian life not being edible, there was no possibility of fleeing town and living off the land.

Piro said his goodbyes, citing a need to take the rats to be defrosted. Marne lingered in the front hall, and when the door had closed he turned to John. "Look, it was years ago when we sent out that call for help. We're just not in the same situation we were then. I have two apprentices who can handle simple cases now, with supervision. It's important they keep doing that for the experience. The best role for you will be to handle emergencies outside town."

"What sort of emergencies are there?"

"Mainly falls and adverse interactions with wildlife. Now and then a poisoning—that should be up your alley. Having you on call will let us deal with all that without leaving the town undoctored. You understand?"

John understood that he was being pushed to the side. Even if everyone here was both foolish and clumsy, such a little settlement could not antagonize enough animals or fall down enough cliffs to add up to a full-time occupation. It could only be a prejudice against Essians that motivated Marne. The ship had found John fit to see patients—albeit, not the more challenging cases—and he had said so; a colony with only one real doctor could not have less use for him than that. And while, no doubt, Ischnura was more advanced than Essius, Marne could not know how much ships' medicine had been adopted in the cities, and he ought to know that he could not. The two planets were far from each other, and no ship in living memory had made the trip directly. Marne's impression of John's world must be not only secondhand, but long outdated.

And yet, the idea of tending to emergencies was not so unappealing. At home John had practiced medicine in puddle country for a time, before returning to the hospital in Faivai—treating any problem brought to him without the help of specialists, and often with herbs gathered locally; that had taught him how to improvise to meet a circumstance. Field medicine here would be less varied, but it would still allow him a degree of independence. He thought if he insisted on being allowed to see regular patients, it would mean being treated as another apprentice, and that would be galling. So he said nothing more.

Sudharma came into the hall. "I think, since Dr. Maraintha will be assisting me with translation, it will be best if he tends to any other medical needs I have as well. You will indulge those of us who prefer his care even in town, won't you?"

"Certainly," Marne said, sounding apprehensive. Then he managed a more relaxed tone. "Yes, of course, if that's how you want it."

When he had gone Sudharma said, "A man like that might have alienated a few patients. Possibly one could find them. Now if you will excuse me, I am going to adopt the suggestion of a nap."

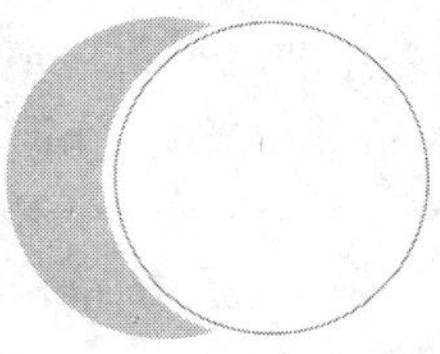

CHAPTER FOUR

Piro returned to show them to the place of the meeting. Sudharma, on hearing his knock, came out of his room with a parcel covered in elaborately printed cloth and tied up with a ribbon of contrasting cloth—a gift, John thought. He wondered if he should have brought a present of his own, but even if he had thought of it, he had nothing to give.

A walk of five minutes brought them to a house whose earthen walls were stained orange by the sunset. The governor answered the door and introduced himself as Michael Ward. He had the coloring of signalberry bark in autumn, when it has faded to a yellowish tan; the lightness of it made a pleasant contrast with his brown-black hair. His nose was narrow and prominent and had an interesting bend at the bridge. When he shook hands his touch was delicate, his manner was reserved. John thought the governor was deciding what to make of him, but whether he had come to a conclusion was unclear.

Sudharma spoke his own beautiful name and added, "That is a *Rose of the Winds* accent, isn't it?"

"Yes," Michael said with mild surprise. "I'm the only ship-born on Scythia—no one else fancied a new colony."

As John came into the room, a feeling of unease washed over him. He knew these were the people he would spend his life among, and he must make a good impression, especially after making such a poor one on Marne; that was enough to make him nervous. He knew, too, that they were probably all married and he must conceal any reaction to that fact; the thought was suffocating. But more than that, he had a sense that some great tragedy had occurred or was about to. After groping in the dark inside himself to find the cause of this dismay, he traced it to the fact that they had been met at the door by a man and led into a room without women. If the meeting had been held in an office he might only have thought that it was, at least metaphorically, a council of war; but since this was a house, he naturally felt as if he were attending a funeral. The last of the mothers had died, leaving the house an empty shell, and it must change now or die too: that was the memory that troubled him. Having named the dread did something to alleviate it, and he managed an appearance of equanimity.

Piro made his greetings and went to sit on the couch. On the other side of the room Marne sat in an upholstered chair, leaning forward with his fingers laced together in between his knees. He had an air of poorly contained restlessness, as if their entrance had interrupted him while he was pacing and he would like to get back to pacing.

Near Marne was another of the same kind of chair, and next to that a man stood very straight, as if he had been stationed there to guard it. He might have been Marne's brother: they were equally fair, equally pale-haired, and quite similar in face. Another Ischnuran, then. Looking back and forth between them, John could pick out a few differences—Marne was a little thinner and his hair, although not long, was slightly longer—but if he saw them again separately he would have trouble telling which one was which. The governor introduced the new man as Zhuyef; he was an engineer but had some understanding of linguistics, and so had led the attempts to communicate with basket-men.

"He's too polite to add, with a complete lack of success. Welcome to both of you, especially my replacement."

In the chair that Zhuyef seemed to guard, a man sat wearing an expression of faint amusement. He was as white as the other Ischnurans, but the shape of his face was softer. His golden hair was pulled back in a braid that fell forward over his shoulder and reached to the crook of his elbow, a few strands being left unbound to frame the face in hanging spirals. He wore a long blue jacket that fit closely from the shoulders to the waist, then spilled out in soft pleats over trousers the color of stone. The intricate braid and the beautiful garment turned the blank paper of Ischnuran sameness into something far more elegant; there was an allure about him that was lacking in the others.

"And this is Iren," the governor said, pronouncing the name with the piercing vowel of 'here' and the soft one of 'then.' "They're a biologist, and have been working with Piro to understand the nature of the basket-men."

Zhuyef put his hand on Iren's shoulder. "Iren is a jess—not a man or a woman. To respect our customs, we ask that you use the pronoun 'they' for them. It's important to all of us."

Iren laid their own hand over his, quellingly. "But we understand, don't we, that you are from different worlds. You may find it difficult to use 'they' in the singular—as no doubt we will stumble over the pronunciations of your names and trample every rule of courtesy you follow. Where there is goodwill on both sides, such unintended blows land lightly."

The formality and measured cadence of this discourse was surprising. John found the other two Ischnurans rather terse and blunt—in Marne's case, to the point of rudeness—and had expected, without realizing he expected, that the pattern would continue. Iren's speech could hardly have been more different. Terran books sometimes described a character as 'courtly,' and though he couldn't have defined the word precisely, something in their manner caught on the tangle of associations that surrounded it and drew it up into his mind. He wished he could meet their complicated courtesy with an equally gracious answer, but, unable to formulate anything suitable, he only managed to say, "We do, actually, use *thee*—that is, 'they'—for a child in the womb, for example, or a figure on a distant hill. I believe I will manage."

Sudharma said, "I suppose I too can manage, although it will be an adjustment. Hearing a jess with a Northern accent, I naturally expect to use the pronoun *yee*."

"Ha! No, the South has conquered us to that extent—we all say *day* and *zhes*, not *yee* and *hoandviif*. And in English we just roll the words back to their roots, so I would say 'they' if I referred to some illustrious jess of history—I am the only one in the world at present, so it hardly comes up otherwise." They looked up at Zhuyef. "Now quit fussing and let's move on to more pressing matters—such as how all of us courteous and brilliant people might manage to die of old age."

This remark produced a silence into which the governor said, "You've heard about our visitor from Earth."

He retold the story anyway, adding a few details. Iren, who must have known it as well as he did, nonetheless listened attentively. It was obvious to John now that the shape of their face was feminine, the line of their jacket inflected by breasts. Their voice was deep for a woman's, but not so deep that one would ever say it was a man's. He didn't see a bed-beetle in their throat—what was it called in English?—an Adam's apple. He had been so certain they were a man that he had not been aware he was making a judgment; it had felt like directly perceiving a natural truth. Now perception informed him, with just as much certainty, that he was looking at a woman. He understood that that was also incorrect, but how? Perhaps there was some difference in the intimate anatomy, but the cut of their trousers was such as to baffle investigation.

He looked up at Iren's face again and saw them looking back at him. He was sure they knew where his eyes had strayed and for what reason. Warmth came into his face and he fixed his attention on the governor, but he held the image of Iren's expression in his mind. It was not, he hoped, a look of deep offense. He thought that mainly they seemed tired. Perhaps there was also a tinge of amusement that by tailoring they had defeated his intrusion, but that might also just be their habitual expression. He could only hope they would consider his rudeness an example of trampling a rule of courtesy through inexperience.

The governor had finished his narration; now he addressed Sudharma directly. "What do you think Earth was up to?"

"I believe you already know. They saw our pod in the sky and thought it might be a threat. It would be useless to attack aiyi with a bomb, but they didn't trust humans to understand that. They had something precious to them and irreplaceable, and instead of trying to hide it, they moved it to the center of your colony. Even if you had all fled town, I imagine any bomb that could damage a Terran vehicle would also destroy enough infrastructure to put your survival on this world in question. Reasonably, Earth expected that would stay the *Folly*'s hand."

"I'm glad their theory wasn't tested. That ship has a reputation." The governor's eyes found John's. "No offense."

"None taken. Your opinion of the captains' conduct could hardly be lower than mine."

Michael didn't look happy to be agreed with. Maybe he didn't think someone not born on the ships should express an opinion about them. But he let the matter go. "Any theories as to what it is Earth wants so badly to protect?"

"The only thing that can't be backed up offworld and restored after an attack," Sudharma said. "Live human beings."

The governor nodded as if he had thought the same. "So we have Terrans, and we probably have sentient aliens. The example of Erav shows that's a dangerous combination, but Dharanendra survived it. What can you tell us about how?"

"In honesty, nothing. Terrans landed on our world, spent some time there, and left. They were interested in the vzdrei, but not particularly focused on them. Dharanendrans never felt we were in danger. It was nearly a century before we found out Terrans had destroyed the human colony on Erav. Most people think the Eravans were judged for their treatment of the indigenous people on their world, and our more harmonious relations with the vzdrei saved us. But it could be that the aiyi who came to Dharanendra simply had different intentions and ideas. They certainly could not have coordinated their decisions with each other, or with Earth—even aiyi cannot send a message faster than light speed."

"Do you have any suggestions for improving our chances?"

"I'd like to understand your situation as a whole first. What can you tell me about your neighbors?"

"We can show you," the governor said. He turned to a large screen on one wall, and though he didn't touch it, speak, or in any apparent way gesture, it sounded a soft chime and brightened, becoming a rectangle of pure white. Colors bloomed into this paleness to become the image of an animal—not a photograph, but a meticulous and detailed painting; it must have been worked on for many hours. Like a rat or a cow, the creature stood on four legs, but it was curiously proportioned—higher at the shoulders than the hips, so that the back sloped sharply downward. The arms were thicker than the hind legs, too, their powerful muscles visible beneath the short gray fur. It had a long face like a rat's, although not quite so pointed. The cheeks were bare of fur and wrinkled, which at first made John imagine it as old; but when the screen zoomed in to show the head alone, he saw they were not creased with age, but rather had a quilted look. As he watched, the ears folded down onto the sides of its face, where they resembled sepals on a bud, then swiveled up and back to stand erect again. The silhouette of a man stood behind it for scale; the head came up about to his waist.

Michael looked back and forth between Iren and Piro. "Which of you wants to cover biology?"

Piro shrugged. "You talk, I'll heckle."

"All right," Iren said, "but if you're too much of a nuisance I'll make you take over so I can interrupt you instead."

Everyone sat down, and Iren began. "This is a basket-man, and I will tell you first of all, don't take the word 'man' literally—that is human guesswork, and says more about us than them. They have no visible genitalia, and though we do have their genome, sex determination on Scythia is never genetic. A plant may choose to make male or female animals depending on the time of year, or how warm is the soil, or whether others of its own kind are nearby. So we cannot say whether the ones we've seen are male or female or otherwise. Perhaps, like jesses, they will tell us their own genders someday."

"Maybe we'll see one of the other sex and it'll be obvious."

Iren acknowledged Piro's point with a shrug. "This is the hand," they said, and at once the image of a hand filled the screen. It had a thumb longer than a human's and six fingers, each one tipped with a thick and curving claw. Cradled in the palm there was a round, brown object that looked like it had been dug out of the ground. Then this vanished, and the hand turned over and stretched out its fingers. "Those claws are made for digging—very common on this world, where every animal at least plants seeds, and many cultivate the ground to benefit their seedlings. Their food, we think, grows underground, so they must also dig that up. Perhaps they live in burrows too, which would explain why we don't see them until they decide to come visit us. When they aren't digging, the claws fold back out of the way"—here the last joint of the fingers bent back sharply, a pad of skin at the bending point becoming the new fingertip—"and the thumb can touch any of these pads, so they can grip objects quite delicately. They can carry things too, and when they're doing that they sometimes walk upright, but to cover distance quickly they will go on all fours."

The screen changed to show the whole of the basket-man again. This time he was wearing a pack woven from plant fibers that stretched the whole length of his back from his neck to his hips. It was curved to conform to the shape of his body so it would be stable, and secured around his arms and waist with thick bands. At the front, a lid of the same stuff had been affixed by thrusting several small pieces of stick diagonally through lid and pack.

"And this is the product of their dexterity: a basket suitable for carrying large quantities of food while keeping the hands free. Every basket-man we've seen has arrived wearing one of these, and left when his supply ran low. They accepted water from us, but ignored any food we tried to give them. It may be that the food they carry with them is the only kind that they can eat, in which case those spheres are probably food bodies made by the plant phase of their own species—that is a common pattern on Scythia. But we have yet to find any basket-man plants. In any case, we can't confirm that they are dining on their relatives, since they don't waste so much as a crumb of their food. At my instigation Zhuyef tried, by gestures, to ask for a piece once. The response was such as you might get if you asked a man to hand over a slice of his testicles."

"If I were walking on a world where I couldn't breathe the air," the governor said, "and only had one tank of oxygen to keep me going, I don't think I'd let even the most well-intentioned alien inspect the mechanism."

"No doubt, but wisdom in a subject of study is inconvenient—hence my preference for invertebrates." Iren paused and then said carefully, "Of course, a carrying-basket is a tool, which might be taken as an indication of intelligence—and I had better yield the floor to Piro now, or he is likely to burst an aneurysm."

Indeed Piro was leaning forward in his eagerness to speak. "I'm going to make the case for *not* losing our minds about the baskets. Humans get all excited about animals using tools, because that's our thing and we've done well with it. But tool use is found in all kinds of animals, including some with brains the size of pinheads. And there are at least eight worlds besides this one where animals make baskets—we just call them nests. They don't carry them around, but that's just another simple behavior. Weaving plant fibers isn't that hard, and it doesn't require any special intelligence. So when I look at that basket, I'm not wondering 'How are they so smart,' I'm wondering 'What problem is that solving, and how are they getting away with such a crude solution?'"

"It seems elegant to me," John said. "I mean, I would be proud to have made a basket like that."

"Sure, it's pretty—that's not the point. The point is it takes time to make, it weighs them down, they have to watch over it constantly or risk losing their food supply. As a way to increase the distance an animal can travel, it has a lot of costs. On Zandahe there's a young volcanic island with a little flying animal called a *gaña* that drinks nectar with a straw made from a hollow plant stem. Why an island? Because no real nectar-drinkers have made it there yet, so an animal that used to eat fruit found a quick and dirty way to fill the niche. But they waste a lot of their time making straws. As soon as something with a long, narrow beak or tongue shows up or evolves, they'll probably go extinct. This is *not* an island. So if basket-men are really going to all that trouble just to travel further from their plant-stage relatives, why haven't they evolved to store more body fat or have a varied diet instead?

And if they can't, why hasn't their niche been taken from them by something that can?"

"I'm sure you will enlighten us," Iren said. They were enjoying themself, John thought.

"Because they *are* males, they're here looking for mates, and what they're carrying isn't just food for the road, it's a courting gift. They're going to offer it to any females they can find. That way it makes perfect sense—males do costly and ridiculous things for mating all the time. It's not like some other animal can come along and outcompete them at mating with their own species. Even the basket itself might be a courtship display that females will evaluate. But I'm sure Iren wants to tell us all some paradox that proves me wrong."

"Well, I would like to, but the *gaña* has disarmed me. I wouldn't dare to go against you without marshaling up some equally charming animal." They thought for a moment. "I could tell about the hound who tried to lick the gypsum dunes because he thought anything white and sparkling must be snow."

"Does that mean 'You don't know until you experiment'?"

"Not a bad principle, but I think it means that we are far from home and should be careful in interpretation. And, also, what do you think the hound did, after he spat out his mouthful of sand? Did he stay in the dunes, to admire them? They are very striking—a human might linger. A hound is smart, but not too smart to be pragmatic. Seeing there was nothing for him there, he would leave to find prey and water. The basket-men see a marvel too—us. A useless marvel, offering no food they can eat, no chance of copulation, and nothing of the mutual understanding or companionship that another of their species might provide. Yet every one stays. If they are searching for mates, why would they waste time and eat up their dowers just for us? Mating is important! Animals pursue it with great dedication—humans too, or so I'm told. But they are fascinated. They try to learn our language, imitate our ways. They can't tear themselves away till imminent starvation forces them to leave. Only intelligence could produce behavior so ridiculous."

Sudharma cleared his throat softly. "I think that, while interesting, this debate won't affect my work much. No matter what theory says, I will still try to communicate with them. I would like to hear what you have tried so far, and what the outcome was."

"Well, thank you for stopping us," Iren said. "I would never have gotten the last word with Piro otherwise. I gladly yield the screen."

Zhuyef sighed and sat up straighter in his chair. "The video I'm going to show you is of last year's attempt to teach a basket-man ships' English. I haven't tried to learn their language because they never speak it in front of us. Maybe they don't have one. They act like they want to learn ours, but . . . well, you'll see how it works out."

Unprompted, the video began.

"This was in a small educational farm just outside town. It's used to test new strains of crops and to teach people how to farm with only simple tools, in case we have to do it all like that someday. That's usually where basket-men show up first. They'll stop to watch people work, sometimes even try to help by imitating us. They always give up after a few minutes, though."

On the screen Zhuyef pointed to a plant and said the word 'pumpkin.' A basket-man, on all fours, examined it closely and pressed his face into the leaves. Then he turned toward the camera and sat up. His right hand rested on the ground; the left came up to grip one of the bands of fiber that held the basket on his back. It was a very human gesture, John thought. When Zhuyef repeated the word, he opened his mouth but produced only a vaguely bisyllabic mutter. Then on the third try a high, childlike voice said, "Pumpkin." John shivered, because the basket-man's lips had not closed on the consonants *p* and *m*. It was as if the word had come from somewhere inside and his mouth only pretended, unconvincingly, to be the source.

"I knew from previous years that they can easily distinguish Terran plants, and plants or dryads are easier for them to learn than objects or people's names. Also, they always assume I'm giving them the name of the species. I've tried teaching them categories like 'plant' or 'candle' but it didn't go well."

Zhuyef repeated the teaching process with a pepper plant, a sweet potato, a squash, and something called a tomatillo. Then he gave a quiz by pointing to different plants of the same species in a different order. The basket-man answered all of the implied questions as readily as if he had been speaking English his whole life. Next Zhuyef pointed to himself and spoke his own name. The alien repeated this on the first try, but with an *f* that sounded like *th*. Then, as if dissatisfied, he repeated it several more times until the consonant was correct.

"Trying to give them more than one person's name or teach the word 'human' just confuses them. I skipped that in hope of getting further this time."

The basket-man was standing upright now. In this pose he looked more human than animal, even if by 'animal' one meant the Terran kind that wore hair instead of armor. Zhuyef gave him a stiff rectangle, hinged in the middle and covered in some soft material on both sides—rather like the cover of a book with no pages. He held it close to his face and opened his mouth twice without speaking, as if considering how best to shape the sounds of its name, then repeated the word Zhuyef had given him, which was 'library.' Next came a clawlike tool that Zhuyef called a cultivator; again, after a few false starts, the basket-man learned the word easily. A hoe gave him more trouble. He examined the blade and started to speak several times, then turned it around and repeated the same process with the handle before finally saying 'cultivator.' He was sure of this identification and repeated it six times before finally conceding to Zhuyef's insistence on the word 'hoe.'

"By this time I was wondering if he thought 'cultivator' was the word for 'tool.' But watch this."

On the screen, the offering of a garden trowel was enthusiastically identified as a library.

"Wait," Sudharma said. "Could you pause that?"

"Yes," Zhuyef said, and the image paused.

"Why did you hand him each object, rather than just hold it up for him to see?"

"They want to handle things and examine them closely. Otherwise they just ignore the word I'm trying to teach."

"Were all those tools made of the same materials? The same metal, the same species of wood?"

"That's not my department, but I would think so."

"And who did they belong to?"

"The farm, as far as I know." Zhuyef was puzzled by the question and so was John. "There's a toolshed. Piro's wife Laura was there—I think she had taken them out to use."

"Not the trowel, however," Iren said. "That one is mine—I use it to dig traps for invertebrates."

"What about the library?"

"That was mine, too. I prevailed upon Zhuyef to give it to the basket-man, so he would handle it and it could read his DNA."

"Good," Sudharma said. "Continue, please."

Zhuyef, with difficulty, managed to convince the basket-man that the trowel was a trowel. Then he handed him a plastic cup, and the alien at once asserted it was a trowel too.

"Pause, please. Whose cup was that?"

"It was Laura's." Iren's tone was guarded, as if they suspected Sudharma of playing some trick on them.

Sudharma frowned; John thought the answer disappointed him. "All right, please continue."

The basket-man could never overcome his confusion about tools. He learned the word 'cup,' but then when the trowel was presented again, he identified that as a cup too. Later Zhuyef tried a rake that—as he volunteered without being asked—he had taken from the shed himself. The basket-man repeated the word 'rake,' but then, after another round of hesitation, he also said "Zhuyef." Eventually he decided that every object handed to him was Zhuyef. Yet when quizzed again on plant names he recited every one correctly.

"That was it for that day. I kept trying as long as he stayed in town, but his heart wasn't in it. I don't mind admitting I'm out of my depth, but it looks to me like plants are all he understands and his mind can't get a grip on anything else. I don't suppose you have a better idea yet?"

"I have another idea, at least. If I were wise I would wait to share it until I have confirmed it. But perhaps, by coming up with a hypothesis so quickly, I can create an impression of brilliance that will linger even when I turn out to be wrong." Sudharma went to stand at the center of the floor. "Michael, if you would indulge me by joining me here? Thank you. Now, imagine we don't have any languages in common and you want to teach me the word 'window.' How would you do that?"

The governor looked like he was feeling awkward. Probably he thought this demonstration was beneath his dignity. Nevertheless he pointed and said, "Window."

"Yes, that would work on me, because I understand your gesture. If you tried it on a vzdrei—at least, one who hasn't spent time around humans—he would just look at your finger. To point out an object to him, you would have to do this." Sudharma curled the fingers of one hand into a tunnel and placed it in front of Michael's eye so that he looked through it. "If you would close your other eye, please—a vzdrei would do that instinctively."

Michael made a small grunt of surprise. "It's like you put it in a frame."

"The gesture I just made is called *dashkvaut.* It might seem cumbersome to us, but if you're trying to point out well-camouflaged animals in the forest, it's superior to any method humans have. So I can use that, and a vzdrei will look where I want him to. The next question is, what will he see? If he's never been in a human house before, he won't know what a window is. Now, at night, he might think 'window' means a reflection, or he might see himself and think it's our name for his species. If I tried again during the day, he might see the sky, or the house across the street, or someone who happened to be passing by."

Sudharma turned to Zhuyef. "The basket-man did know what it meant to point with a finger—as long as you were pointing at plants, he understood you. When you gave him objects, he brought them close to his face and then opened his mouth. I think he was smelling them. Humans leave traces of our scent on things we touch, especially when it's a hot day—you were visibly sweating by the end of the video, and somebody weeding a field, or digging holes out in the desert, would be sweating even more. So when he holds the cultivator and the hoe, he smells Laura, and he's confused that you insist she is two different people. On the library and the trowel, he smells Iren. On the rake, which I imagine had been in the toolshed for some time, he smelled only you, so he said your name. Eventually you had been handling all those objects enough that he smelled you on everything."

"You mean all that time, all I had to do was wear gloves and give him unused tools?"

"That might have helped, if I am right. But it wasn't modesty that led me to say I would turn out to be wrong—it was that cup. The cup was Laura's, so he should have associated it with the hoe, not the trowel. Iren, is it possible you touched it before it was given to him?"

"Why yes, I did. I passed by the farm on my way home from digging traps. Laura had brought ice water and took pity on my overheated state. I held the cup and drank from it—I even pressed it to my brow to cool myself. Then we saw the basket-man up on the hill, so I stayed to see what would happen. The cup would certainly have had more of my scent on it than Laura's."

"Then, when a basket-man next comes to town, at least I will have an idea how to point properly. There will be many other barriers to communication after that, no doubt. But I have every hope of being able to talk to them in the end."

This appeared to John to bring the subject to a close, but Piro was still discontent. "Doesn't that just prove Zhuyef was right that their minds are limited? The basket-man had plenty of chances to figure out 'trowel' meant the tool in front of his face and could never grasp it. A lot of dryads tend their seedlings and some of them do it communally—maybe they only use language for that. Names of plants that need to be dug up, other basket-men he can work with, animals that need to be killed or driven away. Us, but we're probably counted as basket-men."

"That might be. It might also be that they expect to learn a language in a certain way, and we confuse them by not following the rules. When I was five years old I wanted desperately to speak with vzdrei. I noticed that when important announcements were made on the radio, they were always said in Dharanendran and repeated in the local vzdrei language, which was called Kveidenzsat. No one had told me different languages had different grammars. I thought if I wrote down what I heard and matched up the first word to the first word, the second to the second, and so on, I could gain enough vocabulary for a conversation. The first four words of a Dharanendran weather alert, translated literally, are 'Warning: A severe storm' and the Kveidenzsat begins 'Aurally attend because-of danger,' so you can imagine that the vzdrei I tried my language skills on were confused. Later, when I was taught those same words properly, I learned them with no trouble."

"Even so, if they made tools by experimentation and insight, instead of pure instinct, you'd think they'd be more interested in ours."

John wondered why Piro insisted so much on this point. It seemed to him that all of them were taking miracles for granted. A basket-man could speak words; it could weave fiber; it could hold food in its hand. He had barely gotten used to seeing animals with fur.

"There are different kinds of intelligence," Sudharma said. "As a translator I'm not here to evaluate theirs, but to try to have a conversation. If they only talk about gardening, I will find out what they have to say about gardening."

Michael said, "The only definition of intelligence we need to worry about is Earth's. That's what's going to tell us which side of the airlock we're on." And of course, all these people were only afraid. Piro was afraid and it made him search for reasons that the basket-men were of no interest. If Terrans had truly killed all the humans on Erav then the fear was understandable, but it seemed that had been more than a century ago—an unthinkably long time to pursue a feud. On Essius the neighbors' mothers would have put a stop to it long ago.

"I'm afraid I don't know anything about what definition they use, or whether intelligence is what they care about. Have you tried asking them?"

"They made it pretty clear they didn't want to talk to us."

"What were their exact words, if you remember?"

"'We are not here to communicate.'"

"I would take that literally: contact with you was not the purpose of their visit. That doesn't mean that contact is forbidden. It is simply not possible that we could annoy Earth humans by trying to talk to them. They have conscious control over their senses and attention—ring a bell next to their ears, and they can choose not to hear it. As for the aiyi, they would no more be distracted by our voices than by the flowing of a river on the other side of the world, which, we must assume, they also hear. But if the idea worries you, let me visit them first. When I have returned safely, you can choose whether to go too."

"You'll be infected with their technology."

"That happened on Dharanendra, yes. When people had been near an Earth human, engineered microbes and machines as small as microbes were found in their bloodstreams. It's simply part of how they perceive us. Here in your house, that lamp shines on me—in theirs, a light will be shed on my inner workings. The microbes die within a day; the machines cease functioning and are eventually eliminated from the body. The people this happened to lived and thrived, and their descendants still thrive. I don't fear it. But if I did, I certainly wouldn't expect distance to protect me. If Earth wanted me infected with something harmful then I already would be."

Sudharma looked over the room, and seeing that his words had alarmed everyone, he added, "As difficult as it is, we must see our situation clearly. If the aiyi choose to harm us, we can do nothing to stop them. We can only hope to influence them, or failing that, at least to find out what they want. To do either we must start talking, and right now, while Earth humans are nearby, is our best chance. Can I walk to where they are?"

"Absolutely not," Michael said. "You've made your case—we have to try talking—but you don't know how to stay safe in the desert. You could get killed trying to get there."

"That does create a complication. *Dashkvaut* is very difficult for humans to perform—our brains don't calculate the angles naturally. Mine has been altered so it does, but other abilities were affected. It's not at all advisable for me to drive."

"I can drive," John said. "And I'm not afraid if he isn't. We are the newcomers, so Earth can put the blame on us if we are trespassing. That way none of you will have to risk yourselves."

Michael said, "This isn't like driving on city streets."

"I spent two years driving around puddle country—that means 'the backwoods,' more or less—tending to families with no other access to ships' medicine. The terrain there was quite rugged."

"But there were roads?"

"It was forested, so I could only drive where somebody had cleared a road. The roads were always dirt—or mud when it had rained enough. I kept a saw and a machete on the front seat to cut saplings that had grown up in them."

"Piro, what do you think? Can he manage it?"

"Assuming the Terrans haven't moved, it's not a bad drive, but the stretch of river that crawler is camped on is lousy with snake-trees. They're going to need a crash course in desert safety first."

"How long will that take?" Sudharma asked.

"Half a day would do it—if you two are willing to get up early and spend the morning walking around the desert. Then you can make your visit in the afternoon."

"Certainly," John said. "That suits me."

"I think I had better spend the morning reviewing the history of Dharanendra's contact with Earth humans, to be as prepared as I can for the meeting. I trust John to protect me from snake-trees, whatever they are. To protect us from conflict with Earth will be my concern."

"All right." Michael looked unhappy but resigned. "For the moment at least, you're our ambassador. Piro, you'll make arrangements with John?"

"Sure, I'll message Laura and find out when she wants to start."

These words, though seemingly innocuous, produced a sensation. Marne and Michael looked worried and Zhuyef shocked. Only Iren was unbothered; there was the trace of a smile on their lips.

Piro, with the air of someone struggling to be civil, explained slowly: "I'm a biologist—she's a desert safety instructor. He doesn't need to understand how candles change albedo in the summer, he needs to know how to tell the difference between insects and snake-trees and which one to run away from. Laura will teach him the basics with no unnecessary digressions and have him ready to go by lunch. If asked nicely, she might also provide lunch."

"Maybe you should go with them, to provide the expert view," Michael suggested.

"No, I shouldn't, because it isn't necessary, and because Iren and I are going out to collect specimens for our genetic survey tomorrow. Remember, if something out there has genes for concentrating arsenic and we miss it, we might not have to worry about *Earth* wiping us out."

Iren, who was no more disturbed by Piro's annoyance than the ocean would be heated by a fallen candle, spoke serenely. "Piro and I are as one on this. If we must die, I intend to die as I lived: with a great backlog of undescribed specimens. But we might bend our route to go along the ridge, and look down on the river to find out whether the Terran myriapod still lingers where it was before. If it has moved and we can spot it, we could call home to discuss some unrelated matter, and you could make a note of our position when we called. In that way we might save our embassy some time in searching."

"Good. We'll do that."

"Well," Zhuyef said, "I'm an early riser. Perhaps I'll take the opportunity for a good walk and a refresher course—"

"I trust my wife and I don't see that it's anybody else's business, so you can all just cut it out before I decide she's been insulted."

John understood at last that the dispute was about marriage. The men—except Piro—imagined that if he was left alone with a married woman she would surely agree to a visit, in defiance of her vows. It was interesting to see that even they knew that monogamy was unnatural. Why else would they expect it to crumble so easily? At home there was no need to keep men and women apart in case they should decide to get married. It was interesting, too, that the idea of John going into the desert alone with Piro did not produce equal alarm. In principle, marriage constrained all its inmates, but perhaps the summer captain had been right that it constrained men less.

"Well, I suppose that's settled," Michael said. "Dinner should be in about twenty minutes—let me just go and check on that."

"May I review that video in the meantime?" Sudharma asked. "There are a few details I would like to make sure of."

"Certainly. Zhuyef can help you if you need it."

Sudharma seemed already to know how to operate the screen. He turned it down to a much lower volume, explaining that his hearing was acute. He sped through the video, then played brief sections of it over and over, sometimes slowing them down until their movement decomposed into a series of still pictures. John thought he was examining the basket-man's body language rather than his speech.

"Ru is bringing food," Iren remarked to the other Ischnurans. "She wouldn't take no for an answer—told the governor it was favoritism to feed the newcomers on only Zandahean cooking."

"I wonder who told her the governor was asking them to dinner," Zhuyef said, in the tone of one who doesn't wonder at all.

"I did, of course. A noble act of Northern solidarity, concealing a great craving for her *meribred*.—That's a dessert, young man," they added, to include John in the conversation, "and you should save room for it. But how will you manage, after this dinner? Marne says you and Sudharma are lodging together. Will somebody bring you your meals? Or on Essius are boys taught how to cook instead of girls? For I hear everything there is done upside down."

"We were given some cooked dishes to begin with. But yes, I did learn to cook. Not all men do, but it was part of my training as a doctor."

"Not so much upside down as sideways, and yet what a good idea. Marne, you'd see me more often if you cooked me a hot lunch before the exam."

"On a good day I might manage a cold sandwich."

"What about you?" John asked. "I mean—being born a jess, were you taught to cook?"

Iren raised an eyebrow. "No one is born a jess, young man. We don't slide out of the womb with hair already braided."

"I beg your pardon. On the *Folly* they spoke of a gene—I must have misunderstood."

Iren leaned forward and inclined their head, regarding him intently. John wondered if that look was the last thing an insect saw before it was caught and pinned to a card. "Who told you that and what did they say exactly? If you remember."

"It was another doctor. The words were something like . . . 'on Ischnura there's a gene that makes some of them neither man nor woman.'"

"Is that all? I am eager to know what the ships say about jesses when Ischnurans aren't around, and will be grateful to you for carrying the message even if it is insulting."

John wondered if their resolution not to be insulted would survive hearing an insult. But they had asked directly and he felt that he must answer. "He said you've tried to breed the gene out of the population but you weren't systematic enough about it."

"Ah." It was hard to say what Iren's expression meant. He thought they were upset, and then again that maybe they were satisfied. "Well, you did misunderstand what they said to you. No harm done, and you weren't to know. But also, fuck the ships in general and *Edgar's Folly* in particular, because what they said was both incorrect and unkind." Noticing Zhuyef's expression, they added, "Oh come on, is it so shocking for a jess to say the word 'fuck'?"

Piro, who had been listening from the couch, said, "You do say it like you found it on the ground and are just trying it out to see what it does."

"Then I guess I need more fucking practice." Iren spoke with an ease that suggested such joking was common between them and Piro; but perceiving that Zhuyef was still out of countenance, they sought at once to soothe him. "Forgive me. I am feeling undone by the *Folly*'s sacrilege and will take a minute to braid up again." They fell silent; but after only a few breaths they said, "I worry that Ru has no one to help her bring her dishes here. I'm sure she'll have cooked more than one person can carry."

Zhuyef stirred at once as if to rise, then hesitated. John thought that Iren was trying to get rid of him and probably he knew it. But he did rise, and said graciously, "I will go and see how she is faring."

"That's kind of you, Zhuyef—and you will find me less scandalous on your return."

When he had left and closed the door behind him, Marne leaned toward Iren. "Ru will not thank you for that."

"She will understand the reason for it," Iren said blithely; then, reconsidering, they added, "And I will make her a dress in apology."

John was puzzled, and Iren must have realized it. "Zhuyef is a good man, truly," they explained, "but not one I can have at my elbow if I am to tell you the true meaning of the braid. He is very full of opinions on the topic."

"All of them from a previous century," Marne said.

Iren didn't look at him, but pointed a thumb in his direction. "This one also has opinions, but the opposite. I have to pick the one that best suits the occasion, like a woman's jewelry."

Marne threw up his hands. "Do you want me to take a walk too, or would standing in the corner be enough?"

"If you can bring yourself to listen with the deference you'd expect of me if you were teaching medicine, I will be glad of your company."

John thought that Marne didn't like the comparison to medicine, but he mastered his irritation. "Fair. I'll observe the operation and keep my hands out of the sterile field."

"Well, then, now that I have cleared enough space on the ground to sit down with my skirts about me, let me tell you a story." This was evidently an expression; they remained in their chair, leaned forward slightly, and smoothed their trousers down over their legs with their hands. "I was born into a sex, as you were. I was raised in it, as much as anyone could manage. But from an early age, I felt the call of a tradition that has shaped Ischnura's history more, perhaps, than any other. I asked my parents for permission and received it. There were months of planning and a considerable expenditure of money, which, luckily, better-off relatives helped to defray. A location was booked. A large number of chairs were rented. Flowers were arranged, ribbons were threaded into lattices, and hangings of embroidery were on display. There was a feast and a dance and a series of heartfelt but overlong speeches. And somewhere in the midst of all that pageant, I, a little waif in a blue jacket, under the eyes of my family and friends and a dozen or more jesses I had never met before nor would again, allowed an ancient jess to braid my hair, and spoke a vow nearly as old as our world, swearing to hold myself apart from sex and gender. With that oath, I became a jess.

"Now, if I liked, I could have told you a different story. I could have said that from an early age, I had a sense of being something else: not a boy, not quite a girl. I could have told you I felt that my body was wrong, and especially once puberty began, the shape of it tormented me. We call that kind of feeling a memory. If Zhuyef were here, he would be eager to inform you it was literally a memory of the form I once wore in that other world where, he believes, we all live before birth and after death. I'm not religious, personally, but it's true that it is *like* a memory. If you woke up tomorrow a half meter shorter, you would feel odd and unlike yourself, because you could remember being otherwise. Well, in the same way, I experienced a *not-myselfness* born of longing for a body and a way of being I had never had. Once I had taken the vow, I could begin to change myself to fit my memory, using medical techniques that are reserved for jesses only.

"But to tell the tale that way would be to change the focus from the social to the merely individual. Others come to the braid by many different paths. Theo the child of Toviian, the inventor of the artificial testis, took the vow as a way to change their name and appearance, hoping to elude their creditors after the failure of their first laboratory. No one ever praised their wisdom for it. Still they were a jess, and in the end a good one. Our reasons don't matter—what matters is that we speak the vow, and by it we're made new."

"Then why do the ships believe otherwise?" John asked.

"Because ship-folk never understand what is important. I think perhaps you've seen that at first hand."

"Certainly, I have. But how could anyone mistake a ceremony for a gene?"

"Here is the logic, if it can be called that. You've noticed, I'm sure, that Ischnurans are poor in variation. That is because, in the early years, our population crashed to only a handful of people. So at one time, before mutations and transplants from the ships brought in a trickle of diversity, all of us were blond and all of us were fair and all had the allele known commonly as anamnesis. We know, today, that those who have it are more likely to take the vow. The ships suppose that this inheritance is the only reason that the braid exists. And yet, most jesses don't have anamnesis and most who have it are not jesses. That doesn't trouble the ships—finding the theory doesn't match the facts, they would alter the facts to fit. So they propose, there should be testing: anyone with anamnesis should be urged to braid—they don't say 'forced' out loud—and anyone without it must remain sexed. Eventually, they imagine, anamnesis will die out and then the vow will be forgotten. Which goes to show we of the worlds are nothing more than cattle to the ships and they would breed us to their liking. They will never understand what matters: that to take the vow is joyous. It's a transformation we embrace with our whole selves. When I stood up before all my family and friends and recited the old words, a gene did not speak. *I* spoke. And we are richer, all of us, for being three instead of two."

John could easily believe the *Folly* would seek to suppress a custom they found inefficient or distasteful. But he still felt he was missing something. "Why do the ships think the gene would die out, if everyone who had it braided?"

"Ship-folk assume that jesses don't have children. Next time the *Folly* comes back to Ischnura, they will find out that idea is out of date. Then they will have to come up with some other reason to declare our ways irrational."

"But what does a change in hairstyle have to do with reproduction?"

"I am sorry—I see that Zhuyef's squeamishness made me too circumspect. When I said we hold ourselves apart from sex, I should have been clear and said fucking. Jesses are celibate."

"I see," he said carefully, trying to conceal his dismay. He had heard of celibacy: it was the most restrictive form of marriage, in which, instead of renouncing the whole world except for one person, the unfortunate spouse swore to visit with no one at all.

Iren was examining his face closely. "I think now for the first time I have shocked you. The word 'celibate,' was that it?"

"It's only that I don't see why, just because a person is neither a man nor a woman, they shouldn't be visited—or visit, according to preference, I suppose."

Halfway through the sentence he began to worry Iren would be offended at the implication they might be involved in sex, even couched as a general statement. But when he had finished, they smiled. "It is, in fact, my preference not to visit. You needn't imagine me pining. But also, celibacy is at the heart of what a jess is. It is the very substance of the vow we take. And so, as I love the tradition, I uphold its essence."

"Iren," Marne said, "I swear I am not trying to backseat-drive your gender, but you can't really expect the rest of us to pretend we all walked here from the year 200."

"My friend would like me to inform you that, in his part of Ischnura in particular, not every jess is as traditional as I am. And at home, where everyone already knows what the vow says, variations in observance might not threaten its survival. Here, I am the only jess that many people have ever met. If I explain the vow in words and contradict it by my conduct, how will they ever learn what being a jess means? We must also face the probability that a colony as small as ours will lose most of its technology, as your world and mine and Zandahe all did when Earth became enraptured by aiyi and ceased to send aid to its colonies. The ships have been warned Earth is here, or anyway the *Rose* has, and word will spread as fast as light. They all will stay away. So our machines will break down, no one will dare to bring us new ones, and we will have only what we can make for ourselves. As a few hundred or few thousand people huddled in a town, we will be vulnerable to disasters, and our tools will be poor. We must become millions, as soon as may be. A world in such a situation makes great demands, especially of those it sees as female. There will be those who cannot bear the universal fate of marriage and children, and for them, the vow won't be a sacrifice. It will be a refuge. So while, yes, in latter years and warmer climes, some jesses no longer observe their vows strictly, that is the act of those who have the luxury of being modern. It will not be so for our descendants, not for a long time. The tradition must be kept very strong and very clear, if it is to survive for those who need it."

John saw that Scythia's future was as bleak as its landscape. It disturbed him to think that women might escape the harshness of a wedding vow by swearing an even harsher one. And yet, for all the horror of it, he could see that such a choice was better than no choice at all.

He was trying to find a way to say as much without either offending Iren or betraying his own principles. Then he perceived that Michael had returned, and was watching them as warily as if a fate's-dagger had crawled into the room. Iren didn't turn to look, but they must have realized the governor was there from John's expression. At once the intensity fell from them. "But to answer your question at last," they said lightly, "yes, I can cook—though since I came to Scythia I rarely do so for anyone but myself."

Trying to match their casual tone, John asked, "And is it because you are a jess that you speak that way?"

Iren raised an eyebrow. "Why, whatever do you mean?"

"Well—copiously, I suppose, and colorfully, and often with a tinge of irony."

Marne blew out breath in an expression of disgust. "Iren is from the North—and from Iisles, no less. I used to work there. I can promise you there's not a man or woman in that town who can be serious at a funeral or wish you a good day in less than sixty seconds."

"Marne didn't like our Northern weather," Iren said, unruffled. "He got stuck in a snowdrift and his manners froze off."

They liked each other, John thought—despite their conflicts, despite their origins on different parts of Zandahe, despite the man's inherent unpleasantness. Iren and Piro had a fondness also, though they were from different worlds, and though even their gender was foreign to him. The problem facing John was to discover how to live among strange people with disturbing ways, and Iren had, in some measure, solved it.

Sudharma hoped to solve that problem too—not to learn to live with foreign people, but with basket-men and representatives of Earth. That should have seemed more difficult, but it did not.

A knock at the door stopped his train of thought. The governor went to answer, and admitted an Ischnuran woman in a long but sleeveless dress. Her whole left arm was covered by a shell of shining metal, cunningly designed not to restrict the normal movement of the limb: the elbow, the wrist, and all the small joints of the fingers were articulated like an exoskeleton. An arrangement of canvas straps, depending from the sheathed fingers, held two covered vessels stacked together. Zhuyef followed her in, bearing a third dish that would easily have fit atop the other two.

Michael introduced the woman as Arunikha, to which she instantly added "Ru." He added, as an afterthought, that she was an agricultural scientist. When he had given her John's and Sudharma's names she said, "It's a delight to meet you. I hear you are both very intrepid, and *you*"—she nodded toward Sudharma—"are some way toward being a sorcerer. I am sorry I missed the show."

"Your timing is perfect—we're ready to move to the dining room," Michael said. "You two can bring the food directly there."

In the dining room they found a small, dark, pleasant woman whom Michael introduced as Zohia, his wife. John's heart sank at the word in the usual fashion. She must have been in the kitchen the whole time they were talking. John saw no reason that the meeting could not have been held either before or after she began to make dinner so she could attend, but she gave no sign that she was sensible of being disrespected. In any case her presence, putting a last dish of food onto the table, and directing everybody where to sit, made the household feel less arid. John wondered if she and Michael had children somewhere. They were of an age when children might already be grown up, and so have moved to their own houses; that custom was common among marrying people, who by every indication must despise each other's company.

John found himself seated across from Ru. She was older than the other Ischnurans, he thought; her hair had streaks of white, though since the yellow strands were pale, one had to look closely to see it. Her face was softened by wrinkles but not yet hardened into them. On it was that look of exasperated indulgence sometimes seen on mothers in reaction to some mischief from their children—but Ru directed it instead at Iren, who paid no attention. She had no ring around her finger, but one hung, round and golden, from a chain around her neck. Possibly she had removed it so the metal covering would fit over her hand.

Zohia sat down last and addressed Sudharma. "Everything I cooked is meat-free. It couldn't be otherwise—our preserved beef all spoiled years ago if it didn't get eaten up first. And I left out any vegetable that grows under the ground, because I read Dharanendrans don't eat those either. The only native foods we use are cooking oils and those only come from the plant stages of dryads, but I wasn't sure if that would count as an animal so I used vegetable oil instead."

"Indeed, I will have to learn more about dryad biology to be sure," he said. "Thank you—that was very thoughtful."

Ru said, "I followed the same restrictions, being carefully schooled by Zohia, so you need worry about nothing on the table."

Sudharma thanked her as well and the transferring of food to plates began, less formally but more efficiently than at the winter captain's feast. When Ru had served herself, she used her armored hand to pick up a fork that was on the left side of her plate. John noticed that in reaching for it she overshot the mark a little and had to correct: the arm was a prosthesis. It was a well-made one and she was skilled with it—the amputation was not recent—but naturally she passed the fork to her right hand to use.

The meal Zohia had prepared was coal-black beans; mushrooms and vegetables bathed in a red sauce; and a dish of thin strips that, despite their purple color, turned out to be cabbage. The cabbage was sweet and the other two dishes were pleasantly spicy, though he thought they needed to be even more so to offset the barely flavored bedding they were served on, a pasta cut into small ovals like seeds. Arunikha had brought two vegetables John didn't recognize, possibly native Ischnuran. One was hard and overly bitter, the other bland yet satisfying in its texture. Glancing around the table, John detected a general lack of enthusiasm for the food that politeness could not quite conceal. As people used to eating meat, the colonists must have felt the loss of livestock keenly, and additional restrictions on ingredients could only make the resemblance to familiar foods more tenuous. Sudharma, however, ate with every appearance of enjoyment. Probably he found nothing amiss, but John was sure that he would not have shown it even if he had.

When everyone had finished, Ru retrieved her third dish—the one Zhuyef had carried. "This is a kind of dessert bread," she said as she uncovered it. "Where Iren and I come from, it's made in the late summer with wild berries, sweet roots, and a great deal of animal fat. I replaced the roots with sugar and the fat with a vegetable shortening, but I warn you that it's barely any lighter than it is at home. Only the strawberries are fresh this time of year, but they are *very* good strawberries."

John took a piece when the dish came to him. Though it was firmer in the hand than the word 'bread' implied, it came apart in flakes when bitten into and then melted in the mouth, releasing soft pieces of berry that were varyingly sweet and tart. It was wonderful. John saw that everybody thought so. And at this moment of harmony and satisfaction, Sudharma laid his present on the table.

"This is a gift for everyone—the whole colony—but Michael, as governor I think it would be fitting if you opened it. Piro, if you would pass it to him?"

When Michael had received the package he set it down and untied the ribbon. The cloth fell away to reveal a stack of paper packets. He picked up the topmost; it was covered with tiny handwriting on both sides. Puzzled, he began to read, holding the packet some distance away—he was of an age to need glasses, but had not yet given in to the necessity. Then his expression changed to startlement. "Seeds," he said.

"We had to guess what plants another world wouldn't already have, so I'm sure some of them will be redundant."

"Even so, more genetic material can never hurt." Ru had stood up immediately on hearing the word 'seeds.' Without asking permission she seized the packet on top of the stack. Zohia took one too and squinted at the text. "This says it is the most digestible of beans," she said. "Does that mean it will improve the odor of my family?"

"I think that is the implication, yes. My mother wrote those notes. Her opinions are not everyone's, but the recipes are excellent."

It was the perfect gesture: a permanent improvement to the world's diet, and at the same time, a connection to Sudharma's roots. It was a letter of recommendation, too—by entrusting him with her recipes, his mother had vouched for him. Sudharma had brought this gift along when he boarded *Edgar's Folly*, not knowing on what world he might wind up, only trusting that whoever he might meet would see the value of it. John had expected to return home, and so had brought nothing. In any case, he had no mother to write for him.

Ru tapped the packet she was holding. "I know what this is. Not by this name, but a resin that stinks until it's fried in oil? That's asafetida. I didn't know the plant had made it off Earth. This says it wants a cold desert, not a hot one, so it will take some engineering to make it grow here—then we wait five years to get a harvest—but I think it can be done." She smiled slightly. "Asafetida has something of the character of onion or garlic, doesn't it? Useful if you are forbidden to eat those things."

"You see through me, I'm afraid. I've brought you a great deal of work, of which I hope to get the benefit, and tried to pass it off as a present."

This was, John thought, like something Iren might say. Sudharma had adopted Northern irony when speaking to a Northerner—much as, at the harvest feast, he had spoken Clear Lakes dialect. But he had done that to keep the ship-folk from understanding him. This time he must be trying to create a sense of fellow feeling. Maybe that had been part of his reason on the ship, too.

Ru seemed to be charmed. She answered him in the same mode. "You've brought me the kind of work I like the best, and no gift could be better than that. So I thank you. I suppose the others will too, though all they get out of it is better food."

Nothing would do then but that everyone thank Sudharma individually and that every packet be read over and discussed. Date palm produced the greatest excitement, though Ru warned that it would be a long time before any fruit could be harvested. John supposed the sweetness of the fruit was easier for the colonists to imagine than the taste of unfamiliar spices, but he thought the spices would improve their cuisine more.

When at last they left the governor's house, the night was cooler than he would have imagined. Ru had stayed behind to help with cleanup; it would be even chillier when she emerged, and in her sleeveless dress he thought she would be cold on the right side.

Piro caught up with them as they came out onto the street. "Laura says she'll come to your house at six AM, if that's all right."

"That's fine." John hesitated. "How would I set an alarm to wake me?"

"There was a tag left for you on your nightstand. You can use that." Piro saw that John was at a loss, and added, "A card, about this big." He marked off the dimensions with his fingers in the air.

"Oh, yes."

"Maybe I should come back with you and show you how to use it."

"I worked out how to set an alarm earlier," Sudharma said. "I'll show him."

"Okay. You can find your way home?"

"Of course," John said.

Piro bade them good night and they walked back to the house.

"That went well, I think," John said once they were in the door. "You were very well received. And they took pains to be gracious hosts to you. I certainly like it better than the ship's behavior at that awful dinner."

"I told the captains that I prefer not to eat from a kitchen where meat is prepared, that I would go into cold-sleep right after the feast in any case and so would need an empty stomach, and that I preferred no fuss be made about it."

John considered the harvest feast in this new light. "Even so, I like it better."

"Yes," Sudharma said.

"Is something wrong?"

"No. I was just thinking that I like these people and I hope I won't be at odds with them."

"Why should you be?"

"The outcome of talking to Earth, and to basket-men, may not be to everyone's liking."

"In that case, you should avoid accepting any more dinner invitations."

"I'm not worried about being poisoned, only about becoming unpopular. But in fact, I will prefer to dine in. I am sensible of Zohia's kindness in trying to cater to a Jain diet, and her research was more accurate than I would have expected, but I also want to avoid cooking or eating before dawn or after sunset; to forgo cauliflower, broccoli, eggplant, mushrooms, yeast, and honey; and to filter or boil water before drinking it or cooking with it. I will also avoid green vegetables on certain days, and from time to time fast entirely. And, as I said, I will not eat from a kitchen where meat is cooked or stored. That last in particular may become a source of conflict, once rat becomes available."

"What is the purpose of all these restrictions? If I may ask. You mentioned leaving a good soul."

"That phrase was probably misleading. The goal is, rather, to avoid doing harm."

"I can see how eating an animal might be called harm, but why an onion or a potato?"

"Plants contain souls of the same nature as animals' and ours, though far more limited in their ability to perceive the world. It is not possible to live without some harm to them, but one can seek to limit it. Some vegetables, particularly roots and bulbs and tubers, contain very many souls, so naturally those are to be avoided. Furthermore, in harvesting a root crop one usually kills the entire plant, and by digging damages the earth and the creatures in it, so that altogether the harm done is very great."

"But why such scrupulousness?"

"To do harm to other beings is also to damage our own souls—to cause them to be tainted by a substance known as karma, which blocks their natural perfection and omniscience. Furthermore, it affects the soul's fate when we die and are reborn."

"In the other world that Iren spoke of?"

"That is an entirely different set of ideas. Most Ischnuran religions refer to a singular other world. In Jainism there are many places one might be reborn—this universe is only one of them. But, like Ischnurans, we believe that after rebirth we might take other shapes than the ones we have now."

"You could become a dryad?"

"Certainly."

"Well, I suppose I can live with avoiding carrots and all that. We can take our meals together if you like."

"I can't imagine that resolution will last very long. But for as long as it does, I'll be glad of your company."

CHAPTER FIVE

John had expected to wake after too little sleep and lag through the morning's walk as if weighed down by heavy baskets, but when he set his alarm he discovered additional time in the night. The greater length of Scythia's day compared to Earth's had been accommodated not by altering the duration of the second, but by stashing the excess in one great heap in the dark hours, so that the clock went all the way to 27:48 before it wrapped around to 00:00. So he rose without resentment of the tag's chime and was bathed, fed, and feeling reasonably energetic by the time Laura knocked at the door. The translator was awake too, but, by the sound of it, reciting something in his room. It would, John thought, be rude to interrupt. Sudharma would know where he had gone.

He opened the door to find a woman of about Piro's age, whose finger was encompassed by a band of gold. Her hair was as dark as his, but her skin was lighter—the Zandaheans, he thought, were nothing like so uniform as the Ischnurans. Under a wide green shawl her blouse was white; her full skirt was sun-faded blue. She was smiling up at him with a delight that the prospect of a long walk through an arid landscape hardly seemed to justify.

"Good morning! I'm Laura Torres." She put out her hand to shake. He saw, then felt, that there were calluses at all the bases of her fingers.

"John Maraintha."

"You'll want another layer. It's still chilly out."

He put on a light jacket from the rack fixed to the wall. Then, after considering a moment, he took his bag down from the shelf above and settled it onto his shoulder. Laura examined it with an attention that worried him, but she only asked, "What did you bring?"

"Medical supplies. The load is light—I could only bring medicines that would survive the trip to Scythia—but I can clean and bandage wounds, at least."

"That's a good idea. This would have been a better one." She was carrying two bottles in covers of drab fabric, hanging at the same hip; she disentangled the straps and held one out. "Lesson one, always bring water. Even when it isn't hot, the air here is still dry—you'll dehydrate faster than you think. Now, did you bring your tag?"

"No."

"Go and get it."

He retrieved the card, brought it to the door, and in her sight tucked it into his jacket's breast pocket. "Why is it called a tag when there is no way to attach it?"

"Because it tracks your location."

"What, all the time?"

"Not if you turn it off. But don't, in the desert. Lesson two, make sure people can find you."

She led him up the main street, which was nearly empty at this hour. Ahead, a single cone rose far above the buildings. Like the one at the pod's landing site, it had a circular hole near the top, and a weedy beard hung out of this, falling almost halfway to the ground. As they approached, an animal with a furred face like a rat, but larger, peered out of the hole at them. It climbed out headfirst onto the tangle of leaves, unfolded hairless wings that were the color of a well-baked fish bun, and leapt off into the air. The wings were broad, and supple as a soul—not beating stiffly like the glassy wings of Essian birds, but flexing to caress the air, then spreading out to glide. As it descended it turned in a wide arc, and when it had the rising sun behind it, light shone through its wings so that the bones stood out in black. Then it was near the ground. Its wings tipped backward until they stood vertical; the legs swung forward and touched down. Its momentum carried it along so that it would have fallen on its face, if the wings had not buckled and folded in half—at the bending point of each one was a little hand, and with these it caught itself. John realized he had been holding his breath.

The animal came toward him. Its legs were short, and bound by flaps of thick skin to the tail; it couldn't walk on them, but used its folded wings like crutches, planting both its hands in front of it, then swinging its legs forward to a new standing place. Even folded up the wings were very long, so this gait, though awkward, narrowed the distance between them rapidly.

It cried out—a high and piercing sound—revealing long teeth at the corners of the mouth.

"Don't worry, that's just Alma. She's a candlehawk, and she's getting entirely too tame. The kids won't stop killing lizards to feed her."

As the creature got close she slowed down, looking up at him with eyes that were a vivid yellow except for the little black dots of the pupils. She stretched out a wing until it almost touched his shin, then drew it back shyly.

"Does he look stupid enough to give you food?" Laura asked her.

Alma tilted her head as if she thought the question difficult, but then deciding in the negative, she ran past him. He turned in time to see her stab the ground with both her wings at once and vault into the air. She rose and circled the cone twice. Then she landed, grabbing the edge of the hole with her feet and folding her wings just in time as she dove in. John had felt—and only realized now he had felt—that animals born out of plants should be crude and unfinished, like blocks of wood carved roughly into figures. Such an idea could not survive the sight of Alma. The design of her might be fantastical, but there was nothing lax about it: in every way she was exactly herself.

"So now you've learned one thing about dryads. When you see a big cone like that that has a hole in it, there's probably going to be a flying predator living inside. Alma's an oddball because she's been around humans too much—most of them don't like us getting close to their candles. I'd give them a good ten meters to be safe. They'll yell a warning if you get too close, so if you hear that, back off slowly. Now we're about to go into the real desert, and some of the wildlife out there is aggressive, so stay close to me and don't touch anything I don't tell you to touch."

She led the way along a trail, distinct at first, that faded until John was not sure if she still followed a path that she could see, or one that she only remembered. In the mild light of early morning, the world was not so harsh and glaring as it had been yesterday; the shadows of boulders and columns were soft, and all the grayish greens were warmed with amber. Still, one could see the desert's stinginess. Most of the plants had tiny leaves or none at all, and between them were stretches of gravel and sand too dry for life to take hold on. The land was cut up into hills and valleys, so their travel could not be direct, but must meander to avoid more strenuous terrain. Even so, there was some walking up and down slopes, and the exertion overheated him, so that he took his jacket off—only to put it back on and wish it were heavier when they returned to the shade of a hill.

"I warn you," Laura said, "there's going to be some botany. It might seem like a lot to learn for one little drive through the desert, but you need to build a solid foundation."

"I would want to understand the world I'm on, even if I never intended to leave town. And in fact, I will be attending emergencies out in the desert, so I will need a complete knowledge of its hazards."

"You mean, on top of seeing patients, or instead?"

"Instead."

"Was that your idea?"

"It was Marne's."

"He changed his mind when he found out where you're from, didn't he."

"So it seemed," John admitted. "But I will be assisting Sudharma, and that will absorb much of my time. Perhaps once that is finished, I will take patients in town."

"Don't do that. You have to fight Marne on this now. Ask any woman on this colony if you don't believe me."

"Why a woman?"

"We know all about being pushed out of good jobs.—Hold on, we have to take a detour here." She led him carefully around a large patch of pale soil, at the center of which stood a few shrubby plants. By the time they reached the other side he thought she might have dropped the subject, but setting off in a straight line again, she told him the story.

"Zandaheans came here two by two like animals off the ark, all married couples. *Grandfather's Axe* insisted on that, so we could start having babies as soon as we had houses to raise them in."

"Did they think that without marriage there would be no children?"

"Well, no, probably not, but they wanted to ensure a stable home life, which to us and to the *Axe* means marriage. And they also made sure all the women had a skill, something important we could do, because Scythia needed both—the colony had to be built as well as peopled. So at first, we were all working in our specialties. But then we started having children, and surprise surprise, it turned out that the burden of providing that home life I mentioned fell on us. There was no older generation to help—not even any teenagers to babysit, at first. When we took time off from work, the men flowed in to fill the gaps. And the kinds of jobs that needed doing kept changing all the time as the colony developed. I was a food scientist—I specialized in making human food from native life."

"That sounds very important."

"Damn right it is. Too bad it's mostly impossible here. I figured out how to make cooking oils and shortening from the plant stages of certain dryads, which nobody will remember. Then I'd run through all the possibilities of that, and I had a baby to take care of. It was like that all over the colony. Men had the time to learn and adapt to new roles, women didn't. By the time we got ready to focus on work again, we were stuck with the leftovers. Like teaching part-time and helping run the educational farm."

"I met a woman last night who was an agricultural scientist."

"Ischnuran women learned from our misfortunes and set up childcare sharing right away, so they did a little better. But yeah, Ru kept her whole job. She lost her husband a few months after they landed, and never did remarry. God knows I wouldn't change places. But what I'm telling you is, you can't drive an ambulance for a few years and then come back and say 'Remember how I'm a doctor?' People need to see you are and they need to keep seeing it."

"I will think about it," John said. In truth he felt no great attachment to the role of doctor in the way it was defined by colonists and ship-folk—certainly none great enough to make him willing to work closely with a hostile Marne. If Marne's disgruntled patients presented themselves then that would be different, but he could hardly go around the town asking if anyone disliked the man.

"How many children do you have?" he asked, to change the subject.

"Three sons, all grown up and married. One daughter still at home."

"Is it hard, being separated from your sons?"

She looked back at him as if the question surprised her, but she answered easily enough. "It's a small town, it's not like I never see them. And they've been moved out for years, you know—they were all born before the famine, Tali was after. I guess I still miss having them around the house once in a while, but I like to see them thriving, making their own way. I don't miss cleaning up the bathroom after them. It's the great thing about marriage, you foist that off on other women.—Here we are, this is where the lesson begins."

She stopped in front of a little bush, spiked with short twigs and furred with narrow leaves. "Look at this branch," she said. "See how these seams divide it into segments? I'm going to break one of the segments off." She did so; nothing objected to the assault. "Now you do the same. Don't worry, the animal stage of this species is ungrateful—they won't lift a mandible to defend their mother."

The bush was more robust than yesterday's, but with some effort he managed to break it.

"Now let's strip off the leaves."

When he had finished this task, he held a thin twig, roughly the length of his hand with the fingers extended. It was stiff and covered in smooth bark. Six smaller twigs, arranged in three pairs, branched off to the sides along its length.

"What you're looking at is called a stick figure. It's the basic building block of plant-stage dryads. Each figure is a separate organism—a clone. What looks like a plant to us can be made up of hundreds of clones, but they all share water and nutrients and work together like they're one. The central part of the figure is called the body, the bits that branch off are called limbs, and the first thing we need to do is count them. In this case, six limbs tells us the animal offspring are going to look something like this."

She slipped one of the limbs of her stick under the belly of a little animal, which, finding its feet unsupported, clung in panic to the implement that was abducting it. She brought it close to John's face so he could see it better: a long-bodied creature in a metallic red exoskeleton. Each plate of armor was outlined with yellow, and thorns of the same yellow jutted from the head and back and the first segment of each leg. "Piro would want me to teach you the word 'anthousai,' but everybody else just calls these bugs or insects. With a couple of exceptions that I'll show you, they're not dangerous unless you get bitten by a lot of them. Don't tear down the plants or crash through them and you'll be fine. Sometimes you can identify them by their buds—they're the only kind of plant where young develop up off the ground. But buds aren't around all year, so you also have to look for figures with six limbs. It's easy to remember because six limbs equals six legs."

"Is the number just coincidence?"

"No. A long time ago some Essian animal sprouted appendages from its body, probably for swimming. Later some of its descendants split their life cycle into two phases, one that moved around and one that stayed in place. Now the two phases have diverged so much they don't even look like they belong in the same kingdom, but there are still some similarities in how they grow, and some of the same genes control their body plans. So the number of limbs and legs is often the same."

So then a stick figure was, in a sense, still an animal—stiffened in whatever shape was needed, fastened to its neighboring clones forever unless someone tore them apart. And the world was full of such creatures, thousands of them all around, even in this desert. The thought was horrifying; and he imagined himself silenced and hardened too, unable even to cry out, made into just another plant in the bleak landscape.

"Don't count on limbs and legs matching a hundred percent of the time, though," Laura added. "There are insects with twelve or eighteen or dozens of legs, because they're made of several clones that fuse together during development."

"Then are there additional heads trapped in the middle?" he said, unsettled by the image.

"No. The extra heads get reabsorbed, Piro says. And plants can lose some or all of their limbs, while the animal still has the usual number. You'll see examples of that later. For now let's move to the next lesson. Take out your stick figure and break off the middle two limbs, like this. Find me a plant like that—exactly four limbs on a figure. They aren't as common, so it might take you a while."

After another half an hour of walking, he sat down on a rock to fold his jacket and tuck it into his bag. The sun was high and any little charm the morning landscape might have had was now bleached out of it.

"Drink some water while you've stopped," Laura said. "You should drink small amounts throughout the day, especially if it's hot. Don't try to hoard it for later—that just leads to dying of thirst with a full canteen."

As he was screwing the cap back onto the bottle, a plant on the slope in front of him caught his eye: a mass of green stems, defended by long curving thorns of the same color. It had no leaves to cover it, which made it easy to see that each stem branched exactly four times.

"Is that what I am looking for?" he said, pointing.

"That's right. Four limbs means the animal that comes from it will have bones instead of an exoskeleton and be covered in scales or bare skin. They don't linger near their mothers or tend to their children, so the plants are safe to approach—even to touch, if you're careful of thorns. As you can see, they tend to be prickly. Officially they're called daphnaiai, but you'll hear words like 'reptile' or 'lizard' more."

Of these words only 'reptile' was vaguely familiar; John thought it meant something like 'cold' or 'indifferent.'

"You've got a good eye," she said, offering him a hand up from the stone. "Did you take botany in school?"

"I learned to gather medicinal herbs. Of course the plants at home are very different, but they also have a structure and there are patterns to it one can learn."

"Well, you seem to have the hang of reptiles, so let's move on to the next page."

She broke off the two lower limbs from her stick figure and he did the same. "Find me something with just one pair of limbs on each segment. And when you find it, don't get close to it."

A few minutes later John stopped and pointed. "I am certain that has two limbs per segment, but not quite sure it's a plant." It looked more like a collection of forked sticks, such as one might use to prop up fishing poles on riverbanks, all thrust into the ground at random angles. Their bark was smooth and greenish and they had no leaves at all.

"It's a plant, all right. That kind gives birth to animals with bones, warm blood, and fur—like basket-men. They're called meliades, or mammals if you aren't fancy. Most mammal mothers stick around to defend and take care of the plant, and some of them are dangerous, but in this case they're small and won't bother us."

"How do the adults care for the plants?"

"They weed around them. Work the soil, to make sure the growing babies aren't deformed by rocks or tough roots. Some species even water them."

It was recognizably a mother's labor—not so different from the way that Essian women dug and tended farms, to give their children safer foodstuffs than the wild woods could provide. But the plant child that a mammal worked to tend would always be silent and still, more like a crop than a child. And against his will, the image came to him of a mother in Essian dress cradling, not an infant, but a bundle of thorned twigs, the thorns piercing her breast so that blood flowed instead of milk.

"Do they feel, in the plant stage?" he asked. "Do they think?"

"No. They don't have brains or nerves. I wouldn't have torn off an animal's leg just for a visual aid.—If you want to see a mammal, there's one that's out on a mission."

It took him a while to find the animal she pointed at; it was not large and its fur blended in with the sand. In the end he found it only by the motion of its forelimbs as its claws dug a miniature hole. "What is it doing?"

"Planting seeds."

"Where do the seeds come from exactly?—*Are* they seeds, in truth?"

"Like a seed, in that it has a coat. Like an egg in that it's laid out of an orifice beneath the tail. But that one isn't, strictly speaking, going to lay seeds—he's not a female. In his species the male swallows the female's seeds, passes them through his gut, and sends them out the other end along with feces. Fertilizer. I'd suggest we stay awhile and watch the planting, but I don't want to make you late, and anyway, it isn't appetizing." She held up the stick figure. "Ready for the last stage?"

He nodded and she broke away the last two limbs. "What does this look like now?"

"A stick?"

"It's a plant we've been seeing all day."

He could think of no answer; the riddle was too deep for him. She held the figure up to the horizon. "Up there, on the ridge."

It still took him a moment, and then he felt foolish. He knew that waxy plants were plants, but it was hard to think of them as such. "The columns."

"Exactly. Those are a type of candle, which means they're insects. They've grown fat with water and lost all their limbs, but aside from that, they're put together just like other plants. Do you see the seams?"

"Yes."

"And in a few weeks you'll start to see buds on them. In the meantime you can recognize them by their fleshiness. Can you find me another?"

This task was easy; he pointed out a cluster of thin waxy stems that arched and twisted upward nearly to the level of his eyes, as if a mass of green worms had decided, by unanimous agreement, to stretch out toward the sun.

"Good. Candles are like most insects—you can walk close, but if you touch or damage the plant you might get a nasty surprise. Just remember if you touch a candle you get burned."

"I would only be burned if I touched the flame."

"That's true, but for the sake of the mnemonic pretend it isn't. Now I'm going to show you something that you'll wish didn't exist. Remember to stay close to me."

She led him around a small hill and then stopped; her raised hand told him he should stop too. "What do you see?"

At the base of an outcropping to their right, a litter of leaves without visible stems clung to the rocks. "What is that?" he asked, pointing.

"Just worms. They're never anything to worry about. Notice anything unusual about that tree ahead?"

He examined it: a little gnarled insect, standing alone in the sand.

"One branch is thicker than the others."

"No it isn't. Look again."

"Is it two branches growing together?"

"Good guess, but not quite."

"The lower branches are very crooked."

"Yes. But you're still missing something. Let me see if I can get it to declare itself."

She chose a stone from the ground—a red one that fitted the palm of her hand—and with a good stance and good motion threw it toward the tree. As it passed by the branches he started. Something had twitched, he thought, but there was no animal to be seen.

"Did you catch that?"

"I thought something moved, but now I'm not sure."

"That's because my aim was bad. You try this time. Aim for the branch that looks thick. You don't have to hit it—just come close."

He hadn't thrown anything to hit a target in years, not under gravity—and never under Scythian gravity. Nevertheless he found a rock of a suitable size and threw it as hard as he could. The stone flew too high, striking nothing, and yet the branch split. The top part of it swung toward them and stretched out straight, a long tube covered in green bark. It had eyes and they were open. It was trying to get to them, John thought, but its tail was trapped inside the trunk, and it was not long enough to reach. At last its body slackened, became a zigzag, then folded up tight. Slowly it crept out along another branch, a downward-angled one; the way it moved was liquid, like a trickle of water or oil. Its color and its pattern matched the plant's bark so exactly that when it became still it was invisible.

"What was that?" he breathed.

"It's called a snake-tree and it's the deadliest thing in this part of the world. Luckily their venoms don't work on humans, but they can still kill you. They'll latch on to an arm, sometimes a leg. The teeth are curved backward like hooks, to hold on. They'll pull you closer so you don't have time to get away while they let go, then bite you in a different place. You noticed Ru's arm, of course."

"Yes."

"She had to tear away three times before she got free. If you like all your limbs, I recommend not getting close to one in the first place. That means checking every tree before you get any closer than we are now. Snake-trees come in lots of species, different sizes, colors, shapes, some with leaves and some without, so you can't go by any of that. What you can count on is that the main branches will be very crooked. That way the snake can lie along one and be fully supported, even though it's long enough to reach beyond the tree. But there can be other limbs the snake doesn't use, that help it mimic other plants. You can see this one has branches with fake buds and even fake seams, to disguise it as an insect."

"What is it really?"

"Closest to reptiles, but a distant relative." She answered offhandedly; she was studying his face and, he thought, making some judgment. "I'm going to tell you what I tell the boys who take my class, because you're older than they are but I'm not sure you're enough older. Seven people have been bitten by snake-trees since we got here and all but one of them were young males. Why, because either you're doing something stupid to show off, or you're trying to kill the snake to protect other people, which is also stupid and a way to show off. If you find a snake-tree, use your tag to mark the location—I'll show you how later. If it's in a bad place we'll send out a team of at least four to remove it. If you want to kill snakes, the place for you is *on that team*, not lying half-eaten making them step over you to do their jobs. Do you understand?"

"Certainly. I would never approach something dangerous unnecessarily."

"I'm glad the women on Essius raise sensible sons."

"I should hope so. Our world is so full of poisons that a reckless boy would never become a man."

"Hm. Well, keep that in mind when you get close to the Earthlings, because that riverbed they're in has snake-trees on both banks. They like to live near springs or rivers, mainly because water attracts animals—the snakes don't have to drink if their roots can suck up enough water. You'll have to look for a gap wide enough to pass through safely. The river's very low right now, so you should have room to walk along the water from there, but you do *not* want to be wrong about that, because a snake-tree near water will try to drown you. By the river they're a lot bigger and stronger than this one, so they can push you in and hold you down, and their mouths are big enough to grab you by the throat when they do it. Every segment of the snake has spiracles to breathe through and they all share air, so they can keep you underwater as long as they need to. To stay safe you'll have to find the snake, figure out how long it's going to be when it unfolds, then multiply that by one point five, because it's hard to judge exactly. If you can't find a snake, it might have died and not regrown yet, but assume it's just well hidden and it's long enough to reach the end of the longest resting-branch. You'll remember?"

"Yes."

"Let's go around this one, then. I have one more thing to show you before we start back."

She brought him to what looked like the remains of a fallen tree, long dead and dried out; its leaves and bark were gone, leaving only weathered wood. The trunk was in segments, most of which had separated. Each one had short, unbranching limbs that became gradually shorter nearer the top. "This is what's left of a cone like Alma's. We call it a skeleton because it holds the plant up, but it's made of wood, not bone. Those are real limbs on it—they're buried in flesh when the plant's alive, but they help support its bulk. How many limbs per segment do you see?"

"Six."

"And what kind of animal do you think Alma is?"

"If not for the wings, I would say a mammal."

"The wings are just legs that grow funny. She's a mammal, all right. So how did a plant that looks like an insect give birth to a mammal?"

He thought of the cone-candle, the hole in it, and the incongruous leaves emerging. "It didn't. The leaves aren't part of the cone—they are a parasite."

"Good job. That's exactly right. Alma dug out that hole and sowed her seed inside the candle. Her plant-child takes water and nutrients from the host plant and makes chicks every year for her to raise. The cone's own children are a lot of little insects that bud inside it, and when they hatch, they crawl down through tunnels in its flesh to the nest below. They benefit from having Alma there, though—she scares off animals that might dig them out. That's probably why the cones grow so tall, to attract protection. Now one more question. Why do you think I told you candlehawks don't come from candles?"

"So I could understand the biology?"

"That's why Piro would have told you. I told you because I wanted you to understand that this world will surprise you, and not everything is what it seems. Also, the farther from town you go, the thinner our knowledge gets. So remember the rules and follow them, but even when the rules are telling you that everything around is safe, be careful and keep your eyes open."

"I will."

"You can start practicing that now. We're going to walk back to town, and you'll take the lead. Do you know which way to go?"

"Approximately. We've had the morning sun on our left when we were not avoiding obstacles. It is still morning, I believe, so keeping the sun at our right should take us home."

"Good enough. I'll be right behind to warn you if you're getting too far off course or are about to feed yourself to a snake-tree."

The return under his guidance went smoothly in the main, though twice he mistook furled leaves for buds, and once he failed to recognize a dangerous insect he had not been taught about. Little white buds that were borne in great masses, that was the warning sign. Another time a blue-black insect landed on his forearm. He raised it to his eyes to see more clearly, and was startled when Laura slapped her hand down on his arm to crush it. She said that kind cut into skin to plant their seeds, which sprouted and then died, since their roots could not draw sustenance from human flesh. On a dryad they would branch and put out buds, from which would hatch more flies that laid more eggs, so that you might see a mammal or a reptile with a miniature forest growing out of its face and the back of its neck and in between its shoulders, those being the places the animal could not reach to pull out the seedlings with its teeth.

They made it back to the town, arriving at Alma's cone. The candlehawk looked out at them briefly but retreated back into the shade of her hole. John wondered if she understood she was a protector of unseen insects, and if she cared.

"Do you have time for lunch before you go?" Laura asked. "When are you and the translator leaving?"

"I don't know. I think it depended on when my lesson was finished. I should probably go and tell him that it is."

"He can hardly expect you to fast, can he? I'll whip up something quick. He can always send a message to your tag if he's impatient." She hesitated. "I feel like you need tips on surviving the Earth people more than the snake-trees, but I don't have any."

"I must trust in Sudharma for that."

"Well, come on. Torres house is at the east end of town."

Now that the sun was high, there were more people on the street, and Laura stopped several times for greetings and introductions. John felt there was an air of disapproval in the way everyone spoke to her, but her replies did not acknowledge it. For himself, he was as carefully polite as he could be and spoke as little as he could get away with. He had no idea how to talk to these people.

They came to a large building whose arched entryway was set into a three-story tower, surmounted by an ineffectual-looking weathervane. A man dressed all in black, who had been eating his lunch on the front steps, put down his plate and wiped his lips with a napkin hastily, then crossed to the sidewalk with long strides. He introduced himself as Father Adzere. John wasn't sure if Father was a name or simply an unusual piece of information to volunteer.

"John has finished his lesson and done very well," Laura said, "so I am going to feed him some lunch before his adventure."

"I see." John didn't know why so innocuous an announcement should cause an expression of such concern. But whatever troubled the man's face didn't affect the words he spoke. "I won't keep you, then. But, John, you should come dine at my house when you're able. I would like to hear you tell about your homeworld. Also, my wife is an excellent cook."

"Certainly. I would be delighted."

As they went on, Laura covered her mouth with the back of her hand.

"Is something wrong?"

She didn't answer until they had reached the next block. "No, not at all. It's just Adzere being Adzere." He could tell by her voice that she was trying not to laugh.

"In what way?"

"He thinks it's improper for us to be alone together. Well, everybody thinks that, but Adzere is a priest of the Church of Zandahe, so he thinks it ought to be his job to guide me back to a more decorous path. Too bad I'm a Denier and won't listen to him."

"Is it forbidden for any man and woman to step away from supervision, or does that rule only apply to Essians?"

"We're getting extra scrutiny because you're Essian. A whole morning alone in the desert followed by an invitation to the house might raise some eyebrows even if you weren't. But you don't have to worry about it—no one really believes anything is going to happen. The message they're sending is 'Oh Laura, what will everyone else in the world but me think?' After all, it's ridiculous. I'm much too old to be at any risk of interesting a man your age."

"I don't see why, but I have no such intentions."

"Well, I'm glad of the second part of that, and more glad that nobody heard you say the first."

She laughed out loud. The encounter had left her merry, he thought; because she and the priest were at odds in some way.

"What is a Denier?"

She stopped in her tracks. "Oh Lord, how to explain Denial?" She resumed walking but stared fixedly ahead of her, so that he was glad the sidewalk was in good repair and without obstacles; if a creek had crossed the road, he thought she might have fallen into it. “Okay,” she said. “To begin with, do you know what sin is?”

“I think it means a fault?”

“Yes, that’s right, but not just any kind of fault. Sin is an offense against God.—Do you know what God is? I mean, you understand that when Zandaheans say God, we are talking about the one God who created the universe, and not . . . wandering spirits, or anything of that kind?”

“I’ve heard of the idea.”

“All right. I’m going to simplify this as much as I can, but it might still be hard to understand. Because of how human beings are, our nature, it’s impossible for us to live without sin. And sin is a barrier between God and us—one that we could never overcome on our own.”

This assessment of humanity was curiously harsh. John thought that people acted well enough as long as they were raised right. But then, in a culture corrupted by marriage, no one could truly be raised right. It was also possible their god was just too easily offended. A god would suffer from being constrained to marry, perhaps even more than a human would; it might tend to make them irritable.

“So God,” she said, “being merciful, decided to heal the rift. And He did it in a very special way. He sent His only son to become human, and to live with us, and—well, He died for us, too, and that opened the door for us to be reconciled with God. But we still have to do our part, which is very hard. And so the Son, while he was with us, also gave us help. He created an authority on Earth, that could interpret God’s law for us, so that we wouldn’t be led astray. They could . . . bring us close to God, by certain rituals. They could forgive our sins, and we’d know that God forgave them too. And those powers were passed on through the centuries, from one to another, by laying on hands. This was called *apostolic succession*.”

She glanced at him, and, seeming to divine that he was not quite keeping up, she tried another tack.

“Imagine you didn’t know how to make fire. But one day lightning struck, and you picked up a burning stick, touched it to wood, and used that to cook food and keep warm. And after that, you had to carry coals with you wherever you went, and make a new fire from the embers of the old one. People on Earth may have lived like that once. But the spiritual fire, you could never make that by striking flints. It could only come from God. Can you understand that?”

“The fire would have to be preserved at all costs.”

"Yes. And that brings us up to the time that my ancestors left Earth for Zandahe. We were a different kind of colony. We didn't come from a single place on Earth, like you or Ischnura—we came from everywhere, but we all believed the same. We had faith in God, and in the Church, and of course we brought His fire with us.

"But starting on a new world is hard. Accidents happen. We didn't lose as much as a lot of worlds did, only the most important thing of all: the fire was snuffed out. At first we thought we might get it again from Earth, but that was around the time Earth gave in to the aiyi—there's no hope there anymore. It was devastating for everyone. And over time, most of us came to believe that God would want us to have fire, so it must be that we did have it. They made up a story to explain how that could be. It was never true. But still, if people sit together around an unlit fireplace, they'll feel warmth, won't they, just from being close to each other. And God might see their longing for the sacrament and grant them some kind of a spiritual encounter with Him—we have to hope that. But they don't have the full . . . union with God that He gave us on Earth, or the certainty that sins have been forgiven. Nobody has those anymore. Those of us who know it are called Deniers."

The longing in her voice was obvious and he could not help being moved by it, but it seemed to him the Zandaheans had fixated on a single god to an unhealthy degree. His own encounter with a god had been memorable, and of course he had wished for a closer connection, but to dwell on the matter so long could only lead to misery.

"Since that time, the Church of Zandahe took its one bad idea about the succession and spun it out into a lot of other bad ideas about how things are different on different worlds. If they ever say the word 'provision' to you, you're about to hear a heresy. Never mind, you don't care. On our side, without a religious authority to keep us united, Deniers did exactly what you'd expect and started disagreeing about everything—starting with exactly how hopeless our situation is. There are some who believe God deserted us entirely, and there's no point in praying anymore. You don't care about that, either."

He did care, in that he could tell that these matters weighed heavily on her mind, but it was difficult to make sense of the details.

"What do you believe?" he asked.

"Oh, I don't believe in God, not really. But the rules are the rules and their priests are still fake."

They had come to the end of the town. The last building was behind them, and ahead was a small hill of stone that was marked with fine bands like some layered pastry.

"Did we go past your house?"

"No. It's just a little farther."

The street became a trail and curved around the hill, disclosing a two-story house that overlooked a gentle downward slope. Below, the river curved in a long S before settling back into a straight course.

"I know it's a bit of a walk, but we like the view. Let's go in through the garden—I want to check on something."

The garden was compact and orderly, with straight paths separating the square and rectangular beds. The dark soil, surely much augmented, contrasted with the hard pale earth around. Laura moved along the paths, glancing down at several of the beds, but stopping only at a large one full of staked vines. She bent over, searching in the green, and straightened again with two red globes in her hand.

"Thirty-eight days from transplant!" she said, shaking out her skirt to dislodge the bits of gravel that had clung to it. "I'll have to tell Ru.—We have long days here and we have an agricultural scientist who really likes tomatoes. They get earlier every year."

From the garden a door led, conveniently, into the kitchen, which was spacious enough to accommodate a small table and chairs. On one side, a gap between cabinets and counter looked onto another room that was for sitting, and a doorless frame led into it. He saw that for this family the life of the kitchen must intermingle with other activities of home, whether or not such a closeness was wanted. The stove and the refrigerator were the same as in the house he shared with Sudharma.

"Were these appliances brought by the ships?" he asked.

"No, made here. *Rose of the Winds* brought us an unfolding treasure box. Robots to farm and to mine and build, machines to make machines to make machines. I'd say don't get used to it, but maybe it doesn't matter—the technology might last your lifetime. Still, it'll run down in the end. The ships wouldn't give us technology that could keep going forever, would they? Then we wouldn't need their help anymore, and they couldn't get away with interfering with our lives. We don't have enough people to keep everything working by ourselves, and by the time we do have enough, it'll be much too late." She laid the tomatoes on the counter, then drew a small amount of water from the tap into a kettle and put it on to boil. "Do you want to sit down and rest until lunch?"

"I'd rather watch, if I may. I haven't had many chances to observe cooking with Terran foods."

"Of course, whatever you like," she said, but she didn't move to begin preparations. She was looking at the strap of his bag. "Is that an ancestor?"

"No," he said; and seeing her relief, he nearly said nothing more. But that wouldn't have been honest. "Only women become ancestors. But yes, the strap of my bag is a part of a soul."

"You believe the human soul lives in the skin?"

"No, in the brain." He realized this would make no sense alone, so, though he dreaded her reaction, he explained. "When someone dies, the women of the family heat the brain in water and place the skin into the mixture to soak. Certain herbs are used, too, if it is a man's soul, to give the skin some stiffness—because men's souls become useful objects like this strap, which would stretch out in use otherwise." He didn't know why he had thought this detail would make the preservation of souls easier to accept. He could see she was disturbed. "If you'd rather I left, I can always get lunch at home."

"Please stay. I'm sorry, I don't mean to be unwelcoming. But . . . would it offend you if I asked you to put that in the other room?"

"No," he said. He went through the door and laid the bag down on a chair where it would be out of her view. There was no reason for him to feel ill-used. He would have reacted no better to an exhibition of the boxed dead.

When he returned she had washed her hands and was drying them in front of the counter. "Who was it? Or . . . who is it? Is it all right to ask that?"

"Yes, certainly. The soul is my great-uncle's."

"Did you know him in life?"

"I was quite young when he died, but yes."

"And you believe soaking a skin in a brain makes the soul go into it?"

"I believe it preserves the leather." These words came easily, but they were not the whole truth, so he tried again. "I feel he's there, when I touch the soul. I can't justify that as a fact, but I believe it."

She nodded thoughtfully, then said with an apologetic smile, "I know perfectly well a piece of leather can't contaminate my kitchen, and yet look at me."

Laura took yellow flour from a canister and put it in a bowl, tossed in a pinch of salt, then added water without measuring. She stirred it thoroughly and kneaded it with her hands. Several times she put the bowl under the tap and let a little water flow into it before kneading it again. When she was satisfied, she wetted a small towel and laid it over the bowl. "That'll need to sit a little while."

"Does it rise?"

"No, but it takes time for the flour to fully absorb the liquid. Do you like hot peppers?"

"Yes, very much."

She took down one of two hanging objects on the wall that he had thought to be mere decorations: long shaggy worms bristling with red and yellow spines. He realized he had been smelling them since he came in, but he would never have connected those twin ropes of withered fingers with the glossy fullness of the peppers on the ship. "Are they dried?"

"Yes. I'll revive them."

She cut two of the yellow peppers from the worm with scissors, paused to consider, then snipped off a third. She pulled the stems from them, cut them open, and scooped out the seeds with her fingers. Still using the scissors instead of a knife, she cut the peppers up into a bowl. By this time the kettle was steaming exuberantly. She poured in the boiling water, then nested another bowl inside the first.

"Why the second bowl?"

"It keeps the peppers down inside the water. If they floated up they wouldn't hydrate evenly."

She opened the refrigerator, crouched to reach into the bottom of it, then emerged embracing a sealed jar, a parcel wrapped in paper, and two vegetables John didn't recognize. One had long tubelike leaves emerging from a small white swelling that was growing a beard of roots. The other was a tight bundle of stalks, colored light green, with a ruffle of leaves at the top. When she broke off one of the stalks, he saw that it was curved in a familiar way. "What is that called?" he asked.

"Celery. Is it new to you?"

"Yes, though it reminds me of a vegetable we have at home called full-and-crescent. The outer stems have that curved shape, the innermost are round. You slice them up together and they look like moons in different phases. Children like it. Well, everybody likes it, I suppose."

As he spoke she had been cleaning off the celery in the sink; she laid it on a cutting board, sliced off a piece, and held it out to him. "Taste."

He bit into the rigid flesh and was surprised by its juiciness and the intensity of its crunch. "I don't know why I expected that to taste the same. Full-and-crescent is sweet."

"It'll be sweeter when it's cooked. But I'm using it mostly for texture. I'll just be putting in a little bit, cut into small chunks."

"There is an interesting bite to it, like . . ."

"Black pepper?"

He had been about to say young-man's-hem, but both comparisons were equally unsatisfying. "Yes, maybe."

John heard a door open and then slam. "That'll be my daughter," Laura said, and at once a slender, long-limbed girl came into the sitting room. She was panting and her face was flushed, as if she had been running. Her hair, which was long and black and loosely curled, had been tied with a ribbon and the tail stuffed down the back of her dress, but half of it had slipped out of the collar and now spread out messily. A few strands were stuck to her neck with sweat. The dress was a little too large for her, and the strip of cloth intended to be tied around the waist had been left loose, leaving it shapeless. She came into the kitchen, hugged her mother, then turned toward him. Laura raised a hand to the back of her neck to fix her hair, then thought better of it and let the hand fall.

"John, allow me to introduce my daughter, Catalina Torres—"

"Tali," the girl said.

"—and *Tali*, this is Dr. John Maraintha. Now do like I told you."

"It's very good to meet you." Tali held out her hand—sardonically, John thought, but he shook it in all solemnity.

"Now that's how you meet a new person. You can practice again when you're introduced to the translator."

"Who else am I ever going to use it on, a baby? The ships aren't coming back."

"Well, the future might surprise you. And if someday they do come here and you don't have any manners, they may blast right off again, so don't forget. Now wash up and help me with these." She picked up the tomatoes and brandished them.

"Sweet onions?" Tali said hopefully.

Laura shook her head. "Not for a while—the tops haven't fallen over yet. But we have scallions, and I traded Aline for some mushrooms."

Laura chopped up the vegetables with the long leaves—which, by process of elimination, must be scallions—turning them into little coins and separating out the white ones from the green. She washed and sliced the mushrooms, then poured oil into a heavy pan and put it on the stove. While it was heating up, she fished the slices of pepper out of the water and laid them to drain on a dry towel. She held her hand above the oil, spreading the fingers wide, to feel the heat of it; and finding it ready to receive them, she put in celery, mushrooms, the white coins of the scallions, the reconstituted peppers, and small chunks of potato from a package in the freezer. The odors of all these things filled the air wonderfully. Then she retrieved another pan, a wide and flat one that had merely the suggestion of a rim, and put it on the hot stove without adding oil. She took up a portion of the dough, rolled it between her palms into a ball, and by tossing it back and forth from left to right, gradually flattened and expanded it; these movements were so practiced that she hardly had to look down at her hands. She dropped the golden disc she'd made into the pan and took up a spatula, waiting for it to be ready to turn. She was happy, John thought. Her wedding ring was on her hand, a small fetter. But he had seen the night before that Piro, though placed by marriage in the position of a tyrant, was not tyrannical by nature; probably on Zandahe that was the best that could be hoped for. And she had her daughter, and was cooking for her. That most essential of connections was intact.

"Bring me three plates and then put napkins, forks, and water on the table," she told Tali.

The flatbread cooked quickly, developing brown spots and speckles. She added some of the vegetables that she had fried, covering only half of it. Then she opened the jar and spooned out a thick yellow-orange sauce.

"What is in that?" John asked.

"Beans, potatoes, carrots, onions, broth, deactivated yeast, some spices. It's a substitute for cheese. Have you ever eaten cheese?"

"No."

"Good, then you should like this."

"Mama is in mourning for cows," Tali explained.

Laura folded the flatbread in half over its fillings and cooked it a little more on each side. Then she slipped it onto a plate, topped it with tomatoes and the green coins from the scallions, and handed it to him. "You're our guest, so you get the first one. Don't you dare wait for us, they're best right off the griddle. And you'll need that fork—if you pick it up it'll just fall apart. The sauce doesn't glue it together like real cheese would."

John sat down, laid his plate on the table, cut out a bite and lifted it to his mouth. It all blended marvelously, the soft potatoes coated by the rich and unctuous sauce, the dark deep flavor of the mushrooms brightened by the peppers' fire. Mushrooms were said to smell and taste like Earth, which

John supposed must mean that they abounded there, their scent enveloping the world. No doubt a dish like this emerged from a tradition next to which even the oldest Essian recipes were new.

Tali had finished her task and was standing at Laura's elbow, watching the progress of another yellow circle. She turned to look at him. "How do they cook on the ships when there's no gravity?"

"Some ships spin, so they have gravity all the time," Laura said. "At least, enough to keep the tortillas inside the pan."

"The *Folly* doesn't, though. We studied it in school."

"Yes, that's right," John said. "They have several ways of cooking in summer. There is, for instance, a pot that is round like a ball, that they fix to a rod, which turns like a glassblower's pipe, and the spin presses anything put in it out to the edges. That will keep the foodstuff to be cooked within the water or in contact with the oil. It is convenient because to stir it, they can just pause the rotation and let the pieces of food float into new positions."

Tali thought about this. "It has to be all closed up, right? Or everything would get flung out. So how do they put the food in?"

"There is a hinged part, like a lid. They open it up to fill it, and a latch keeps it shut when it's spinning."

"Then how do they know when it's done?"

"There is a sensor that tells that, but I don't know how it works."

Laura gave Tali a plate and she sat at the table to eat, which distracted her from further questions—fortunately, since he had nearly exhausted his understanding of shipboard cookery.

"My daughter will be asking for seconds. Would you like another one too? There's plenty of filling left."

He had barely half eaten his first, but he answered without hesitation, "Yes, please. This is amazing."

"Mama's *gezo* is the best," Tali said complacently.

John finished just in time to return to Laura with his empty plate. When Tali had received hers too, Laura cooked and filled a final round of dough, then turned off the stove and sat down. By then Tali had already finished her second. She put down her fork and asked:

"So what's it like being a man on a world where women rule?"

John looked up, startled. He saw that Laura was watching him closely. "I think," he said carefully, "you may have the wrong idea. Unless you mean that women rule themselves, in which case, of course they do—they have no husbands to rule them."

Laura looked like she didn't care for this reply, but whatever her objection was, she let it pass. "But who makes the decisions?" she asked.

"That depends. Usually women decide in matters of the home, of farming, of money or at least of its expenditure. Men in fishing, and in trade if it is at a distance. And in war, of course."

"I thought you didn't have war." Laura was ignoring her food entirely. Somehow these questions were important to her. He couldn't see why customs on a world that she could never visit should be of so much interest.

"Of course there's war. There was a war over the fishing in Yles Lake the month I left home. A dirty business—they were going from house to house burning the ancestors. Some three hundred living souls were lost, and I don't know how many of the dead. But I shouldn't speak of such things here. I beg your pardon."

"What about in business? Who decides there?"

"Where I was born, it's simple. Business is a matter of money, and it's conducted at home—unless products are taken to market, which would probably be done by men, but even then the choice of what to keep and what to sell would be guided by women. They have a more intimate knowledge of the family's needs. In the cities, where businesses have outgrown the home, there is confusion of domains, so that many jobs can be done by either men or women, though one expects they are done rather differently."

Laura looked disappointed. But she only said, "Sounds better than our history, anyway. Or any other world's I ever heard of, after technology got lost. I don't suppose you know how Essius got to be that way."

"It's said that the women refused to be wives, and everything else stems from that."

"Well, good for them," Tali announced.

"You had better run," Laura told her. "You'll be late getting back."

"Can I study at Lili's after school?"

"Yes, but be home in time for dinner or you'll miss out on the rest of the mushrooms."

"Then can she study here and stay for dinner with us?"

Laura thought for a moment. "Yes, they'll stretch that far."

"Oh, Sii is going to clear out a couple of ohnos tomorrow—"

"Siinen is reckless and you're too young."

"It's only two. They don't get dangerous until they make a pack."

"I said no and you're going to be late. Get going."

When Tali had departed, an expression of deep worry crossed Laura's face—quickly extinguished. John thought of how she had suppressed the natural impulse to resettle her daughter's disordered hair; and though everything that he had seen of Tali had suggested vigorous good health and more intelligence than it is altogether comfortable to face in one so young, still he felt that in some way the child did not thrive.

"That one wants to fight dragons with the pinking shears," Laura said. "I need to see some proof she knows she's mortal before she does any weedkilling." She cut a bite and ate it. "The tomatoes are good, at least."

"It's wonderful altogether." He meant not only that the food itself was satisfying, but that it was a comfort to be cooked for—cooked for individually, and not, as on the ship, as part of an impersonal process in which the face of the one doing the work was rarely seen. In this way the same meal fed two different hungers. But he must remember that to eat was also to be vulnerable. No matter what Sudharma thought, to be at odds with neighbors was to be at risk of poisoning, and they would have to take precautions.

"Would you teach me how to cook like this?" he asked. "I mean, with Terran foods. I know how to measure out and cut things up—I suppose I could follow a recipe. But I see I must rely mainly on foods in season, and that argues for improvisation. I need to learn the grammar of it, I suppose."

"You could get people to feed you, you know. You don't have to cook for yourselves if you don't want to."

He wondered if that was true. After the impression Sudharma had made last night, he would probably be welcomed as a dinner guest at any house, but if John was not trusted even to sit in a kitchen alone with a woman, he doubted he would be received with as much enthusiasm. In any case, he could not let Sudharma expose himself to meals cooked in a series of different houses, any of which might be hostile. But Laura mustn't know that he feared poisoning—that would be an insult to the colony. Neither could he justify home cooking on the basis of the additional dietary restrictions Sudharma had told him about, since the translator had chosen not to reveal them more widely himself. John would have to invent an innocuous reason.

"I hope to persuade him to eat at home, however. I care about him, and cooking is a way that I can care for him."

"Oh." Laura looked shocked. She lowered her voice, though no one else was there, and said, "Look, things may be different on Essius, but you *cannot* talk about that here."

His heart sank. She had seen through him. At least she didn't seem to have taken it personally, and clearly she did not intend to spread the news to others. "Of course. I wouldn't want to give offense."

"It's not offense, exactly, it's . . ." She waved a hand in the air vaguely. "Well, close enough." She sighed. "All right, look. At my age a whiff of scandal with a young man is more flattering than plausible, but there are limits. You can't be in and out of the house all the time when Piro's not around. I can let you come over at five o'clock on Sundays and help me get dinner ready. Piro and my daughter are home then, and Iren usually comes over, so it won't look so odd. You can eat with us too. I wouldn't want you to develop an onion and garlic deficiency."

"Thank you. That suits me perfectly."

Laura ate the rest of her lunch, slowly. He thought something preoccupied her. At last she folded up her napkin, put it on the table, and looked him in the eyes. "I'd better tell you, or you'll just hear it worse from somebody else. A lot of the Ischnurans think Tali's going to take the braid. Zandaheans are not going to tolerate that. Do you understand why?"

"They want her to marry instead?"

"That, too. But mainly it's about what this world's going to be like. Making jesses is not our way, it's not our faith. It was one thing when it was just Iren. I mean . . ." She frowned and seemed to choose her words carefully. "Iren is Piro's best friend, I guess I know them pretty well. I can't imagine them being any other way, and obviously no one else is ever going to be like them. I think Adzere just figured the custom would die out. I make fun of Adzere, but he's the priest you get when the ships have a veto—he's been willing to hold his tongue to keep the peace. But one of our own, plucked right out of the church pew—even if her mother's a Denier, and of course they'll blame that. Or both of us, for letting Iren in our home. Never mind, that doesn't matter. What you need to know is, if someone asks for your opinion, they're not wondering what they should think of jesses, they're wondering what they should think of *you*. You won't do yourself any favors by picking a side. Also, it's a matter for the family and everybody else should butt out."

"Of course, I understand completely. I will say as much, if anybody asks."

"Do. And take this seriously. You and me walking alone in the desert together is a nonsense scandal that will blow over—this is not that. Figure out how far you need to be from the explosion and multiply by one point five."

"I will," he said, disquieted. He understood the worry he had seen in her face now. It was the look of a mother whose son was going to war.

CHAPTER SIX

The van provided to convey them out of town was long and wide, and raised so high on its huge tires that they had to climb up to it with stirrups. He had never driven anything so large before, but the controls were familiar—a ships' standard, he supposed. In front was enough room for three to sit easily. Unlike the van that had taken them from pod to town, it had no second row of seats, but crates of food arranged around three edges of it were of a height to be sat on. Tiers of shelves above held plastic jugs of water, lashed into place by their handles—enough for all the people sitting on the crates to drink for days; the pillows and blankets stacked up in the corners would be sufficient for them to sleep. The van was packed for an evacuation.

John feared at first that, being so high above the ground, the van might tend to tip, but when he turned it felt quite stable. This emboldened him to try going over rather than around small obstacles, and soon he was driving in nearly a straight line across the terrain, though at times this made the cabin tilt dramatically and plunge again. Sudharma gave no sign of being worried either by his driving or its destination. He sat quietly, hands folded in his lap, watching the landscape through the windows. An animal caught his eye—like the one John had seen clinging to a column yesterday, but larger, its sides striped in the colors of mud and bone. It was digging a hole underneath a bush, wary of their passage but not daunted by it. It scratched in the earth with its claws, raised up its long head to look, then hunkered down to scratch again.

"That is a reptile," John said, "but the bush is a mammal. It must be digging up the developing young to eat."

Sudharma received this news in silence.

They mounted the ridge and drove along it the prescribed distance. The crawler appeared below, long and dark gray. Lying in the riverbed, with the shining line of water underneath it and its many legs splayed out on either side, it was like a row of sutures on a wound. There was no hint of a head at either end. It was on John's side of the van, so Sudharma leaned over him to see. He smelled of the soap they both used, sharp and clean, with a trace of some sweet richness underneath.

They worked their way down to the river and drove along the line of trees on the bank, looking for a place that they could pass through. John stopped the van about half a kilometer upstream of the crawler.

"This will do, I think. But I must show you what we are avoiding. Stay close to me." John led Sudharma to a place closer to the bank. "The two trees in front of us are innocent, but look at the next one over to the right. The snake is on the bottommost branch."

"Yes, I see it."

"I'll go down first, and when you see me safe, you follow exactly the same path."

John walked slowly to a spot that he judged neither of the nearest snakes could reach. He paused to wonder if the bank was too steep to climb back up. No, he decided; the slope was short and there were good handholds. Still, it would be easier to slide than to step down. He turned to the side, lowered one foot to the slope, and let gravity take him, his boots raising a plume of dust as he descended. Nothing moved to strike him.

"I'm all right," he called out. "Do it exactly as I did."

Sudharma came down without hesitation. Near the bottom he lost his balance and might have fallen, but John caught him around the shoulders and kept him up.

"Let's walk at the edge of the water. We should be out of range of the snakes, but we'll check each one anyway."

They progressed about a hundred paces without incident. Then John stopped. Ahead of them a snake, its whole long body stretched out toward the river, scraped soil out of a hole that it was making and pushed it into a pile; there was a ridge below the mouth that seemed made for this purpose.

"It can't reach us," Sudharma said.

"I want to know what that thing is doing before I turn my back on it."

John approached it as closely as he dared. For perhaps another five minutes it dug methodically, peering down into the hole once in a while to examine its work. The fourth time, it looked for longer and did not return to digging. Its mouth opened so wide that he thought it would turn itself inside out. A wave went through its body—a convulsion. Then, with a wet tearing sound, it vomited up a brown mass in which John thought he saw fragments of bone. Of course, the snake's feces would have to come out somewhere. By expelling them through the mouth it could choose whether to place them near or far, and so fertilize its roots as much or as little as they needed. The adaptation was ingenious. He wished he had not stopped to watch.

They moved on, but not fast enough to avoid seeing the snake close its mouth and calmly drag soil back into the hole.

They rounded a turn in the river and found a fallen tree blocking their path. It had broken from its roots, slipped some way down the slope, and now lay like a bridge across the water. They walked toward it slowly until John could see the snake, hiding under the branches on the near side.

"It might be dead." He found a stone and threw, hitting a branch close to the snake, which reared up and looked at them, swiftly: it was not merely clinging to life, there was still vigor in it. It was very long, and he could not judge exactly how long, because it lay not stretched out on a branch but loosely in a pile. He made a guess, increased it, and then multiplied by one point five. They could not get by on either side without risking its attack or coming into range of snake-trees on the banks. "We will have to go back and approach from the other direction."

"Let me try something." Sudharma looked past the tree to the crawler, filled his lungs, and said: "People of Earth, and honored teachers, we are new to this world, and have come to greet you as our neighbors. We find it difficult to get to you. If you are willing to help us, we would welcome it."

There was a moment during which John guessed that someone—or something—mulled over the request. Then the crawler stirred and walked toward them on its many legs. When the legs were raised they ended in a point, that spread out when it touched the ground, becoming a round foot. It came near; it was enormous: even the long belly of it was above the level of John's head. It splayed its frontmost legs and lowered the end of itself down to the ground, so that they were confronted with what should have been a face but was, instead, a flat blank wall. The gray of it was glossy and reflected their images back at them, dimly. The crawler hid much of the fallen tree from view, but since John heard no splintering of wood, he thought the snake had not been crushed. He didn't know whether this scrupulous regard for a dying monster's life should reassure or frighten him.

As they waited for something more to happen, one of the snakes on the bank flowed downslope like a rivulet of blood, then shot forward to bite the crawler's leg. Its teeth went through as if the leg were made of water. It tried once more with the same result, then swiftly reeled itself back in. The crawler never twitched, but suffered the assault in stillness.

He was still watching the retracted snake when motion caught the corner of his eye. The wall before them was sinking inward, becoming concave. As it changed shape it quivered, as if it were made of hot soup and some giant, by blowing on it, opened up a hollow.

"We're meant to enter there, I think," Sudharma said, and he did so. He turned to where John was still standing and added, "Don't worry. Just think of it as an elevator that will take us inward as well as up."

John didn't care for elevators either, but had learned to tolerate them. He tried to step into the dimple in the crawler with the same composure. As soon as he was in, the hollow deepened to become a chamber; they went further, and the wall closed up behind them. The substance of the crawler seeped in underneath their feet to lift them up. It was dark now and they were completely enclosed. Earth could kill them by doing nothing at all, just leaving them sealed up to suffocate or die of thirst. They would perish in secret, like those birds that never escape from their cocoons, but are found when the leaves fall, the dried-out husks, when opened, revealing nothing but a suit of armor and a puff of dust.

"Patience," Sudharma said. "We will be let out presently."

John wondered how he could possibly know that, but nevertheless he was comforted.

Without knowing exactly how, he sensed that they were rising. Then they stopped, and the light increased. He thought the wall ahead of them was glowing, then realized it was becoming thinner. It peeled away from the air and was gone, revealing the interior of the crawler: a great hall empty of all furniture or ornament. The walls and floor and ceiling were the same gray color as the outside, but they had a rougher texture, like unpolished stone.

At the center of the room stood a woman. She was barefoot, in a yellow dress that fell down to her ankles. The fabric of it was loose everywhere, yet so compliant to the contours underneath that when she walked toward them he had a clear impression of her shape, boyish except in the curve of the hips. Her hair was black, and straight as if a plumb bob had been fixed to every strand; her skin was brown and warm. She had a face made for amazement, high of brow and low of cheekbone, as if the whole province of the eye could widen in delight—yet she kept closing her eyes for long moments, as if she were fighting off sleep.

She stood in front of them, looking them over with interest but saying nothing. Her silence was not hostile or contemptuous, John thought. It was as if she didn't know that conversation was expected.

"I am Sudharma Jain, and this is my colleague, John Maraintha." When she didn't respond to this opening, Sudharma added, "May I ask your name?"

"How would I know that? You haven't said it yet." Her voice was gently teasing. "Shall I guess?" Not waiting for an answer to this baffling question, she exclaimed, "Oh! I'm told you mean a name affixed to me at birth, and that I do have one and that it's Izavolizet." She pronounced this without any pauses; it might have been one name or four. "You can just say 'Vo' if you like. This is to make you comfortable."

At home *vo'* meant a little boat, the kind used to fish in ponds and rivers in the Clear Lakes—a comforting image. It could also mean a bone, but John set that idea aside.

"You are guests, so I should offer you refreshment. I heard that's a custom. Do you like chocolate?"

"The plant never made it to my world," Sudharma said. "But I would gladly try it."

Without waiting for John to answer, she went to the nearest wall and touched it, causing a part of its substance to flow away. Behind was a rectangular compartment holding two glass cups, each filled with a thick brown drink. John wondered uneasily whether this fluid had fallen from some duct inside the wall like water from a tap, or if it was secreted by the cups themselves, like nectar in a fly-soup flower. Vo returned and handed cups first to Sudharma, then to John. When he glanced back at the compartment it had sealed back up; no trace of its existence could be seen.

Carefully, he sniffed the air above the cup. The fluid gave up a dark and complicated odor, unfamiliar to his nose not only as a whole but in all its parts, like a book written in an unknown alphabet. It might mask any number of poisons; it might be, itself, a poison. But Sudharma was already drinking, raising the cup just high enough to sip, his eyes level with hers.

"You may as well drink too, Doctor. If she wished to harm us she would not need our cooperation. In any case, the drink is excellent."

To suggest out loud that a guest might poison them was shocking, but Vo took no notice. She didn't know what hospitality was, he thought—except that an unseen presence at her elbow taught her as she went. He imagined that her upbringing among aiyi had been extremely strange, and so she had far more excuse for ignorance than the people of the *Folly*.

He looked into his cup with foreboding. Even if it was not lethal, it was likely to be psychoactive; a drink so layered up with scents must have some purpose other than its taste. Still, he could hardly refuse now. He sipped it sparingly, finding it deep and rich, with a sweetness that smoothed but did not overbalance the spices. It was, in fact, excellent.

"I am surprised to find you alone in such a large space," Sudharma said. "How many Earth humans are with you on this world?"

"None. It's just me."

"And how many aiyi?"

"They're not *countable*. You can't *enumerate* them." Her tone suggested the idea would be offensive if it weren't so absurd. Then a thought occurred to her. "If you mean how many humans did they arise from, then one."

"Do you mean they are like your children?" John said.

"Oh no, I've never engendered aiyi. To do that you have to die, and I don't want to."

Uncertain what to make of this response, John sipped his chocolate. It was awkward to drink and converse while standing, and he wished he had a place to sit down, but the aiyi—if it was they who advised her on etiquette—had neglected that lesson.

Vo frowned at him, puzzled. "You can shape here," she told him. "Don't you see that?"

"I'm sorry, I don't understand."

"Like this," she said, and three chairs rose out of the floor. They were the same color as the inside of the crawler and made out of the same substance, though the floor that had birthed them remained undiminished. "You can do that."

"I am quite sure I cannot."

With the air of one deciding that some mystery was too trivial to investigate, she shrugged and sat down in the chair behind her. John and Sudharma stepped forward to sit in theirs. The chairs were softer than they looked, and John could feel, even through his pants, that they were warmer than the air around. Probably the whole inner surface of the crawler was like that, he thought—it was not the stone that it resembled, but a kind of flesh.

Sudharma put one hand flat on his lap with the palm facing up, and rested his cup on it. "What is your purpose here?" he asked. "I mean on this planet, the one humans call Scythia."

Though the words were probing, his voice was mild, and she answered readily. "The aiyi are here to represent the life-forms on this world."

"You mean, to speak for them?"

"I don't think so," she said. "I mean to record them? To make something of them. To preserve them, but not in a literal or exact way. It's an art form, like a painting or a sculpture. Humans can't perceive it, though—it's not made for our minds."

"Then what do you do, on this world?"

"I'm here with the aiyi. We couldn't be apart. Our connection is very intense. But in particular, I help when the art needs a human body."

"And do you, or do the aiyi, have any concerns about the human presence on this world?"

She blinked in puzzlement. "Why should that concern us?"

"You are making art based on the life here. Human activities must affect that life."

Vo closed her eyes and seemed to think for a long time. Then she opened them again, but they focused on nothing. Her face was transfigured by joy. "Things that are changing are beautiful."

"But, I can't help noticing, you are on Scythia, which humans have changed little, and not on Earth. And being from Earth, you may have different ideas about change than we do. All of us have made our worlds more hospitable to human life by our efforts, whereas Terrans made theirs much less so."

"Oh, that was a long time ago. But on Earth, now, most of the life is invented by aiyi, or at least re-created. It's already a representation, so it's not as interesting to represent. We'll have moved on to another world long before anything like that could happen here."

"Do you know, or do the aiyi know, what happened to the colonists on Erav?"

The question was pointed; and it was rude, John thought, to pepper their hostess with so many questions one after another. But Vo seemed not to care. She thought for a second or two and replied, "I'm told they only know what humans have said about it. If the aiyi there sent any message to Earth, it wouldn't have arrived until after we left to come here."

"You understand we are worried that the same fate might befall humans on Scythia."

"Yes," she said. "I can see that."

"If such an action were considered here, would you be involved in the decision?"

"I doubt I'd be asked in words, if that's what you mean. But I'm involved in everything. As I said, our relationship is very close. We're *interpenetrating and penumbrally synonymous.*" She spoke this phrase with emphasis, clearly enunciating every syllable, as if it represented an incomparable distinction and gave her immense pleasure to recite; but then, growing dissatisfied with either the words or their reception, she added, "Like tea leaves seeping out into hot water—although I don't know what that looks like. Oh! It's pretty."

"Are you happy?" John asked.

Vo looked at him and smiled. He felt that for the first time she had turned her full attention to him—that she saw him in a way she had not before. "Yes. Very."

"I'm glad," he said. "It seems strange, and hard, to be alone on a world for so long."

"I'm never alone. Even on the ship between the stars, I had the aiyi, so I didn't need anything else. But it's even better here. I like the things there are to see."

"What have you seen?"

"Oh, everything. I've been to the tundra and seen animals dig out a nest of snow around their seedlings, then lie curled up inside it to keep them warm. I've been to a rain forest and watched them catch prey with a net woven out of their mother's vines. I've swum in the deeps of the ocean, where the animals shine in the dark, and seen a fish give birth to clouds of spores that rose up to the light."

The mention of a forest made him think at once of home. He imagined tall stingbark and eight-o'clock trees lacing the tips of their branches together, with the white bells of laurel's-tears scattered beneath. Such a landscape existed on Scythia, even if there were no true flowers here and the plants bore only green leaves and not orange. But any such richness must be very far from the desolation he was trapped in.

"It was beautiful," she said. "But the trees around us now are also very beautiful, especially the way they move. I'll be glad if we stay here a long time."

Such serenity and joy suffused her voice that to find beauty in the liquid creeping of a snake seemed only natural. He thought she was more willing to be pleased than anyone that he had ever met. It was difficult to say whether that openness might translate to a more specific kind of welcome. But she had told him she might linger near the town awhile. Perhaps there was a reason she had mentioned it.

"I find the snakes unsettling, to be honest," he said. "They are known to attack humans. And there is something quite unnatural in their behavior."

"Well," she said with a compassionate amusement, "you only see them with your own eyes."

That was true, but he hardly knew how to respond. When he had thought about it for a while without locating words, Sudharma filled the gap in the conversation.

"May we ask that if the aiyi are considering some action against us, they communicate with us first?"

"They don't talk to anyone but me," she said.

"If you, then, become aware that the aiyi object to something humans are doing on this world, will you tell us?"

"All right. But I can't imagine that would ever happen. It's just not the way they think."

Sudharma stood, placing his cup on the seat of his chair. "Thank you. You have relieved my mind—not altogether, but as much as you are able."

"You don't look relieved."

"I am, however—relieved of fear of the aiyi."

John got up from his chair. To take their leave now felt abrupt to him. But Sudharma knew about Terrans, and so John ought to follow as he led.

"May we return later, and speak with you again?" Sudharma asked.

John was still holding his cup, and as Sudharma spoke Vo had moved to take it from him. Their fingers touched briefly, and she looked into his eyes as she said, "That's all right. Come here anytime you like." It might have been coincidence.

"There is another who may want to meet you."

"That's all right too."

Her tone was cheerful but her back was turned; she had walked a little way away from them. She dropped the cup deliberately to the floor, where it shattered. The floor flowed over the pieces and drew them down, removing any trace of them. The other cup merged with the seat of the chair and then all the chairs sank.

Vo never turned back toward them. The interview was over.

They passed through the moving chamber back out to the riverbed, walked to their entry point, and made it safely up the bank. When they had climbed into the van, John didn't start the engine right away.

"Well," Sudharma said, "I am tempted to believe it. The aiyi simply do not care about the basket-men or us. A landscape painter sets his easel on a high hillside; when in the valley below the animals begin to build a fire, he simply adds it to his composition. . . ."

"She struck me as entirely honest."

"We must remember that she is conjoined with the aiyi. They might manipulate the muscles of her face as a musician plucks the strings of an instrument. They are not animals, as we are—they do nothing by instinct or accident. Still, I don't know why they would bother to conceal their wishes from us, when we can do nothing to thwart them. So probably it was the truth."

"How long ago must she have left Earth, to be gone when a message from Erav would reach it?"

"At least two hundred and thirty-eight Terran years. And if it's true that she and the aiyi can't bear to be apart, she won't have used cold-sleep—the Terrans on Dharanendra had a horror of it. Time dilation on the way here might account for eighty years or thereabouts, but even so, we may assume the aiyi don't allow her to age."

That was obviously impossible, but perfectly in character. She didn't want to die and so she didn't.

"Can she read thoughts? It seemed that way."

"On Dharanendra they could. They couldn't hear words—or so they said—but they could sense feelings and impulses."

John thought she might have sensed a few of those from him. If so, it hadn't seemed to bother her.

"I had a notion she might welcome a visit."

Sudharma stared at him. "That is perhaps the last reaction to that meeting I would have predicted."

"It seems very logical to me. She is strange, no doubt, but since I left home everyone is very strange. I think at least Vo would not confuse visiting with marriage, or expect it to lead to marriage."

"You might be right about that part." Sudharma sighed. "I cannot tell you what to do. But you must realize there could be no question of equality in such a relationship. It would be like visiting a god."

"Well, there's nothing wrong with that. It happens all the time. People say it's good luck—I don't know if that's true. Even if it's not, gods by their nature are very appealing. I missed my chance with one once and I greatly regretted it. But he was nothing like her at all."

"The point is, she is extremely powerful."

"No doubt. I don't think she would use her power for harm."

"You are staking a great deal on a first impression."

"If she did want to harm me, would distance help? Would she need my cooperation?"

Recognizing his own arguments turned back on him, Sudharma tried another tack. "You wouldn't be able to keep it a secret. Your tag transmits your location—"

"I already know about that. Tags can be turned off."

"This van is likely tracked as well. I don't know who looks at the data, but an unannounced visit to the representative of a power that could kill us all will draw attention. The governor, in particular, would want to know what you discuss with her, to monitor the status of the relationship—"

"All right, I understand," John said. "That's enough." He had dared to imagine a visit to Vo might be uncomplicated, but the tangling roots of marrying culture infiltrated everything. Everybody's visiting was everybody's business. He sat without speaking a while, his frustration rising in him like a dough with too much yeast. It burst out, at last, in a random direction: "Will you at least tell me how I am supposed to help you with whatever you're planning to do to yourself? Because I am entirely at a loss."

"Let's go home, and I'll show you." Sudharma's voice was gentle, and at once John regretted his ill temper. But he only started up the engine and turned back toward the town.

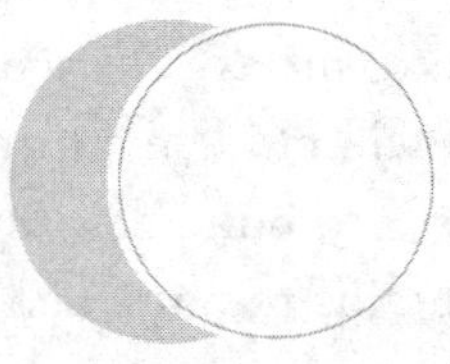

CHAPTER SEVEN

John knocked at the door of Laura's house, greeted her, and washed up at the kitchen sink, his thoughts haunted by glowing images of brains.

It had been three days since Sudharma, holding a lit screen in both hands, told him what he was expected to do. "We speak and understand partly by learning, partly by instinct, and partly in virtue of the kind of animal we are: the senses that we have, the concepts we develop by interacting with the world in human bodies. When I learn a human language, my instincts and my embodiment are right for it, and I can become fluent. With an alien language, I could probably communicate to some degree, but haltingly and with errors. I would be trying to overcome a mismatch of instincts and bodies through learning and reason—it might be like solving a difficult math problem for every sentence. For fluency, the instinct must be changed."

"And the body?"

"In a way. In the translation that made me able to perform *dashkvaut*, I didn't change my hands or my eyes, but rather the way my brain uses them. My body feels different to me now, and I live in it differently. I might need to do that again for some other reason. Besides that, I might need to process input from artificial senses so I can perceive in the way that the language demands. It might mean carrying around some kind of instrument, but I hope that will not be the case."

"How is any of that possible?"

"I have small machines inside my brain, like the ones that we were host to in the crawler—descended, in fact, from Terran machines that Dharanendrans managed to resuscitate. They will make parts of my brain more pliable, as they were at birth, or perhaps even more pliable than that. Some parts might be restructured, or reassigned to different purposes. I will prepare a program in advance for the machines to follow, so you will only have to administer sedation, monitor me as I change, and intervene if something goes wrong. Afterward, you will guide me through a prescribed education to regain the abilities I've lost and build new ones." During all this talk the screen displayed a series of brains rotating and splitting into cross sections to show the harm that had been done to them; each one was labeled neatly with the purpose of the damage.

When Laura set him to cutting up vegetables for a soup, John was grateful for the task. The household's knives were admirably sharp, so keeping his skin whole required a mindfulness that kept his foreboding at bay. He remembered what his mother used to say, when some childish crisis moved him to distract her from her work: "Even if the world ends tomorrow, we still have to eat tonight." Probably, when the first smoke of the wildfires reached her nose, she had worried and cooked dinner anyway. Probably cutting up stalks of ocean-crest or baby's-tooth had comforted her too.

Laura sat at the kitchen table, looking up a recipe. "I'd save myself a lot of trouble if I just made the same dishes over and over," she told him, "and my family would be just as happy if not more so, but I get bored." On Essius such restlessness would have endangered the whole family, leading the cook to seek out new ingredients and methods rather than sticking to those known safe. Here, it could do no more than increase the challenge of the evening's preparations.

"It's convenient for me," he said, slicing up celery. "I want to learn everything I can."

Heavy feet came down the stairs, and Piro appeared. To John he said hello, to Laura nothing, but he rested a hand on her upper back briefly. She tilted her head to brush his arm as it moved away. There was familiarity in the gestures but no trace of passion; if such intensity had ever burned between them, it had died out long ago. Perhaps now they were like brother and sister, and could raise children together in the ordinary way, without being distracted by visiting matters. If so then they were fortunate. For lovers pushed by law and custom into an unnatural proximity and forced to stay there past the proper time, the outcome could have been far worse.

"Iren will be here any second," Piro said. Laura acknowledged this neither by word nor expression.

The doorbell rang, and Piro went to answer it. Tali ran downstairs at once; John could hear her eager stream of talk and Iren's calm replies. They all came into the sitting room, and after a little persuasion Tali sat with Piro on the couch to read and discuss a book, which seemed to be about the care of sheep. Since there were no sheep on Scythia, it was unclear what purpose this study could serve, but both of them were absorbed by it. Iren looked on with fondness, but never sat down. After a few minutes they drifted over to lean against the kitchen doorway. They wore a formfitting dress of a clear greenish blue, marked with a pattern of pale orange flowers. A white wrap, fastened with a gold pin in the likeness of some flying animal, covered their shoulders and chest. They smiled wanly at John and then addressed Laura.

"The air's a bit heavy with incense. Is there anything here I can help with?"

Laura, who by then was gathering ingredients from the refrigerator, barely glanced over her shoulder at them. "You can set the table in the dining room. For five, and we'll need bowls."

"All right." Iren sounded disappointed, but they readily opened a cupboard, split five plates from a stack of eight, and held them in one hand as they arranged glasses on top. Though they were unsure of their welcome in the kitchen, they knew where to find things in it. When they had finished going back and forth to the dining room, they settled down to watch Tali study and did not try to help any more. Later, however, when Laura went to tell everyone dinner was ready, they came into the kitchen without asking and helped carry food. Before they sat down at the table, they unpinned their scarf and folded it onto an empty chair, revealing the fine sculpture of their shoulders and their collarbones.

When everyone was seated and all plates were filled, Iren asked him, "Did your cooking lesson go well?"

"I think so," John said. "I can make one suitable meal, at least—although I don't know where to get ingredients."

"The grocery's on Main Street, about half a kilometer west of your house."

"Wouldn't I need money for that?"

"Not in the least. Take what you like from the front, and if you need something you don't see, just ask in the back."

"We don't have a money system yet," Laura explained. "Though we're at least a decade overdue for one. As it is, whoever's popular with the grocer or the manufacturing people gets the best of everything—or whoever has a favor to call in."

"She means me," Iren said. "It's true I have a store of favors owed me, but I mainly use them to have fabrics made, half of which go toward sewing clothes for other people."

"And the other half toward showing off at my dinner table."

"I never knew it bothered you till now. Next time I will come to dinner in my humblest dress if you prefer, or my most traditional jacket—or I fill out a suit nicely, too. In what clothes am I innocuous? You have only to pronounce."

Laura looked flustered by the question. Iren was enjoying themself, John thought, but in a way that was not altogether kind. To soothe whatever tension was between them—but out of a real curiosity too—he asked Iren, "Is there some philosophy to when you wear women's clothes, or is it quite at random?"

"Me, wear women's clothes? What an idea. This is a jess's dress, young man—the proof of which is, that I am a jess and I am wearing it."

"Is there some difference in style?"

"There might be, but there needn't." They paused, holding their fork straight up; they were considering how to explain. "When you learned English, were there words that sounded like the words you knew but meant something quite different?"

"Such as, 'veil' is not a fluid made by the liver?"

"That's a good one. Well, women's fashion and jesses' are two different languages, and the words of them are garments and accessories and makeup, all of which can be false friends too, and bamboozle the unwary. So even if a woman had the same dress—which she couldn't; I made this one myself, and I'm not making any more—it wouldn't mean the same thing as it does when I wear it."

"What does it mean on you?"

"That I like blue and I look good with my shoulders bare."

This was undeniable, but left him none the wiser. He liked Iren, but he felt sometimes their conversation was deliberately unilluminating.

The next morning, when Sudharma had completed whatever ritual he performed in his room and emerged, John announced his intention to go to the market and gather the makings of dinner.

"You should let me cook for us," Sudharma said. "I have little to do for now—you are studying to help me translate. When basket-men arrive you can take over, if you like."

"Will you be able to manage, without the plants whose seeds you brought?"

"I studied how to cook with limited ingredients, while I was still on Dharanendra. It was a topic of great interest to all of us translators leaving home."

John had looked forward to cooking as a reprieve. When you worked in the kitchen every evening, you could think about it and plan for it during the day, which would buffer his mind against the thought that he was studying to help do injury to a healthy brain. But he couldn't deny Sudharma was better suited to the task for now. Perhaps after a few more Sundays spent at Laura's he could plead his case.

"Let me do the shopping, at least," he said. "I don't want to be stuck in the house all day, when there's not even snow on the ground."

Sudharma agreed readily. But John quickly came to regret the arrangement. It was interesting, at first, to be out at a time when people went to work or school, to see their faces and how they dressed and who they walked with—Ischnurans with Ischnurans and Zandaheans with each other, for the most part, though when he saw Tali she was often walking close with her friend Lili, an Ischnuran girl. He thought it would be well to be seen out on the street, to speak to those he passed and so become familiar in the town. Surely, in time, people would perceive he was no threat—not even to the chains that they had placed upon themselves; he would never have induced someone to violate a vow they still believed in, however foolish he might think them for embracing a constraint. He found instead that it was mainly young men and boys who would engage him, and the only subject that they wished to talk about was visiting, which they imagined in the crudest and most self-regarding terms, supposing every cabin door on Essius would be open to them. Nothing could have been less likely. When he deflected their insinuations, they only became more offensive; mistaking him for the kind of man who brags about his visits, they thought to draw him out with personal questions, until one day a youth on his way to school, without greeting or preamble, asked him for a detail he would not have vouchsafed to his closest friend and a sum that he could not have calculated if he tried. He would have ignored the question and walked on, except that Iren, coming up behind the boy, grabbed him by the shoulder to turn him around. "Adhnan son of Roalin, shall I take you to repeat that to your mother?"

"No, Dama. I didn't mean anything. I was just curious."

"Exercise your curiosity in your science classes, young man, not by prying into your elders' private business. If I hear you've done it again I'll tell your parents myself."

When the child was out of earshot, Iren sighed. "I apologize profusely for Ischnura's wayward son."

"I am sure you have done nothing to apologize for."

"There you are mistaken. I used to babysit that brat. Any of a hundred times, I could have taken his bassinet out in the desert and left him to die, yet I failed to. They're cute when they're small, so you don't think of it, and once you notice they've turned into monsters it's too late. But he will grow out of it presently. I'm sure you know what boys are like."

John couldn't imagine an Essian male of any age saying such a thing, but not liking to suggest that his homeworld was superior to theirs, he nodded.

Despite Iren's intervention, he shifted the beginning of his walk a half hour later in the morning, by which time the streets were largely the domain of women and the store entirely so. No one then began a conversation with him. When he had trouble finding Sudharma's requests in the unlabeled bins and barrels of the grocery and asked for help, the women either answered as if sensible of their own daring in speaking to him, or else in tones laced with contempt. Two would not acknowledge him at all, though it might have been the same one twice—he still couldn't tell Ischnurans of the same sex apart.

He saw that without having visited anyone on Scythia, he was entirely defined to these people by visiting. He wondered if even a lifetime of abstinence would change their opinions. He certainly wasn't going to try the experiment.

Every week, John went to Laura's house to help her cook. Iren always arrived two hours before dinner, though they had little to do except to watch Piro and Tali studying their book—which by this time he understood to be about the god that Zandaheans so greatly favored. They always sat where they could look into the kitchen, but no longer tried to enter it. At dinner Tali often asked them questions about jesses on Ischnura, which they answered gravely and with care, sometimes glancing at Laura to gauge her reaction. John thought Laura would have preferred that these subjects did not come up.

One evening Tali asked, "Why does there have to be a jess at every wedding?"

This time Iren's eyes shifted toward John. They had some notion of how Essians saw marriage, he thought. "After the wedding vows are spoken, we confer a blessing on the happy couple, wishing them eternal love and harmony both now and after death."

"But why jesses?" Tali asked.

"Some say it's because of our connection to the other world. Others would have it that, being apart from the two sexes, we can build a bridge between them. It also helps that we have no experience of marriage, and so can pronounce such improbable sentiments with a straight face."

On the fifth Sunday, Tali left early to dine with her friend Liliana. Iren and Piro made each other laugh in the sitting room; Laura hummed a tune as she made tortillas. At table her conversation with Iren was nearly amiable. When everyone had eaten but still lingered, not conceding yet that they would not take more, John asked Piro the question he had been wanting to ask all evening. "When Sudharma and I went into the desert, you made one of the vans recognize me and start for me. Would it still do so?"

"Sure—I never rescinded permission. Why, what are you planning?"

"Nothing. But I am meant to respond to emergencies and I suppose that is how I would do it."

Iren leaned forward. "So Marne decided you'd be a field medic and did nothing at all to make that possible?"

Laura plucked the napkin from her lap and laid it by her plate. "When did that man turn into such a snob?"

"In the womb, probably. Still," they said, frowning at John, "I'm surprised he didn't try to dump all his most irritating patients on you."

"I'd say you dodged a bullet," Piro said. "You'll get fresh air and sunshine and miss out on Zhuyef's monthly visit to complain that he can't get it up for women."

"Now, Piro, I know you are making up stories. You surely can't believe he tries that often."

These remarks seemed both gratuitous and unkind to John, and Laura was of the same mind. "Ignore these two," she said. "My husband had to come twenty-two light-years to find someone who appreciates his sense of humor. It's a great stroke of luck for the two of them only."

Iren didn't look at her, but kept their eyes down, minutely adjusting the silverware laid on their plate. "You're right, of course—I shouldn't laugh. I am suitably chastened. And as I am chastened, Zhuyef must remain as he is."

Laura rolled her eyes at this, but John didn't think that she was seriously displeased.

"In all sobriety," Iren said, lifting their gaze to meet John's, "go see Marne and make him equip you. I doubt he's trying to be inhospitable—he is more likely overtaxed by all the work he won't let anyone else do." They turned to Laura. "On an entirely unrelated matter, are you going to let me help you with the dishes, or is your soapy water liable to be tainted by exposure to strange vows?"

Laura stood up and resignedly began to gather tableware. "Come on then."

Iren leaned over to pluck John's plate from in front of him, then rose with it. "How pleasant to again be put to use."

The next day, and all the next week, John made breakfast for Sudharma. He had asked to take over this task, a simple and pleasant one: it was only a matter of making fresh roti and stir-frying whatever vegetables needed to be used up, along with a rehydrated pepper—Laura had shared some of her hoard. Every morning in his room, Sudharma performed a ritual called *pratikraman*, about which John knew nothing except its name and the time it ended. As long as some vegetable new to him did not take longer to cook than he expected, he could have breakfast on the table at the moment that Sudharma would emerge.

The next Sunday Piro let him in, and he found Laura at the kitchen table, staring at nothing in particular. "What's wrong?" he asked.

"Yesterday Tali brought Iren home to ambush me and ask if she could take the jess vow. I didn't say yes, so they are both going to hate me until further notice."

"I am sure she doesn't hate you. She's your daughter."

"You have no idea what a daughter can feel toward a mother," Laura said. Then she waved a hand at him in vague apology. "Sorry, but I can't take the view from Utopia right now. Just multiply by one point five, all right?"

"All right," he said. "Are we cooking?"

"Can't say I feel like it, but Piro and I are still eating, at least. And I have tomatoes that aren't getting any fresher."

"I will do something with them. Just rest for now."

"Don't expect Iren to show up or Tali to come down."

"I will make enough for them in any case."

The meal he made was simple and did not take long. No one was inclined to linger over dinner. When he left he turned his tag off, got into the van, and set out to find Vo's crawler.

CHAPTER EIGHT

The crawler had moved only far enough to lie down on its belly without crushing the fallen snake. John approached it slowly, trying to work out whether to speak to it or to knock. But before he reached either the front of it or a decision, a trembling crater had already formed. He supposed that was a welcome, so he entered. After some moments during which he was in darkness, the wall in front of him diminished to a thin film, like the skin of a soap bubble, and then burst. Vo was standing close, wearing the same yellow dress as the last time. Maybe she had a closet full of them, hidden somewhere inside the walls. Maybe the fabric formed around her every morning out of vapors in the air.

"You came back," she said.

"To visit, if you'll have me."

"I can see that." Her head was tilted. He thought she was amused, and maybe that she was deciding. Then she raised both her hands to his chest—not touching, but hovering close with the palms toward him, as if she were trying to feel the heat of his body through his clothes and through the air. It was such an odd gesture he didn't know how to respond. He stood waiting there until, with sudden resolution, she grasped both his shoulders and kissed him. The kiss was tentative until he brought his fingers to her face. Then she became insistent, pushing him back against the rear wall of the chamber he had come up in. Her hands and body pressed him into it with such an urgency that he began to wonder if she felt him only where they touched each other, or if the soft, warm wall behind him was a second skin and felt the imprint of him too. But in the rush of desire and relief, such a thought could not stay in his head for long. He felt as if all of his muscles had tensed up the day that he landed—or before that, at the moment that he learned he would be cast down from the *Folly*—and finally relaxed only now. Though she was strange, yet this was simple and familiar—a conversation in a universal language.

He felt her plucking at his collar ineffectually. Probably she didn't know how to unfasten buttons and was trying to work it out by touch alone, since to look down she would have had to break the kiss. He was just about to help her when she figured out the trick of it and quickly opened the shirt all the way down. The purpose of this was to burrow her hands beneath the fabric and slide them around to the small of his back. One small warmth pressed into the hollow while the other quested upward, clutching and releasing. Of course, he thought, she would be starved for contact. He hadn't made a visit since the captain called him to the old bridge, more than two months ago now, and the time seemed very long to him; but Vo had been alone with her aiyi a hundred and fifty years. It was unthinkable.

He pulled at her dress, hauling the hem of it up like an anchor, until he could hold her waist between his hands. Then he followed the rise in the flesh down to the generous curve of her buttocks, and with spread fingers he enclosed them. No undergarment impeded this. He pulled her in tighter, felt the soft pad of flesh above the joining of her legs pressing against him. She shifted her hips, and even this slight friction brought a cry into her throat that she broke the kiss to release. Her eyes had closed and her head was thrown back.

Suddenly she pulled away from him, gasping, working her mouth like a caught fish, her irises swimming in white. "Oh, that was weird!" Waving her hands near her face in distress, like someone who just bit into a slice of ring-root that a careless cook left in the stew, she collapsed to the ground and sat staring at nothing.

He crouched down near her, but not too close. He wasn't sure that he should touch her. But he laid a palm against the floor, and maybe that was contact. "What's wrong? Are you hurt?"

"No. No, it's just a panic." Already her voice was steadier. "It's over now—I killed the instinct." Her breathing slowed gradually. Once she was calm she perceived he did not understand, and explained further: "There's an instinct, a modification. Suppose you like to be touched in a particular spot, it's like my hand wants to move there? And when my hand finds the right place, I feel a satisfaction—as if it fits into a notch made for it."

"You mean you look into my mind to find out my desires."

"*I* don't, the instinct does, and it makes a . . . taxis, that's the word. I move by a taxis. But the idea is that we both have the same instinct, and it negotiates and finds something we both like, so everything just works out. And you don't do that? Oh, you *can't* do that. I'm told the instinct was never meant to work with an unmodified human partner, because there hardly are any on Earth. So it went out of balance, and I kept getting pulled further and further into what you wanted. Like a riptide."

"You didn't want to kiss me, you were . . . made to? By my thoughts?"

"I wasn't forced, it's not like that. I was estranged from my impulses. Anyway the desires I was feeling weren't bad, just *not invented here*. Too much of the outer self and not enough local animal, so then I started to delaminate. But like I said, I killed the instinct, and the aiyi helped me dampen down the memory, so I'm fine now."

Her words swam randomly inside his head, like stick-wing insects underneath the surface of a pond. The only fact that he could grasp out of the whirl was that somehow, without knowing, he had exerted an improper influence on her—worse than the giving of gifts to create a sense of obligation; less bad than binding a lover with promises, perhaps, but only in that the effects were short-lived.

She was wrong about the nature of the influence, he realized. It could not have been the placement of her hands on back or shoulders that her artificial instincts plucked out of his mind—he had no requirements so specific. Her instinct must instead have sensed his hope that she would want him, be eager to touch him and awakened by his touch: which meant that all of that had been a lie.

He thought that he should leave. But she was as calm as if nothing had happened. "Let me find a better setup, and then we can try again." Her eyes closed and she laid a hand against her collarbone. With the expression of a woman trying to find a distant station in the static of a radio, she tensed and loosed her fingers by the tiniest increments, pausing for a long time in between, as if every activation of a motor neuron had to be considered like a move at chess. Surely, if her actions were so careful and deliberate, the adjustments she was making must arise from her own true intent.

She opened her eyes wide and turned her head to take in the empty hall. "Is this how you see the world all the time? Oh, I'm told not really. Even so . . ." She looked into his eyes with wonder. "It's so strange. I can't tell what you're going to do."

"Nothing, until I'm sure you want it, truly and completely."

"I do. All of me." She said this with a calm and condescending air, like a mother comforting a child who shrieks because a bird has landed on his arm. She stood up, took her dress by the back of the neck, and pulled it off over her head in a single motion, as if dragging a dusty blanket from a mattress in a disused cabin. She spread it on the floor, lay down on it, and stretched out on her side. "Will you try again with me? Please?"

Cautiously, still fearing that his touch might cause some further avalanche, he put his fingers to her cheek. She rubbed her face against them, so that without moving he caressed her cheekbone and the long line of her jaw. Reassured, he drew his hand along her neck, over her shoulder, then down her body as far as he could reach without rising from the crouch that he still held to. All the way that his hand went, he let his eyes follow. Most people liked to be looked at carefully and with a thorough appreciation; a few would flinch away. She was not one of the shy ones.

"I can't feel what you're thinking, but I can see it in your face," she marveled.

"Not a difficult deduction, I imagine."

"No . . . but if I couldn't see you, you'd be able to *surprise* me." Abruptly she rolled onto her back and closed her eyes. "Will you touch me like this?"

The enthusiasm in her voice could hardly help but charm him; and after all, compared to some requests that had been made of him on the ship, hers was hardly peculiar at all.

She received the service she had asked for with an inexhaustible delight, each new caress eliciting the same small gasp, as if a spark of electricity had jumped between them. There was no urgency about her now, and so he was unhurried. When he had thoroughly explored the possibilities he began again, kissing her skin in all the places he had touched. Eventually he focused the attentions of both mouth and fingers on the place where they might do most good, and finally he entered her—turning her onto her side and lying behind, the better to continue to employ his hands. Yet everything he did drew out the same response, a diffuse excitement tending to no conclusion—until, disengaging, and leaning in to murmur in her ear, he asked, "What do you need?"

"Come when you like. I'll do it with you." She turned onto her back and opened her eyes. "Like this, so I can see."

"You mean to read my mind."

"It's not reading. It's just seeing."

"The last time, that ended badly."

"This is different. It's not taking what you feel into me, it's just watching and mirroring. As if you started a song, and I joined in because it's nice to sing together, and if I didn't want to anymore then I would stop."

He wished she would just teach him how best to unite their bodies. He wanted natural communication, flesh and nerve, and not this mysticism. Still her metaphor of singing made the idea sound oddly pleasant, and despite misgivings he agreed. He could not help thinking that her eyes, when she looked up at him, were like the sensors of some apparatus of ships' medicine, and the sweet sounds that she made were just the imitation of his pleasure by an artificial process—a heartbeat turned into the beeping of an EKG. It was unnerving. And yet she was beautiful, lying beneath him. She was wholly given over to a feeling he had made in her, even if not in the ordinary way. And after all, it had been a long time. So in the end the natural urges of his body overwhelmed the hesitations of his mind.

Afterward, he lay beside her, and she turned to face him. She would not have needed any extra senses to perceive he was unsettled, but no doubt she used them anyway. Even so, a tenderness intrinsic to the situation made him lay his hand upon her hip.

"I could visit you next time," she said.

"I think that would alarm the others in the town."

"I don't mean I could go where you live. I mean I could penetrate you. Isn't that what 'visit' means?"

"It can imply that, yes," he said. But how could she know that, unless Earth kept a watch on Essius? He was sure he hadn't used the word in such a colloquial way since he came to Scythia, except in his thoughts, which perhaps she could see more exactly than she let on. Neither theory was reassuring.

"Do you like to be fucked?" she asked.

"Once in a while, certainly."

"Well if you want to, come over early. The alteration takes about two hours."

"Alteration?"

"I can use a prosthesis instead, if you'd rather—the aiyi can simulate sensation in my mind. I just think growing a natural organ would be more companionable. After all, you'll be using one."

He was entirely at a loss. He had pictured one of the instruments by which women in puddle country sometimes visited, always hand-carved and, one assumed, used on themselves if nobody knocked at the door. If he had thought it through he would more likely have imagined the kind found sometimes in Faivai, and more often on the ships—better made, of softer material, and often attached to the body by straps, which he supposed was what she meant by a prosthesis. To create one from her own flesh should have been impossible. It should, he thought, especially have been impossible to do it in two hours. If the growth that she proposed were instantaneous, or on the other hand as slow as the emergence of a steepwood seedling, that would have offended his reason less grievously.

"You do like them, don't you? The natural kind."

He surrendered altogether. "I suppose I can hardly deny it."

"Good." She sat up. "Come by anytime." Then, as if struck by an idea, she bent down and kissed him on the cheek. He wondered if the aiyi had reminded her. It might be their idea of manners: a beverage for a guest, affection for a visitor.

He returned home to find Sudharma at the table, studying something on a screen—a text in a language John didn't know. Since he had left Laura's early, he was not so very late; he could have made some excuse. But eventually, he thought, everyone would find out he was visiting, and then Sudharma might guess he had lied. John sat down at the table across from him.

"How would Vo, or the aiyi, know a secondary meaning of an Essian term, when I haven't used it in that sense since we landed here?"

Sudharma responded without surprise. "We all learn words from context. With her abilities she would be very good at it, and aiyi even more so."

"It wasn't like that. She used the word first. I mean, she was the first to use it with the meaning that she used it for."

"I have books on Essian, and my own notes. I have recordings of radio programs too. All that would be easily accessible to the aiyi."

John sat back and loosed the tension in his shoulders, tempted to relief, but then he hesitated. She had said 'visit,' which was merely the ships' prim translation of an Essian phrase that literally meant to enter a cabin. "Would your books and notes give ships'-English equivalents of Essian terms?"

"Certainly, if we know them on Dharanendra. If you tell me the word, I will check for you."

"I don't want to say. But you must be correct. Thank you—that is much less alarming than any theory I had come up with. Though I do feel one should ask before one borrows a book."

"I quite agree, but Terrans don't perceive information as private or as capable of being owned."

"Including the thoughts in our heads."

"Yes, insofar as they can see them."

"What is a 'taxis'?"

"It's a movement in response to stimulus. For instance, an animal might move toward or away from light—that is called phototaxis."

"A movement by reflex?"

"That might be implied. What was the context?"

He would have deflected the question; but if she didn't see information as private then there was no point in keeping her secrets. "She had some . . . software, I suppose, that senses another's desire and helps the user to fulfill it. She said that when using it, she moved by a taxis. I thought that was an explanation, but I see now it was just a restatement." He realized suddenly what his words must cause Sudharma to imagine. "I hear the implication. It was not like that at all."

"I am not trying to peek into the windows of the cabin."

"I know you aren't." He should have gotten up and gone to bed; he meant to; but he found himself still talking. "Sometimes when a pregnant woman mistakes rainleaf seeds for lesser silvercup, she bears a child at full term who can take the breast but gain no nourishment from it. The babies are given to suck so that their mouths can learn the habit, while their real food is flowing through a plastic tube into a vein. If the poisoning is mild they may recover, but usually they don't live long. That's what I keep thinking of." He paused, beginning to regret what he had said. "She feels no lack, that's obvious. She's contented. Just because she expresses herself strangely, that doesn't mean that she feels nothing, does it? Probably I'm wrong. But even so I can't stop thinking of it."

His need to speak had burned through the last of its fuel, and now he was appalled with himself. A visit should be private. Even if Vo didn't know that, he still did. "This is distasteful. I don't want to talk like this."

"I don't want to know anything you don't want to reveal," Sudharma said gently. "I do need to ask you one question. Will you go back to her?"

"I don't know." He sighed. "Probably."

"Then, if you will tell me anything you learn that affects the colony's safety or its future, I will convey that to the governor, and I won't ask you any questions. I hope the governor will agree not to ask you either. I will stress the delicacy of the situation as forcefully as need be."

"Fine. If I overhear a declaration of war, I'll pass it along."

"I will impress on him also that if he tried to prevent you from going to her, Earth might take it very much amiss. For that reason, if you decide to stop visiting, it would be a matter calling for the utmost sensitivity."

"If she were the sort to pine because her door goes un-knocked-on, do you think she would have left Earth for a world empty of humans?"

"Probably not. But it's one thing to be alone by choice, and quite another to be left once her emotions are engaged."

"I'd be likelier to catch the ocean in a net. If I don't visit her she'll forget I exist. I've listened to enough absurdity for one evening. I am going to sleep now."

Lying in bed he regretted the outburst, and in the morning he would have apologized. But he heard the chime of a tag during *pratikraman*, and though Sudharma completed the ritual, he left without his breakfast and without more words than these:

"A basket-man has come."

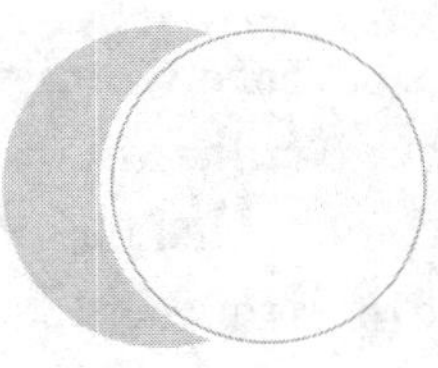

CHAPTER NINE

John finished his own breakfast, then spent four hours rehearsing for a program of translation that would soften and reshape Sudharma's language centers for a grammar that made no distinction between parts of speech. The language was entirely hypothetical, and he did not see how it could work, but he did identify a hemorrhage in the simulated brain in time to stop it. Rising from the table with relief, he made a curry out of lentils and sweet corn, packed it up with the roti and vegetables that Sudharma had flown from the house without eating, and carried it to the educational farm. Sudharma stood before the basket-man, holding out a leaf to him with tongs. John settled on the strip of ground between two crops to watch. The man would have to eat sometime.

Twenty minutes later, Ru, who had been working some distance away, stood up and stretched her back, putting both hands to the small of it to press at the offended muscles. She wandered over toward him. "Are you waiting for an audience?"

"I'd hoped to bring him lunch, but he may outlast my patience."

"Well, if you'd like to make yourself useful, there's weeding and a bit of planting to be done. We can't have students running around here distracting the one with the claws from his lessons, but my experimental corn strains need their sisters."

"I've never farmed before, but I will help if you can teach me."

She took him to a toolshed to find gloves that fit, then showed him a bed of small plants with long straplike leaves.

"This is corn—it's rather distinctive, so you should have no trouble recognizing it. Anything else that you may see around it is a dryad and needs to be pulled up, root and all, so that it won't come back. I'll show you how."

"Will something come to their defense?"

“Not likely. If something does then we might get a little excitement, but don’t expect to come out of the conflict with an arm like mine.”

She demonstrated how to pull a weed out of the ground, using a forklike tool to loosen up the soil if the roots threatened to break rather than come free. She worked efficiently, pulling with her right hand and wielding the tool with her left, so that when he tried to imitate her he felt clumsy by comparison.

“That looks better than any prosthesis we have on Essius.”

“It’s not bad,” she said, curling the fingers with an air of satisfaction. “Awkward for fine work, but it’s as strong as it needs to be.”

“I suppose bulk is the trade-off.”

“Oh, it could be slim if I wanted it slim. My first one was twin to the right arm, colored to match and all that, but it didn’t move the same way as the right, which always bothered me. So I bribed Roalin with berries and tomatoes to make me a different design. A little clumsiness is natural in a gauntlet. And he made good use of the extra space—look here.”

She pressed on a rectangular panel in her upper arm, which popped out at the top, revealing itself as a compartment. She pulled this free of her arm altogether and slid the contents out into her hand: a little folding knife, a ribbon for tying up the hair—additional to the one that she was wearing—and a little steel flask, curved to match the contour of the arm, that must have held spirits, since so small an amount of water would not have been worth carrying. Underneath it were two white pads, individually wrapped in clear plastic. Though they were thinner than the ones he was familiar with, their purpose was still obvious. She must have realized as much; with a slight embarrassed smile she scooped everything back into the compartment and returned it to its lodging place. “Not so many years until I have room for a bigger flask.”

The work had to be done on the knees and bending down, which was hard on the back. Yet it was satisfying to pull at the base of a stem, using a firm and steady tension so as not to break the roots, until they came free of the branching passages they hid in and he held the plant whole in his hand. Once he had managed this a few times, Ru moved to the opposite corner of the bed to weed, and together they finished more quickly than he had expected. Then she showed him where to plant black-eyed peas, at the corner of each cluster of corn seedlings; the corn, she said, would support them as they grew and they would nourish it by fortifying the soil. A third sister, to be planted later, would shade the ground with her broad leaves to cool it. In this way an arrangement of seeds would grow into the shape of a story—a very old one; Ru said it came all the way from Earth. He could have thought about it pleasantly for another hour or two of work, except that their activities had drawn the attention of the basket-man, who came toward them with a slow four-footed gait. Sudharma followed, matching his pace, staying close without crowding. Could a basket-man perceive his gentleness? Could it see how in his every movement he was the embodiment of calm? Would a basket-man be soothed?

"Let him smell you if he wants to. I will make the introductions."

The basket-man approached John first. The muscles in his arms moved smoothly as he walked; his claws, folded back so that they didn't touch the ground, were thick and sharp. It was frightening to think of what those muscles and those claws could do together. He drew close to John and reared up on his hind legs. Lifting his long head, he put his mouth close to John's face and took in air with three soft gasps. He stayed close, considering, and John smelled his fur and his breath: wood and hot iron and flowers and rich soil newly tilled and the scent of a man at the end of a day's work.

"John," Sudharma pronounced; and with his face still close enough that John could feel the breath against his cheek, the basket-man repeated "John." Though equally high in pitch, his voice had a more resonant quality than that of the basket-man in the video. So like humans, they had individual voices. Or maybe it was only that recordings could not reproduce the eeriness of that timbre, suspended undecidably between old woman and young boy.

He sat down on his haunches. For the first time he looked into John's eyes—briefly, as you might peek at something forbidden. Then he turned away. He glanced at Ru, and seemed to consider whether he would go to her. This took most of a minute. Then, moving slowly and deliberately, he walked over and put his face as close to hers as he had to John's. After thinking a while longer, he carefully sniffed each hand too. Ru bore up under this investigation with good humor.

The basket-man learned Ru's name, then moved off a little way. Finally John could approach Sudharma. He still felt he owed him an apology for last night, but they could hardly discuss the matter in front of Ru. So he only said, "I brought you lunch, but I'm afraid it will be cold. I didn't like to interrupt."

"Thank you, John." Sudharma's voice was kind; John felt he was forgiven. "I realize now I'm very hungry, but I don't want to eat in front of the basket-man—at this stage he might be confused by foods with more than one ingredient." A clinking sound caught his attention: the basket-man was trying to pry the cover off one of the dishes with his claws. "I see I have no choice, which is a relief to my stomach."

He drew the basket-man's attention and removed the cover. The basket-man sniffed the outside of the dish first, and after some contemplation, spoke the word "John." Then he put his mouth above the curry, sucked in air, and thought, his eyelids half-shut. Basket-men ate only one vegetable, and that one uncooked; what would he make of its complexity? Finally he spoke a single word: "corn." The stir-fry, after more deliberation, he identified as "squash." The roti he considered but said nothing. This inspection being complete, he allowed Sudharma to eat unbothered, but he watched every bite closely. Now he knew that humans could eat many foods, and not only the provisions made by their own mothers' bodies. His stance and expression betrayed no reaction to this news, or at least none that a human could discern.

John returned the next day with more roti and another dish of lentils, this one enlivened with tomatoes and hot peppers; the latter had come into season and he found them even better fresh than dried. Ru intercepted him at once. "I thought you might come back," she said, and dropped a hat onto his head—one with a wide brim and a string under the chin to stop it from blowing off. He saw that Sudharma was already wearing one of the same kind. "Now you won't get blinded by the sun. Are you taking sunscreen?"

"Yes."

After that he brought lunch to the farm daily. Ru was often there, and when she was, he helped her until it was time to go home and start dinner. As they worked she talked about the plants they tended, seeming to mention whatever facts came to her mind, so that without any system and probably without intending to, she taught him a great deal about Terran plants and their cultivation. In turn he answered her questions about Essian agriculture as best he could, though, farming not being men's work, he could only say what he had learned from either gathering or medicine. He knew, for instance, that run-further berries, picked and eaten from the roadside, would cause agonizing headaches, while their seeds, brought home and planted, yielded wholesome fruit, but he had no idea by what means women's care might turn them innocent. She was pleasant company, and the labor, though tiring, was a much-needed distraction. He began to make enough lunch for her too.

The basket-man continued to acquire English vocabulary, but like his predecessors, never vouchsafed a word of his own tongue. One evening John asked Sudharma, as casually as he could manage, whether it would be necessary to alter his brain after all, if basket-men spoke only English. Sudharma answered that he thought it likely; they would use words in a way appropriate to their minds, and so even though the raw material of their speech was harvested from human language, the result might well be alien enough to require change. But 'might' was not 'would,' and so there was room to hope.

The next morning, when Sudharma had left for the farm, John walked to the van and—after looking around to make sure he was not observed—mounted and drove it away. Someone would notice that it was gone, probably, but he doubted anyone kept track of every errand the town's vehicles were sent on.

The crawler opened for him in the usual way. At the center of the hall, a rectangular block had risen up out of the floor, and Vo stood behind it. It might have had the function of a table or a counter, though nothing was on it and there were no chairs. She didn't come to him, but she smiled. "I started the alteration when I saw you headed toward me, so we've got about an hour and a half left."

He went to join her at the table, but by the time he got there she had closed her eyes. On her face was the expression of a woman listening on a telephone to someone loved and missed. She didn't speak, but once she made a soft sound, halfway between hum and laugh. He was sure she had forgotten he was there. Just as he was about to clear his throat, her eyes sprang open, as if the intention alone had been enough to startle her. She stared at him a moment and then said, "Let's go outside."

When they stepped out of the crawler she turned and would have climbed the bank at once, except that he grabbed at her hand to stop her. "Be careful! There are snake-trees."

"Don't worry, I've been bitten by those enough. I'm going to slip between them—there's just enough room."

"I can't judge the snakes' length as well as you can."

"Stay close to me, then."

He followed her, careful to put down his hands and his feet exactly in the places she had set hers. The snake on his left shifted, lifting its head up off the branch it rested on to look at him. He froze, expecting its bite. But the snake must have concurred with Vo's geometry. It laid its head back down and didn't strike.

"How did you come to be bitten?" he asked when he had reached the top.

"By going close to trees. On purpose, for the art."

"Didn't that hurt?"

"Of course it did, but never more than I could bear. If the pain got too bad I could always turn it off, but I try not to. It's one of the reasons I'm here, to touch things and be touched by them. An aiyi can't experience what a human feels when being bitten. The more fully I feel it, the more of me will make it into the work. Anyway that's what I like to think."

Vo spoke casually, as if describing some slight discomfort—touching a sewing needle to the thumb to test its point; but it must have been agony. And she should have had the marks of vicious wounds, which she did not. In fact her body was as innocent of the small scars and blemishes that everybody builds up in the course of life as if she never left the shade and safety of the crawler's insides.

She stood examining a little tree whose boughs were bent down by the weight of yellow buds. "I haven't been touched by these yet. But stay back, since you don't like being bitten."

She held her arms out wide and walked into the branches, pressing against the tree as if she would merge with it. Yellow insects flowed onto her, covering all her bare skin; they moved under her dress like bed-beetles beneath a sheet. Blood was trickling from her arms. Then she backed away, calmly brushing off the little bodies, which, finding themselves on the ground, paused to collect themselves and crawled back to the tree. She turned around and John could see the wounds seal up without a scar. The blood seeped back into her skin and disappeared.

"That was a strong defense! They're really fierce. And I felt the tickle of their legs, and once a wing fluttered against me. All of that can be used too."

She searched his face, inviting him to share in her excitement. He was sure there had been blood staining her dress before, but now it was immaculate.

She shrugged. "But if it bothers you, we can just look."

After that, she wandered and he trailed after. She obeyed none of the rules of safety Laura had taught him, and she never suffered for it. Once she even reached out to touch a mammal-tree she passed, apparently for no more reason than to feel the roughness of the bark against her hand; yet she was safe. John was careful to stay close, and so was safe too. He thought that her perception and her understanding of the world were so much greater than his own that she could tell whether a mammal lurked inside its burrow or ranged far. Or maybe the aiyi, walking in front of her invisibly, calmed them to make her path smooth.

Once he stopped in his tracks, noticing an animal that stared up at him from a candle shaped like a fan. It had six legs, but instead of insect armor it wore fur, and its tail was like a lizard's. "What is that?"

"It's just the aiyi, watching us." She bent and stroked its small head with a fingertip. When she rose again her gaze was shy, as if he'd caught her doing something embarrassing. "I like to touch the aiyi's bodies, even though aiyi don't care about that kind of thing."

Soon after that a little papery wing flew by, and then another. Vo caught one and turned to show it to him: a seed rigged with a sail so that the air would take it up, as the wind tugs the seeds of catch-my-ribbons from the dying flower. "They're seeding!" she said. "We have to go watch!"

She ran back toward the bank, and he could not choose but run after. When the river came in sight it was an unfamiliar section. The snake-trees here were widely spaced and tall; their leaves were delicate. She led him close enough to one to clearly see the winged seeds growing from the boughs at every angle. The snake bit them off their stalks, gathering four in its mouth. It raised its body, curved in the shape of the letter S, and waited. When the wind picked up and all the wings still on the trees bent down and shivered, it shot forward and released its darts.

All along the bank, other trees were casting their seeds on the air too. In their repeated motion, bending and then straightening, there was a liquid grace. The little wings glided and drifted anywhere the wind would take them, aimless, and yet capable of sowing death wherever they might land. Of course, many poisonous flowers were beautiful.

"The seed grows from the plant and not the animal," he said. "I thought that didn't happen here."

"I'm told the snake injects its seeds into the bark using an ovipositor inside its mouth. The seeds draw nutrients from the plant and grow a wing around themselves."

So every snake-tree began life as a parasite on its own grandmother. It was only in character.

"That was a zap," Vo said. He didn't understand until he saw that she had laid her palm over her pubic mound. "Like an electric shock. It means the nerves are starting to hook up. Let's go back—I'll be ready by the time we get there."

They walked along the bank with snake-seeds coasting through the sky above their heads. She clasped his hand, as a mother might when walking with a child. Her palm was cool and dry and it was strange but not unpleasant. She didn't disengage until they reached the place where they must slip between the snake-trees and descend.

In the dark as they passed through the skin of the crawler, he wanted to draw her close to him. But he couldn't stop thinking of how she had pulled away, just at the moment she had seemed to want him most.

"I still don't know if I should kiss you," he admitted.

"You should."

The chamber wall sublimated away, and in the light that it let in he cupped her head. She responded to his kiss with interest but without reciprocation, as if she would reserve her judgment until he had made his case; and so, at length and with a slow insistence, he declared himself. At a suitable moment she drew his hand down between her legs, so that he might feel how the organ she had made for him, though artificial in its origin, still gave the natural evidence of desire. After that there was no difficulty. She responded to his touch, light through the softness of the dress, with such abandon and surprise that he was sure the feeling must be new to her, traced out on flesh that she had never worn before; but once she entered him it was impossible to think that this was so. He had had no great opinion of women as visitors, finding them usually too tentative, and when encouraged sometimes too abrupt. But Vo was both attentive and assured, and the sounds she made communicated clearly, without words, that she sought her own pleasure as much as his. In the end he reached his destination before she did, and sated but receptive, listened to her cries until she ceased and fell away.

Under more normal circumstances, he might have been content to open the door for her every time, never reversing their roles. But on Scythia he had little hope of forming other, balancing relationships; and since being visited was for him more a spice than a staple, he knew he would become dissatisfied.

"We can make it work the other way around," she said, exactly as if he had spoken. "I just need the right setup. It will be easy because the aiyi will help me now."

"They didn't help before?"

"They were sulking. They don't think it's a good idea for me to visit with a baseline human, so they ignored me while it was happening, except that when I started to delaminate, they helped me recover. Now they see my mind is made up, so they've given in."

This was the first time she had hinted that aiyi might seek to influence or control her. Yet it was not so different from how ancestors guided the living at home. If you bought a boat against their advice, you could hardly expect them to send your sails wind. Even so, they were your ancestors and in time their foolish kin would be forgiven.

"What exactly is a setup?"

"Oh, setup is everything about how my senses connect to my brain—innate senses and mediated ones both—and how I process what they tell me. What I'm feeling, too. If I decided to be in love, for instance, that would be part of my setup. I won't, of course. I mean it's fun if you're sixteen and want to write a lot of bad poetry, but I'm a grown-up and have better things to do."

While it was wise to avoid too intense an attachment to visiting partners, he felt the control that she claimed went beyond the sensible and into the uncanny. Of course that was not a thought that he would speak aloud. She would not care to have her emotional management criticized, and he would never risk seeming to make a demand that she love him.

"Did you use a setup when you let the snake-trees bite you?"

"I use a setup all the time—there's no way not to. Even if I turned off all my senses, that would only be another setup. But yes, I used one that is good for bearing pain."

"That the aiyi gave you?"

"One of the first ones they taught me. It helps me trust in them and know that I'll be healed."

He remembered the blood running from her arms and was again disturbed. And yet he was not tempted to agree with the ships' judgment that to live in close communion with aiyi was to be unfree. As with Christianity among the Scythians, her devotion might seem excessive to him, yet he thought that it was *her* devotion and not something forced on her. Touching a mammal's bark, running to watch snakes seed, Vo seemed to be entirely governed by her own impulses.

"Is that a boat that you see when you think about me?" she asked.

"A rowboat. That's what *vo'* means, at home. You can see pictures in my mind?"

"Sometimes, dimly. I can't always tell what they are, but if I see the same one a few times it's easier. Does that bother you?"

"No," he said. The image, a little boat bobbing on water, was homely and comforting. It was pleasant in a way to think of sharing it. But, he realized, other images that came to him repeatedly must be as visible to her as that one; in particular, the hospital scene that he had unwisely described to Sudharma. Just remembering that conversation brought the image back, and panicking he tried to make himself stop picturing it—the doomed infant suckling uselessly, the liquid flowing into the vein. He succeeded only by fixing his mind firmly on the twin black arches of her eyebrows, which made her smile. He wouldn't call a lover unnatural, or tell her that the way she lived was horrifying. Yet he had felt those things at times—and even knowing that she could sense feelings, it had never occurred to him he might be doing harm.

"Have my thoughts been cruel to you?" he asked.

She looked away and didn't deny it. "I think your mind just talks to itself," she said, in the tone of one who shows compassion for another's failings. "You know, for company. It doesn't have anyone else to talk to."

"I will try to be kinder from now on."

He came home and cooked lunch. When he delivered Sudharma's portion he said quietly, "I learned nothing this morning that threatens the colony."

"Thank you," Sudharma said, taking the covered plate, and neither of them spoke of it again.

But by the end of the week it seemed everyone knew. Probably someone had noticed the van's unscheduled absence and been curious enough to find out where it had gone. It didn't matter—the secret would have come out one way or another. Inconveniently, Sudharma had lately decided that a limited number of students could come to the farm, so long as they were warned not to approach the basket-man. Laura came with them and kept them focused on their tasks; as much as possible, John worked close to Ru and away from them. Even so, on the third day of their presence one Ischnuran boy found enough liberty to seek him out and ask him quietly, "So is she made like other women or is it just a nest of wires down there?"

"You should watch what you say," John said. "She can easily hear you."

He only meant to remind the child that words could hurt—or if he was too ill-raised even to care about that, that women listened and they talked to each other, so that a man who spoke without respect would find every door closed to him. Young men, even when not quite of an age to visit, understood these things instinctively. But the boy froze in shock; his pale face went even paler; he turned and pelted between rows of artichokes back to his classmates.

When the students had dispersed Laura stayed behind to ask him, "What did you say to keep that brat so quiet? I need to know your secret."

"You would have to have a visitor from Earth to use it."

"I see. Well, terrorizing them isn't the best tactic, but I understand the temptation."

"I miss dinners with your family and with Iren. I wish there could be some reconciliation, so they might resume."

"Me too," she said, and took her leave.

He did have an engagement that Sunday, however: he was finally to dine with Father Adzere, who had reminded him of the invitation. The evening was not, as he had feared, a primer on monotheism; the priest mentioned his church only once or twice, preferring to ask questions about Essius. None of the subjects of his inquiries related more than distantly to visiting, so John could answer without inhibition. His wife Zera, an elegant dark woman with black hair wound up in a bun at the nape of her neck, barely said more than hello, but listened to her husband with a quiet respect that made John uneasy. It was not natural for women to defer to men like that; it spoke of some corruption in the relationship. Families made by marriage lacked the natural affinity of blood, so harmony could be achieved only by domination, if at all. But toward the end of the meal Adzere seemed to ponder each question for longer and longer, leaving his wife to fill in the gaps in the conversation, which she did as if drawing up words from a deep well and finding very little in the bucket. When John asked about the squash with basil and tomatoes she had served, she only said "It's an old family recipe" and could be drawn out no further. He thought she was a person who looked inward so entirely it was hard for her to call across the chasm between her and others. At last Adzere laid a hand on her arm—not to silence her, John thought, but to grant her reprieve—and said, "John, I'm embarrassed to reveal I've been listening to gossip, but I worry you have put yourself in a dangerous situation."

"If anybody is at risk it is Sudharma. But the basket-man has shown no tendency to violence."

"I mean through your connection with the Terran woman. You must see that she's immensely powerful. If that power were turned on you . . ."

"She too has shown no tendency to violence. Why does everyone off Essius assume that anyone involved in visiting will act as badly as they can? Is it so impossible to judge a person's character? If we are all to close the door to anyone with power to harm us, I suppose no woman could admit a man again, which would be a sorrow to both and catastrophic for the species. For that matter, gods are powerful, and yet they visit humans all the time. They are benign as a rule, and so their attention is much coveted."

"How do you know they are benign?"

"One just knows. With the god I met, it was quite obvious.—But you won't want to hear about that," he said, recollecting himself. "I know you don't believe that gods are many."

"It's true, there is only one God, but not to get hung up on words. What you mean by the word 'god,' I may know under a different name, or it may even be something unknown on Zandahe. God is the creator of every world, but He provides for each one differently, and just as the animals are different on your world and mine, the spiritual creation may be different too. I would be interested to hear your story."

"Well, if you want to know, it was when I was traveling around in puddle country—which is to say that I was traveling with difficulty; there settlements are far apart, and little traffic moves between them. There was a village in the woods that no road led to, so I had to walk to it along a trail. After about an hour I came to know that a man was walking just behind me. He moved in perfect silence, even though the trail was much invaded by the plants on either side of it—I certainly made noise stepping over them or brushing past. I didn't turn to look at him."

"Then how did you know he was there? Or that he was male, for that matter?"

"I just knew. It's a difference between gods and humans: I could sneak up on you if I were quiet enough, but a god never could. Even with your eyes closed, you would know where in the room he was. And so we walked along, for, I would say, about an hour. Then he caught up, so he was walking right beside me, and he took my hand. I was shy—I don't know why, it is unlike me—and couldn't bring myself to look at him directly, though every time I looked down to avoid some vegetation I saw his legs moving and his hand clasping mine. After a while he let go and fell behind, and that was that. The people in the village told me that he visited a great deal in those parts, and that those chosen often had a good catch or some other piece of fortune the next day, although—" He had meant to say "I was not lucky enough to be visited," but thinking better of it, he substituted "although I can't vouch for the truth of that."

"He never displayed any supernatural power to you?"

"Not unless you count moving silently through undergrowth, which I admit is only suggestive. I expect he could have if he wanted to. But that is beside the point. Gods are often powerful, but it isn't power that makes a god. A god is a being who lives in a body differently from the way humans and animals do. We exist as brains connected to a body by nerves—in effect, we are machines with wires, sensors, and motors. Gods inhabit a body as—" He stopped himself from saying "as we do when the brain has soaked into the skin after death." Metaphor would be less shocking. "As water inhabits the body, present in every cell. Or as wind would inhabit a house if you threw all the windows and doors open. They suffuse themselves, and any power they have is incidental to that mode of existence, which is called divinity. With Vo it is entirely different. She is a brain that pilots a machine, as we are, but the connections between her and it are infinitely flexible and can be changed at any time. The body also can be altered, as it cannot be for us. Although," he added, "it might be that the aiyi lives in her in a more godlike way. I had not thought of that, but it is probable."

The priest exchanged glances with his wife. "Well," he said, "I am glad you did not speak with him. I don't claim to know, at this distance, what exactly you encountered, but the bad possibilities are very bad. It's good to be careful around anything possessing unusual powers and, especially, not to assume its intentions are what it claims they are."

"Not at all. A god could never lie or misrepresent their nature. They are always entirely themselves. That was certainly clear with the one I met."

"How do you know he was himself, when you only met once?"

"I don't know. But you would have felt it too, if you had been there. Really, there was nothing to fear, and I wish I had not become shy. So there is no need at all for your warning. I assume you meant it to apply only to gods and not to Vo—it would be tedious to have to defend a lover from such an insult."

Adzere flinched as if he had raised a fist. At once John was sorry; he liked the priest and had no wish to intimidate him. "I meant only that I dislike having to explain Vo to those who know nothing about her. She is strange in her ways, but entirely guileless. If you would like to have an opinion on her honesty you can go and meet her yourself."

"I think that would be unwise," Adzere said.

At that, John gave up. If Scythians could find no other attitudes to take toward Vo than fear or disrespect, then let them be afraid. It was not his fault, or hers, that cowardice prevented them from meeting her.

When he came home, Sudharma looked up from the notes he was reviewing. "How was dinner?"

"Excellent, if only the food is considered. Rather wearing in other respects."

"I can't say I'm surprised. It's widely known that Christianity loves company."

John took a few seconds to decipher this remark. "Oh, no, he didn't try to press a copy of the sheep book on me. It's just that he agrees with you that Vo is likely to coerce me into . . . I don't even know what. Maybe one of you will tell me."

Sudharma ignored the invitation to an argument and merely said, "The governor went to see her today."

"Good for him, I suppose. That has nothing to do with me."

"I mean he went to speak with her, not to visit in the Essian sense."

"Well, the same remark applies."

"He didn't care for the experience and I suspect she didn't either. Eventually she stopped paying attention to him altogether."

"She gets distracted sometimes. You just have to remind her that you're there."

"He did eventually manage to rouse her, but his pride was injured, I believe. He is a man used to authority and the solicitude that comes with it. I encouraged him to return anyway, but I fear he's too inflexible to manage more than an austere sort of diplomacy with her. You have learned to accommodate her eccentricities, haven't you?"

"I would say, we are learning to accommodate each other's."

"You are fond of her?"

"What makes you say that?"

"You are protective of her. You respond when she's disrespected. I heard what you said to that boy at the farm. Were you gentler with Adzere?"

"I thought so, but he didn't." John sighed. "I suppose I am as fond of her as one reasonably could be after two openings of the door. You promised not to ask me questions about my visits."

"Forgive me. I meant to ask about communication, but the two subjects are intertwined. Let me say one thing—a statement, not a question—and then I'll keep my peace. Vo is the only one the aiyi speaks with, and you have a rapport with her that no one else is likely to develop. That may become very important. No one will ever give you an official title for it, but you are our ambassador to Earth."

"I don't want that," John said.

"I know, but it remains true anyway."

John went to bed irritated. He resolved to put the matter from his mind. Let others imagine what uses they liked for his visits; he would ignore them and keep his behavior correct.

He set the tag's alarm and went to sleep. And in the cool of the next morning, he went to her again.

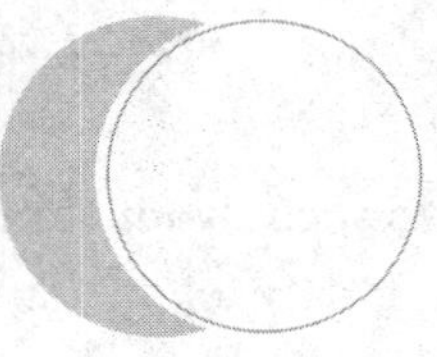

CHAPTER TEN

John had made it a habit to run his daily simulation in the morning; that way, he reasoned, he could enjoy the whole rest of the day without feeling the dread of it. He had, increasingly, also made it a habit to spend ten or fifteen minutes convincing himself to press start. No matter how many times he rehearsed the mutilation of Sudharma's brain, it never got easier. One morning he had nearly reached the twentieth minute of procrastination when he remembered, with an access of relief, that Iren had suggested he go talk to Marne and he had not done it yet. He would walk to the clinic at once.

He found Marne wary and defensive, but when he explained he only wanted the equipment and medicines he needed to deal with emergencies in the field, the doctor visibly relaxed. He led John to a storeroom and put up no fuss about sharing his supplies.

When John had filled his bag, he slung it over his shoulder. It was once again as heavy as it would have been at home, and that was comforting. "How often should I expect to be called on for help?"

"It varies. You might get two emergencies in a month, or none for six."

"That is very little work."

"You should talk to Michael. He can figure out another job for you that's compatible with being on call."

John considered the idea. "In fact, I am not lacking for employment at the moment. I spend much of my time studying to assist Sudharma with his translation. I am also helping out at the experimental farm. Besides that, I am taking care of all the cooking and cleaning for our house, now that Sudharma is working with the basket-man."

This drew a sympathetic wince from Marne. "You two could find families to put you each up, you know. You don't have to play wife."

"I am certainly not practicing, or counterfeiting, marriage. The idea is abhorrent."

"I meant, you don't have to spend your time slaving over a hot stove."

'Slaving' was a shocking choice of metaphor, but when women were chained to men by vows, no doubt it was an apt one. Still, if Ischnuran men held the work of cooking in such low esteem, it was hard to see why anyone would do it for them.

"The kitchen is the heart of life," John said. "It's an honor to keep it beating. Besides that, there is a pleasure in it. It is a way to express caring."

"When the summer heat sets in, you might change your opinion. But suit yourself. It's none of my business."

By this time the basket-man had built up a vocabulary of some six hundred words, of which more than two-thirds were species of dryad or plant. Sudharma had managed to teach him a few categories, but others eluded him. He easily learned the words 'insect,' 'reptile,' 'mammal.' With a little more trouble he mastered Iren's term 'dayfly' for insects that did not eat as adults, but only bred and died, and he applied the same word also to the plants that produced them, though they were not closely related to each other. He could not, on the other hand, learn to group tomatoes, potatoes, eggplants, and peppers into a botanical family called 'nightshade.' He had acquired some adjectives, but rarely used them in exactly the same way as humans did; for instance, he would only apply the word 'tall' to candles, and only those between about eight and ten meters in height. When Sudharma tried to teach words for colors, hoping at least to learn something about basket-men's vision, he seemed to acquire 'blue' readily—the first examples being a passing insect and an investigating reptile. All human crops were green to him, even a red slice of a ripe tomato. Humans were green too. Dryads were either blue or green, apparently at random. Even plant-stage dryads of the same species could be blue one time and green another. After a long session in which Sudharma had tried to discover the pattern without success, the basket-man pointed at himself and said "blue" again. Sudharma doubted that this was an act of self-naming, but one had to call him something shorter than 'the basket-man,' and so it stuck.

Blue could rarely learn verbs as verbs. When Sudharma used a series of flying insects as examples to teach the verb 'to fly,' he seemed to grasp the concept, but would not apply it to a candlehawk. After some trial and error and an appeal to Piro, Sudharma worked out that he thought the word meant an adult insect, that being the life stage at which species that had wings unfurled them. The few verbs that he had learned—such as 'walk,' 'follow,' 'look,' 'drop,' 'smell'—were all actions he could take himself, and he understood them only as imperatives, so that if he heard "John follows" he would try to follow John. When Sudharma pointed at a small green-armored animal nibbling on a dryad leaf and said "Insect eats"—for simplicity, he was teaching a version of English without 'a' or 'the'—the basket-man, after a long pause, removed a food-sphere from his pack and took a bite. He never tried to give commands himself, and indeed he never joined a verb with a subject or object. After an ill-advised use of the word 'dig' led to the destruction of several of Ru's squash plants, Sudharma did not try to teach verbs anymore.

"Blue will be leaving us soon, I think," Sudharma said that night, over a dinner of John Corn. "His store of food is running low."

"I'm sorry you didn't get more time."

"It may be for the best. I'll have a year to work out what mistakes I've made and figure out some better ones to make next time. As it is, we have a lot of words and no communication. I fear his mind expects a different kind of grammar, but since he won't speak his own language to me, it will be difficult to work out what he needs."

The afternoons had grown too hot for farming, so John walked with Sudharma to the field every morning, helped Ru for two or three hours, then went home and made a cold lunch to bring back. Often the meal's highlight was one of the sweet ground-borne fruit the farm was then producing in abundance; these were sweet and dark and heavy in their flavor, wonderfully cooling in the sun, and large enough that even when all three had eaten their fill, there was enough left of the orange flesh to chop up with a ripe tomato and make curry for the evening. Blessedly, this dish required the stove to be turned on for only about ten minutes.

One day the sky was thick with clouds. John thought that it might rain, but such hopes had been dashed many times before. All morning Blue would not attend to his vocabulary lessons or to Sudharma's attempts to engage him in conversation. Every few minutes he reared up and swiveled his ears toward the town. Even when not listening to whatever distracted him, he wouldn't stop twitching his ears.

"Is something going on?" John asked Ru.

"Valeria's daughter Lia is in labor. Having a hard time of it, is what I heard. Must be, if she's still going."

He went home, prepared lunch, and started back. As he came down

Main Street with his covered dishes, an Ischnuran man, walking with two Zandaheans, greeted him and remarked, "I see you've done some cooking."

One of the Zandaheans covered a smile; the other was trying not to laugh. John ignored their odd behavior and replied politely that since the day was so mild, he had made something hot. It was not the first time he had noticed odd reactions to the idea of his cooking, and the thought of it lingered with him as the lunch was eaten.

After lunch Sudharma returned to his futile attempts to work with the basket-man, who paced back and forth between the rows of peppers and ignored him. As Ru began to pack her garden tools to return home, John quietly asked her, "Why would my cooking be a subject for hilarity?"

"For who?"

"For everyone, it seems."

"Oh, don't worry about that," she said. "It's only rumor running around town in circles. Soon enough it will tire itself out and lie down."

"What sort of rumor?"

Ru looked reluctant, and he thought she might not answer. Finally she said in a soft voice, "About you doing women's work for Sudharma."

"What are men living without women meant to do, if not cook? Pick weeds from the roadside and chew them as they walk along?"

"No, of course not. It isn't just the cooking—there are other men who do that—but people say you *make a home* for him, and that you do it because you like to."

"Then, it would be all right for me to take care of the obvious necessities of life, if only I were miserable about it?"

"When you put it in that way it sounds ridiculous, and I suppose it is. They are saying unimportant things in a suggestive tone and with a certain emphasis and making something out of nothing. But the purpose of the nonsense is to hint that, well, I don't know how to phrase it. That you and Sudharma are *not chaste* with each other."

It was a galling thought, that he was universally believed to be Sudharma's visitor when nothing could have pleased him more or been less likely. "What does everyone here have against men visiting each other? One of the captains on the *Folly* used the word 'homophobia.' Is it a fear in truth? A fear of what?"

"Oh, well." She looked dismayed at the question. "For Zandaheans it is mainly a religious taboo, I think. For us . . ." She thought for some time. He thought that she was genuinely at a loss. "Maybe it *is* fear, in a way. Parents worry that their sons will pursue other men, and never marry or provide them with grandchildren. Women fear their husbands may sneak off with men, and so lose interest, or leave them to bring up their children alone."

Of course—it all made sense now. For a culture based on marriage, and insisting on monogamy, for men to visit men would seem a threat to the very institution by which children were produced and raised. It would be more sensible to recognize that families formed without the bond of blood were fragile by their nature, but if they let themselves admit that they would no longer be marrying people. Such a liberation was too frightening, and so they had to find an evil in the ordinary workings of desire. But as he admired the flawless glass sphere of this insight, he found that it cracked in his hand.

"If a desire for grandchildren is the trouble, why do Ischnurans approve of jesses?"

"That's an exception, I suppose. Although the state of jesses isn't quite so perfect as Iren might like you to believe."

"What do you mean?"

"Sometimes I think Iren is trying to build Utopia by pretending that Ischnura already is one and urging us to replicate it here. But don't listen to me. I am probably wrong about all of it."

He felt little wiser than he had been before he began asking questions. But when he had turned the conversation over in his mind a little more, it came to him that he had told no one but Marne that he liked cooking and cleaning for Sudharma. Marne had started the rumors. That, at least, was interesting. John wondered if the man was merely loose-lipped or if he had intended to be unkind.

"In any case," Ru said in a much lighter tone, "you cook for me, too, don't you? I certainly hope you enjoy that."

He would have reassured her on this score, except that at that moment they both jumped: Blue was charging toward them on all fours. He ran past, close enough that John could feel the wind as he went by and smell his rich and pungent odor. He disappeared behind tall sunflowers. Then a rustling told them he was crashing through the lima beans, and he shot out in the direction of the town.

"Oh, mists and veils," Ru said, and ran after. John shouted a brief explanation to Sudharma and then followed. He passed her as they reached the clinic and burst in to find a knot of frightened family members in a waiting room. "Marne says stay out and don't agitate it," a man said. John ignored him and followed his ears to a room where a terrified girl lay with parted legs in a high bed. There were no mothers there, only Marne and his two apprentices—both backed into a corner; only Marne had stood his ground. Blue stood at his utmost height, frozen, watching as the baby's head was born.

It had seemed very important that John get into this room, but now that he was here he had no idea what he could do. Trying to drag Blue out would put mother and child at more risk and not less.

Ru banged through the door and said, "Will you get out of here? Can't you see you're bothering her?"

John nearly complied with this sensible order, but then understood by the direction of Ru's gaze that she was not talking to him. The basket-man turned at the sound of her voice, but her sentences were far beyond his comprehension. She must have realized it. "*Follow me,*" she said, and stepped out, holding the door open. Blue walked after her as if compelled. John went out too, feeling profound relief. Sudharma, who had made it to the waiting room, joined the procession and they all emerged onto the street, where the basket-man stumbled back, as if a fishing line connecting him to Ru had snapped. He faced them, standing tall, and walked backward a few steps. His eyes were wide and staring. Then he dropped to all fours and walked away up Main.

"He is going to leave town," Sudharma said. "I will follow on foot and try to keep him in sight. John, get the van and come after us, as quickly as you can."

"What makes you think he will leave?"

"He saw that human beings give live birth to each other, in violation of the universal rule of Scythia. What would you do if you discovered a creature that violates natural law—one that might use its uncanny form of reproduction to spread out over the world, replacing all life with its alien crops? He's going to tell someone. We need to follow him to that someone. The matter is now urgent. We cannot wait a year."

"You two might be out there for a while," Ru said. "Tell me what to pack for you and I'll send another van out to deliver it."

They both wanted as many changes of clothing as could be managed. Sudharma requested a book, a small broom, a stack of white cloths, and a supply of white strings, all of which could be found either in his dresser or on top of it; besides those, he asked for water filters from the kitchen. John, with some misgivings, told Ru where to find his bag. It was impolitic to ask an

Ischnuran to handle it, but he had filled it with what medical supplies Marne allowed him, which might finally now be needed. If Ru knew what the strap was made of, she gave no sign.

The van was not far from the clinic. John started the engine and caught up with Sudharma just outside the town. He stopped to let him climb aboard. The basket-man had stopped too; he turned and sat down on the sand to watch.

"He could easily have left me far behind by now," Sudharma said. "Maybe he wants to show us to his fellow basket-men as proof that the monsters he speaks of are real. Let's show him that our speed is greater in the van than on foot, so he can move as fast as he likes. Accelerate and catch up with him, but don't aim the van directly at him, and don't get too close—we don't want to frighten him off."

When John had followed these instructions, the basket-man, framed in the side window, regarded them coolly. Then he moved forward swiftly on four legs. His pace was greater than a man on foot could long sustain, but when John matched it in the van he felt that they were only creeping forward. He began to wonder just how long this trip might take.

"Why did you say it was urgent to follow him?"

"He is going to find his people and give an account of us. It will be better if we are there to account for ourselves."

After some two hours more, a black shape in the rearview mirror caught John's eye: another van. He stopped and it pulled abreast of them. Iren slid over to the passenger side and alighted with a practiced ease; their right foot had no sooner touched the stirrup than the left swung toward the ground. John descended with a greater care to meet them.

"I have some things of yours, and a few presents for the road." They pulled down the ramp from the back of their van, strode up it, and threw the doors open. All three of them began to carry objects from the one van to the other, and Iren helped secure and stow them: first their luggage, then some extra water and spare power cells for the van.

"With these you will have a range of two thousand kilometers," Iren said, "which means turn back after a thousand if you want to make it all the way home."

"The cells already installed may be a little less than full."

"I made allowance for your diplomatic missions in the calculation. Use the radio in the van to check in, morning and night—if you miss a call, someone will come out to find you."

"How long would it take rescue to arrive, if we are a thousand kilometers away?"

"That all depends on the terrain your quarry decides to lead you through, but I doubt there is a route so long in this much-crumpled desert that could be achieved in less than four days."

This was hardly reassuring. But they would not likely make it that far, he thought. The basket-man's provisions would not hold out long enough.

Iren stepped up on the stirrup of her van and retrieved a folded rectangle: a library. "Now, John, this is mine and I want it back, but since I understand you are the woods-guide of the pair, you may take charge of it till your return." They opened it out flat and handed it to him. The cover felt as soft as a well-cared-for soul against his fingers; the inside was hard and yet porous, like wood. "Look out into the desert and hold it up in front of your face."

Like a window, the library showed the landscape that it blocked. Each bush and candle was distinguished by a colored outline, and small letters below gave the name of the species.

"White are reptiles, yellow are insects, red are mammals. Now tap the image of a dryad—any one."

He chose a tall cylinder nearby. Instantly in response to his touch, the screen changed to display a drawing of a similar candle alongside its corresponding animal, a pale insect with a bulbous head. Words wrapped around the image explained the dryad's mode of life, its identifying marks, its evolutionary relationships, and the threat that it posed—none, except to crops unwisely planted in the territory of the subterranean insect horde.

"To go back, swipe on the screen like this," Iren said, demonstrating. "I've also set the guide to appear automatically when the library is reset. Should you wander outside it and lose your way, just close the cover, tap on it three times, and open it again—you will find yourself at the beginning. Now, this part is important. If a dryad has a sparkling outline, that means the guide doesn't recognize it. Try going closer if it's safe, or looking from a different angle. If it still sparkles, you may have discovered a new species. Try to harvest a leaf or some other small sample—again, if it's safe—and do this."

They took a leaf from their pocket and laid it on the inside of the library, then closed the covers, pinching them together tightly. After a minute the library emitted a soft chime. When they opened it, the screen displayed a tree next to a scaly animal that hung upside down by all its four legs from a branch.

"That species is not novel, but if it were, you would see a preliminary image, along with any information that can be gleaned from genetic sequencing or from the library's observation of the living dryad. If you can save the sample and bring it to me when you return, that is also well. You may come out of this with a few species named after you." They handed him the folded library. "Of course, if you can find the plant form of a basket-man, that would be the great prize."

Sudharma had gone around the two vans to check that the basket-man was still waiting for them. He returned to the small shade cast by the nearer one with an appearance of relief; it was nearly the hottest time of the day. "Blue is asleep now. We ought to sleep through the heat too, or at least rest. We don't know how late he will wish to travel."

"What if he wakes and departs without us?" John said.

"I don't think he will. But to be certain, we might sleep in turns this first time."

"I will leave you to your naps, then, gentlemen, but I have one more gift first." They retrieved a covered dish from the cab of their van and hopped down with it. "This is lunch, prepared for you by Laura. As one of you is well aware, you could ask for nothing better as a last hot meal—except that it will make you hate the travel rations even more ferociously. Sudharma, I am bidden to tell you it conforms to all your dietary restrictions, including the ones that John is aware of and Zohia is not."

"Thank you," Sudharma said. "Do you know if the rations are likewise suitable?"

"I can't imagine they have garlic or onions in them, as that would tend to impart a flavor, but as to the rest, I don't know. I will find out the ingredients and call you on the radio."

When Iren had pulled away Sudharma said, "Let's eat over there in the shade of the hill, if you think it's safe. We can sleep there too, afterward."

"That bare stretch to the left ought to be all right."

"If you will carry the food, I will get us some blankets to keep the sand off. You can leave the library here. That, too." He pointed to the pocket where John kept his tag. Though puzzled, John complied, climbing into the van and laying both tag and library on the middle seat where they were safe from accidentally being sat on.

Sudharma had found silverware as well as blankets. Apparently there were no plates, so they sat in the shade eating with two forks from one divided dish. The meal was simple: cubes of white potato sautéed until crispy, mixed with generous amounts of fresh green pepper and tomato, topped with Laura's cheese sauce and accompanied by fresh tortillas and black-eyed peas. It ought to have been comforting, but John was waiting with some apprehension to discover why he had been asked to leave the tag and library behind. At last Sudharma finished eating, laid down his fork, and spoke.

"I wonder if you understand the course that this colony's future is likely to take. The technology the colonists brought to this world is designed to be resilient, but even so we can expect it to break down while the population is still small. Without help from the ships, which is unlikely, everyone or nearly everyone will have to be a farmer, just to grow enough food to prevent famine."

"Iren said as much, the day we landed. It's not unlike what happened on my world when Terran ships did not return."

"On mine as well, though we were recontacted by the Free Ships sooner than you were. Ischnurans and Zandaheans both experienced the same kind of fall. It's a standard feature of worldly history, and to a degree unavoidable. But if the Scythians had someone else to do their agricultural labor—such as a species that shows a keen interest in farming, tries to help without being asked, even spontaneously takes human orders—then at least they could focus on maintaining what technology they can. This thought must have occurred to some of them before now. Probably it's why Zhuyef was so eager to teach the words for farming tools. But today Ru, in the hearing of at least a dozen people, gave the basket-man an order and he obeyed. The whole town will be talking about it by nightfall, and for a long time to come. Many who hear of it will think of other orders that might be given."

John knew that a number of marrying cultures on Earth had kept slaves. Probably, having adopted one form of servitude, they were always at risk of developing others. And yet marriage was slavery mystified, disguising itself as the natural outcome of love. It was one thing to be fooled by the obscuring rituals of rings and vows, quite another to invent a novel form of servitude with no cloak of tradition to conceal the naked truth. "It is hard to think that of the Scythians I know."

"I agree. I like these people. I don't believe they mean harm. But they are in a frightening situation, and may convince themselves that what they want is also good. They could come up with an arrangement that seems mutually beneficial to them, and press it upon basket-men who understand it only partly. Over time they would become dependent on extracted labor, and resort to ever more desperate means to retain it, each step seeming a small difference from the last. Some future generation might consider it quite normal to sow basket-men in the ground like a crop and rear them without knowledge of their own culture, speaking only human language and knowing only subjugation. When we landed I worried that some such scenario might draw the wrath of the aiyi down on the colony. Now I am more worried that it won't."

"What can we do?"

"First of all, you and I must keep our vision clear. We have a stake in this world whether we like it or not, because we have to live here, but the colonists are also committed to the settlement of Scythia as a project, and we are not. We mustn't let our sympathy with them lead us to adopt their viewpoint."

"My sympathies are more complicated in any case."

"I know they are. That's one reason I'm confiding in you. The other is that I need your help. The colonists can hardly extract labor from the basket-men without a supply of food they can eat. Most likely, that food can only come from the plant that gives birth to them. Iren asked you to search for that plant. I am asking you to make sure the search fails. No doubt it will be found someday, but let us put that day off as long as we can."

"I will avoid taking samples of likely prospects. That's easy to justify—touching the plant phase of mammals is frequently unsafe. Is that all?"

"For now. Depending on the outcome of this journey, I may need you not to notice certain changes in the way I work with basket-men."

"Why?"

"Slavery requires communication. The communication may be very crude, but one must have some way to give an order. I fear I have established just enough vocabulary to say 'dig up these dryad seedlings' and be understood, but I am far from being able to convey 'agreeing to the colonists' requests will lead inevitably to your subjugation.' If we meet more basket-men, I may have to confuse them about the meanings of some basic words so that any orders humans try to give them will be misconstrued. You have observed my methods and will notice the difference. Please understand I would not sabotage my own work lightly, and I will repair the damage as soon as it is safe to do so."

"I won't say anything. But I think Ru is as likely to notice as I am. I know she listens while she's working."

"I will have to do it when she's not around and hope for the best." Sudharma sighed. "I know this is difficult, but I am relieved at least to have an ally. We can talk about it more any time you like, but not near any of the colonists' devices, including the van. I don't know if they listen, but they easily might."

John didn't care for the idea that his visits with Vo might have been spied on. Of course he knew the aiyi perceived everything; that didn't seem like spying but only presence. For colonists, not present, to listen in was an entirely different matter. Perhaps he would ask her if the tag was trustworthy or not when they returned.

"Do you want to nap?" Sudharma asked. "I will keep watch."

"You go ahead. I doubt that I would sleep."

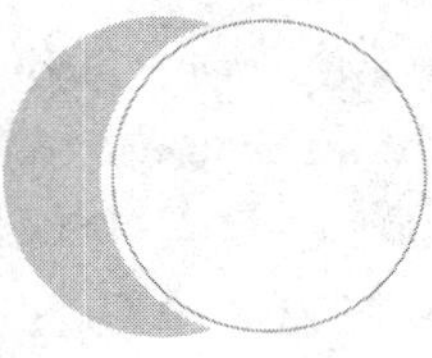

CHAPTER ELEVEN

Every morning in the first light of the dawn, Sudharma laid his book down on a pillow and stood upon a folded blanket facing it. With a white cloth fixed in front of his face by a string, and pressing his hands together in front of his chest, he began to recite. The ritual was not in English, and John's ear could hardly even tell where one word ended and the next began. Even so, he came to know the different rhythms of the different parts of it, to recognize repeated phrases, to anticipate when Sudharma would sit cross-legged and when he would kneel and bend down. All this he absorbed by a kind of osmosis, without, of course, sitting down to watch as if the ritual were a performance for an audience. He would have liked to. In the light of the sunrise Sudharma was even more beautiful.

He had little to do in the early mornings now. He could not cook, since the food provided for their journey, a compressed dry biscuit, neither required nor admitted of any preparation. He would have been grateful to take the extra time to sleep—the long days of driving exhausted him—but both of them slept in the back of the van for safety from night-roaming wildlife, and in that confined space Sudharma's alarm woke them both. John had never been good at returning to sleep. So when he had tidied up their sleeping area, he took the library from his bag—he always wrapped it in a shirt for padding and tucked it away safely in a side pocket—and walked around showing various plants and animals to it. He never went out of sight of the van, but even so he found several new insects and a reptile, proving each discovery by pressing a leaf between the covers and putting it into his bag to bring home.

Blue always woke about two-thirds of the way through *pratikraman. He* had no qualms about playing the spectator. The first morning he watched with his eyes fixed and ears forward, head slightly tilted, his nostrils twitching now and then. Though Sudharma had warned John against trying to read emotions on an alien face—they were likely to be false friends—he could not help seeing this as a keen, but bemused, fascination. When Sudharma repeated the ritual at sunset, he watched for the full hour and fifteen minutes with the same expression. He never paid *pratikraman* the slightest attention again.

All day, except during the scorching middle hours when they all slept, Blue loped through the desert, traveling generally east but in a zigzag that suggested he didn't know quite where his destination was. Often he sniffed the air and examined the landscape. Sometimes he would climb up to some stony height from which the world could be surveyed. From one of these ascents he came down cradling a round vessel, brown and rough on the outside and with a little bulbous neck at the top. The library identified this as a food body that a plant had made to feed its children—not, however, the same kind that Blue used for food. He carried it carefully, walking on two legs to hold it in his hand, but even so it spilled a little now and then, and so John understood it had been hollowed out and filled with water. The next morning Blue was slowed down by his upright gait, but he gathered plant stems as he walked and, in lieu of his midday nap, sat down in the shade and wove a basket. When it was finished, it cradled the vessel safely and formed a handle at the top. After that he went on all fours again and carried it in his mouth.

"I think we can discard the notion that they only weave for courting gifts," Sudharma said. "It would be interesting to know if that vegetable was already opened and the flesh eaten when he found it, or if he hollowed it out with his claws, or if he used some other tool to scrape it out."

"I would like to know how he found anything growing at all on that hill. It's not much more than a bare rock."

"He found a source of water. Plants might grow around that."

John had to accept this as reasonable. Yet as the days passed, and over and over Blue came down some slope or bluff bearing a refilled vessel, he grew puzzled again. It offended his sense of order. Water ran down hills, collected in rivers and basins; you went down to find it, not up. Now and then some might seep from the side of a mountain, but it was not to be believed that Blue could find so many flowing springs in such modest outcroppings of stone. Unswayed by this logic, the land continued to supply the basket-man with water.

Every day in the late afternoon, around the time that back in town he would have come home from his work with Blue, Sudharma closed his eyes.

If at that hour Blue was off seeking water, he would sit on the ground in a cross-legged pose; if they were travelling in the van, he would simply remain sitting and become still. Either way, he placed his palms face up in the center of his lap, the right one resting on top of the left. He recited certain syllables and phrases, then remained silent for forty minutes. He called this practice meditation, and explained that it had several stages, the ones that he emphasized most being perception of breathing and of body. When John wondered what the purpose of it was, Sudharma said it helped in balancing the mind and banishing uncontrolled emotions; moreover, it would ease recovery after his translation. After hearing this last, John did not ask questions about meditation anymore.

Later, when the sun drew close to the horizon, they sat outside and ate, and talked awhile before they went to bed. Blue always listened from a little way away, but never tried to join the conversation. Sometimes Sudharma would talk about his work with the aliens on his own world. He often mentioned one that everyone called Three-Legs, with whom he had "something as near as a human and a vzdrei can come to friendship." John assumed at first that the alien was missing a limb, but Sudharma said no; "He had once, after killing an animal, devoured an entire haunch of it before reuniting with the hunting party to divide up the meat. I don't know if he meant to insult them, or if he was driven by great hunger—it would have been impolitic to ask. But plainly, he was never to be allowed to forget the incident."

"They are meat-eaters, then."

"Oh yes. They are obligate carnivores—they can't digest anything else."

"Is it because you became friends with them that you don't worry about other humans' customs? 'I look after my own soul and take others as I find them'—I remember you saying that."

"I would say, rather, I could not have become close to vzdrei in the first place, if I had not already been a person who could long for a connection with a carnivore." Sudharma's face took on an expression that, John had learned, meant he was considering whether something that he wished to say was worth the time it would take to explain. Deciding in the positive, he began: "Millennia ago there was a man on Earth, Lord Mahavira, who achieved omniscience, and afterward showed others the path to their souls' liberation. But not so many lives before that, he was reborn as a lion. Do you know what a lion is?"

"I've read the word in books, once or twice. As far as I could gather, it's someone who receives a large share."

"I suppose a lion would, if you had something to divide with one. They were—or are, if they survive on Earth—very large and fierce animals, and like the vzdrei, they must eat meat to live. Such a birth should have been a calamity—the violence that a lion commits in order to survive would have led to an enormous influx of bad karma. But, luckily, two monks came to remind him of who he was and how the universe works. He saw that there was only one solution: he stopped eating altogether, and purified his soul by austerity. In time he starved to death, and so continued his soul's journey. From time to time humans take it into their heads to urge the same course of action on vzdrei. If I were the sort of person who attempts that, rather than the sort who approaches vzdrei as much as possible on their own terms, I would certainly not be here."

"It must have been hard on your relations with them," John said. "To have other humans wandering in and telling them to kill themselves, I mean."

"You would think so, but in fact, they never take it amiss. Often they simply don't understand, because the would-be teachers' language skills are lacking. If they do manage to decipher the bad Kveidenzsat . . ." Again he debated with himself whether the destination of his thoughts was worth the long road he must take to get there, and decided that it was. "Vzdrei have a practice called *zgauridei*. The usual translation is 'madness,' but that word is just the fossil remnant of a misconception. In fact *zgauridei* does not arise from a disorder, but is a task engaged in voluntarily: for an hour, or a few hours, or rarely as much as a day, one of the vzdrei speaks only nonsense and absurdity. Often the mad will urge others to unreasonable acts. I have heard one insist to her fellows at dinner that they should be taking in food through their nostrils. She gave many complicated reasons, that might resemble logic if you looked at them from a great distance with your eyes half closed. Then without warning, and without acknowledging the contradiction, she switched to telling them that they should all eat through their anuses. So vzdrei regard the human proponents of their starvation as making a lackluster attempt at madness, and answer them in the appropriate way: address them as elders no matter their actual age, and thank them for their teaching. Needless to say, the advice of the mad is not actually followed."

"Is madness a sort of humor, then?"

"Some translators have thought so, but I doubt it. As far as I can tell, they treat it as a solemn matter. I asked a few what the purpose of madness was, and they only said they did it when it seemed necessary or when it felt right.

When one, in return, asked me why humans joke, I can't say my response was any more illuminating."

Every night John prepared the back of the van for the two of them, spreading and smoothing out blankets one at a time until the stack was thick enough to hide the hardness of the floor. Blue would move off to find a resting place—he had slept next to the van the first night, but after being awakened when John passed by to relieve himself, he had decided to keep his distance. Then John and Sudharma would lie down. With Sudharma in such close proximity, it was only natural that John's thoughts when drifting off to sleep, and during the day as well, should gravitate toward him. When they returned to town and he could feed his senses with a more varied diet of human beauty, no doubt this unproductive interest would recede into the background. For now he only had to make sure he did not look at Sudharma with too obvious an attention.

As they traveled, the landscape had changed. The hills now had the texture and color of mud, sun-dried and flaking off a boot. Tall cones such as the one Alma inhabited had been replaced by squatter ones whose gray-green skins were rucked up into wrinkles; when John approached as closely as he dared, he saw the wrinkles had a texture like the braided fibers of a rope. The library called these 'lava cones' and said that Piro had discovered them. The familiar columns yielded gradually to a still taller cylinder bearing branches nearly as thick as itself, that grew high on its sides, bent down to the ground, and took root there. Sudharma suggested that the branches were to brace the plants, so that they wouldn't fall in strong winds. John wondered if the plant also had insects that budded inside it, as a cone did; if so, the branches would provide them with more points of access to the soil. Many of these braced columns had the telltale hole and leafy waterfall that showed there was a candlehawk in residence, so whatever insects they gave birth to were protected.

Sometimes, as John drove along, he imagined Vo walking beside the van. He felt sure, without knowing why, that she would effortlessly match its more-than-human pace. She would look at the desert in that way she had, as if everything around was wonderful and everything must be investigated. She would touch all the plants and let animals crawl on her, or even taste her if they liked. She, alone of all humans, belonged in this landscape, and could walk in it without the vigilance that he had to maintain. He missed the comfort of his visits to the crawler, the familiar pattern of them—enjoying each other for a time and then parting, never giving gifts or asking favors, not promising fidelity or permanence or seeking to extract such promises. He missed the soft warmth of her body and the shape of it. He missed, also, the bafflement of her, the way that he could never guess what words might come out of her mouth next or what she might suggest to him they do. He missed walking with her in the desert. And while it was perfectly correct behavior for a visitor to simply stop showing up, he wished he had had time to say goodbye.

One day, as the day grew hot, the candles turned white in patches, as if afflicted by a rapidly advancing vitiligo. It started with the smallest ones, which bleached first on their tops and then along the raised parts of the pleats. Soon the plague reached even the lava cones and the braced columns, the latter fading fastest on the outsides of their legs. In three hours every candle was blindingly white. Laura had described this to him: the heat of summer was so great that they changed color, reflecting the sun's light away before they could be cooked by it. The day that this first happened was called candlelight, which, Laura said, should really be a holiday or festival, except that it was always far too hot to think about a celebration.

Blue's basket was down to a single sphere. He had been eating more and more sparingly, but conservation could not help him much longer. He no longer paused his questing to climb up and find water. When he had had nothing to drink for half a day, John took a fresh jug from the back of the van. He shook it so that Blue could hear it slosh, opened it up, then held it out for him to smell. When this was done he replaced the lid and held it out again so that the handle faced the basket-man, who carefully wrapped his clawed fingers around it. He gripped the lid with the claws of the other hand, looking to John to see if he approved this action, as a boy tying his first fly checks his uncle's face for confirmation of each turn and knot. He pulled the lid off and refilled his carrying-vessel. Gravely, he returned the remaining water, then held out the lid on his open palm. There was no way to say that if only Blue would carry his water in the jug, sealed against evaporation, it would last longer. Anyway, it didn't matter—the expedition would never last long enough for the van's supplies of water to run out. Blue's food was entirely gone now. He would have to find his people soon, and they would give him food and water. If he did not or they did not, then he would die. He carried his head higher now, and his nostrils flared often. It might have been fear.

On the morning of the second day of Blue's starvation, he stood up on two legs, pointed his face into the wind, sniffed the air as he had done a thousand times before, and stiffened. He walked forward a little and sniffed again. Then he dropped down to all fours and ran. John turned the van to follow, but had to stop when a braced column with widely splayed legs, occupying a pass between hills, left too little space to squeeze past. He realized that until now Blue had been moving through the landscape like a fishing guide who shows town-dwellers where to find the idling redback: taking easy ways, avoiding sites that would require the customer to slide down slopes or push through brush.

"We could try to follow on foot," he said halfheartedly.

Sudharma considered the suggestion; probably he was tempted; but he shook his head. "No. *Tsia'*," he said, which was 'Let's eat' in the Clear Lakes. "We'll wait for him."

They found a shady place to sit, ate their tasteless rations, and did not talk about Blue. There was nothing to be gained by speculating or by dwelling on it.

They rested, but John couldn't sleep. Instead he asked the library about the plant Blue's vessel came from. It would respond to spoken requests, usually in a sensible way. But that evening, as sometimes happened, it had ideas of its own, and though it did show him the dryad he had asked for—a long mammal with white stripes slashing diagonally down its fur—the moment that he paused to think, a photograph unfolded to take over the whole screen. It was of two people sitting in chairs and talking to each other. The one at the right caught his eye first, even though the photographer had stood behind and to the side of them, so that one saw only a crescent of their face. Instead of hair they had long tendrils sprouting from their scalp, of such a vivid red it seemed that blood must pulse in them. Each one was set with short, flexible barbs of the same color, closely spaced along its length in pairs. From their points of emergence the tendrils arched back toward the nape of the neck, where a wooden comb, carved with the image of some glowering animal, held them together. From there they fell in a loose twining tangle, held together only by the barbs, which curved to grip each other. The set of their jaw showed that their mouth was open. They were raising their hands in a gesture with fingers spread wide; they were pleased with what they were saying.

Across from them a jess with a neatly trimmed beard sat in a large chair with orange-brown upholstery. The chair leaned back, but they were leaning forward. They were waiting for the right moment to speak, he thought, with the look of a chess player who knows his next move will be mate. They had laid a trap that was about to be triggered. And yet there was no malice in them; even the one with the strange hair would laugh. John would not at all have minded being the object of a gaze like that.

A third jess, younger, sat on the floor next to the bearded one. They had some sewing with them but had let it fall into their lap. Their hand covered their face as if to shield them from the sight of some embarrassment, but he could see that they were smiling. It might have been Iren, or not.

That evening the library returned to the same photo over and over, and though John was frustrated by its willfulness, he could not help looking every time. Iren and the other jess, and the one he surmised was an alien jess, all seemed happy. It was only one instant recorded, and not their whole lives. It certainly could not prove celibacy was no hardship to them. But perhaps, if Tali did take the vow, she could somehow be content.

At sunset Sudharma performed *pratikraman*. No matter what else might happen, the ritual had to be observed. He was just bending down for the last time when John heard footsteps crunching the gravel, looked around, and found Blue in the moonlight. A long wound ran diagonally from just behind his eye down to his jawline, and his basket was three-quarters full of food. He must have taken it by force from others of his species. He stood up on his hind legs and looked at John with his ears hanging down and his long muzzle angled up, an expression John had never seen before. It might have meant triumph. It might have meant regret.

John turned on the headlights of the van to see the injury better. It was not as deep as he had feared, but it would heal more neatly if stitched up. John imagined trying to bring a needle near Blue's eye and pierce his face; he would be lucky if he lived to make a second suture. Well, it would heal. He ought at least to clean the wound, but for all he knew an antiseptic meant for humans might irritate or burn Blue's flesh. In the end he only washed out the red trench with water from a newly opened jug, and gave Blue the rest to replenish the vessel he still carried between his teeth.

The next morning Blue continued east. John suggested they could try to find the victims of his raiding, but Sudharma preferred to keep following Blue.

Now that Blue had gained some food and might gain more, there was no telling how far he might travel. They would have to manage their resources in order to follow him as long as they could. By counting empty jugs and full ones, John worked out that they were more constrained by their supply of water than by that of fuel or food. After consulting with the town by radio to find out the minimum that would sustain life, they limited themselves strictly to four liters of water per day: one jug apiece. It meant feeling a little thirsty most of the time. It also meant abandoning the habit of moistening a cloth to wipe off the accumulated sweat and dust, and giving up the hope of ever washing clothes. This last distressed Sudharma in particular, since *pratikraman* called for cleanliness, but nothing could be done about it.

Their way was more direct than it had been—not precisely a straight line, but as like one as could be expected, considering the complications of the terrain. Blue had gained confidence from the success of his raid, John thought. Or maybe he had always known where he was going, and only bent his course to look for food along the way. Of course, he still had to seek water. Twice, when he climbed up to a height, John tried to follow him, but he was fast and agile, his feet able to grip the rock nearly as well as his hands could; John was left behind quickly.

The next time Blue approached a hill, John brought him an empty jug, hoping he might fill it at whatever secret source of water he would find there. Blue only sniffed the jug and dropped it in the sand. But he began again to gather plant stems as he walked, made half-finished baskets that he carried with him; and three days later, he returned from a climb with two extra food bodies full of water, sheathed with weaving and tied to the basket he wore. These he removed and presented to John, who thanked him seriously but sniffed them with unease. Water carried inside a plant husk might have soaked up poison. He let a careful drop fall on the opened library, which, when closed and reopened, gave him a list of impurities, including several compounds whose properties were unknown. John decided not even to venture to wash clothes in it. Not wishing to appear ungrateful by discarding the gift, he poured both vessels out into a jug, but instead of lashing the jug to a shelf, he put it in an empty food crate so it could not be mistaken for drinkable water. He gave the vessels back to Blue, who continued to present them filled with water every time he filled his own.

John regularly found new species for the library to sample. Once while walking he came upon a curious shrub or tree, in shape resembling the bare skeleton of an umbrella. A dozen or so woody stems, emerging in a cluster from the ground, clung tightly together until they reached the height of John's head, then split apart and radiated out in all directions; each one curved gently up, then downward, as it spread. Little round leaves like coins clung tightly to the trunk and branches, striping them with green. The library identified it as an insect, but John could not see how it knew—there were no buds, and the chained dryads that made up each stem had no limbs at all. Cautiously, he took a leaf and pressed it, confirming that the library had been right. As they drove farther the umbrellas became common, then dwindled and disappeared.

One morning the sky filled with clouds, and at midday it grew dark. The candles never lit. A few drops patted gently at the gravel, and then it was a downpour. John cut open jugs with his knife, creating a large gape to catch the rain, yet leaving the handle attached. In this way he could grip each one to keep it from being knocked over by rain and wind, until the water in the bottom weighed enough to hold it down. His clothes were soaked, his hat brim dripped continually, and he was happy.

In a little more than two hours the rain stopped. John had collected almost three liters of water—enough for each of them to wipe himself a little cleaner, and for Sudharma to wash the face masks that he used for *pratikraman*. Cheered out of all proportion to the real improvement in their state, they moved on. The ground dried quickly. The only lasting effects of the torrent were a crop of green leaves on the plants they passed and the emergence of new buds on certain insects.

The landscape was changing again. The cones were now covered in spherical swellings and circular pits, as if they had boiled in the heat and then hardened while bubbling. When he approached one cautiously, he saw that each pit was the entrance to a passageway. Most of them were occupied by animals whose girth exactly filled the hole's circumference, so that nothing could go in without removing them. All of them faced out, with long curved mandibles protruding like twinned thorns. He did not come any closer after that.

The hillsides, too, displayed a pattern of rounded depressions. Some were so eaten away by small holes that the stone remaining had the airiness of lace. Others had only a few great ones, which, when high up, might resemble nostrils, or eye sockets in a skull. John wondered if these, too, were niches for animals—though any animal that could plug such caverns with its body would be large enough to crush a man under its foot. Sudharma, however, thought that all this excavation was the work of water or of wind; there were mountains on Dharanendra afflicted with the same hollows.

The kind of column that braced itself against the ground had vanished from the world, replaced by a towering cylinder that had two arms growing straight out from its sides. These occurred in groups of four to seven that grew in a circle and leaned toward each other as they grew. In almost every cluster was one sibling—usually a little taller than the rest—that had a hole near the top and a cascade of leaves descending, which, depending on its location, suggested either a long beard or flowing hair. Though it was only a chance resemblance, John could not help seeing the bearded ones as men and the long-haired ones as women.

When the columns in each ring were tall enough they grew together. In the configuration that John took to be ideal, the arms reached toward each other, met at the tips, and fused, so that each sister or brother in the ring was well supported and could grow tall. But such perfection was a rarity; more often the familial harmony fell short. In many rings there was a pair, or two or three, in which the arms grew past each other and kept going, until, groping, each one found its neighbor's trunk and curved around it. Then it was as if each brother threw an arm around the other's chest or shoulders. Sometimes the arms missed altogether and the column, tipping too far forward, would find one of its siblings to lean into, as if pressing its forehead into the other's chest. If the trunk missed too then the unlucky column would begin to fall, but be caught by the fused arms of siblings. Usually a column leaning so far over did not thrive, but withered and sagged down over the arms that held it up; its weight would pull at the survivors that had tried to save it, forcing them to turn and bend, as if they looked toward it and mourned. There were some, also, that had toppled to the ground and become skeletons, leaving their siblings to try to close the circle by leaning closer and growing their arms longer. In one cluster only two columns remained standing; both their arms had found each other, and they gripped hands tightly to resist the tendency of grief to pull them down. Their long necks had twisted together and fused, as if they were merging into one being. Thus every cluster was a different dance, a different gesture sculpted in green flesh; each one was frozen at a different moment in some sacred ritual. A tree on Essius might have a presence and a personality, but John could not remember seeing any as expressive as these giants. He thought they were to other plants as gods were to human beings.

The library could not identify the rings of columns, but it took them to be insects, even though the single pair of arms suggested mammals. John didn't trust its judgment and would not approach the dancers closely, though he longed to.

The days stretched on and every one was much the same: driving for long hours, creeping through the desert, waiting while Blue climbed to look for water. It should have been boring, yet John was content. He wanted to see what new disfigured cone or monumental dance would be revealed around the next hill. The light in the morning was like liquid gold. And though their mutual filthiness had dampened the erotic character of his thoughts, he was happy just to lie down near Sudharma, to sit with him, to discuss what they each saw in each new cloud or ring of dancers. He liked to hear what Sudharma would tell about the human languages he knew or the lives of the vzdrei or his own youth. Thus in these tedious days he knew a perfect happiness—as long as he could manage not to think that everything he cherished in Sudharma might someday be destroyed by his own hand. When he could not, the knowledge pressed on him with ever greater weight. So one day in the morning as the van set out—unsure whether he was building up a tolerance to poison or just picking at a scab—he asked:

"When you are changed, you will become like a basket-man? Is that it?"

Sudharma answered as if this were a topic like any other, merely a way to pass the time. "I will become better able to speak with them. Whether that means being more like them is more than I know."

"How could it be otherwise?"

Sudharma tapped the body of John's bag, which sat between them. "Consider the library you carry around. It draws dryads like a human illustrator, doesn't it?"

"Very much so."

"If I met a human who could draw like that, I might infer that they had a great love of the natural world, and probably had had it from a young age. No doubt they made a careful study of anatomy, so that when they drew they understood the disposition of the bones and muscles underneath the skin. Over the years they would develop an intuitive sense of every animal as a whole, and know just how to highlight the uniqueness of each one while staying faithful to its true appearance. Now I don't know how that library works, but it must not be an aiyi, or the ships would never have let it on board. So it doesn't have those intuitions or that understanding, let alone that love. Probably it just applies an algorithm to a photograph, and doesn't even know what an animal is—not, at least, in anything like the way we know it. Because it is a different kind of being, it accomplishes the same task in a different way.

"Of course, a basket-man and I are much more similar than an artist and a library. We have organic brains, we walk through the world, we eat and drink, we manipulate objects and make tools. Still, our ancestors emerged from different waters and our brains are organized on different lines. So maybe when I change, I will acquire some echo of how they think and feel—or maybe I can only emulate an intuition with an algorithm. I won't get to know which. All I can know is that communication will be easier, and that must be enough."

"What about aiyi?" John asked. "Are they as different from us as a library is?"

"As much or more so, I would think. Their intelligence is of another order, and their embodiment, if you can even call it that, is nothing at all like ours."

"But they partake of Vo's embodiment."

"How?"

"I don't know. I think at least they can perceive sensations through her, as if she were a sensor or a microphone. And maybe their spirit enters into her . . . commingles with hers, in some way. I could ask her, but I don't know if I'd understand the answer."

"Well, if you don't know I certainly don't. But if she is more than a microphone, it must be an experience of profound transformation for them. Much greater than the one I'll undergo."

As John drove through the desert he tried to imagine what such a transformation would feel like. The problem was beyond him; he could make no headway on it. But long after his mind had moved on to less baffling subjects, Sudharma spoke again.

"I think, when I was small, I did have some idea of becoming vzdrei. But of course, I didn't want to be carnivorous. And when I was old enough to find out how they reproduce, I certainly didn't want *that*. I wonder if it's even possible to truly want to become alien, or if we can only imagine ourselves as some humanized image of them. If it is possible, then I was not up to the task."

They were coming to the foothills of the mountains. If one could dare to judge an alien's mood, Blue was in good spirits; his head was always high, and often he sniffed the air, then pressed forward with renewed speed. He seemed to know where he was going now, but where he was going was into the mountains, and the way was every hour more difficult. On the morning of the sixteenth day he led them to a path so steep and so uneven that John would not drive up it.

"We might radio home and ask what the van's limits are," Sudharma suggested.

"I don't care what its limits are, that slope is beyond mine. If I overturn it out here, or slide backward and crash, we are a long way from help."

He had expected an argument, but Sudharma gave in. "Drive the front wheels up it a little way and let the van roll back, to show him what the problem is. Then we will both get out. Perhaps there is an easier route to where he's going."

But Blue had not the slightest interest in discovering a different path. He came toward them and seized each of them by one wrist. John felt the curve of the hard claw against his skin.

"Be calm," Sudharma said. "This is not an assault, it is communication—more than we have had from him before."

Blue pulled at them, but not so hard as to force them forward. He let them go and ran to the back of the van. John followed to find him pulling at the latch, which worked by turning. "Let me do it," he said, and though this was not a sentence Blue could understand, he stood aside. When John opened the door he went in, cautiously despite his urgency. Perhaps he felt as unnerved there as John had been on entering Vo's crawler for the first time. But when he saw the jugs of water lined up on their shelves, he was emboldened and went toward them. Though they were lashed in place, he got one free, fraying the rope considerably with his claws before he managed to undo the simple knot. He placed it at Sudharma's feet, and then another. He put another two at John's, and then he stopped.

"He wants us each to take two jugs," Sudharma said. "That could just be because we walk upright, so we can carry one in each hand. But if he's noticed we allow ourselves one jug a day, which I can well believe he has, he may be saying the trip will last no more than two days."

"Two days to get there, or one day there and one day back?"

"That's a good question. Could we carry four each, in case it's the former?"

"Up a mountain? I should think we'll be doing well to manage two."

Sudharma picked up a jug in each hand, feeling the weight of them. "Yes," he admitted. He stood thinking for a while. "I could never teach him any words related to time, but if he does mean we should take water for two days, he must understand duration in something like the same way that we do. Maybe communication without words will work better."

He went out and trudged a few steps up the steep path. He turned so that Blue could see and mimed drinking from one of the jugs, then put it down and started back.

Blue would not allow this drama to continue any further. He ran toward Sudharma, squeezed past him, retrieved the jug, and pressed it upon him. "*Carry*," he said. He didn't want to discuss the details; he expected to be listened to.

Sudharma accepted the jug but walked back to where John was standing, though Blue was at his heels saying "Follow" the whole way.

"I think all we can do is go with him and turn back when half our water is used up. I will radio the town and let them tell me why we shouldn't. Will you pack anything that we can't do without, in some way that allows us to bring it along?"

John went to the back of the van, closing the doors behind him so that Blue could not harass him as he worked. He counted the water jugs still on the shelves and repeated a calculation he had made every day or two since they set out. In most of the terrain they had to cross, he thought the van could go at least twice as fast as Blue's walking pace, probably more. On the way back they would not zigzag or take detours or pause to get unexplained water from hills. They could run the air-conditioning and drive through the heat of the day. It would be grueling, but he thought they could get home in eight days at the most. They would have enough water for ten. And they could call for someone to come meet them in the middle with supplies, so, truly, even multiplying by one point five, they would be safe.

He wished the answer had been otherwise; although the hike would not be long, the prospect of it filled him with unease. Nevertheless he looked around the back of the van, considering what to take. On the first evening of their journey he had searched through the stored crates and found, in addition to food, some supplies for survival, notably several good knives in sheaths; he had added the longest of these to his bag, with no intention of returning it when they got back to town. Now he opened the same crate, took out a coil of rope, cut off two lengths, and put them in. He thought with these he could contrive a kind of harness that would let them carry their burdens of water on their backs. One could not use such a makeshift for long periods—no doubt it would be brutally uncomfortable—but for short times when both hands were needed for climbing, it should suffice. He packed food for two days into his bag, and two blankets, and two flashlights, plus a cup for Sudharma and a piece of filtering cloth large enough to fit over it. He left in the most important medical supplies and, after some fretting, the library. He worried what might happen to it if the bag were dropped; but the library, by identifying a dryad, might save their lives, and that was more important. To reassure himself he cut another and much longer piece of rope, coiled it around him, and tied it so it pinned the strap to his waist; that would keep it from slipping or swinging around. And if the terrain became too difficult to carry their jugs even in a harness, this rope would help them to haul water to a height after attaining it.

Then he was ready. Unable to find any further reason for delay, he took a jug of water in each hand and joined Sudharma, who emerged from the cab of the van when he saw that John was outside.

"I dissuaded them from sending someone after us right away, but they will do so if we don't check in again by nightfall tomorrow."

"Good," John said. He would readily have agreed to an immediate intervention, but at least there was some prospect of help. "Did they say how long it would take rescue to arrive, once launched?"

"They will send a team of two and drive continuously—perhaps even at night, when the terrain allows it. They thought three days with luck, and four at most."

The first hour of their ascent was strenuous, and it was not long before John had to attempt the harness. After some trial and error he managed to secure Sudharma's water to his back, and then to talk him through the steps of tying the same rigging onto him. It answered as well as he could have hoped. There was no reason that the success of this trivial invention should make him feel more optimistic about the outcome of their journey, but it did. His spirits were lifted further when the slope of their path gentled and finally became almost flat. The way was wide and bounded on both sides by rocky hills, often with insect shrubs scattered about their bases. Gravel crunched beneath their feet, and sometimes their boots sank deep into sand, which made the walking sluggish. Blue moved ahead with urgency, impatient of their slower pace. When they took advantage of a patch of soft sand in the shade to nap and wait out the hottest part of the day, he tried to urge them on, but they persisted in their calculated laziness. If they exerted themselves too much in the heat, they would only sweat out their water and have to turn back sooner.

They rose from fitful naps, a little earlier than John would have preferred, and pressed on. Soon walls of stone rose on both sides of them. They had that look of many-layered pastry that the rocks by Laura's house had, but they were more irregular, each layer's edge protruding a bit farther or less far than the one just below it. It was as if the two sides of the canyon had been broken from each other roughly by some great force. The gravel became patchy and then disappeared, so they were traveling on smooth and naked stone. Here and there a small hole pocked it, and Blue lowered his head to examine each one before passing by. Then after peering into a larger hole, he called out "Follow," which, John thought, must be the closest word he knew to 'come.'

They caught up with him and looked. The hole was tapering in form, and at the bottom there was water.

"It's rain," John said, feeling the shiver of a revelation. The rainstorm they had driven through, falling on sand and gravel, had soaked in and been lost, but rain that fell into a pit of stone was trapped and must stay there till it evaporated or somebody drank it. That was the answer to the paradox: Blue went up to find water because in the desert, stone jutted up high. "It's just rain," he said again. "It should be drinkable."

They used Sudharma's cup to dip out water and poured it carefully into an empty jug. John drank, and Sudharma filtered water into his cup and drank. Blue stuck his head into the hole to lick the rest out, and stood up brushing bits of sediment off of his tongue.

"If he can show us more water," Sudharma said, "we can increase our range."

"I only packed food for two days."

"We could survive awhile without, if we have water."

John didn't care for this mood of risk-taking. He felt Sudharma was developing an obsession. For the rest of the day he was careful to remember every turn they took, in case they had to go back without Blue—though indeed they were following such a wide and obvious path that there would be no difficulty in returning. It occurred to him to wonder how this boulevard existed, and as soon as the question was posed, the answer was obvious. Like the riverbed that Vo lived in, it was a course for water, yet it lacked even the shining ribbon that survived drought there; it must become a river only when rain filled it. Water had deposited the sand and gravel and had washed the hard stone clean. Water tore out any seedlings that might take root at the middle of the path; it nourished the insect shrubs around the edges. And walking in this insight, he seemed to see the great brief river rush around him, to feel the force of it trying to tear him off his feet. The vision faded, but it left him feeling that the stone and sand around him—a landscape lacking everything that made his own home beautiful—could be as vibrant as a forest, that like a tree its stillness flowed with secret life.

In the shadow of the canyon walls, the darkness came on early. They had found nothing, and had nothing but bare stone to camp on. Possessing no bag suitable for hiking, Sudharma had not been able to bring his book, but he recited *pratikraman* anyway. John waited through the customary sounds, which, though they might flow in one ear and out the other, had still left an imprint, carving their own creekbed in his mind. In the morning they would have to turn around. He feared Sudharma would not want to. He wondered if it would be best to discuss that now, or if he should wait until morning. Before he could decide, it was too late. Sudharma was lying down and closing his eyes.

Hot as the day had been, the night grew chilly, and one blanket each was not enough. When each found the other wakened by the cold, they combined their covers and returned to sleep together in a double-layered cocoon. This would never happen again, John thought, but he had little time to think about it. The day had been too strenuous. Almost at once, he fell asleep.

After Sudharma's morning ritual they both ate their awful biscuits, and John said what he had to say.

"We must go back. The risk is too great."

"I know."

"There will be other years and other basket-men. You must preserve yourself to meet them."

"Those are wise words, and I don't feel very wise. But even so, I will turn back."

This was as ready a concession as John could have hoped for. But Blue did not accept the plan so easily. Already, as John was packing up the blankets and winding his rope around him, Blue was taking slow steps up the path and calling "Follow." When instead they started downslope toward the van, he charged past and stopped in front of them. He lunged at John, who stood motionless, expecting to be taken by the wrist again. Instead Blue hooked a claw around the handle of a jug and tore it out of John's grip. He held it up and with his other hand, he laid two fingers on it, just below the level of the water.

"He must mean that's all the water we'll need," Sudharma said. "Two finger-widths. He's saying we're close."

"It doesn't matter if we are. We must go back."

"We didn't start until midmorning yesterday, and we were traveling uphill, which is slower. We can go a little farther and still make it back today. Between the late start and the preserved rain that we drank, we haven't used quite half our water yet, so there will be enough left for a morning drink tomorrow even if we don't."

"You are cutting things entirely too fine," John said, but he knew he had already lost the argument.

"Give me three hours—that is all I ask."

They rose above the canyon walls and came out on a nearly level plain. High peaks rose ahead of them. The course of the missing river could be seen as a depression in the ground and as a gap in the pattern of plant life. They followed it upward. John used one of the shorter pieces of rope to lash his full water jug together with the one that was now empty, and carried them both with one hand; this allowed him to pull out his tag to check the time, and he did so frequently.

At two hours and forty minutes, Blue broke into a run. Sudharma ran to catch up, and so John did too. Scattered among insect shrubs on both sides of the riverbed were mammal-trees, leafless and brown, small enough that one might stand and look down on their tops. Blue was sniffing at the nearest of them. John would have said that they were all dead, but in the desert it might be that they were only waiting for more rain before they sprang to life.

Blue walked as far as the last tree, which was perhaps as much as forty paces, and came back to the place John and Sudharma stood. "Blue," he said. He set his vessel on the sand, then stood up tall on his hind legs. Raising his muzzle to the sky, he made a startlingly loud whistle. With ears held high he listened for an answer. Finally he dropped to all fours and went along the riverbed again, individually inspecting all the trees. John and Sudharma followed, watching how he poked his face into the branches to examine every twig. When he had nearly reached the end, he found one little withered berry, dark red-brown and barely visible against the dark brown bark. He folded back his claws to pluck it gently with his fingers. Slowly, as if reverently, he placed it on his tongue. He lay down, basket and all, on his side. After a minute he closed his eyes.

John crouched down beside him and put a palm up to his nose to feel the wind of his breath. He was alive. Perhaps his respiration was a little shallow, but who could say what might be normal in a basket-man?

"Blue? Are you all right?"

He didn't stir. John waited, hoping that Blue was merely in despair at having found no others of his kind here, and that soon he would regain hope and stand up. Then he remembered that they had a deadline, and reached into his pocket for the tag. It had been three and a half hours.

"We have to go now," John said.

"Yes."

"Do you think these plants are his own species?"

"I think we should be very careful not to find that out."

As they left, they passed Blue's vessel sitting in the sand. John picked it up, carried it back to him, and put it near his hand so he would have the water if he woke. It was all that he could think to do.

On the walk back it was easier to see the plants that grew up on the tops of the canyon walls. All the ones John could identify were insects; he supposed mammals and reptiles were too wise to gestate children so close to a precipice. In the evening, as they neared the place the canyon walls would end, he noticed a depression in the wall-top, bare of plants but flanked by denser growth: another empty riverbed. A smoothing of the stone below it showed where water must have plunged down from a tributary.

By the time they reached the steep part of their path, the sun had nearly set. They discussed camping on the trail again and finishing their journey in the morning, when the footing would be easier to see. But the idea of spending the night within shelter held too much allure. They would be warm and safe, then in the morning they would start for home. They turned on their flashlights and went down the slope sideways.

The smaller moon was out, and in its light they saw the van ahead. The hood was open, and empty water jugs lay on the sand around. John ran to look into the engine compartment. It was fouled with something brown that he supposed was feces. Short lengths of wire, all frayed by chewing, were scattered around in the filth, and two plastic reservoirs that must have contained fluids were cracked and empty. The side doors were still closed, but the front window had been broken. He warned Sudharma to stand back and then pounded the side of his fist on the driver's door, ready to flee if something came out. He heard nothing. He banged on the back of the van—its door too was closed—but still there was no protest or attack. So he climbed up to the cab, finding the seats and the floor mats sodden, strewn with clusters of excreta that had softened and expanded in the wet. He could see bits of severed wire on the floor mats; a few still hung down from beneath the dashboard. When he sat, his weight squeezed water out of the upholstery and it pooled around him and soaked into his pants. He pressed the starting-button, realizing a second too late he was sitting in water near damaged electrical wiring. It didn't matter—nothing happened. The van was lifeless and the radio was too.

The dividing door between the cab and cargo sections had been opened, and he ducked through it. Not a single full jug was left on the shelves—the ropes that had secured them were chewed through, and they were lying, lidless and dented, all over the floor. None contained more than a vestige of water. The floor was damp with what had been spilled, but any standing water must have dripped out through some gap. One crate of food was broken and the packets of food from it had been perforated with small holes, then clumsily torn open. The contents, spread around the floor, had softened and expanded like the feces they were mingled with.

John tried to comprehend what creature could have caused all this destruction. He pictured something numerous and small, crawling in the gaps of the van's workings. They would push water jugs off all the shelves, even though that made the lids pop off, because they couldn't reach them from the ground, and they would spill the lidless ones while trying to carry them. But it was hard to imagine some Scythian version of a rat breaking the window, even with a rock. Perhaps it had been a larger animal, that could reach wires in the recesses of the engine with long fingers and long claws. He thought that basket-men would have been more careful with the water, and furthermore with their own feces, but then he only knew one individual; they might be just as various as human beings. Someone who had only met Essian people would never have imagined ship-folk could exist.

John let Sudharma into the back to survey the damage. He did so in a few glances and did not waste time on lamentation. "Where do we spend the night?" he asked.

"I don't know how to identify a place of safety at all, let alone in the dark. I think we had better clean this up as best we can, then lock the dividing door and sleep in here. Whatever did this hasn't learned to pick a lock, at least."

Neither of them said that locking the dividing door before they left would have kept their water safe, and either of them could have done that. They both knew it, and there was no point.

"Some of these jugs have a little water left," John said. "We should salvage that first."

They both searched through the mayhem, tested the water left in jugs using the library, and poured any that was uncontaminated into the jugs they had brought home from the canyon. Along with what was already in them, it came to one full jug, another three-quarters full. That was more than he had thought, and it was not nearly enough.

"I think I know where to find more," he said. He told Sudharma of the imprint of a waterfall that he had seen, which must surely be the issue of some temporary river. "Any pit or pocket on the river's course would fill with rain. I'm sure that natural reservoirs like that are how Blue has been filling his vessels. I will go tomorrow, early, and climb up."

"We should consider the water Blue gave you first. That wasn't in the crate that's broken open, was it?"

"No. But we don't know if it's safe."

"I'm quite sure that climbing the canyon wall is not. Have you climbed mountains before?"

"I've climbed trees."

"That's rather different. How much water did Blue bring, in all?"

"Five jugs and a trickle more, I think."

"With what we have here, could that be enough?"

Spread out over four days, it would come to a little less than they had been drinking. They would no longer have air-conditioning, but at least they could rest in the shade all day—somewhere apart from the van, in case the spillers of the water came again.

Was it more dangerous to risk ingesting poison than to climb the rocks? There was no way to quantify. John could only say that he would rather die here, with Sudharma, than lie broken at the bottom of a canyon wall alone.

"All right," he said. "I will try Blue's water, as cautiously as haste allows. If there is any sign of poison, I will set off for the canyon in the morning."

"*I* will try Blue's water. I like your chances of treating me for poisoning better than mine of treating you. And if you do have to climb the canyon walls, it's better that you not be sick."

"There is a method to the trying."

"Teach it to me."

John felt in his bones that he should be the one to try anything dangerous. But Sudharma's logic was irrefutable. "Let me clean up in here first."

He used a folded blanket to push deliquescing food and feces out—they came apart as they were pushed, and he had to rub the blanket against the edge of the door to scrape the remnants free. With another blanket, wadded up, he mopped the floor dry. After that there was no more excuse for delay.

"Come outside, and we will do it by moonlight."

John put a filtering cloth over Sudharma's cup and filled it halfway with safe water, then carefully, holding the cloth over the jug-mouth, poured a little of Blue's gift into an empty jug. "Let this run onto the inside of your wrist. If it burns or itches or you see a rash, flush it with the pure water at once." He sighed. "We ought to wait overnight for a skin reaction, but I will set an alarm for two hours."

They shut themselves up in the van and he laid his head down. He worried about poisons, and the worry became a dream in which the smooth skin of Sudharma's wrist wrinkled and twisted and turned gray, becoming monstrous as the lava cones. The alarm went off and he woke in a panic, certain that he had forgotten some precaution, left out a step of the testing, and Sudharma would die for it. His heart slowed when he identified the source of the emotion. Sudharma had not done *pratikraman*. Of course everything felt wrong.

They both slipped out and John took Sudharma's hand to examine his wrist. The skin was smooth and free of blemishes, even when he shone the flashlight on it to be sure.

"Did you sleep?" he asked.

"A little."

"Take a drop of this and rub it on your lips."

Sudharma obeyed.

"Do you feel any tingling, burning, or itching?"

"No."

"We will wait fifteen minutes."

At the end of this time Blue's water had shown no sign of corruption, so John gave Sudharma more.

"Take this in your mouth and hold it there for fifteen minutes before swallowing. If it tastes bitter or soapy or you feel any other reaction, spit it out and rinse your mouth with the clean water right away."

The allotted time passed, and John heard Sudharma swallow.

"Now we have only to wait. I would like to keep watch, but I had better sleep, in case I have to climb tomorrow. I will set an alarm to check on you in another two hours. If you feel anything amiss at all, don't hesitate to wake me up."

They went back inside and lay down, and John fell asleep at once.

He woke to the sound of the door being opened. Then he heard the sound of retching. Outside the van, Sudharma was wiping his mouth.

"It's good that you brought it up," John said. "I'll give you something to reduce absorption of whatever might be left."

He mixed activated charcoal with clean water to create a slurry. As Sudharma was drinking the last of it, the tag in John's pocket chimed its alarm. He had administered the charcoal at two hours after exposure. That would limit its effectiveness, but he was still glad he had given it.

"You should sleep," John said; and by the slowness of Sudharma's breathing in the dark, he thought he did.

His alarm went off again an hour before dawn. Sudharma was not there; he was outside, leaning with one hand against the van. "I had a nasty bout of diarrhea just now."

"That can be a side effect of charcoal. What was the consistency?"

"Thin. Almost like water."

That did not sound like a side effect, but John tried to receive the news calmly. There was no point in causing Sudharma to panic. John was afraid enough for both of them. He worried that the plant husk had contained some toxin deadly even in a small amount, like blue bookshelf or sister's-mittens. But nothing so dramatic would be necessary to kill; all the poison had to do was make Sudharma waste the water in his body when he had nothing left to drink. John would have to leave now, in the dark. He had no time to lose.

"You can't stay in the van during the day, or you'll cook when it gets hot. I'm going to show you to some reptile trees you can take shelter under. Lie still as much as you can, and if anything comes along don't move a muscle." He mixed four sachets of rehydration salts into the jug that was still full and gave it to him. "Drink this slowly, but do drink it—don't try to conserve it. I *will* be back with more."

He put as much confidence into his voice as he could manage, but no doubt Sudharma knew as well as he did what he meant. He would find water because not to find it was unthinkable. If he didn't, he would not have much time for regret.

He took his bag, removing the blankets and some other inessentials to lighten the load. He took two empty jugs and the one that was still part-full of pure water—pausing to pour out the one Sudharma had been poisoned by, so it could not be mistaken for innocent, and to stuff the tainted filtering cloth inside. He tied the coil of rope around his waist again, and following the faint disc of the flashlight's beam he set off.

CHAPTER TWELVE

In the moonlight the steep section of the path was treacherous. He forced himself to take it slowly, carefully identifying every place that he would set a foot or hand before he tucked the flashlight back into his pocket and moved forward. A sprained ankle now would be the death of both of them. He could not tie a proper harness on himself, but he had lashed the jugs together by their handles and slung them on a rope over his shoulder, tying it to the coil around his waist when the way became so difficult as to require both hands. He had less than two-thirds of a jug left, so the burden was not very heavy. By the time he got to easier terrain the flashlight's power was used up, but the sky was light enough that he no longer needed it. After that he moved quickly and reached the dry waterfall in good time. The day already felt quite warm, at least to one who had been hurrying up a slope, but he would have a few hours to search before he had to find some shade and rest. He only had to climb the wall first.

It was, at least, not so high a wall here as it would be farther up the canyon. He chose a spot where the ascent looked relatively easy; the layered stone rose at an angle of fifteen or twenty degrees from vertical for the first two-thirds of its height, and at that point was a shelf wide enough for him to stand on. In places he could see the stone was crumbling, but when he pulled down on a few potential handholds, nothing broke away.

If he paused to judge the chance of falling during this climb he would never begin it. He put one foot up on the stone, and both hands. Cautiously, testing the stability of every toehold and gripping-place before he dared to shift his weight to it, he ascended, and his feet achieved the shelf.

The worst was still ahead. He had been pleased to find a section of the wall with a favorable slope at the bottom; he had not considered that the climb would be hardest at the top, when he had farthest to fall and his arms were most tired. He allowed himself a few minutes to rest his muscles. But the day was getting hotter, his water jug was low, and Sudharma was sick and alone.

With his arms and shoulders aching and the stone barely supporting the tips of his boots, he got his right hand up on the top, then the left arm. Groping blindly, he found a place that he could clutch at. He heaved himself up, and his chest and belly flopped onto the rocks. At once a bush next to his shoulder hissed and rattled; he held his breath, but it did not attack. He lay still there for another minute with his legs hanging over the edge. Then he slowly pulled them up, got them under him, and hurried away from the bush. Now he could look around.

There were no stone walls to bound the flow of water here, but a smooth riverbed angled away from the canyon. It made a good path to walk up. Before long he found a round depression in the stone that would catch rain—not deep enough to have retained the water, but it gave him hope. Then there was nothing else.

He was beginning to sweat profusely. It was time to find his shelter from the worst heat of the day. But that would last five or six hours. Even if he found water the moment he rose from the shade, he didn't think Sudharma would survive. He pressed on.

He stopped looking at his tag to check the time; there was no point in it, since he no longer had a schedule to abide by. He would go forward until he had filled his jugs, then he would turn around, walking by moonlight if necessary. His shirt was soaked through, which was heartening—at least there was some water left in him to come out through the pores. That would probably not remain true for much longer. His water jug was empty.

Then he saw it. Sunk into bare stone, there was a rounded hole full of clear water—a bounty of water, enough to last months. Beside it was a tree whose roots clung to the rocks beside and underneath it. From this base it rose up to perhaps twice as much as John's height, and its branches spread more than halfway across the water. It was split deeply, from the top down to the level of the lowest branches, and from the cleft a yellowish scar of missing bark ran down the trunk; the upper branches were all dead, and some were missing. Perhaps it had been struck by lightning. Yet the crooked branches toward the bottom were still vivid green, and a slight shifting of the bark on one of them told him the snake was still alive.

There was no hope that he could creep up to the edge of the water; undoubtedly its mouth could reach anyone close enough to drink. But there were a few small holes in the stone around the great one that might hide some water in their depths, and the nearest of those might be safe. He tried to visualize the snake's full length and then extend it by one-half to be sure, but couldn't seem to settle on an answer. He thought if only he could wet his throat he would be able to think better, and so—expecting the snake's strike at every instant—he crawled on his belly toward the little water hole and lay down to put a hand into its depths. There was not much, but he scooped up everything he could to drink. Then he paddled his fingers in the silty remnants and dabbed the moisture on his face to cool it, over and over, until his fingertips no longer came up charged with water but only a poultice of wet sand.

He backed away and rose into a crouch, watching the snake-tree. He felt that it was mocking him. Stretched out at ease in the shade of itself, well within reach of good water, it had all the time in the world. He had to act quickly, but also correctly. Lying near his feet, a vessel like the one that Blue had carried, still bearing the tattered remnants of a basket, showed that another had been desperate here and died for it. He examined the landscape, imagining every possible path by which he might approach the water. It was hopeless. He could not avoid the snake's bite.

Could he survive it?

He knew one who had done so. He wished she were here to advise him, or that Laura was. Ru had torn away from the teeth that clutched at her, which would do him no good, since it left him without water and the snake able to strike again. But he had a knife, he remembered—and the thought, like a splash of cold water, startled his brain awake. When the snake bit into him its neck and eyes would be within reach of his blade. He could walk toward it with his left arm held out, apply a tourniquet beforehand to reduce the bleeding. He might have to get back down the hill with only three limbs fully working, but if he could find somewhere to secure a rope—

Maybe he wouldn't have to. He opened his bag and took out the library, still safely wound up in a shirt; he laid it carefully on a flat stone. He dumped the rest of the bag's contents and grabbed the knife out of the pile. Unsheathing it, he used the point to carefully unpick the stitches that fastened his great-uncle's soul to the canvas on one side. He wrapped the body of the bag around his forearm, then wound the strap around that. Holding the loose end in his hand, he examined the result.

The armor was too thin. The snake's teeth would easily pierce through it. He wished he had brought the blankets—they would have made a better padding. But he had the shirt the library was wrapped in, and the one he was wearing. He took off his pants too, but restored the boots for traction's sake. From pants and shirt and bag, he made as neat a swaddling as he could. With the extra thickness, the soul was not long enough to cover his arm well—there were unprotected spaces in between the windings—but it would have to do. Uncoiling the rope from around his waist, he tied one end near his elbow, making an awkward knot with one hand and his teeth. He wound it around his forearm in a spiral to create a final layer of armor. At his wrist he tied another clumsy knot, and then cut off the excess length. The casing would stay in place now, so he could keep his left hand free. He had thought of a use for it.

The rim of the hole was smooth and rounded, and the snake would easily drag him in to drown—except that at one place near the edge, the stone was piled up like a stack of cushions. That, he thought, might serve him as a bulwark; if the snake pulled him close to the water, he could drop to his knees behind it. He circled around, keeping his distance, until the stone barrier was between him and the tree. Then he had to search for the snake in the branches all over again, until a telltale thickening showed him where it hid. It was so well camouflaged against itself that if he looked away from it, it disappeared.

He paused to go over his plan one last time. It wasn't a good idea. He didn't have a better one.

He advanced with his padded arm held out in front of him, the hand curled back as far as it would go. One short step at a time, he came forward. The snake rearranged itself so it lay facing him, though the movement made it easier to see. It was counting on his desperation rather than its camouflage to bring him within range, and it was right. He expected it to strike, but even so it was a shock when it launched itself toward him, the creature's speed giving him only a moment to feel his heart stop before it latched on. The jaws squeezed hard and he felt the teeth piercing his arm, but not deeply. Quickly, he raised his knife. Then he saw that the snake's eyes were closed, shuttered by armored lids. Of course, it must expect the animals it preyed upon to fight back. Everywhere the scales were thick and overlapping, keeled like the bottom of a boat, which would increase their strength. Given time he could slide the edge of the blade beneath their points and pry or slice them off until he made enough room for the knife to enter, but he doubted he could hold a thrashing snake so long. If it got away then it could wait until he came up to the water and pull him in before he had the time to stab.

He hadn't given Laura enough credit, and he was going to pay for it. Of course, if knives had been the answer to snake-trees, she would have told him to carry a knife.

The snake yanked hard, so that he stumbled forward. It let go, but before he could pull his arm away it took a new grip, close to the site of the last. It bit down hard and he could feel blood trickling from the punctures it had made. It shook its head from side to side, tugged back and shoved forward. It was trying to open up gaps in his improvised armor. Again it yanked and changed its grip. Any further and he would have to brace himself behind the pile of stone to keep from being drowned. If he tore away now, how badly would his arm be hurt? At the back of the long mouth, where the teeth gripped only air, he could see how wickedly curved they were—

The back of the mouth. He gripped the snake hard with his left hand, as close to the neck as he could reach, and at the same time shoved the knife blade in between its jaws. Sawing with all his strength, he cut back through the corners of the mouth until something, bone or scale, stopped the knife dead. The expanded gape gave him more room to work, and he turned the blade to cut at its flesh from inside. The snake was trying to let him go and get away, jerking back wildly in a panic; its lower jaw came loose, but the thrashing of its body only drove its upper teeth deeper into his arm. It was bleeding but not enough to kill it quickly, and though the muscles that tightened the jaw might be damaged they were not, he thought, entirely severed—it might still manage to attack him again. He slipped the knife blade into the thing's throat and stabbed blindly, over and over, at anything the point could reach. The mouth gushed blood and the snake's flailing slowed. Then it was still.

He stood gasping in shock and relief, feeling no impulse to do anything at all. He had killed a snake-tree by himself. Surely that was enough, and nothing more would be required from him. Finally a deep aching in his arm reminded him that there was still work to be done.

He dropped the knife and detached the bloody head from him, carefully drawing out the teeth along the curved tracks they had made in his flesh, then pulling them out of the ruins of bag and clothing. Almost, he cast the grisly thing away, but just in time he realized that its bleeding might contaminate the water. Furthermore, the body, if left stretched across the water hole, would fall in when it rotted. He carried the head off to the side of the canyon, keeping the body stretched out taut, and laid it down where it could decompose safely. Eventually some flood would carry the remains of the monster downhill and away.

Steadied and calmed, he unwrapped his arm to examine it. He had done quite a bit of bleeding from the tooth-wounds, but there was no risk to the function of the arm, so long as infection did not set in. He went to one of the small outlying water holes, and using his largest syringe and a blunt needle, he flushed the wounds with water, tweezing out some bits of skin and fabric that would not be washed away. There were, surely, no bacteria in either mouth or water that could feed on human flesh, but since those that lived on him and on his clothes might become troublesome, he sprayed the wounds with antiseptic and applied a generous amount of antibiotic cream. He bandaged up his arm to stop the flow of blood and washed his hands as best he could. Then at last he could go to the great water, the one that the snake had protected. He took up the three jugs, hanging together from their rope like fat fish from a stringer, and walked toward it with the fervor of a man who visits for the first time after being long at sea. It felt like months since he had drunk his fill. He was so lost in anticipation that he didn't see the other snake until it struck.

The teeth sank deep into his calf. It yanked, and he fell on his side, hitting his shoulder hard against the stone. It began to slowly pull him toward the water—it was going to drown him. He tried to dig his fingers in but found so little purchase that he couldn't stop his progress. The knife was no more than a meter from his hand—it might as well have been a light-year. He kicked wildly at the snake's head with his free leg, though every impact was an agony that made the teeth tear at his flesh.

Then he stopped—stopped kicking and stopped sliding toward the water. The heel of his flailing boot had caught in one of the small water holes, just outside the major one. It was not salvation, but at best a stalemate; the snake could still bleed him until he was weak, or if it had enough wit, bite the other leg and pull his foot out of the hole. But the stoppage gave him time to raise his head and see that the new snake's body was anchored not in the trunk, but in a low branch. From there it angled across the water and down to his calf. There was not much slack in the body—it must have stretched out to its very limit to bite him. If he tore away quickly enough, he might be able to get out of range. But that would leave it in possession of the water, and him with such a serious injury that he might not make it back to Sudharma.

The tree was injured too, he thought. Injured enough, perhaps, that it now functioned as two separate plants, each one supporting its own snake—which might mean that the two were joined only by old rotting wood. At once he raised his torso and bent double, stretching out his arms to seize the snake as far down on its body as he could. He leaned back until the long body was taut, then heaved with all the strength he had. Nothing gave way. It came to him that he might tear the snake apart before the tree, and then its blood would foul the water. He still didn't have a better plan.

The snake let go his calf and sank its teeth into his side instead. That let him turn onto his back and get both heels into the hole. He bent his legs so he could grip the snake still farther down, then straightened them, using the long muscles of the thighs together with his back and shoulders. This time he heard and felt a snap. A final heave produced a splintering, and his back slammed down against the stone—the snake had come free. A branch and a piece of the trunk had broken off along with it; they had fallen into the water, as had most of the snake's body. He grabbed the snake around its neck before it could try biting him in his, and dragged it against its own thrashing and the weight of the sinking branch to the place where he had dropped the knife. Again he cut back through the corners of the mouth and stabbed into the throat, and it was dead.

He approached the water warily this time, examining each branch until he was sure every one was innocent. Hand over hand, he pulled the snake and severed branch out of the water and thrust them behind him. He rinsed his hands off in the hole his boots had lodged in. Then he went down on his knees at the edge of the water, and finally he drank.

He was bloated with water by the time he rose; his face was washed and he had splashed himself all over to cool down. Then he picked up the stringer of jugs. The first one that he filled went to cleaning the punctures in his calf and his side. Taking supplies from the place he had dumped out his bag, he sprayed and coated and bound up the wounds. He filled up all three jugs and put their lids on them.

He could not put off the worst task any longer. He went to where he had removed the windings from his arm, crouched over the tangle of fabric and rope, and examined what he had not let himself think about, the damage to the strap. There were punctures in it and two grievous tears, one nearly long enough to split the soul in two. He touched it and still felt his great-uncle's presence, weaker, but discernible. The leather was not emptied of him, not quite. But it would never hold up the bag's weight. John would never again raise his hand, with an almost unconscious gesture, to take comfort from its strength, but at best would keep it in a drawer to be handled with great care once in a while. He ran his fingers over the wounds, mourning the loss.

Then he took a breath and made himself stop fussing. His great-uncle had protected him. It was what he would have wanted, what all men's souls hoped to do.

He wiped the knife clean on his underwear and severed the stitches that still bound the soul to the bag, then rolled it up carefully and cocooned it in a self-adhesive bandage to keep it safe. With sutures and a harness-rope, he fashioned a new strap. The bag-body was intact enough that so long as the smallest objects were kept safe in pockets, nothing would fall out, and the clothing had soaked up most of the blood; in the arid heat, the few drops that had made it to the bag were nearly dry. He packed it carefully, with the library and the soul in the middle, surrounded by soft things so they would not be damaged on the journey home.

As he worked he began to wonder if he had some affliction other than the obvious: the backs of his hands felt tight and hot. It was not a spreading of some poison from the snake's bite, because it affected both hands and only the hands. When he touched the skin he found it tender, and the diagnosis came to him: he had forgotten to take sunscreen and was burned. Furthermore, he discovered, on searching the bag, that when he winnowed its contents he had left the pills behind. He put his clothes back on, even though the blood on them was not yet dry, so that at least the condition would not become general over his skin.

He put on the bag, then lifted the jugs by their rope and laid it over his shoulder to carry. He was about to set off when a last thought occurred to him. He slipped the library out of its niche in his bag and showed it the tree, the snake-body still attached to it, then the separated branch and snake. The outlines of all of them sparkled: a new species. He dipped one finger in the snake's split mouth and drew a bloody streak across the screen. He closed the library and put it back into its place. Now he was ready.

Rather than retrace his steps, he went directly toward the canyon and walked along the top of its wall until he found a good place to descend. There was a wide ledge to which he could lower the water before he climbed down to it, once he had cut away the portion of the rope the snake had damaged and spliced the rest together. From there he could walk down backward, as if the stony layers were a steep and shallow staircase. After that he had only to walk. He switched the rope that held the heavy jugs from side to side every few minutes so that each shoulder could rest. It was hard to get the water down the steepness at the end, but as he labored through the task he felt more and more hopeful. He saw the van down in the distance, no more damaged than before; likely the wreckers had not come back. He had brought home water and now everything would be all right.

Sudharma was asleep under the reptile trees. That was well, if he was only sleeping. John crouched down and said his name. He didn't answer. Nearby a stain of diarrhea on the ground, black like the charcoal it contained and with a length of paper stuck to it, showed he had been just well enough to clean himself but not enough to cover it with sand. John called louder, then shook him gently, as his mind flicked through an inventory of the equipment in his bag, trying to devise an apparatus to rehydrate him if it could not be done by mouth. But the ineffectual contraptions in his mind evaporated; Sudharma's eyes were open.

"I brought water," he said. He helped Sudharma sit, and supporting his back with one arm, raised the jug so he could drink a little. Then he went to mix up a liter of rehydration fluid. He gave this to Sudharma slowly, one mouthful at a time until it was all gone. A little reptile watched impassively from a low branch. Finally Sudharma roused enough to speak.

"I see you had some difficulty."

John glanced down at his torn and bloodstained clothes. "A little. It doesn't matter."

"I'm sorry I doubted you."

"That doesn't matter either. There is much more water where this came from. We will have enough."

He tried to make his voice sound confident, and thought that he succeeded. But dread was swirling up around him like a tide. So long as the poisoning symptoms persisted, they would go through water rapidly; he would have to repeat his journey every day. He wasn't sure Sudharma could survive being left alone so long again.

When enough time had passed, he made another liter of solution and induced Sudharma to drink most of it. The sun was setting and the reptile still examined them. He sat considering what he would do in the morning—whether he ought to go out right away for more water, or wait to see how Sudharma might fare.

A shiver washed over him. The reptile's head had been on the right, facing away from the tree's trunk. Now the head was on the other side, and yet it hadn't turned around. He had fallen asleep, of course that was it—the real lizard had blended itself with a dream. No animal, not even one birthed from a tree, could stretch its head out to a point and pull its tail in to become a head. But such a translocation might be possible if it was no dryad at all, but an appliance of the aiyi, differing from the crawler only in its size and in the shape it happened to have taken.

"Vo," he said. "If you can hear me. We are in trouble and we need your help. Please help us."

The reptile cocked its head at him. Then it flailed its tail, leapt off the branch, and vanished. The movement was so reminiscent of the first reptile he had ever seen—upside-down on a column, the day that they landed on Scythia—that he lost all hope at once. It was just a dryad after all. It could do nothing for them.

The night was warm. He fell asleep on the ground and woke with his arm around Sudharma's chest. He removed it at once, feeling a double stab of guilt at the unintentional intrusion and at his negligence at not putting Sudharma safely to bed in the van.

The lizard was watching him, perched on a little flat stone in the moonlight. As soon as his eyes had lit on it, it flowed backward, leaving behind a clear glass cup the size of a thimble. It was full of water. John knew the cup could not have been concealed beneath the reptile's chest—the creature was built too low to the ground for that. It must have made a vessel for the water it had brought by giving up a portion of the substance of itself. So small a sip could do nothing to help them, but this token gift must mean he had gained Vo's attention, and that gave him hope. He drank the water and put the cup back on the stone for the reptile to reabsorb.

Sudharma vomited as soon as he was wakened—though very little came up—and John made him drink more solution. He managed to walk to the van on his own, but John could see that the strength had gone out of him.

The rest of the night held more worry than sleep. Shortly after daybreak, John gave up on any further rest and decided to go out into the light and check his wounds. He opened the back door. On the ramp and all around it, animals of every kind and size crowded together in a throng. Guessing what they had come to do, John took down four empty and undamaged jugs, uncapped them, and sat them down on the van's floor. At once the animals began to fill them. The insects' donation was small, but two or three of them could sit on the rim of a jug at the same time, looking outward as they squirted water through their tails. Miniature reptiles crawled up the sides and made deposits from a spiracle that opened in their necks. A mammal, round and short-limbed, climbed up on a giant reptile's head and squirted out more water from its mouth than its small body could have held; when the two turned away, they were no longer separate. The last animal, a rangy mammal with a blunt nose, added a liter or so from the center of one paw, then used its claws to pry open a crate and took out two of the remaining jugs of Blue's water. Placing one on the ground, it narrowed its head to form a tube and inserted it into the jug's mouth. The tube extended to the bottom as the tail shortened to compensate. The creature sucked up the contents, its sides swelling enormously, and spat them back again into the jug. It repeated the procedure with the other one and screwed the caps back onto both. Before it left, it wandered over to Sudharma, still asleep, and sniffed him thoroughly. He stirred when the snuffling came close to his ear, and John held his breath, but he did not wake. John didn't know why he was glad. To let Sudharma see these creatures change and flow, freed of the constraint of mimicry, would have been like bringing a third person to the cabin during a visit, he thought. But on reflection this association made no sense, and so he let it go.

He opened the library. A brownish dust fell out—the dried blood of the snake; he had forgotten about it. None of it had stuck. He let a drop of water from each jug drip onto the library's screen. They were, of course, all pure.

When Sudharma woke he looked around him at the filled jugs. "How long did I sleep?" he asked.

"Not so long. I didn't bring all that—it is a gift from Vo."

"Is she here?"

"No. The gift came by unusual means, but it is safe. We will have plenty."

Sudharma didn't ask any more questions. He drank some of the rehydration fluid but he threw it up at once.

"That's all right," John said. "Wait awhile, and then just sip it." He dampened one of his dirty shirts to take care of the mess. Afterward he looked after his wounds—no sign of infection so far—and changed into clothes that, though reeking with old sweat, at least were not snake-bitten or stiffened with dried blood.

When the back of the van grew too warm, they went to the shade of the reptile trees. Sudharma had to be supported to walk, and barely managed the distance. He could keep down fluids if they were given slowly, but could not take food at all, even a moistened crumb. The diarrhea was more frequent and as thin as tinted water. By afternoon John had to clean him up after each bout.

Rescue from the town might come as soon as the next evening, but their arrival in itself would hardly help Sudharma, unless, by foresight, they had thought to bring the means of intravenous feeding. He would have to make it all the way back home to reach the instruments and expertise required to treat a novel poison. Fervently John hoped that Vo would send some better rescue first, a new creature that could cleanse the blood and heal the bowels. And though his great-uncle could have no influence on the aiyi, being a very different kind of spirit, still he took the wounded strap out of his bag, freed it from its self-adhesive bandage, and held it, still in its tight roll, against his heart.

He sat watching the horizon until the sun went down. Then he said Sudharma's name. Sudharma didn't wake, not even when shaken. His breath was steady and his pulse was not alarming, but he would not respond. John thought of carrying him, but the muscles in his arms and back and shoulders had all stiffened up from the exertions of the day before, and even the hoisting seemed too much to manage. He shifted him onto a blanket, and gripping the corners, he dragged it off toward the van.

He heard the approach first, a rumble with a rhythm to it, and felt it too, a trembling in the ground. Then the thing coming toward them charged over a hill and showed itself, large and with many legs, faster than anything moving on feet ought to be. It was the crawler. Reflections on its back and sides repeated the orange and blue wash of the sky. It slowed itself smoothly, opened up a deep hole in the place its face was not, and tilted the rim of the crater forward as it reached them to cover and trap them both.

He was still holding up the blanket by its corners, but in the dark he felt the weight lifted away from it. When he emerged into the great hall, Sudharma was not with him. A long block in the shape of a coffin was rising up out of the floor, and John ran to it, finding Sudharma still asleep beneath the transparent top.

"What happened to him?" Vo said.

"He drank poisoned water."

"Well, that was silly."

"Is he going to live?"

"Of *course* he's going to live! His brain isn't damaged at all. He's just anesthetized while he gets a couple of organs repaired. You people aren't very good at healing on your own, you know."

At these words all the horror that had weighed on him sublimed away. His heart felt whole. And finally becoming aware of her as a warm and living presence, not merely as an effigy made to deliver bad news in a nightmare, he caught her up and kissed her. She responded willingly enough, but he felt she was indulging his exuberance, not sharing it. Then she held him at arm's length and looked him in the eyes. "And what have *you* done to yourself?"

"I was bitten, and a little sunburned, but I will be fine." Then he realized he no longer felt pain from any of his injuries. The scabbed wounds in his arm were gone, and his fingers could tell even through his shirt that the ones in his side were healed too.

"Yes, I know, all that's already fixed. I mean your mind, you ridiculous person. Why did you fall in love?"

"For once you are mistaken," he said gently. "That kiss was an expression of relief and happiness—and gratitude, of course—not some escalation of romance. I am very fond of you, but I am not in love with you."

"Of course not with me! Why did you fall in love with *him*?"

John felt the breath had been knocked out of him. It was true and he knew it at once, but he found himself saying by reflex, "No, I am not . . ." Then he gave up, because anyone could see that it was hopeless—hopeless to deny love and hopeless to pursue it. Sudharma had never shown the least awareness of him as a man.

She was peering at him as if baffled by some mystery, the answer to which was written in small letters on his forehead. "You don't always know what's going on inside you, do you?"

"Hardly ever, it would seem."

She sighed, giving up the matter as beyond her understanding. "Well, from now on, if you need me, just say my full name. *Isavo Lizet.*" This time she pronounced it with exaggerated care and he could clearly hear the space between the two names. "I'm going to make sure I always hear that, so I can help. He can say it too. I don't think you two take care of yourselves very well."

"I suppose I must concede the truth of that." It meant that the aiyi would listen to him all the time, and watch too. But he was sure that they already did. They had been watching when he put Blue's water in a crate, and that was how their creature had known where to look for it.

"Anyway, as long as you're here, do you want to visit?"

"Not while he's lying there unconscious." He should have been appalled at the idea, but there was never any point in being surprised by Vo's behavior; it would take up energy he didn't have. "And not while he's here and awake, either." Then a thought struck him. "How far off are our rescuers from the town?"

"They'll be here the day after tomorrow, in the morning."

"And how long until Sudharma heals?"

"Three hours."

"I am sorry to ask this, but would you make sure they don't see you here? And don't tell the governor or anybody else you meet that you saved us?"

"Of course," she said.

"I asked because I worry about what the people in the town would think, if they knew parts of him had been remade by Earth. They are afraid of you. They would not be if they knew you, but I don't think any argument from me would be believed."

"It doesn't matter what they think."

It occurred to him for the first time that he had asked a lover for help, which was not right conduct; worse, he had accepted her ongoing protection, which would complicate putting an end to the relationship when it had run its natural course. Though in principle the errors were serious, he thought he had done no harm to her. Vo could not be bound—there was nothing in her heart that one could fix a rope to. No relationship could trouble her by ending, because the aiyi would soothe any feeling of loss. For his own part, though he knew his time with Vo would always have a special vividness in memory—she could never fade into the background as just one of many women visited—he was confident that if she stopped opening the door for him, he would not disgrace himself with his response. He only wondered what had led her to rush all this way when he asked her for help. Certainly, it had cost her nothing; whatever medicines she had given Sudharma did not, as in an Essian clinic, come out of a limited supply, but flowed from an inexhaustible spring. And she was exactly as content here as she had been in the riverbed, since the aiyi was with her wherever she went. Was it only that?

"Would you have come if someone else had asked for help?" he asked.

She looked bewildered by the question. "Who else would ever call to me?"

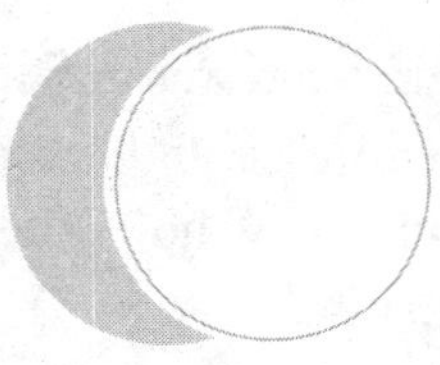

CHAPTER THIRTEEN

They came home in the afternoon. John put down his suitcase in the hall, unwilling to deal with its contents yet. He glanced at the refrigerator—surely a museum of mold by now—and didn't open it for the same reason.

Sudharma went directly to his room. He was physically in perfect health now, but his mind no doubt remembered what it had been through. It would be wise to wait to speak to him until the memory receded, John thought. But he knew this scrupulous concern was no more than a costume for the same dread that had kept the door of the refrigerator shut. There would never be a proper time to declare love. There would never be a better chance of being answered in the same kind. He should make his case, and then at least it would be over.

He did wait until both of them had showered, however. In Vo's crawler they had ceased to stink, and all the dirt and oils and residues of three weeks without bathing had evaporated or sublimed. But he would not feel clean until he scrubbed himself with soap and water, and probably Sudharma felt the same.

He tapped gently at Sudharma's door.

"Come in."

John thought he heard a note of resignation in Sudharma's voice, as if he knew what was coming. He was sitting at the edge of his bed. To sit on it with him would be to presume too much, so John settled for leaning against the dresser. That put him too far away—he would seem detached—but to change his place now would reveal that he was nervous, so he stayed as he was and began.

"I think you may know what I'm going to say."

"I have an idea."

John couldn't put a name to what was in Sudharma's tone, but it was not a welcome. He should excuse himself and leave. But he had to be sure.

"Recently—or really, I don't know how long—I have begun to feel—"

"John. What you want can't be."

"Oh," he said; and something in him that had hoped despite all reason—some bird-shaped brightness lying at the center of his chest—curled up its many legs, shed its clear wings, became compact and heavy as a stone.

"I've never felt that kind of love for anyone, and I believe I never will."

"But that doesn't matter at all! I said I love you—well, I didn't say it, but I meant to—only to be honest, not to demand the same from you, as if it were some kind of trade. Fair exchange is a requirement in the marketplace—to give love in the cabin is its own reward. I am content to visit you in any way you will allow. I don't need love of equal weight piled on the other pan of the balance."

"I think maybe you do," Sudharma said. "But in any case, it is impossible. I value your friendship greatly, and your company. I hope I will not lose them. But I won't visit with you." His voice was gentle and that made it worse.

"Is this about leaving a good soul?"

"Yes."

"Visiting would be a . . . sin, or something, because we aren't married?"

Sudharma seemed, for the first time since John had known him, to be at a loss for words. "You might say that is part of the problem," he managed.

"If you believe that, then why don't you have a spouse?"

"In part, because I could not feel love for one—though it was the strong opinion of my family that I should have married anyway."

"Have you never thought that exploration of desire might lead to love?"

"It isn't like that. Not falling in love is simply part of who I am."

"So, then," John said bitterly, "it's just another thing translation might change?"

Sudharma's back straightened. "I certainly hope not." He looked at John with a new wariness. "Please understand this is a very disturbing conversation to have with the man who may soon hold my brain in his hands."

That was not what he had meant at all. He didn't want to alter Sudharma for his own convenience—the idea was horrifying. He wanted him to stay just as he was forever. If that meant they could have nothing more than friendship, it would be no price at all to pay.

"How could you think such a thing of me?" he said. He wanted to say more, but he knew he had argued far too much already. He had received a clear refusal; he should have accepted it at once. And as much as he felt wounded by Sudharma's lack of trust, he knew that he had wronged him too. He had acted as if love could justify making demands on the one that he loved. That was part of the ideology of marrying people, he realized. Living surrounded by them had corrupted him. He had held the door fast against marriage, but it had slipped in through a window.

"I will go get us some groceries," he said. "If I hurry we can still have dinner before sunset."

He walked to the store seeing nothing around him, passed through the aisles in a trance with his basket empty. He stopped short in front of an unfamiliar kind of squash, round in shape and deeply pleated. It was very like one of the spherical candles found everywhere in the desert around town, except that the green of its skin was rich and deep. He didn't know how to cook it. He could ask somebody in the store, but he didn't feel like hearing whatever thoughts about him would be in their voices.

He could leave now and go to the crawler. Or no, he couldn't, because the only van that would start for him was sitting ruined far away, but he could walk out of the store and call Vo's name. He could, in fact, go away with her and never come back to the town. But he had told Sudharma he would make dinner.

He took a firm grip on his squirming mind and held it still until it made a plan. He hadn't started any beans to soak, but he had lentils at home, which would cook quickly from their dried state. He selected tomatoes, zucchini, ears of corn, hot red peppers and sweet green ones. He would make a curry. On impulse he took some fresh basil leaves to put into it. They were not an herb Sudharma ever used in his own cooking, and possibly there was a reason for that, but the scent of them had always intrigued John. And he doubted Sudharma was speaking to him, so if the experiment failed he would not have to hear criticism.

He paused with the leaves in his hand and revoked the thought. Sudharma was not, in fact, prone to complain about food, but easily pleased. Even if John's heart was broken, that was no reason to be unjust.

When he was nearly out the door he turned around and took one of the pleated balls. It was a squash; he would figure it out. Like the snake's head, he would cut it open and find out what was inside.

At home, he unpacked his groceries onto the counter and stared at them, feeling a vast disinclination to begin. The doorbell rang, and with a mixture of relief and dread he went to answer it.

"Is it true you killed a snake-tree with your bare hands?" Piro asked.

"No. I used a knife."

"We want to hear everything," Iren said. "And I want my library back."

"Come in then. We can talk while I make dinner. But I want something from you first." He led them to the kitchen and held up the squash. "Can either of you tell me what to do with this?"

"You can roast it," Iren said. "Don't try to peel it—just cut it in half lengthwise, scoop out all the seeds, and make thick slices."

"All right. Give me a few minutes to get started, and then we will talk."

At Iren's suggestion the two biologists moved to stand on the other side of the counter, where they could speak and listen without being in the way. John replaced the piece of filtering cloth over the faucet with a fresh one. He rinsed the lentils, drowned them in a pot of water, and put it on the stove to boil. Then he scrubbed the green skin of the squash and got out a knife. "Which way is lengthwise on a sphere?"

"Cut along the trough between two ribs."

The rind was tougher than he expected. "Are you sure I shouldn't peel this?"

"Trust me. The skin will be soft when it's roasted."

"Can't be harder to cut through than a snake-tree's scales," Piro said.

"No." John pushed the knife the rest of the way through the vegetable body, then retrieved a spoon to scoop out seeds with. He saw that they were both impatient, so he started. "The matter was simple. We had to have water, and the snake-tree was guarding the only source. I padded my arm as best I could, let it bite me, cut its mouth open, and stabbed into its throat until it died."

Iren and Piro exchanged a glance; they were amazed. The killing had been impressive, he supposed, even if the triumph of it had been overshadowed by the greater quantity of water brought them by the aiyi's creatures. The really important thing that he had done was to observe which way a lizard faced, and he could tell no one about that.

"Were you badly hurt?" Iren asked.

"Not too badly," he said, holding out his arms to show them. He had asked Vo to restore some signs of puncture to his arms and leg, partly so he wouldn't be suspected of making up the incident, and partly because it seemed right to him to bear the scars of it; but even so he had to downplay the injuries.

Piro, standing by the table, leaned forward to see. "How did you run out of water in the first place?"

John described the walk up the canyon with Blue while he sliced up the squash. The slices had a pleasing shape, a curve with a zigzag edge, like segments of the flaming aureole that children draw around the sun. He coated each one with oil. "What spices go with this?" he asked Iren.

"The dish would welcome oregano, sage, or thyme if you have them, but salt and black pepper are all you need."

"I have four out of the five." He took out salt and spices from the cabinet, sprinkled them over the squash, and put it in the oven. Then he put flour into a bowl with oil and salt, trickled in water, and began to mix the dough for roti. "On the second day, we came to a place where little trees lined the dry riverbed. Blue became excited, ate a berry from one, and fell unconscious. We were at the very limit of our water supply and had to leave him there."

"Tell me you got a sample of the trees," Piro said.

"No." John realized this failure would require a better explanation. "They were mammal-trees, so something might have shown up to defend them. Also, I thought they were important to Blue in some way—a kind of sacred grove, perhaps—and so I didn't want to desecrate them."

"Well," Iren said, "the one reason is only prudent, and the other speaks to your perceptive and considerate nature; but I could wish you were more reckless and more heedless and less kind. Those trees may have been the parents of basket-men."

A little blade of ice formed in his chest, beneath his sternum. He should never have told them about the trees. On the ride back to town, Sudharma had only told their rescuers that the journey was a failure and they had learned nothing. John had followed his lead then, allowing their mutual reticence to be put down to illness, injury, and exhaustion—which was not far from the truth, for all that they had slept and rested in the crawler; there was a deep weariness in them that couldn't be relieved so quickly. He should have used the same excuse to shut the door to Iren and Piro. Now he would have to repair his mistake, and quickly.

"Oh, that couldn't be," he said, keeping his eyes on the hot peppers he was cutting up and trying to make his voice sound unconcerned. "On Scythia a berry isn't a casing for seed, is it? It could only be a way for plants to feed their offspring. We've seen the food bodies basket-men eat, which are scaled to the needs of a creature their size. What good could it do to add a tiny fruit to that?"

"You have a point," Iren admitted, "though nature is often surprising."

John went to the sink to wash off the juice of the peppers, and to hide his face while he did. As he was drying his hands on a towel he turned, struck by another thought. "Also, food made for him by his own species wouldn't cause him to pass out. Probably I misinterpreted his mood—he wasn't excited, but agitated that he hadn't found what he was looking for. In despair he ate something he shouldn't have and suffered for it." He knew this was unlikely; Blue had not been out of food. But Iren and Piro didn't know that, and he could ask Sudharma not to tell.

"Maybe you're right," Piro said.

John thought he had dampened their interest. Now it was time to move on to a safer subject. "We came back to our van after sunset and found it ruined."

Piro listened to his description of the scene with growing horror. "That sounds like what the tumblers did to our equipment in the first colony."

"What do tumblers look like?"

"They're mammals. Mostly small and do their harm by chewing. About one in fifteen is a big brute that knows how to use rocks to smash things."

"That fits the damage I saw."

"If you really ran into tumblers or their desert equivalent, we need to find out what their range is and stay well out of it. Those things are the devil."

"We should talk about that later, Piro, but first I would like to hear the saga of the snake-tree. Every detail, if you please, John, and if you can manage unrhymed hexameter, that is traditional."

"I have to stir-fry now, but I will tell you—in prose." He turned to the stove and raised his voice so they could hear. The oil heated as he climbed the steep part of the path, began to shimmer as he reached the top. He added spices as he scaled the canyon wall. He killed the first snake, put in the tomatoes, and covered the pan. Then he turned back to them. "I know it was not a good plan and I'm lucky to have survived. I still wonder if there was a better way I didn't see."

"You had rope," Piro said. "If the snake's head was enough wider than its body, I might have tried to lasso it. You could have pulled it out to full length, held it there by the rope, and used the knife when it couldn't bite you."

"Lasso? What is that?"

Piro explained while John was putting the rest of the vegetables into the pan.

"I suppose that might have worked. But whoever would come up with such an idea?"

"A person from a culture that keeps livestock," Iren said. "Essians have only seafood, Piro. Throwing a lariat at a fish would get you nothing but a wet rope. Anyway, I doubt that even someone who has practiced could lasso a snake. It would see the rope coming and dodge, or it would slip out while you're trying to snug up the noose. If you'd like to make a wager of it, you can have a hundred tries."

"In any case," John said, "I don't have the skill, and I was in no condition to learn it by trial and error. I think I must have been close to heatstroke, or I would have seen the second snake coming."

He checked on the squash while they exclaimed. The vegetable wasn't done yet, but in a little while the biologists were. He confirmed that, yes, he did mean a second snake from the same tree, and explained how he had killed it.

"I don't suppose," Iren said with poorly disguised eagerness, "that after all that you were in any state to think of getting a genetic sample."

"Not one to bring home, but I did feed the library some blood. I showed the snake-tree to the library too, though it was in a disassembled state by then. Let me get my bag."

He retrieved it from the shelf in the hall and put it on the counter. He took out the packet of samples and the library and handed them to Iren. They and Piro examined the illustration of the snake-tree, then called up a summary of its genetic information and pored over it for some time. Then Iren, by some means John didn't see, caused the library to display a video of the tree and the dead snakes.

"I don't know if you can tell," he said, "but the tree was lightning-damaged. I thought that might have been the reason that it grew a second snake."

"A shrewd hypothesis—though one can also see the value to the tree of having two moving limbs instead of one, if there is food and water to support two. There might well be species that do that." Iren pointed with their chin toward his open bag. "That canvas has seen some battle."

"It was part of the padding I used to protect my arm."

"Was the strap lost?"

"Not lost, but too damaged to use anymore."

"May I see it?" they asked. They didn't know what a soul was, he thought. He could not hand them his great-uncle's skin, lest they find out later what it was and become horrified; he would have to find some excuse. But then they added, "Should I say 'it' or 'he'?"

"Either," he said with relief. "The strap is 'it,' the soul is 'he,' they are the same, so either."

Seeing that he still hesitated, Iren said, "I'm a biologist, John. I handle dead things all day. Rarely the remains of human beings, but it's the same principle."

"Yes, then, you may look, but please be careful. It is near to tearing in half."

"I will treat the soul as carefully as my own," they said, accepting the rolled strap in their upturned palm. "Maybe a little more so." They unwound it slowly, examining the damage. "Well done, old warrior," they breathed; and then looking up at John, they asked, "Would you let me mend him for you? It would be my honor."

"I can stitch it up myself. Well enough that I can handle it without fear of tearing it all the way through. I know I'll never dare to use it as a strap again."

"I'll give him some help to support the weight. But you'll be able to wear him—I have no doubt of that."

Their eagerness was strange in an offworlder, and he didn't know what to make of it; but tears stung his eyes at the prospect of having his great-uncle over his shoulder again. "That would be a comfort."

"Is the bag itself of sentimental value?"

"No, not really."

"I will have a new one made, then. I will have to have the proper threads made, too, which may take time. You should keep him until then. He wouldn't be as happy if he stayed with me, I think."

John considered what he knew of his great-uncle. "Not if he knew you were celibate." Immediately he worried that this remark was impolite; but Iren laughed. He took back the strap and wound it in another bandage for protection. Then he uncovered the dough and rolled out roti.

"So, Piro," Iren said, "I think everything we've heard tonight tends to the same conclusion: we must learn more about the desert to the east, and soon."

Piro nodded. "I'm up for some driving."

"You went out alone the last four times. It's my turn to make some discoveries."

"Don't act like it was my idea to be the designated explorer," Piro said. "You kept having things to do in town."

"Not anymore."

"You sure there isn't something here you need to fix?"

"Do you think you can set me a task, old man?"

There was a warning in Iren's voice John didn't understand. But it made Piro sigh and give way. "All right, fine, it's your turn. Happy hunting."

"Good. I will start, then, by retraveling the intrepid doctor's route and finding his sacred grove."

"What?" John said, and then to cover the true reason for the outburst, he said with a fear that was not at all feigned, "The tumblers—if that's what they are—may still be there."

"He's got a point," Piro said. "It isn't safe, especially not alone."

"You know you can't come with me on such a long trip—what if some new pest invaded all our fields while we were both gone? And I trust in my own wits to keep my skin intact. But, John, if you would like to lend your memory and resourcefulness to the expedition, I would be glad of the company."

John barely heard what Iren was saying. He had ruined everything, betrayed Sudharma's trust, and for no reason. He had been so preoccupied by his distress, he hadn't even thought of lying about the grove's existence. No, it was worse than that. He had been flattered by the two biologists' attention; they had treated him like one who has accomplished a great deed, and that had made him want to tell them everything.

Then, belatedly grasping that he had been offered a chance to leave town for some time, he considered it. Iren would find the grove even if he stayed home—they had only to go to the ruined van, then walk along the watercourse—so it could do no harm for him to come along. And for as long as the journey lasted, he wouldn't have to face Sudharma every day. "Yes, if you insist on going, I will come with you. When will you leave?"

"The sooner the better, from my point of view. But I'm sure you will want time to rest and recover."

"Can you leave tomorrow?"

"I would be glad to, if that's what you want."

"You should both stay for dinner. You will be doing us a favor—this squash is too much for the two of us. With that, and if I make some extra flatbread, the curry ought to stretch."

Piro said he was expected at home. Maybe it was because John's hands had held a soul before they touched the roti; maybe it was because Laura was—without a doubt—a more accomplished cook; maybe Piro just preferred the company of his own family. In any of those cases John took no offense. But he was grateful that Iren had accepted. He would have to tell Sudharma what he'd done, but at least he could put it off until they were alone.

John tapped softly at the bedroom door to signify that dinner was ready. He wondered if Sudharma would, like Tali, decline to appear, but it was not long until the door opened.

"Thank you, John."

"Iren is joining us."

The dinner went well enough. John wasn't satisfied with the experimental curry, but the other two both praised it, and proved their sincerity by the amount they ate. Iren was full of questions about what they had seen in the eastern deserts, and having already told his own story, it was natural for John to let Sudharma talk. When Iren mentioned the trip they would start on with John the next day, Sudharma did not react.

Afterward, Iren excused themself quickly, citing a need to pack. John got up to clear the dishes, but before he could escape back to the kitchen, Sudharma stopped him.

"John. I believe I misunderstood you earlier. I do trust you."

"You shouldn't," he said, standing with a plate in each hand. "I've done something terrible." He sat back down and everything came out—his indiscretion and the reasons for it and his failed attempts to mitigate the damage. His eyes were pointed at the table all the time he spoke. Finally, and with difficulty, he looked up. Sudharma's face was troubled but his voice was not unkind.

"I asked you not to read the trees' genes. I never said to pretend they don't exist."

"Doesn't the one concealment imply the need for the other?"

"Perhaps, but even so I should have settled on a story with you, so you would have it ready to your lips when need arose. Anyone can see that you are not a natural deceiver."

"And yet I seem to lie and hide things all the time."

"This world doesn't fit you. It bends you out of your true shape. And yet truth has a way of coming out when you're around, which I must learn to take into account." He put his palms flat on the table. "Well. Between the pair of us we've made a mess of this, but the basket-man life cycle would never have remained secret forever, and we are still in the lucky position of opposing an evil that has yet to manifest. We will just have to keep our eyes open for ways to make sure that it never does."

"I'm sorry I'll be gone for so long. I agreed to go with Iren because I worried about them running off alone toward whatever spilled our water. They're as reckless as you are, I fear."

"See how they manage in the desert first, and then judge."

"I think Laura would be happy to send meals to you while I'm away."

"You know very well I can cook for myself. And I have no other pressing obligations, at least until another basket-man appears."

"Well. I am sorry to leave you with whatever is in the refrigerator. I have to pack—and now I think of it, I have to wash the clothes I'm going to pack—then get up early in the morning, so I won't have time to clean it out. I'm afraid the mold will be horrible."

"Will it? Whatever decomposes native vegetables surely couldn't stomach ours. Do you suppose Terran spores hitchhiked here on the ships, or rode in cold-sleep with the colonists?"

"I have no idea."

"Let's look now, and find out the worst."

Carefully, John opened the refrigerator. It was gleaming clean, and empty except for a single dish. He read the note attached: the food came from Zohia. He could see that it had mushrooms in it, and cauliflower, which she must have thawed especially for them, since it was out of season; both were forbidden to Sudharma. "We should really start locking the door," he said.

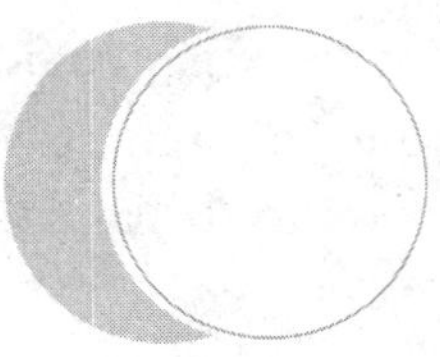

CHAPTER FOURTEEN

In the morning he made roti again and ate one with Zohia's cauliflower and mushrooms, which in fact were very good. He left two for Sudharma and took the last, along with Zohia's gift, out to the van. Iren had already eaten breakfast but was glad to have them, cooled to the temperature of the air-conditioning, as a lunch.

They talked very little. He stared out the windows at the landscape, which still resembled the one Laura had led him through more than it did the greater strangeness of the eastern deserts. It was familiar now, and legible, each plant calling its corresponding animal at once to mind. He recognized the living nests of birds growing on tree branches, and the small holes drilled by candlelarks in columns. Even in the harsh light of the day, the shape of the land was beautiful.

Iren sat in the driver's seat, wearing a blue button-up shirt and brown trousers, working the pedals with a rugged boot. They had tossed their wide-brimmed hat onto the dashboard, but, finding themself irritated by its pale reflection in the windshield, plucked it off and stowed it underneath their seat instead. For most of the day they let him watch the world go by in silence, glancing over now and then with a slight smile. The sun was low in the sky when they asked, "Have you made better friends with the desert, then?"

"What do you mean?"

"When you first came to Scythia you seemed dismayed. I thought . . . well, that you might love a great variety of different people but one landscape only, that was my impression."

"Was it that obvious?"

"Probably not, to most people, but I love this world and so am sensitive to any slight against it."

John couldn't remember any time they could have gauged his response to the desert. He thought the observation must have come to them from Piro, who had caught his first reaction to the landscape, when he was too dazed from cold-sleep to guard his expression.

"You're right, I was dismayed. And I do like it better now. I suppose it just took time to see it properly."

They smiled fully then, and left him in peace to look out the windows. As he did he thought that what he'd said was not quite true. The stone like lace, the rings of gods, the layered walls of the stone canyon, all had made their arguments for Scythia's grandeur, but he might have been insensible to all of them if he had not been in a blissful and receptive state, with love not yet admitted, and so not yet understood to be impossible. Now the towering cones and columns, standing each alone, seemed to reflect his hopelessness and make it monumental and austere. When he looked at them his heart felt calm and empty, and he was glad to be away from home.

At night Iren slept out under the stars, in a quilted pouch of amethyst and cobalt squares that sleeved their body all the way from neck to foot. John considered taking blankets and doing the same, but remembering what had happened to the other van, he decided to lie between crates in the back with the dividing door securely locked.

Iren was a confident and daring driver, and discovering that John was less so, they insisted on driving from dawn to dusk; they would turn the wheel over to him only grudgingly for an hour or two's rest in the afternoon. In this way the van covered distance quickly, so that it was only lunchtime on the second day when the first lava cones appeared. His journey with Sudharma had seemed long, but the distance was not far at all, a single stitch along the waistband of the world. Blue had made the way slow by walking it, by clambering up hills and searching for food. John missed him, and wished—although with little hope the wish would be fulfilled—that they would find him live and healthy when they reached the sacred grove.

That evening, when the light was golden on the hills, Iren stopped next to a tangle of insect bushes. They retrieved a backpack from beneath the seat and slung it over their left shoulder as they lowered their foot to the stirrup. "Come on. You can help me—then we'll be done faster."

"What are we doing?" he said when he had come around the van to their side.

"We are setting up traps for invertebrates." They opened their pack and took out a long piece of thin metal, sharpened along the bottom edge and flanged along the top, so that in cross section it had the shape of a nail. They stood this on the ground and pounded it in with a mallet until it stood firm. Then, with a trowel, they dug a cylindrical hole at one end and fitted a plastic cup into it. They handed him a second trowel. "Now, you do likewise at the other end."

The hole he made was too large and too ragged, but they shrugged that off. "Just put the cup in and then fill the extra space with soil or gravel. It will hold well enough." When he had done this they poured liquid from a bottle into each cup. "Finished."

"How does it work?"

"Simply enough. A creature wanders up to the steel barrier"—they demonstrated this with one hand, walking on its thumb and fingertips—"tries to go around, and when it comes to the end, falls in." They dipped their fingers down into the cup, but not far enough to touch the fluid. "There the killing solution makes sure the captives don't escape or eat each other. Of course, some invertebrates will just fly over the barrier, but considering its simplicity the trap is quite effective."

Together they made two more traps in the area, well spaced apart. Iren showed each one to the library, which, they explained, would record the locations so they could retrieve the dead insects on the way home. Then they went back to the van, took out two jugs of water, and left them together on the sand, showing this arrangement to the library also. "If things go very badly and we have to walk back, this cache of water will sustain us."

"What would we drink for the rest of the way home?"

"We're within a day's walk of the river here. We could find that, and then follow it right back to town."

After that they stopped often to dig: at the bases of hills where the insect-shrubs gathered, between the rooted branches of a braced column, in the shadow of a lava cone at sunset, and in undistinguished places chosen for no obvious reason. Then as the sun went down on the third day, Iren stopped the van and stared ahead and didn't get out. The first ring of gods was in sight, a black silhouette cut from the orange sky. Iren started the motor again and drove past it slowly. "Like something remembered from the other world," they said.

The next morning they sighted a ring of five—all standing, though one leaned its head against another's trunk—the tallest of which had no leaves, only a large empty hole in the back of the head. Iren drove toward it at once. "That one has no candlehawk to object to me." They walked toward it cautiously, with frequent glances at the ground to see whether some fierce and numerous insect might be coming to repel them, until they stood at the very center of the ring. They turned to look at all the gods, examining each one for a long time. When they had completed their rotation, they knelt down and made a trap there.

On the fifth day they came to John and Sudharma's van. Iren pulled right up to it, got out, and without comment on the devastation, looked under the hood. With a flashlight in one hand and plastic tweezers in the other, they peered around the tattered wires and feces-streaked devices in the engine compartment.

"What are you looking for?" John asked, coming to look over their shoulder.

"A way to get a DNA reading without smearing shit on my library. And here it is." From a crack in a fluid tank they pulled a little tuft of reddish fur that bent and straightened in the wind, and would have blown away if tweezers had not pinched it tight. Taking the library from their pocket, they pressed the fur between the covers, waited and then opened it. "Score one for Piro—that's a near relation of the tumbler. I suppose I'll never be so lucky as to find they're still nearby."

John could think of nothing less desirable, and would have said so, except that they slammed the hood shut so abruptly it startled him out of speaking. They settled their pack over both shoulders, tightened the strap, and by climbing from stirrup to running board to hood to roof, attained the summit of the wreck. From this high point they scanned the land around them, then took a large pair of binoculars out of their pack and went over it slowly again. When they lowered the binoculars their face was disappointed. "Well, perhaps I will attempt a search when we get back. For now we should get started up that hill."

"Surely leaving our van here is begging for disaster?"

"We're not leaving it, we're taking it. Get in and I will drive us up that slope."

They were as good as their word. Though the uneven ground bounced them around in their seats, it never threatened to make the van overturn. Several times they lost traction, but Iren calmly braked, rolled down a little way, and started up again along a different course. Once they had made it to more gently sloping ground they traveled quickly. As the canyon walls rose up around them John said, "You won't be able to turn around in here."

"I'll go down backward if I have to," Iren said. "Show me the place you climbed up, when we reach it."

He pointed out the waterfall and then the spot nearby that he had scaled. Iren slowed down to look, ducking down so they could peer up through the side window and see the top. "I'm not bad at a scramble when I have to be, but I wouldn't care to try that."

He didn't want to talk about it, and Iren didn't press him to. They drove the van right up onto the plain and stopped it in sight of the sacred grove. There was no trace of Blue. He might have died and been carried off by animals. He might have revived and moved on.

Iren walked up to the nearest tree slowly, watchful but unafraid. They crouched down and scraped a little of the bark onto the open library. They showed him the result: it was the same species as basket-men.

Iren slept out on the plain that night, while John lay restless in the van. The next day, he thought, they would dig up a tree to take home, or cut off a stick figure that could be persuaded to take root. But in the morning they hardly even glanced at the grove before rolling up their quilted bed-sleeve, stowing it in the back, and climbing to the driver's seat. John rode back down the canyon concealing his relief. Humans would learn to propagate the plant stage of a basket-man someday—perhaps they would even find seeds, or be given them—but at least the threat was not immediate.

When they had descended, Iren said, "Let's see if I can figure out which way all your tumbler-kin went." They walked around the area, examining the ground, until they had worked their way some hundred paces from the ruined van. "A fucking waste of time," they said when they returned. "Wind has long since effaced any tracks."

"You use that word quite fluently, for a novice."

"What word? 'Effaced'?"

"'Fuck.' I heard you try it for the first time, remember."

"Oh, I've been using it since I first heard it—out in the desert, and among friends. English swearing is adorable. What you heard was a test to see whether desert Iren might be able to come indoors once in a while. A mixed success, alas.—Without tracks it will be difficult to find our quarry, but I will make a little search."

They drove south for half an hour, then north for a full one, looking for high vantages from which to scan for tumblers. John thought it unwise to seek out a creature so destructive, but they brushed off his concern. "Piro's tumblers were afraid of people, and I think yours must be too. They stayed away once you and Sudharma had come back, didn't they? Even when he was incapacitated? In any case, they can't outrun a van."

"One that crawled into the engine would be carried along."

"We won't get close enough for that."

When Iren decided they had gone far enough north, they turned the van to the southwest. From the top of the first hill, they searched the land below and called, "Come look!" Without taking the binoculars from their eyes, they slipped the library out of their pocket with one hand and passed it to him, sliding two fingers between the covers to fan it open. The screen was drawing a thicket of waxy plants, each one shaped like a column with a little bulbous head between two upraised branches. The shape suggested a man in miniature, with two arms flung up in excited greeting. Most of these figures were stuck individually into the ground, but here and there one would balance on the hand of another. The arms of the upper ones reached nearly to the shoulder of the human figure that the library, as usual, provided for scale.

"How do you know it is the right species?" John said.

"Look." They gave him the binoculars, pointed out the location of the thicket, and waited until he found it in the lenses. "See that double-height one near the center? Look in front and to the right of that."

"I can't see anything."

"About a meter in front and just a little to the right. You'll see a plant with the right arm held higher than the left. Look down at the base of it."

John couldn't find the plant that they described. After some time of fruitless searching and a repetition of the same instructions, he realized he had started with the wrong double. With that confusion sorted out, he found what they meant him to see: a red tail sticking out from behind a trunk. It was the color of the fur that Iren had tweezed from the van's engine.

"I wish I could get a sample of those plants, but I fear the tumbler-cousins might defend their nests. Even so, there's no doubt in my mind—we've discovered the first succulent mammal."

Iren was elated all day and into the next. Someday the tumbler-kin might run amok and end civilization on Scythia, but for now they had discovered something interesting and new. He could feel their excitement every time they stopped the van to check a trap—pouring the contents of the cups through a mesh strainer, tipping out the captured animals into a cylinder of alcohol, screwing down its lid, and writing the location on its label with a pen. While they were doing this, John picked up the water they had left out on the ground and stowed it in the van.

When they had come back to the land of lava cones, Iren picked up the second cup from a trap, strained out the killing fluid, and then stopped. They took tweezers from their pocket to pick something up, then putting the strainer down on the ground, strode over to show him.

His eyes could not make sense of it at first: a tangle of thin stems and tiny leaves. Then he saw the twelve legs hanging down beneath it. "Is it infested with a parasite?"

"No, this is something new. It is an animal, but the plants that are its offspring grow upon its back, giving it camouflage—and look, they are in bud! It is the closest thing we've found on Scythia to an animal that gives live birth, like cows and rats and you and me." They opened their library and showed the creature to it. "Oh, I wish I had this living! Where were you going, little mother, with your babies on your back? And what are you? One-off experiment, or emissary of some distant empire?" They glanced at him, grinning widely. "You and I are first to see this. Well, the first *humans* to see this. Except your girlfriend, possibly. I shouldn't put on airs. Still, I'll have the naming of it. And Piro will be exquisitely jealous."

They housed the little monster in a cylinder of its own, marked it with coordinates in tiny numerals, and then, in large letters twice underlined, wrote the word PLATYPUS. In the tone of one who undertakes a difficult but needful duty, they pronounced: "That's settled, then. We'll have to celebrate."

CHAPTER FIFTEEN

That evening, Iren emerged from the back of the van, carrying a stack of pillows and blankets pressed against their chest and brandishing a bottle of clear liquid in their hand. "I nearly thought I might get home with this still full, but we will have to drink it up now. It's the customary way to celebrate success in hunting. In the year 26, Jessamyn the daughter of Jerome braided her hair to hunt the boar with the remaining men, so that her people might be saved; it is not written that they toasted their success with her father's wine, but if any was left then they certainly would have."

John, lightly baffled by this speech, turned the name Jessamyn and the word 'braided' over in his mind and asked, "Was she the first jess?"

"She was not a jess at all—therefore the pronoun. In fact, when the food shortage ended, she married and had children. But she became a justifying myth when my first foreparents were demanding their right to exist."

"And what is in the bottle?"

"The drink is a liquor called *maschet,* distilled from grains with an infusion of the choicest herbs and fruits, chiefly *zhuenfloar* from the mountains and *rudhmeree* from the forest . . . horribly parodied after hours on a medical synthesizer. It's uncouth, but you'll like it once it gets to know you."

They handed him one of the blankets and spread the other one out on the ground. He laid his own out next to theirs, leaving a narrow strip of sand between them.

"Is it quite safe to let our guard down here?" he asked.

"If you mean, will we be overrun by tumblers, I still believe they avoid humans. In case I am wrong, *that*"—they pointed at a braced column nearby—"houses a candle-owl of an especially large and ferocious species, which will kill any small scouts that happen by, and warn us through its indignation if anything too big for it to eat comes near. Why do you think I went to the trouble of killing lizards to toss up to it, but to gain its tolerance and make its belly full enough to stay near home? Those bribes provide us with a warning to retreat. If you meant something else . . ." They paused and studied his face. "You do understand, don't you, that I just want to get drunk and look up at the stars? The jess vow has no insobriety exception."

"I understand, yes."

"Good." They put the pillow down at the top of their blanket, sat on it with crossed legs, and drank. He sat down the same way and they passed him the bottle. The liquor had a pungent smell and it burned going down.

"Aren't you afraid of what people will think we've been doing out here?" he said. "Laura wouldn't even allow me to frequent her house when Piro wasn't around. Yet we've been alone out here for many nights."

"I took a vow, and as a traditional jess I am faithful to it. That puts me above suspicion. No doubt some Zandaheans have other thoughts, but I refuse to shrink my life because of small minds. This is the work I came to Scythia to do, and I can hardly bring a chaperone. Furthermore, as I am the only jess in the world, if I impose strict limitations on myself, those would easily become the rules for every future generation of us. So you see I am pursuing my own inclinations very selflessly. Let people talk if they like. Still, I'm glad to have a little time left out here before I have to go back to all that—the buzz of gossip, the pressure of other people's expectations. What about you? Are you pining to be home soon, or do you wish our travels could go on forever?"

"I am ready for real food, certainly."

"So one would imagine. And yet last time you stopped in town just long enough to cook one meal before signing up for more kilometers of biscuit."

"One and a half. I made that flatbread in the morning."

"Indeed you did. That makes it much more understandable." They drank again, recapped the bottle, and put it down next to him. "I was lost in the woods once, as a child. I was twelve years old—that'd be nine or ten, as the ships reckon age. I was on a camping trip with family and followed the trail to the lake, so I thought. It was an animal track, probably. I must have been frightened at first—they said I'd run a long way from the place where I was lost. I don't remember that. I do remember picking berries and being proud of myself for knowing which ones were safe to eat. I found shelter in the trunk of an old fallen tree, and I was proud of myself for that too, even though the hollow in it wasn't deep enough for me to lie lengthwise. I had to curl up inside the circumference instead, knees against my chest. And I don't remember this at all, but when rescuers came by, calling the name that I had at that time, I wouldn't answer them. I just hid in my tree trunk and waited for them to pass by. If someone hadn't seen my wet socks hung up on a twig I might be curled up in that same tree still.—Well, no, it wasn't large enough; I'd have had to molt it and move to another one every year or two. But you get the idea: I was ensconced and averse to being otherwise, or that's what I've been told.

"I used to wonder: Why did I hide like that? Did I love our Northern woods so much I wanted to sink down my roots and never leave them? Or was there something in me, even then, that made me seek a distance from the family that I loved—the same quirk of the brain that brought me to the South, and here? Or did I just forget, when I had fallen out of place and time, that I hadn't spoken the vow already? Because I was meant for a jess and my name was not yet, did I lose track of the name my parents gave me, and refuse to be seen with my hair unbraided? Eventually I decided that this last idea must be true.

"Then, when we were training to come here, one of the instructors was a man who had worked search and rescue, and I thought I'd tell him what I thought I knew. He listened to my story and said, oh, no, it isn't only jesses—children are just like that. They hide and don't answer to people who call them. Even adults often convince themselves nobody could be looking for them—when of course everyone is—and will assume search drones or helicopters are flying by on some unrelated errand. Some lose the habit of human contact altogether. He had seen a man so lost in a woods-madness that he walked right past the search party, and had to be grabbed by the shoulders and shaken before he would come to himself.

"Isn't that strange? Humans are social animals—no observer could think otherwise. We seek each other out, in nearly every circumstance. Yet take us to the deepest woods, spin us around in that green darkness, let us run till we fall panting on our backs, and *then*. As if something in us said: Very well, I am alone now. It was always going to be this way, and after all I am not sorry. . . ."

He lay awhile thinking of Iren in the woods, a blond, braided child curled up in a tree trunk and at ease there. (Their hair had not in truth been braided yet, but his mind rebelled at the idea of picturing it loose.) It was, somehow, a pleasing image. But the contentment he imagined on their face was nothing like what he had felt when he was stranded in the desert with Sudharma close to death.

"It's not the same," he said. "I wasn't lost. And I wasn't alone, either."

"No, of course. You saved his life."

"I was alone, I suppose, when I went back up to find the water hole, but it hardly felt that way." He took another drink of the *maschet*. It was just as bad as the first time.

"How did it feel?"

"As if what I was doing required everything that I am, and nothing was left over. In town I feel much of myself is not needed."

Iren said nothing. They just looked up at the sky, and so he did too. After a time he asked, "If I see a constellation that I think I know from home, is it the same?"

"Most that I thought I recognized turned out to be false friends. But look there: that red star just over the mountain is Betelgeuse, and the blue one up above it is Rigel. On every world that humans live on, both those stars are bright." They took back the bottle and drank again. "I know land animals on Essius run small. You don't have hunting, I suppose?"

"There's birdcatching. You might call that hunting."

"If you catch the birds by setting traps, that's different."

"By throwing traps, rather. You take a length of cord and tie a weight onto each end. Then when birds are hunting overhead—I don't mean picture-book birds. Essian birds are insects."

"Sure, I know the animal. Hatches as a grub, then turns into a flying predator with eight legs that it uses to snatch prey out of the air?"

"That's the one. And if you take a cord with weights just big enough, and throw it up exactly so, they will mistake the weights for prey, seize one and get wound up, then sink down slowly to the ground. They're very tasty when fried up with full-and-crescent. I tried it a few times when I was out in puddle country, but not enough to get the knack."

"Well, Ischnura has real hunting, which is defined as, you can get killed doing it; and the best game in the North is the night boar; and to hunt night boar you need a hound. That's not a picture-book dog, you understand. They're covered in feathers, long of leg and of back, a long smile with a troubling collection of teeth. When they stretch their necks up they can look you level in the eye, and you'll wish they hadn't. They hunt in pairs in the wild, a female and a male together, and if they're hatched and reared by humans then they'll hunt with us instead. But they're jealous when they're bonded, and therefore in the old days they were given to jesses to raise up—no risk of a hunter's wife being savaged, if the hound-keepers are celibate. Well, and the hounds would keep us in line too, no doubt. It's a tricky bit of history, but I've always felt the romance of it. And so, when I was planning to go south for school, I thought I would hunt with a hound just once before I left. Maybe even then I knew that I would never come back. I took a class on use of spears and signed up to spend ten days in the far-north woods in company with fourteen other fools, all hoping that one deadly animal would chase another one in our direction.—I think it's time to lie down and look up now. But drink first, and you won't have to raise your head to do it later."

They drank deeply in demonstration, then handed him the bottle. He took a sparing mouthful. He didn't much like drinking *maschet* but it was pleasant to have drunk it; it gave a tingling warmth, a sense of lightness and well-being. Iren lay down with the pillow underneath their head and went on with their story. He lay down too and turned onto his side to watch them.

"Our guide annoyed me from the moment he first spoke. He introduced himself as a houndwife, which is an old word for a jess, and not a nice one. He only said it to bamboozle all the Southern tourists in the group, which I support as a matter of principle, but I was standing right there. Then he brought out his hound. She had her winter coat already, snow white with a scattering of black. Her eyes were lakes of liquid copper. She was beautiful. And I could tell at once she wanted all of us dead. They say they train hounds better now than in the year 100, and it must be true—you hardly hear of anybody being killed—but just because she'd learned she shouldn't tear people apart for getting too close to her mate, that didn't mean she understood why not.

"Still, there was something I needed to see and to feel in those eyes, in those feathers. So I watched her—just not from too close a distance. She would raise her plumed tail and speak to the guide with the tiniest twitch of it, looking over her shoulder for his reply, which was a slight adjustment of the head or hand. Then she would circle silently around some patch of cover, scream a battle cry, and crash into it, or else she would move on, with all of us trailing behind, clutching our rented spears.

"For a long time there was nothing, except now and then a tuft of down caught in a tree where the guide said a boar had scratched its back, and I still wonder if he lied to keep our interest up. Finally on the seventh day the hound went stiff next to a patch of brush, and I could tell this time was different. Her head was high and all of the long feathers on her neck were streaming in the wind. For the first time those big copper eyes showed an interest in something other than her mate and murder. She was excited. He inclined his head, and she worked her way around the brush more slowly and more silently than all the earlier times. Even so, the boar heard or smelled her and burst out. She gave chase to it, and we to her—not very far, until it dove into a burrow. A horrible screeching and snarling told us it was fighting the inhabitant, a badger, our guide thought. The grunts and the tearing of flesh we heard afterward told us the boar had won.

"Well, hounds don't go in holes. Don't want to spoil their pretty feathers, I suppose. They wait outside until their prey emerges, or they give up and move on. With a belly full of badger, our quarry could stay in that burrow a long time. We all had lives to get back to, and in order to get home on time we had to turn around that day. So we went away and left it, and it came to me that I was glad. No one wants boar meat when you could have beef—it's hard on the liver and smells like a funeral. Jesses of old hunted them so that their families might survive, but that time is over and that world is lost. I wasn't going to become like them by poking a hole in a night boar, or trailing after some sad animal in love with an alien it can't figure out how to fuck.

"And yet here I am. I woke up and braided my hair before dawn to set off on the hunt, helping my people without asking their permission; I set traps as I went along, like any prudent houndwife; I read tracks, or at least I tried to; I kept safe by understanding of the landscape and its denizens. So what if my ice is sand and my sledge is electrified? So what if the animals I trap will go to stuff taxonomies and not warm coats?" They paused and made a gesture with one hand, as if they grasped at something absent in the air. "So what if I had a third example and forgot. The point is this: those jesses were just doing what their world needed. I was infected with a longing for the forms of it—that's nostalgia, and it will just make you ridiculous. But *this* world needs things from me. If I find them and do them, then we are the same in the way that matters." They shrugged. "It might work for you too, even if your heroic past was last week."

It was a pretty speech, John thought, but they had understood him not at all. He didn't long to be heroic. They were diagnosing an ailment endemic to their own home, like a doctor who gives remedies for proudleaf poisoning on a ship far out at sea.

Then Iren added, quietly, "*He* will need something from you, I think."

John thought that after all their diagnosis was exact.

It came to him that he could just tell them. They had guessed enough that saying the rest could do no harm. And there was something open about them, he thought—at least on this night, at this moment, introspective and beginning to be drunk. If he said to any Zandahean, even Laura, *I love him and I am ashamed*, they would connect those facts in entirely the wrong way, indeed would hardly recognize them as two separate facts. He thought that Iren, for all the harshness of their vow, might simply listen. Yet something thick and sluggish in him wanted only to sink back down to the bottom of the lake and hide from speech. Iren would be sympathetic, probably, but there was nothing they could do to help. In the end they would say *You have to let him go*, which he already knew. There was nothing to be gained by letting words thrash in the depths of him and stir up sediment to cloud his heart.

"Well, don't mind me," they said. "I have old ideas and sometimes they ferment; but I know more than you might think of love and its excesses, and I am a prolific giver of advice that now and then is even helpful, and if you want the matter to be poured out on the sand before we go and never spoken of in town, then it will be—if, of course, your brooding manner is for some reason that can be put into English and not just an indigestion."

"I think your advice would be too austere for me."

"You mean because I'm a jess, I suppose." Iren heaved a theatrical sigh. "Look, you *must* get over this idea that I am languishing for lack of dick, or whatever organ it is you think I covet. I have never been troubled by that kind of interest."

"What, never?"

"Not before the braid nor after. I can tell one person has a pleasant voice, another a kind face, a third a well-lathed form, but none of that makes me want to enclose any part of them. I can look at a beautiful painting too, without experiencing the least impulse to put it up my ass."

"Are all jesses like that?"

"No, by no means. Though some have braided for that reason, as a sign to the world they wished not to be bothered. *I* took the vow in obedience to my memory, and to dispel the not-myselfness that I felt by altering my body, which is a privilege reserved to jesses. Being visibly exempt from sex and marriage was a bonus—though far less helpful in the South. But don't get distracted by *why*. I told you before that we come to the vow for many reasons. All our differences are drawn into the braid and made one."

They propped themself up on one elbow and drank. John sipped more moderately; *maschet* was, after all, not bad, but he thought that Iren's tolerance for alcohol was greater.

"It's irritating," they said. "You thought I was an ascetic denying the flesh and now you'll think I am dispassionate, just because the embedding of organs one into the other holds no appeal. But I have been in love, and been a fool for it. I will tell you the story, though it means none of this will be making it back to town." Iren raised the bottle, waved it vaguely in the air, but didn't drink again at once.

"They were a jess too, that I loved, and their name was Kolennen. Kol," they added, pronouncing this nickname like ships'-English 'call.' "It was on Mumeran, which is the wealthiest and smuggest of the Southern islands. I had come there for an education in biology, and for some treatment at a memory clinic—sadly, both are better in the South.

"In those parts when jesses take the vow they go live in a jess-house for a year, away from sexed people. Some of them stay longer, or leave and come back later, especially as college students. I'd always thought of it as Southern decadence—jesses ought to be part of the world, part of families, not members in some private club. But it's an inexpensive way to live, and I had nothing but a little scholarship and occasional sendings of money from home at a bad exchange rate. The house-fee was low, there was always some kind of a soup on, and someone usually attempted tallowbread, so like the nut-mouse in an eggshell I made do.

"Kol had been there for a year before I came, and not for thrift. They preferred to live with other jesses and had done so since the day they braided, changing to a new place as the whim struck. That house was no less than a hundred years old, so it had stood a minimum of ninety-nine before Kol moved there, but I can't imagine it without them. Whenever I came home from school they were haunting a chair in the common room—a rust-colored one with a slanted back, so they could half-recline and seem aloof from all the talk, while listening to everything."

"There was a picture in your library—I didn't mean to pry, but it kept coming up on the screen. The device seemed to have a mind of its own."

"I noticed you had managed to turn on adaptive navigation. It watches your actions and facial expressions, then guesses what you want or need. It's horrible. I hope it didn't torment you too much."

"Mainly it just baffled me, but that picture caught my eye. A bearded jess, listening to an alien?"

"Not an alien, but a person who had benefited from the power and flexibility jess medicine has attained."

"They had a surgery to get feathers?"

"Feeding plumes. And yes, that was Kol. The bearded one, not the one with the sea-creature memory."

"They were very handsome."

"Yes, everyone thought so." They drank from the bottle again and kept hold of it afterward. "Brilliant as well: they were the star of the engineering school, everybody said, though they never left their chair to study and rarely even seemed to go to class. Kol was weightless, I used to think. As if they never had to put in any effort and no ordinary rules applied. Certainly the vow could never bridle them, not on Mumeran where it is commonly defied the day it is pronounced—"

They broke off and made a little sound of protest in their throat, like someone made to wake on a cold morning who would rather stay under the blankets. "I'm making a mess of this. None of that matters. Let me fall out the window and come in the door again. This is how my story ought to start:

"There was a jess named Kol, and they were like my sibling—which is to say that they were irritating, and when they weren't being irritating they were kind. I was off-balance that first year—a Northerner new to the South, and surrounded by jesses with advanced ideas, I didn't make friends easily. No one there was more opposed to celibacy as an institution than Kol, yet only Kol understood how it was with me: that I was starved of touch and of affection, and that other people got those things from lovers but I must find them in some other way. They were generous with closeness and respectful of the limits on it. They were generous with their opinions too, especially those related to the vow, but I never felt they meant it nastily, or that they wanted me to go against my nature. To Kol, I think, remaking what it meant to be a jess was a great work that everybody ought to be involved in. It made me feel important, and so I let them draw me out in argument once in a while. Eventually we shared a room, since they had developed a complicated history with their former roommates. I would read for classes lying in their bed, with my head on their shoulder, propping up my library against their chest. Some nights I fell asleep that way, and in the morning we would braid each other's hair. When I woke from anesthesia, they were the one waiting for me, sitting on the windowsill—they were, I thought, the first person I saw when I was whole. I wanted to see them every time I woke up. I needed that, too, to be whole.

"It seems inadequate, doesn't it? They were close, they were kind, I felt they understood me, and therefore I fell in love? But of course I'm only guessing the *therefore*. Who knows how we are ensnared? Something jostles the cage door, it slams shut, and we don't ever want to be let out.

"But I could never be easy in such a love. I knew I couldn't be everything they needed. There were always others, a succession of beautiful men I had to be polite to. Later, when we moved to an apartment, they would even bring them home for dinner, very civilized. If I had any sense, I would have found another jess committed to the old ways to move in with. But the heart is not a hound, you know, it won't latch on to anyone who bobs their head back. So I cooked the evening meal, made small talk, then went to bed early and tried not to hear things. Some of the men I might have liked, but I couldn't stop wondering: Is this the one that Kol will leave me for?" They glanced over at him and laughed. "Are you making any sense of this?"

"Some." He thought over what he had heard. "It did confuse me that you call people jesses who you say have gone against the vow. Do they not revert to what they were before? I mean, I understand that they don't think so, but I'm surprised you agree."

"Of course they were still jesses. When you have taken the vow, you are a jess until you die or cut your braid. I don't mean literally cut it off—though that's been done. To cut your braid means to renounce, which you can do by proclaiming that you are no longer a jess, or by marrying, since that is an incompatible vow. But the braid will never fall off just from fucking. The vow matters because being a jess has to mean something and not nothing. It's not necessary for every one of us to honor our vows perfectly, though all too many Southerners insisted on hearing me that way. But what I meant to ask is, do you understand me when I speak of jealousy? Or is there no such thing, where you come from? Everyone shares with a glad heart?"

"Of course, there's jealousy—if by that you mean a wish to be the only one a lover visits, or admits."

"Have you ever asked to be the only one?"

"No. It wouldn't be right to pressure a visiting partner that way. Besides, it makes you look pathetic when they say no. But none of that applies to you, does it? You never wanted to visit Kol. You wanted to be the one they came home to."

"Yes," Iren said.

"You wanted to be family and had no way to become that. I understand that problem very well."

"Do you? Don't tell me that's a longing for marriage I hear in your voice."

"Certainly not," he said. "Though I suppose if you believe in marriage, that's what you believe it does. You swear an oath that creates a new family, like growing a new plant from a cutting. If you won't resort to marriage you need something else."

"What is it you need?"

"I don't know," John said. "I never solved the problem."

"It is known to happen, isn't it, that people stay together without needing a vow to fuse them at the navels." Iren's tone was ironic but there was a wistfulness in their voice too. "Sometimes love is enough—or love and fucking in some ratio."

"No," he said, becoming confused, "I am not talking about trying to bind a lover. I meant . . ." He didn't know what he meant. He was both sleepy and slightly drunk, and he could feel the shape of the problem but not reason his way through it, let alone translate his thinking into language they could understand.

Iren gave him a long silence to find words in. When he didn't speak, they said, "Well, let me put the rest of the story before you. You will judge me for it, probably, but I look forward to the strangeness of your verdict.

"As I mentioned, we moved into an apartment. Kol had a falling-out with several people in that house at once, and the hostility spilled over onto me, so it was natural we'd retreat together. I didn't ask them why they wanted to live with me, or what I was to them. I was afraid to hear the answer.

"We held on a few years like that. I started to do fieldwork, which took me far away from home, and every time I worried it wouldn't be my home when I came back. Then one time I was out collecting in the desert—deep Ischnuran desert, baked dry and whipped by windstorms. It makes this place look like a rainforest, but still there are creatures that thrive there."

"I thought Ischnura was cold."

"You've been hearing tales of the North, which is right and proper—it's the only part of the world worth knowing about—but no, on the whole it's a hot place for humans. The middle latitudes are uninhabited except by automated mining operations and a few sweltering scientists, and provide much-needed separation between the North, where a great continent surrounds the pole, and the South, an ocean defaced by an acne of islands. I'd been in that oven for two months and I was worrying about Kol. I was always worrying about Kol.

"Then news came that the *Rose of the Winds* and some other Free Ship had cooked up a scheme when they passed close in deep space. They were starting a new colony, and would take a chosen few to a new world. Immediately I was in a fever. I had to go. *We* had to go. But they said they weren't accepting jesses: they wanted married couples, who could build a world and populate it too. Ischnura informed them they were sadly out of date and plenty of jesses had children now—in fact, jess medicine being more advanced than the last time the *Rose* had stopped by, some of us could have them without outside input, both ingredients for the recipe being made inside ourselves. Then it turned out the problem wasn't fertility after all, but rather that Ischnurans would have to live with Zandaheans, who would never accept jesses. Well, the ships have been doing their best to smash Ischnurans' way of life for a long time, and we know how to dig our heels in. The *Rose* relented: they would take one, no, all right then, they would take exactly two.

"As soon as I heard *two* I went back home to Kol and made the case. We were young enough, with the right skills, fluent in English, able to bear children, and it would make a pretty picture too: North and South, tradition and modernity. With luck they'd never know how *much* modernity, the walls of a jess-house being blessedly opaque, and men who visit jesses often unloquacious on the subject. And, following that appeal to practicality and ambition, I told them I wanted to be with them forever and to make a family. I had never dared to say such things before, but with a whole world as my dowry, I grew bold. I told them all of it: that I loved them, that I couldn't live without them, and that while love in sexed people might seek its consummation in fucking or marriage or both, this love wanted nothing but more of itself. I remember thinking, *This is it: I have blown up our old life, and now we will sort through the rubble and see if there's anything left.*

"They said yes. They wanted the same things, they loved me the same way . . . well, something like. Maybe they meant it, maybe they convinced themself they did. Maybe they wanted to build a new world, and that was worth pretending. I told them right away I'd never ask them for celibacy, but I knew—I suppose we both knew—that the world would. A newly settled colony is like a small town. They could manage some discreet affairs, but they could hardly go away from me and move in with a man.

"Anyway. We passed every test, won out over all of our rivals. It was good, it made us good, being entirely focused on a task together. Lying in my coffin waiting for the anesthesia to take hold, I was imagining how we'd have a house, maybe a kitchen garden, how we'd take turns getting up early to make the children breakfast. I hope Kol was thinking of that too. But they never woke up and none of it happened."

John's brain had grown blunt and its grip on facts clumsy. It took him the length of two slow breaths to understand. "You mean, they died in their coffin? On the *Folly* they told me that cold-sleep was perfectly safe."

"There's no such thing as perfect—everything has a failure rate. Anyway, if someone on the *Rose* has been neglecting maintenance schedules, they're far beyond the reach of lawsuits or revenge. What difference does it make? Kol is gone, everything they would have brought to this world is lost, and I only am escaped alone to tell thee what a jess is. To drive a wedge into your heads and pry open a space where we can live. . . . Sorry, that was disgusting. When I'm drunk I am sometimes too vivid. What I meant to say is, being the only jess in a whole world is sweaty work, hard on the back and shoulders. Two could have borne it better. But I don't know what Zandaheans would have made of Kol. I never had to find that out. I never had to find out whether any of it would have worked. John, will you be honest with me? Do you think someone like Kol—someone who wants what you want, more or less—could have been content with someone like me?"

He thought for a while, looking up at the stars. "In all honesty, the question confuses me. I think you mean, how can two people stay together without sex? Well, how can worms fly without fins? How can birds hear without noses? Semen isn't an adhesive. Family, united by blood and soul, that is the only bond that's permanent."

"And yet I seem to have come loose from mine. So have you, if you don't mind my saying."

"That's different," he said. "I don't have a family. They died long before I left."

"All?"

"Yes," he said. And then, with the feeling of seizing a thread in the dark and following without knowing what it would lead to, he began the story.

"I lost my family when I was fifteen, that's . . . whatever it is in ship years. Our house was in the Clear Lakes region—" He faltered, realizing this would mean nothing to them, and his mind, in place of an account that they could understand, delivering only the impression of one orange leaf floating down a stream. Then a memory of his mother's voice supplied the economic facts, which he repeated: "Clear Lakes is rich in fish, but too far from any city that might import fish to gain much from trade, so there was not a lot of money, but we prospered well enough. The women had scratched out a garden, with a trench dug deep around it to keep out the roots of *lusbain* trees, which are wide-ranging and voracious. My family never had a boat, but even on lakeshores or standing in rivers, two men could harvest enough fish to feed us all. And since I was the youngest boy, it was expected that I would become a doctor, which in those parts just meant that I would look after the household's health. It is adventurous in a way—you range around the woods, gathering wild foods and medicines—but when you come home to prepare them, then you are part of the life of the kitchen in a way most men are not. I liked both halves of that. I thought I would live in that house my whole life and take care of my family.

"But first I had to learn how to tell bundlestalk from full-and-crescent, and to remove the seeds from coilfruit without poisoning the flesh. And instead of an apprenticeship near home, I went to learn the craft at a new school on Via Island, where the education was more scientific. My mother thought—but I should say 'my aunt' in English. My sister-mother, not my *mother*-mother. She was older, so she was the one who decided how money was spent. And she said the true wealth of a family was in its strength, so we should tend to our own health first. I still believe that was wisdom. But in my second autumn at the school, wildfire burned through all the west and the south of the Clear Lakes. The island was spared but my home was lost.

"I made it back there, years later, when blackroot had grown all over the burned wood and vines had swallowed up the chimney. The garden had all turned to golden flagweed, and little birds with red-and-black wings were perching on the highest flowers, darting up to catch flies. There was one of our old neighbors left, still trying to rebuild. She thought my family must have waded out into the river to escape the fire and drowned there. If they had spent their money on a boat instead of my tuition then they might have lived."

Iren had turned onto their side to face him as he spoke, folding half of their blanket over them as they did; the night was growing cool. They did not try to offer comfort nor make any sympathetic noise, and he was glad of that, but they watched him closely. The large moon had risen above the mountains and they must be able to see him quite well.

"Even my name was burned," he said. "At home your last name is the eldest ancestor preserved whole at your house, but they were all lost, the dead along with the living. I use Maraintha because I have nothing else to use, but it's just sounds now. And when I left the school at Via, I had no home to go to."

"Is there no provision made for orphans?"

"In ordinary times, some relative would have taken me in, or possibly an unrelated neighbor. But the whole region had suffered the same cataclysm. They had either died, or at best had lost their houses. If anybody was in a position to take in other people's children, they would have done that at the time of the fire, when I was still away. Maybe if I had been younger, not so close to being a man, I could have gone somewhere else and begged for a name from people who had never met my mothers, but at my age there was no hope in it. Would Ischnura have had a better answer?"

"Jesses take in orphaned children," they said. "Or we did, at any rate. Now that anyone can bear a child whose memory allows it, the custom may have fallen out of use. But don't let me distract you—tell me how you came from namelessness to traveling the stars."

"Well, I heard about a program in Faivai—that's a big city on the coast, the one where the ship-folk come down—that would allow me to study ships' medicine. Since ships' English is the language of it, I studied that too. Then, to discharge my obligation to the neighbors' mothers who had paid for my tuition, I spent three years traveling around in puddle country—that is a large expanse of land with no great bodies of water, to the south of the Clear Lakes, where a few families will huddle up their houses by some little pond that harbors a few fish. They catch birds to supplement their protein, and some try to farm, but the soil is not fertile, so usually they eat a great many wild plants. If they don't gather and cook carefully then they become weighed down with poisons, so that even fishing becomes difficult, and once they start that slide they may deteriorate very quickly. Yet many of them triumph over their environment, and then they are proud and wary of outsiders.

"And when you come to a place like that, as the first new man anybody has seen in many years, not even part of a new household but just passing through, there is a lot of interest and no trust at all. No one can vouch for how you act when visiting. If you did wrong, you could leave town and outrun the damage to your reputation. And—I should explain, in most houses, the ancestors don't like having unrelated men within the walls—"

"They speak to you?"

"Not to me, no. When the ancestors don't like something, that means the women of the house don't. Whether the ancient ones truly contribute their opinions is more than I know. But probably they *would* agree, the living and the dead, that if visitors for every woman in the house were coming through at all hours, rubbing past the uncles at the door and waking up the children, the peace of the family would suffer. So tradition, and the labor of their brothers, provides each woman with a cabin, which in Clear Lakes means a one-room building with a bed and its own fire. In the city it might be a room on a different floor, or a partition on a rooftop—people there live close together and they make do. In puddle country they have proper cabins too, but I nearly always had to walk past them and knock on the house door. I met the whole family, so I could know they all had seen me. Once I received a gratuitous tour of the kitchen that could only have been meant to show me that the family owned a number of sharp knives. Then the woman I had come for would admit me to some room indoors. If the family was especially suspicious, the door might be left ajar so everyone could listen in."

"That sounds excruciating," Iren said.

"It was awkward, of course, but I understood their caution."

"I meant excruciating for the family. But yes, of course one understands. I'm sorry, you were climbing toward a point and I interrupted you."

"Was I?" For a while his mind was dark, but his eyes adjusted and he saw the paleness of the path again. "Well, it wasn't much of a point. Only that on Essius a man without a sister, or some other female relative who's able to bear children, can never truly have a family. Sometimes, if a family is lacking in men, the ancestors will let a man live in the house with a child he has fathered, but more often than not that just means being treated like a servant and kicked out when you're no longer wanted. And so when I was visiting in puddle country, when the mothers sewing by the fire were all inspecting me, or when children up late were playing a game on the floor with some lingering man, I used to think . . . I wished I had come to that house to be adopted, to become a brother and an uncle. If I could have done that, I would have given up the visit without regret. I don't know if that helps. Of course I never imagined giving up visiting entirely. I had no reason to think of that."

"I told you I never asked Kol to be celibate."

"No, I remember. I don't know why I said that."

"You're still fretting about the vow, that's why—and *maschet* is a sovereign remedy for shutting up."

"I suppose so. Mainly I am bothered about Tali braiding. I mean, I can see how swearing celibacy is nothing for you, being as you are—"

"Don't say that. It's not *nothing.* Just because I am a natural jess and didn't struggle with the vow, that doesn't mean I gave up *nothing.*" Surprised by their vehemence, John would have apologized, but anger drained away from them as soon as it had welled up. "What you must know," they said, then paused for a long time. "Kol wanted men. And . . . *he* was a man. Though you could never make sexed people understand that—there's no ritual to make it real. Only among jesses could he be seen as he was, and not always even then; but just the same, Kol was a man. So other jesses who were men too, that was all right, but never somebody like me. I'm too much in the middle, lying between the tracks and feeling the trains rush by on either side. But *if* he could want me, I would have done what he wanted. I would have liked to be the cause of pleasure in him. I would have liked to occupy his whole attention. And after all, if I loved him, how bad could it be?"

"I think, if you are moved to ask that question, the answer is probably 'Very.'"

"Maybe." He heard a smile in their voice; he turned on his side and saw it in the moonlight, the smile of someone with a secret that amuses them. But it faded and their voice was hollow when they said, "Yes, maybe. Because it's not just performing the act, is it? I know how you people look at each other. Not just men, you're all the same, it doesn't matter. I've seen a woman give another woman a look that would strip bricks off the side of a building, and that look would want to see another like itself, wouldn't it? Not find a welcome in indifference, or . . . make do with caring that would feel like charity. In the long run . . ." Their eyes had closed. Then they started awake with a gasp. "Anyway. That is how even a natural jess may be tempted and might fall. I think I'm going to be asleep soon now. If you think of anything you need to tell me in the night, shake me awake, I don't mind."

They didn't close their eyes again at once. After a while they tucked in the edge of their blanket to make a cocoon, then slipped their arm back in under it. "It's a cold night for this far into summer."

"I could get more blankets from the van—or that quilted thing you sleep in."

"It seems a lot of trouble. Maybe my body heat will warm this up, now that it's snugger."

"If we lay closer, we could wrap both blankets around us. Then we would have two layers, plus the warmth of each other."

"That would be pleasant," they said. "Only sometimes I think you have an expression that means things are going to get awkward."

"If you mean, am I attracted to you, I was, or almost was, or might have been, not understanding your nature. It doesn't trouble me and I would never let it trouble you."

They turned onto their back. He thought he had offended them, but then they said quite peacefully, “Is the world spinning for you?”

“No.”

“When it does spin, does it ratchet? I mean it isn’t a smooth motion, it kind of catches every second or so.”

“I know what you mean.”

“Is it the beating of your heart that makes it do that?”

“Maybe. That wasn’t covered in medical school.”

“Hmm. Well, I will move closer to you presently.”

But they still lay looking upward. Their eyes closed and their breathing slowed. They were asleep.

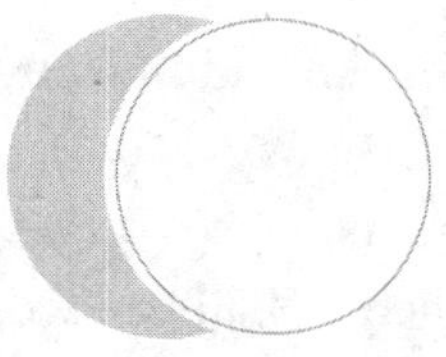

CHAPTER SIXTEEN

When he opened his eyes, Iren had already risen and was taking up their blanket from the ground. They wore an old dress that was frayed at the hem. The color of it must have once been a rich purple, but time and sun had faded it to lavender; the original shade lingered only in the depths of the skirt's folds.

"Not one word," they said. "We left town in a hurry and I didn't want to stay up doing laundry. Just be glad I didn't subject you to the odor of a second-day shirt in this weather instead of digging out this picturesque ruin."

"I was going to say that it's very becoming."

"When I landed on this world it was. Now it's a tincture of its former self."

But something in the gradient of color pleased him, and with a tingle of new understanding he repeated what Vo had once said: "Things that are changing are beautiful."

"Oh, save your flattery for sexed people, John. I don't put poems up my ass either."

There was no wariness in their voice. It was only banter, something to say as they shook the sand out of their blanket and slapped at it to knock off the most stubborn grains. Once they had stowed it and the pillow, John went into the back of the van to wipe himself off with a moistened cloth and to change clothes. When he emerged, Iren was waiting.

"Feeling any the worse for the *maschet*?" they asked.

"Not noticeably."

"You're driving, then. I don't think you held up your end last night—I am more wilted than I ought to be."

They both climbed into the van and Iren sat beside him. "Pass me my hat out from under your seat."

It had slid far back, but he managed to tweeze it between two fingers of one hand and pull it out. When he had handed it over, Iren canted the brim down over their eyes and put their desert boots up on the dashboard. The hem of the dress slipped downward until it was stopped by the swell of their knees, revealing long calves softened by a scattering of golden hair. He saw that Iren unselfconscious would be even more appealing than Iren on their guard, but one just had to ignore it. They closed their eyes and he started the van; they had made sure the ignition would respond to him.

After no more than ten minutes of travel, Iren sighed and their eyes opened. "I won't manage to nap in here. I never do. Piro can sleep in the van all day, even when I crash through the washes on purpose to wake him up. It's irritating."

"At Torres house they raised four babies. Both of them must have learned to sleep whenever it is quiet."

"Possibly that is it."

"He puzzles me," John said.

"Oh? Which of all his many faults bemuses you particularly?"

"Not just him, but all the Zandaheans. Their ideas about gods—or *a* god—are so odd and elaborate, and they are so firmly convinced of them."

"Why should that come as a surprise?" Iren said. "People impale themselves on any number of strange ideas. You would do better to marvel at Laura, who insists she has no faith, yet can't stop acting as if all of it's true anyway. But even that is not so rare. Many on Ischnura too, are too sophisticated to believe what they believe."

He considered their words as he took the van in a wide circle around a cone. Candlehawks would not attack a moving vehicle, but driving too close alarmed them, and he saw no reason to be discourteous. "So you hold that it's all nonsense?"

"I wouldn't go that far. It could be they are right, the universe we see exists because a mind like ours created it—at least, a mind enough like ours that we can say it wants one thing and not another, and when it acts it does so with intent. That's as good an idea as any. But it is certainly not plausible that such a being believes that people everywhere should marry, or that men should never visit men, or no one should become a jess. Look at what they have created. The universe could have been nothing at all, or one atom of hydrogen floating in a void, or a diamond crystal infinite in all directions, if their mind cared for simplicity or tidiness. Instead we have stars and planets and black holes and nebulas. It could have all been cold and dead, but there is life. They could have made one species for each world, or just a few, which could have stayed the same forever, but instead we have millions and millions, all of which are changing every moment, varying among themselves and boiling off in all directions. Such a god is like an artist who fills up a library of sketchbooks with their drawings of strange creatures, and when every scrap of paper in the place is used up, goes back with a different color ink and scribbles over them again. They are obsessed with variation—they gorge themselves with it and never grow full. Do you really think a mind like that could want us all to live in the same way?"

This was a strange and, in a way, a pleasing thought, and for a little while, lulled by their spell of words, he thought it very logical. But the more he turned it over in his mind, the more his credence faded into doubt. "You assume that a creating god has singleness of purpose. Why shouldn't they experience conflicting impulses and harbor contradictory ideas, just as we do?"

"Well, you and I have to live in the world. We're constrained and thwarted at every turn, and that's what makes us complicated. I think an all-powerful god would just do as they liked. But sure, why not, it's possible. Maybe living things are an idea that torments them. Maybe they pluck each one out of the curls of their brain with fingernails, feeling the same kind of satisfaction you and I might get from picking off a scab, and flick them down onto the worlds to die. If so, then they must hate us as they hate all life, and we can hope for nothing good from them, no matter what we do. And the fact that we can't tell which of these possibilities is true shows that we know nothing about what God wants, and we may as well do as we like."

"I see you've picked a destination in advance, and no matter which way you start off, you always turn toward it."

"You should try navigating that way," Iren said with satisfaction. "You'd get lost less."

"I notice also that you use the pronoun 'they' where Zandaheans use 'he,' so you are sure at least the god you speak of is a jess, even if no other fact about them can possibly be known."

"Well, I'm told that this God had a child who was entirely from themself. Everybody *I've* met who can do that is a jess, but perhaps your experience varies."

He thought it might be better not to ask about this. The matter could not be more personal. And yet they had brought it up twice now. "That is what you meant last night, by . . . both ingredients being homegrown, or whatever the phrase was. That meant sperm and egg?"

"Yes." They put their feet down on the floor, removed their hat and laid it in their lap, laid a hand on the brim so it wouldn't slide off as the van tipped and jounced through the rough landscape. "And yes, that fortunate minority of jesses who can rooster their own hen includes me. In theory, anyway. In practice it never worked out."

They said this quite calmly, as if it had little weight; yet what they spoke of was the death of a house. With no relatives on this world, and without even the possibility of marriage, the failure of their own fertility meant they had no means of continuation. He didn't know how to respond to such a tragedy presented in so casual a way, and so reverting to ship-manners, he only said, "I am very sorry."

"Really, it is easier this way. It would take up a great deal of time, being a parent alone—I certainly wouldn't be free to run off to the desert on a whim. And there are politics to think of, too."

"Politics?"

"According to the Church of Zandahe, changing my body was a series of sins and conceiving a child with it would be another one. Children, they assert, are meant to be the product of conjugal love, which means the kind that married people are alleged to have, and not the kind that leads someone to give of their own body so a stranger may be fertile. And also, as you might have heard, long ago their God shrunk himself down and squoze himself out of a woman's vagina—"

"What, as a joke? Or is it some kind of lesson?"

"Not a joke. They take it very seriously. Not intended as instruction either, I don't think." They frowned, considering. "This was the same incident in which they say that the God *made* a child—the child they made was also them, in some way. Ask Laura if you want to know about that. When she tells about it I feel as if I understand, but afterward the edges of the explanation melt together in my mind. The point is, the human subject in this dubious experiment was a virgin, and so am I one; and here they are, all but Deniers, waiting for this same God to start up a brand-new breed of priests, which is something that the son did for old Earth, so for me to bear a child would be a little awkward. They feel mocked by the idea of it, I think. And you know me, I like the quiet life, don't draw any attention to myself if I can help it, so after all it's just as well I am as fruitful as a stone. Much as children were my heart's desire when I was younger, one can redirect that impulse. I focus on my work and on my scientific legacy, and I'm all right."

John doubted such a fundamental need could be diverted from its course so easily, but thought it not a kindness to pursue the matter further. Iren stared out the window, and for a time he thought they would not say any more. Finally they said, without turning toward him, "Still, I've always wished I knew what went wrong. Marne did every possible test, some of them many times over, and never found an answer. Even though I've given up—and really, I am getting a bit old for it by now—I miss the *possibility* of having children. It's part of my memory—which is an explanation that explains nothing, but simply says over again that I miss something I never had." They had turned over the hat on their lap and were toying with the string of it, winding it around one finger and then slipping the finger free. "Did you treat infertility at home?"

"In puddle country I treated everything. There were no specialists to fall back on."

"Well then, what would you have said about a case like mine?"

"There are no cases like yours on Essius."

"I am not asking you to certify the results of my surgery. Marne has done that and found everything in order."

"But . . ." John sighed. "I am sorry to have to speak of this, but that evening we first met, I looked at you in a certain way—"

"Yes, you did, but at least you had the grace to be embarrassed when I caught you, which is more than some of the Zandaheans could say. I came to this world prepared to overlook far worse than that, and have. Consider it forgotten."

"Well. Then, please understand I am not trying to do the same again, but truly, as a doctor, I cannot simply wave away the question of what organs I am treating. You are not coming to me with a sprained ankle. Your reproductive system is quite centrally involved, and I have only the haziest notion of how it could possibly function. For instance, if you are both father and mother, wouldn't the product of the union be more inbred than any human on Essius can be, and so likely never to develop?"

"Yes, all right, I see the problem." They wound their finger in the hatstring one last time; then as if to stop themself from fidgeting, they folded their hands together and set them firmly on their lap. "I have a uterus and ovaries, which look and work like any others, but were built up by machines out of cells cultured from my own tissues. Externally, too, I am as female, and can give natural birth, or so it was intended. I also have one internal testis, which is mainly synthetic, but produces sperm made from the genetic material of a woman—or more probably a jess—who donated it." Their voice, which had been brisk, softened and slowed. "I might have had Kol's, if I had only known to want that sooner. We talked about having my testis changed, after we'd made our declarations to each other, but I could hardly take time off for surgery while competing for passage to Scythia. Anyway, it might have made me seem less chaste to bear a child of both our bodies, even by such sideways means. Instead some woman or some jess I never met would have become one of the founders of a world and never known it."

"Why a woman?"

"Because my chromosomes are XY, and so my eggs, as the products, are either Y or X. Sperm from an XX donor is only X, and that avoids the possibility of a YY zygote, which would not be viable."

John realized they had told him that the child who curled up in the fallen tree had been a boy, or looked like one. This fact, if he had known it when they first met at the governor's house, might have colored all their interactions after, so that he saw them as a man in truth, albeit never to be spoken of as such. But at many different times now he had regarded them as male, or female, or indefinable as either, so the thicket of confusion that surrounded them had grown too tough to cut through with so dull a blade.

"But as I said, it's far more likely the genetic material came from a jess than a woman. Many jesses are happy to give of themselves to help honor another's memory, and if they too seek surgery, that is a natural time for the donation to be made."

"And why is the testis synthetic? To prevent transplant rejection?"

"No—there is still some foreign tissue that my blood must circulate through, so I had to have my immune system reeducated in any case. But a fully organic testis would leak testosterone into my body, which doesn't comport with my memory. Anyway, it wouldn't function well while marinating in the estrogen from my ovaries." They paused. "Do you know the effect of taking estrogen, on one whose body was not formerly suffused with it? Your education in ships' medicine may not have mentioned that."

"I suppose it would be the same as for a girl who never got her period, when she begins to take gods'-palsy root. That is what we call the drug at home."

"Oh come on now, you don't expect me to believe you can just grind up some alien herb and press it out into a tablet and that's estrogen, do you?"

"No—the medicine is made out of the plant, but by a complicated process, in a lab somewhere, I suppose. The same root gives progesterone and testosterone, but for those we use the plant's other names, which are sweetdrop and singeflower."

"If it's made in a laboratory, why do you use plant names?"

"I don't know. It's a convention like any other. Why do you name species in a language that no living person speaks?"

"Fair," they admitted. "As if learning English weren't enough, we have to get familiar with the two little pet languages it drags around on leashes to do science for it. But Latin makes things sound more scientific and official. All those botanical names make it sound like you spend your time gamboling around in fields and putting flowers into baskets."

He had, in fact, gathered herbs into a basket as recently as a month before leaving Essius—no one would miss the volunteer blueblanket growing in the flower beds in front of his apartment building, and there was no reason that patients ought to pay for medicine deriving from a weed—but he chose not to mention this fact.

"Essius is rich in useful medicines. It's something to be proud of. Can Ischnurans get estrogen from a plant?"

"We can, actually, and the other two hormones as well—a Terran plant, the soybean. So long as it survives, the means of honoring memory will be always close at hand. Though if the colony falls hard, as now seems likely, it may be a long time before our descendants can manage the synthesis.—Now, have you learned enough to exercise your diagnostic skills and prescribe me a drug with some quaint floral name that can only be refined on a space station in free fall?"

"We have no space stations, and no ovaries built up of XY cells either. The situation you describe is miraculous to me. You might as well ask me to restring all the chewed wires in the van we left behind."

"You are making too heavy a weather of this. I am asking you only to look into those facets of embodiment that I have in common with others. Suppose you are in puddle country and I come to see you in the shape of a matron, sporting an ample bosom and hips wide enough to hit the doorframe on both sides. Women like that sometimes find themselves infertile, do they not?"

"Yes, Socrates, they do."

"Then ask me just the questions you would ask of such a woman, and if you can't flush any game out of those bushes, imagine me a man and do it over."

"I suppose, first I would take a history and find out if there is truly any reason to suspect a problem. Which is to say, have they been visited regularly by men, at suitable times in the cycle, and was the act of the correct type—"

"Wait, stop a moment. You had patients who didn't know they needed intercourse to get pregnant?"

"No, even in puddle country where there is scarcely a school they did know that much, but folklore in those parts would have it that sperm lives in the body a long time and there is no need for repeated introductions. That *is* true of Essian birds, so the idea isn't as foolish as you might think."

"Well, I don't store sperm but I do manufacture it, so I don't need to be introduced to any more."

"Still, there must be an insemination, mustn't there? What exits the body must be put back in."

"No. If I want to be pregnant I only have to think about it in a certain way, and sperm is delivered to the cervix by a tube created for that purpose. It doesn't *exit*, as you put it, and nothing is passed transluminally."

"That word can't possibly mean 'faster than the speed of light,' but I have no other guesses."

"'Through an opening.' In this case, the one provided to women by nature, and to me by culture. You understand? These are delicate matters, so forgive me for being indirect—as soon as the topic changes, I will be my usual plainspoken self again."

"But . . . why this ingenuity? Artificial insemination is a very simple procedure."

"No doubt, but through internal fertilization I avoid enacting even an analogy to intercourse. Conceiving in this way is more obedient to tradition, and I like it better. Yet all that is beside the point—whatever the reasons I am plumbed in a particular way, so I am and so it is, and the problem remains. Now, what is the next step in your diagnosis?"

"I would ask, also, if more than one man has been admitted. Infertility from chronic poisoning is more common in men than women, so often a change of visitors is more effective than medicine. Of course, even on Essius many women are not interested in taking such advice."

"You may pass over that one. My sperm have been counted more often than bumps on the ceiling above an insomniac's bed."

"Then I would ask after nutrition and the possibility of toxins. You haven't been subsisting on Essian plants, obviously, but is there anything you might have been exposed to accidentally?"

"Well, it *is* an alien planet, and I'm a biologist. I might have touched some toxic animal once, but if so I never suffered any noticeable symptoms. And if you mean chronic exposure, nothing any mother here isn't exposed to just as much."

"In that case, is there anyone who might prefer you didn't become pregnant?"

"What a question! Are you looking for a secret villain to blame? If so then we may narrow it down to an Ischnuran, a Zandahean, or our governor. You and Sudharma are eliminated on the technicality of not being on the planet when I was trying to conceive."

"An Ischnuran?"

"Not everyone is comfortable with the idea of jess childbirth, and those who aren't may not admit their views to me, or even to themselves. That is another reason why I had myself made to conceive without input from outside. For the sake of not ruffling sexed feathers, it would be better if an infant coalesced from morning dew—I came as close to that as medicine could manage."

"Then, does anyone have access to your food or drink, especially on a regular basis?"

"This is not at all the kind of question I expected you to ask me. Do people on Essius really go around grinding contraceptives into each other's soup?"

"It's not common, but I saw a few cases. One in particular stays with me. A young girl, scarcely old enough to have a cabin, came to me with severe cramps and bleeding and a burning in her limbs. Her hands were clenched in fists and she could not relax them. She remembered being served an unfamiliar leafy stalk at dinner, and when I showed her drawings in an herbal, she recognized river doll's-eye. That is an abortifacient of desperation, used sometimes by women who have nothing else. At best it is about as subtle as being run through with a fencepost, and I think she must have eaten several times the effective dose. When I had stabilized her, I drove to her house to tell the family and check for other victims. Her mother came to the door perfectly calm and admitted she had poisoned the child on purpose. She was sorry to use something so harsh, but one constantly crying baby was all that she could bear. At that point I thought an infant was in danger, so even though she said her ancestors forbade it, I pushed my way into the house. I still think that was justified. All the house's souls were strewn around on furniture and on the floor, as if somebody had been rifling through them, and the oldest ones had crumbled into pieces from neglect—it was horrible. I couldn't find any baby.

"By the time I had looked through every room, the mother was treating me like an invited guest. She even offered me some tea, which you can well imagine I refused. She told me the baby belonged to her older daughter, who had gone upstairs and blocked the door to keep her out. When she knocked and shouted a complaint about the noise, this daughter would move the baby to a different room, but she would never feed or comfort it. I had seen from the outside that the house only had one story. When I asked her to show me the door to the stairs, she tried a closet and a pantry, then became so agitated I could get nothing more out of her. According to the girl I treated, there was no baby and her only sister had died at the age of five. She also said that she herself could never have been pregnant, and I certainly believed her. I still have nightmares about that house."

"Now I will too, so thank you for that."

"I'm sorry. I should not have told you about that case."

"It did have its points of interest, but I was unprepared for the abrupt turn from case study to ghost story."

"Oh, I doubt very much that was the cause. An unfixed spirit might explain the crying—if you believe they can make themselves heard like that—but not the damage to her judgment. Occam's razor suggests both had a single cause, which would most likely be exposure to some substance. Very little botany has been done in those parts, so she could easily have found something unknown to medicine, a false friend of some benign vegetable, perhaps. She couldn't or wouldn't tell me what she had been eating, so I couldn't investigate any further than that."

"I feel compelled to ask what happened to the two of them, though I'm certain I'll dislike the answer."

"Well, since the damage done was permanent, custom allows death as a remedy, but I could never have felt easy about assisting in such a case, and naturally the poor girl had no interest in revenge. It was her own mother. I left her with some neighbors, who assured me they would take her to her kin. She did have kin living, so that is some comfort. As for the mother, nobody was prepared to take her in, yet it could hardly be a kindness to leave her in that house alone. All I could think to do was drive her to the nearest hospital, a three days' journey, as it turned out—two of moving forward and one of getting wheels unstuck from mud. She thought she heard the baby crying in the back all the way there, and I had to invent reasons why I wasn't helping.

"I stopped by that hospital again before I left the region. They said the auditory hallucinations had faded not long after she arrived, but she never seemed to fully understand the damage she had done. I suppose that was a mercy. When she left, she told them she was going to live with her daughter. I hope she meant the living one. For the family to take her back would have been difficult, but of course the bond of blood is very strong."

Iren thought over this in silence for some time. Then in a tone of irritation they commanded, "Stop the van and get out. The way you're driving, we won't be home until midnight."

They slid over to the driver's seat while he walked around to the other door. He thought that by this interruption they were putting an end to their medical inquiry, and he was relieved. But after a few minutes during which they gave their whole attention to the route ahead, they told him, "If anybody here had licked the wrong bug and was being vexed to frenzy by an unquiet spirit, I think I would have noticed. You can tick that possibility off the list."

"Of course that was an exceptional case. But I have seen poisoning by contraceptive in more mundane circumstances. The substance used was always tatterwing, which is not the most reliable of contraceptives, but in puddle country where ships' medicine is unavailable, it's the only one without too many telltale side effects—a little nausea and stomach upset in the first week or so, sometimes, but in puddle country those symptoms would easily be passed off as the result of some mistake in gathering food. Each time, I was told that the family could not support another child—there was not enough food, or the poisoned one was irresponsible and the relatives she lived with were too old. Which may have been true, but is no excuse for dosing a woman without her knowledge. Something must have gone terribly wrong in a family that would resort to that solution—the effect of years of poison and privation, I suppose. But, having seen that, any time that infertility has no apparent cause, I have to wonder."

"You can put it from your mind, because I shop and cook for myself. The only people I have dined with regularly are the Torreses, who would never do such a thing or think of it."

"Forgive me, but I noticed some conflict between you and Laura—"

"Not the kind that leads someone to sterilize a husband's friend. Forget her, and them."

"I suppose you get your medications from Marne, and would rule him out as absolutely."

They thought this over, rubbing their thumbs slowly against the steering wheel. "Perhaps not absolutely. It's not an unheard-of opinion, that the ships are right about the need to stamp out anamnesis—the allele that, if you don't recall, makes a person more likely to take the braid—but that since the gene is not the carrier's fault, sterilization would be more merciful than celibacy. And the man *is* a bit of a ship-kisser. Do you have that expression?"

"No, but it explains itself."

"It is odd, the way he reacted to you. Being a snob about your qualifications is in character, but to push you right out of the back door of medicine's house, to sleep curled up in the snow like a hound—that seems excessive."

"He also started rumors about me visiting men. Could it have been to deter people from coming to me as a doctor?"

"Mm. Or to discredit you, maybe, so if you tried to expose him, you wouldn't be believed. That's possible. I've never known him to be particularly homophobic. If he *is* guilty, what a shock it must have been for him, to open up your pod and find, instead of some ship's doctor who would never dream of helping me have children, an Essian with no notion of jess celibacy, no interest in selective breeding of the human herd, and a cultural obsession with poison besides. . . ." They pointed at their backpack, on the floor of the van next to his feet. "My sunscreen is in there, and so is my library. Test the one with the other."

After some rummaging through pockets he found the bottle, tipped out pills into his hand and poured back all but one, then put it on the screen and closed the covers.

"There's a coating," Iren said. "You'll have to crush it."

"Have you anything to grind it with?"

In answer Iren plucked the still-closed library from his hand, raised it to the level of their head, and without slowing down or taking their eyes off the landscape they drove through, whacked it down against the dashboard. John jumped at the noise and accepted the library back, expecting to find it broken and useless. He opened it and brushed away the powdered medicine to find a listing of chemical names on the undamaged screen.

"I don't know how to interpret this," he said.

Iren stomped on the brake, and before the van had even fully stopped, the library was back in their hands. They examined it, then folded it and tossed it onto his lap. "It's sunscreen and perfectly innocent. Marne is just Marne." They lifted their foot from the brake pedal as if they would put it back on the accelerator, and did not. "Of course, he knows I've given up, so there would be no reason to keep tainting the medicine. Certainly, when he refilled the bottle for me after your arrival, he would have made sure the contents were innocent. . . . *No.* Enough. These thoughts are dark and they're uncalled-for—just the effect of a disturbing story on a too-recently marinated brain. You and your fucking ghost baby."

With decision, they drove on. Though the speed at which they covered ground was hardly restful, still the driving seemed to calm them. After an hour or so they said, "We're making good time. I should be able to catch Piro still at work to show him my platypus. I can't show up at Torres house, not anymore, but to intercept him in his laboratory is another matter."

There was a wistfulness about the way they talked of Piro that reminded him of how, the night before, they had spoken of Kol and desire. *That look would want to see another like itself.* Of course, he thought; that mumbled speech, expressing anguish over being in love with someone whose desire they couldn't match, was not only about a jess who had died long ago. Piro was their visitor.

He didn't know what to make of this discovery. When they spoke of being willing to admit Kol to their cabin, they had sounded, on the one hand, abject, and on the other, covetous, as if by yielding they would bind their lover to them. Yet he saw neither of those postures in their attitude toward Piro, which was a mix of camaraderie and amusement at his foibles, perfectly normal in one being visited. John wanted to ask whether they were all right, but he could see no way to do it without letting on that he had guessed their secret. Also, who they admitted was entirely their own business; if a mistake, it was theirs to make. In any case, he was preempted when they asked him, apropos of nothing, "Why *don't* Essians marry, anyway?"

"On Earth there were a number of diseases spread by visiting. The fear of them created inhibition, and then regulation. On Essius we had no need of that."

"That proves a little too much, don't you think? Ischnura left syphilis and all of that behind as much as you did, yet marriage is still endemic in the population."

"Besides that, plant toxins affect the reproductive system—especially they did in the beginning, when people didn't know yet how to eat. If we had all paired up in marriages, many of them would have been infertile. If men, as they were in those days, had chosen the solution to this problem, it might have been horrible—harems, or forced insemination, or something equally appalling—but fortunately women were more numerous and their vision, which is still our way, prevailed."

"Interesting," they said. "But that's an explanation. What's the *reason*?"

"Desire should be free," he said. And then considering their nature and their situation, he added, "I don't mean only sexual desire. We shouldn't seek to bind each other, or ourselves, in any way. It's an absurdity to swear to love forever—no one can promise such a thing. And even if love does persist, you are still likely to regret committing yourself to a roommate you can't get rid of and a job you're not allowed to quit."

"Of course one sees that it is often so, but even on Zandahe not every marriage is the same. Those who are prudent find someone who wants the same things they do, and together the two make of marriage whatever they need it to be. Even you might manage that, with the right woman. You could have sewing by the fire and game-playing on the floor, even if you won't believe it's a real family."

"If I did that," he said, "who would I be then?"

"Oh, well, if that's the worm that's boring into you, then forget I said anything."

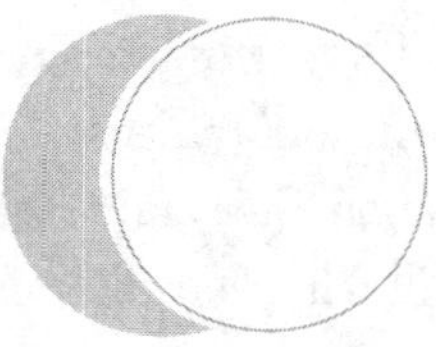

CHAPTER SEVENTEEN

He went back to the house, back to his life. He shopped and cooked, just as before. Sometimes, at the dinner table when the conversation flagged, or when Sudharma spent the afternoon in his room reading, or at random times when it made no sense at all—passing by the bathroom door and hearing the sound of the running shower—John would think to himself, *Sudharma is more distant.* But he could not say how, exactly, he had previously been closer.

At least John no longer had to fear an imminent translation. No progress could be made until Sudharma had another basket-man to learn from. For that reason, and because he had already mastered all the fundamentals of the job that he would have to do, John no longer spent as much time running simulations. Once a week to keep in practice was enough. Each time he finished one he felt a great relief, which lasted usually until he went to bed, rarely for as long as two days. Then the dread of the next one would set in.

There was less work on the farm, too, now that the basket-man was gone and students could roam freely. Ru worked there only a few times a month. When she did, she sent a message to John's tag and he brought lunch to her and helped. Once he tried to tell her about his journey to the east with Iren—omitting, of course, anything they had told him that was personal. When he had tried and failed to reproduce a sentence of theirs about Christianity, he told her, "In all honesty, I am not sure I understand everything they say, but I like listening to them in any case."

"Well, I am hurt. All this time I thought you liked listening to me."

"That, too."

She smiled at him, and blushed to such a slight degree that it would surely have been indiscernible on someone not so pale, and became intent on the beets she was planting.

John visited Vo frequently, finding in her openness a respite from the claustrophobia of town. The moving bubble that carried him inside the crawler, which had so frightened him on first encounter, evoked instead a tingle of anticipation; the long gray hall felt as familiar as a wooden cabin; the strange warmth of the crawler's flesh seemed merely the translation of a roaring fire. Sometimes, still, a remark she made could startle his mind into an unkind thought—as when she mentioned having had an arm regrown after some predatory animal attacked her. Then he pictured the aiyi as a monstrous presence, grasping her wrist to push her hand into a great toothed maw. But she was calm, telling the story; it wasn't even a bad memory. So the hurtful image faded, and she forgave.

One morning John was summoned to the desert. A man had fallen and hit his head while backing away from an angry candlehawk. There was no fracture, but he reported a headache and nausea and so was probably concussed. John drove out, examined the patient, and brought him to Marne's clinic. The whole adventure had taken no more than six hours, and he got home early enough to start dinner on time. It was not so different from what his days might have been like if fire had not taken his family's house—a morning in the wild and then an evening in the kitchen—except, of course, that in the kitchen he would not have been alone, but surrounded by mothers and sisters and nieces. Even so, there was a satisfaction in the thought. But he could not expect such accidents to happen very often.

All in all, he felt his days were no longer as full as they ought to have been, and had resolved to ask Ru if there was anything else he might help with the next time he saw her; if that failed, he planned to go to Michael. But before he had the chance, a message came through on Sudharma's tag: *basket-men are on the farm*. Both of them ran there, leaving breakfast on the table.

There were seven of them, walking around the edges of the plots and smelling everything. Each one wore a basket full of food. One was smaller than the rest, and when the small one turned his head, John saw a scar running from eye to jawline that he remembered as a fresh and vivid wound.

"Blue!" he called out. His heart felt light at seeing Blue alive, and well, and not alone. Blue walked toward him and looked up into his eyes. He pointed to himself and said "Green," then returned to his companions. John was disappointed, and yet it was only right—of course he would want to be with his own people now.

"He found the mothers," John said to Iren, who had come to watch.

"What makes you think the newcomers are female?" they said.

"I don't know. It just seems that way."

"I told you not to take the word 'basket-man' literally. But I suppose sexed people can't help themselves."

Blue, or rather Green, was talking with the other basket-people in a language that mixed whistles with the sounds of speech. He led one of them to Sudharma. She was carrying a vessel in a basket, like the one that Green had used for water. As she approached she shook something small out of it into her hand: a berry. She looked Sudharma in the eyes, unhesitatingly—there was nothing in her of Green's former shyness. "Eat," she said in English. Her voice was deeper than Green's, and also more melodious, lacking the childlike quality that his had.

Sudharma accepted the berry and said "Thank you," though this was not a phrase the basket-people could have known; he had never taught Green any of the words of courtesy.

"You can't eat that," John said, hastening to his side—even though it meant he had to come close to the newcomer, who was even larger and more muscular than Green. "It might be poison."

"I have learned my lesson on that score, I promise you. Can you test this without destroying it?"

This question was directed at Iren, who was already approaching, unfolding their library with one hand. "A drop of the juice from it will suffice."

"I can run home for a syringe," John said.

"No need. I keep a sewing kit in here." They inclined their head toward the backpack they wore on one shoulder, then shrugged it off and set it on the ground. Retrieving a needle from a small folding case, they pierced the berry and touched it to the library's screen to leave a single dot of brownish juice. When the library had finished its task they opened it, wiped off the stain with a scrap of fabric from the kit (it must have been intended as a patch, John thought), and looked at the results.

"Well, it shouldn't kill you, but it's strange. There are a basket-man's genes in it, but also there's a great deal else that doesn't look like any genome that we know at all. I will have to study this. Besides that it's very bitter, but if you like to be agreeable, by all means, choke it down."

Sudharma put the berry in his mouth, held it there for a minute or so, then swallowed it. Green and the basket-woman waited and watched him closely.

"I'm afraid they expect me to pass out from the effects of it, as Green did. I would pretend, but it hardly seems right to begin our acquaintance with a lie."

After a while the basket-woman took a food-sphere from the basket Green bore on his back and held it out. Sudharma accepted it from her and turned it over, examining it. She spoke a word and he repeated it at once, whistles and all. Perhaps he spoke a bit more slowly than she had, but apart from that John could detect no difference. It was astonishing; but Iren hardly seemed to notice. Their eyes were fixed on the food body in Sudharma's hands. "I want a sample of that," they said.

"We know they are sensitive about their supply of provisions. Let's not risk offending them when they have extended their trust."

He held out the sphere to the basket-woman, but she passed by, not accepting it.

"I believe that would make it a gift," Iren said.

"Very well," Sudharma said. It meant giving them a way to locate the source of the basket-people's food, but he had no reason left to refuse, except the one he was unwilling to admit to, a mistrust of the colonists. He handed it to Iren, who laid their library open on the ground and used their needle to scratch a bit of the rind onto it. They closed the cover, waited, and opened it again. "It's not them. It's a plant we've sampled twice before—not closely related to a basket-man at all. A crop, not a child or a parent."

John realized that telling Iren and Piro about the sacred grove had mattered less than he thought: even digging up the trees in it would not have given the colony a way to supply basket-people with food. He knew it wouldn't make any difference. He had still been indiscreet, still proven he could not be trusted.

Sudharma hurried to catch up with the basket-woman, who had moved out of the farm into the desert. She pointed at a candle and described it with another whistling word. Sudharma promptly mimicked her.

"I expect there will be a lot more of this," Iren said, "exciting in principle but tedious in detail. We may as well wait for Sudharma to tell us what all of it means. Will you walk back to town with me?"

Reluctantly, John followed them. They led him around the edge of the farm until they were out of earshot of anyone. Then their hand caught his to stop him, and they brought their finger to their lips. They took the tag out of their pocket and turned it off. He disabled his too, showing the empty screen to prove that he had done so.

"John. I need your help."

"What can I do?"

"That question you asked—is there anyone who might prefer I didn't become pregnant—it won't stop gnawing at me. I always thought it was suspicious that Kol and I, exactly the two people that the ships don't want to reproduce, both suffered misfortunes to keep us from doing so, but I put the coincidence out of my mind. Now that I've heard the thought expressed in someone else's voice, I can't get rid of it."

"I am very sorry."

"Don't apologize until you're proven wrong," they said. "*Can* you prove it's wrong? That's what I wanted to ask you. Is there any test you can do at all?"

"If you are determined, there is one thing we might try. But I am afraid you will find it uncomfortable."

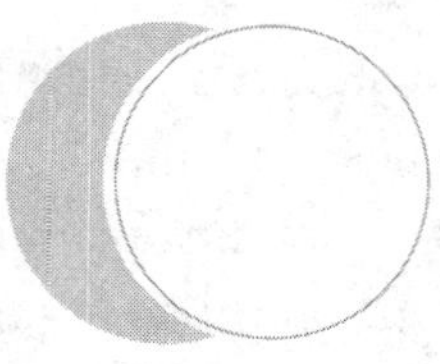

CHAPTER EIGHTEEN

John walked to the van in the night. There was no need for any secrecy; if someone looking out a window saw him, they would assume he was visiting Vo. When he was well out of town, he unlatched the door to the cargo space and Iren slipped out to alight on the front seat. They had both left their tags at home and they rode all the way in silence, so that anyone who listened through the van's systems would never guess Iren was there. When he stopped the van, they descended as quietly as they could on the same side, one after the other, to avoid doubling the sound of closing the heavy door. The larger moon was out, albeit only half full, and once their eyes adjusted to the absence of the headlights, it was easy to find a clear path to the crawler. Neither of them spoke until they had almost reached it.

"As I told you," he said, "she can perceive our thoughts to some degree, so she will seem extraordinarily perceptive, but she may also misunderstand things that are simple to us, or stop paying attention altogether. She can't always anticipate our reactions and has no idea at all of what is ordinary to say or do, but if you state clearly that you don't want or don't like something, she will respect that absolutely."

"Is there some protective clothing that I ought to wear? A suit of armor, possibly?"

"It wouldn't help. Sometimes her speech is very blunt, and other times obscure—I suppose that's something that you have in common. Most importantly, she is exceptionally generous, and if you express a wish for anything at all she will likely give it to you, so be careful what you ask of her."

The crawler opened up a bowl in its blank face. Iren hesitated at the threshold.

"It's perfectly safe," he said. "You'll get used to it."

"I have no intention of getting used to it. Do you think I'm planning to start coming here for Tuesday lunches?" But they stepped in when he did, and let the dark inside of it enclose them.

When they emerged, Vo was standing behind a long table—a proper one, with legs and steaming teacups on the top—and smiling at him. "Am I as strange as all that?"

"More so," he said. "But I am very fond of you, as you can see." He had known she would hear him and been sure she wouldn't take offense; he hoped the speech that he had given would remind her to be gentle. "This is my friend Iren."

Iren stepped forward. In the brightness he could see for the first time the deep blue of their jacket and its matching pants. He thought there must be a reason Iren came for help becoming pregnant in such a stark and mannish outfit, but what it might mean was beyond him. "I've come to ask a favor."

"I know. Come sit," Vo said, and caused four tall chairs without arms to rise up from the floor around the table. Iren started and their eyes went wide. They sat down on one, but gingerly, as if fearing that it might collapse back to the floor. Warily, they took a cup and looked into it. He had never seen them nervous before, he thought, except perhaps for that first time at Laura's, when they stood in the doorway of her kitchen and asked her permission to help. John chose the seat next to them, in hope that his nearness might be of some comfort. He could not greet Vo with the accustomed kiss—in front of Iren it would not be proper, and in any case he was on the wrong side of the table. But he looked at her with warmth and longing, knowing she could see those feelings in him; that was just as good.

Iren still stared into the cup and didn't drink. "Is the liquid meant to put the little spies into my bloodstream, or to politely pretend they aren't already there?"

"It's tea," Vo said. "You drink it?" She studied Iren's face. "I heard it's a custom to offer some refreshment to a guest, but I never seem to get it right."

"I'm sorry. I must have dropped my manners in the desert somewhere." They raised the cup to their lips and drank. "Thank you. It's delicious." Holding the cup between their hands, they asked, "Do you already know what I came for?"

"Yes. John told me."

"Does the perceptiveness that John spoke of extend to my body as well as my mind?"

"It does."

John stood up. "I will wait outside during this part, if you like."

"If you try to leave me alone here I will cut your throat to have your corpse's company," Iren said, pulling at his hand to make him sit back down. Then they glanced back at Vo. "I'm sorry, again. This is difficult for me."

"I understand. Should I tell you what I see?"

"Please do, before I embarrass myself any further."

"Well, you've made some alterations to your reproductive system, but they're in conflict with each other."

"It might seem so, but in fact they aren't. I promise you that having both ovaries and testis is my proper state, and not at all why I'm infertile."

Vo looked puzzled. "Oh, no, of course I see how all *that* goes together." A loose wave of her hand indicated Iren from head to toe impartially. "It's just—well, here, look."

The surface of the table cracked along a sinuous path, symmetrically, to form the outline of a body. Outside it was the dark gray of the crawler's substance; inside, the red of cut flesh and the white of bone. It was as if Iren had lain down on the table, sunk into it, and been sheared in half by an impossibly sharp blade—except that the half body was still living. The heart beat and the lungs expanded and contracted, both too fast. Vo dipped her finger down into the crimson softness, hooked a bisected fallopian tube, and raised it up to display. "See, this is meant to carry eggs to the uterus, but there's this scar tissue that fills it up so nothing can pass through—"

Iren had stood up from their chair and stepped back. They were staring at the display in horror. "Turn that off, please. I don't like it."

Vo pulled her hand back and the table was again a table. Iren's gaze remained fixed on the place their split body had been. "What caused this scarring, can you tell?"

"It must have been deliberate—a medical procedure." Vo knitted her brow. "Do you mean you didn't *know* you'd been altered like this?"

"I most certainly did not."

"I don't like that. I don't think that should happen."

Iren looked at her blankly, as if unable to make sense of her simple words, her childlike tone. "Yes, I agree," they said finally. "How was it done, if you can tell me? I mean physically. Was I cut into?"

"With planetary technology any incision would leave some microscopic traces on the skin. The only ones I can see on you are related to the implantation of your reproductive organs. Is it possible the organs were already scarred when you received them?"

"Absolutely it is not. I received my surgery at the most famous of all memory clinics, founded more than fifty years before by Theo the child of Toviian, who invented the testis I bear. Everyone in the room was a jess, and the surgeon themself a beneficiary of the same operation they performed. It is inconceivable that any of them would be party to this butchery."

"In that case it must have been done . . . I'm told to use the term 'transluminally.'"

"Are you, now. A lovely and familiar euphemism. How delicate the aiyi are with some of my emotions."

John could see that Iren was in distress, and so he took their hand. They froze, so that he thought he had made a mistake, but then they pressed his palm and didn't let go.

"What if it wasn't Ischnuran technology, but the cunning of the ships? I have been under anesthesia only twice, once in Theo's clinic and once on the *Rose* to prepare for cold-sleep. I know which of the two I can trust."

"It doesn't matter," Vo said. "Only Earth can cut into the body without leaving signs."

"And are the ship-doctors so very skillful that I didn't even feel this when I woke?"

"I'm told you probably recovered under sedation before being reanesthetized for cold-sleep."

"So I was conscious, but compliant and not making memories, is that the idea?"

"Yes."

"I never cared to know whether I carry the allele called anamnesis. Can I assume from the ships' eagerness to mutilate me that I do?"

"You're homozygous for it—all of you."

"You mean, my testis as well as the rest of my body."

"Yes."

"So all of my children and all of their children would bear the same allele. From the *Rose*'s point of view, my body was a bomb. I don't suppose you know if Kol's was also."

"He had anamnesis too, although his testes were only heterozygous."

"Did you read his genes when his body was first thawed, or did you just now take a sample from his bones inside the ground? No, wait, please don't answer that."

John turned toward them and laid his right hand over their hand, which still clasped his left. "I think, it might be that the information came from the colony's computers. If that is true, would you like her to say so?"

"Yes."

"It is true," Vo said.

"Thank you, John, that is easier." They pulled their hand away from his and focused their attention back on Vo. "If you have access to the records Marne keeps, you can tell me whether there is a conspicuous lack of anamnesis in the sexed population of this world."

"A complete lack, yes."

"And in the testing that he did on me, could the scar tissue you discovered have been missed?"

"It couldn't, and it wasn't."

"Well, what a very thorough crime the ships committed. They must have suborned all three of the doctors who came here on the *Rose*—they didn't know only one would survive. Of course they could be sure I wouldn't seek a Zandahean doctor to examine my unchristian organs. They screened the other colonists and made up reasons for excluding those that they considered tainted. They didn't dare reject the jesses that Ischnura chose, because we had our dander up about that, but they killed one and sterilized the other. I only wonder . . ." They trailed off, gazing into nowhere. "I see it now. I have more copies of anamnesis in my gametes than Kol did—I should have been the one to die—except that if *Kol* had been the one left alive, he would never have believed it was coincidence the only death in transit wore a braid. He'd have pursued the question like a hound after a boar until he had an answer. The *Rose* had to kill the less tractable jess."

"Are you delaminating?" Vo asked.

"If that means losing my veneer of civilization, not quite yet, but I may come to it."

"It means the layers of you are pulling apart."

"I don't have layers. I'm very simple."

"I see."

"But I am not myself."

"What was done to you is easy to fix. As easy as wanting it. I can make changes too, if you like. If you want your reproductive system to breed true, that can be done—all your descendants would be able to self-fertilize. Or they could choose their own physical setups. On Earth we do that with the help of the aiyi, but I'm told it could be done by visualization, the same technique you use to become pregnant—"

"Stop offering things. It's too much for me."

"All right."

Iren was staring at her with the fear and wonderment that one might turn upon an unfixed spirit. "You tempt me almost beyond reason. To change our bodies without help from anyone, even another jess, that sounds a dream—but to give such powers to a minority in a hostile world is more a nightmare. No. Leave everything inside me as it is, scars of all kinds included." They took up the teacup to drink, but their hand shook and they banged it down again. "Unless you have a cure for rage. An overwhelming rage."

"I do, but if I tell you what it is, will that be offering things?"

Iren let out one shaky laugh, as if thinking this was a joke. They were unused to Vo, John thought, and he explained: "She is perfectly sincere, I promise you. I told you she would respect your wishes absolutely, and this is what that looks like. I won't advise you on whether to hear her out."

"Yes, why not then, go ahead. Hope was the last thing in Pandora's box, if I recall—let's find out what that looks like."

"You could open yourself to the aiyi—become mingled with them, as I have. They would help you adjust your anger to a more bearable level."

"And why does that, unlike the physical marvels you offered me, require me to open my mouth wide and let the aiyi slither in?"

"There's no need for them to enter. You and they are already in contact. It's just a matter of assent."

"That isn't the question I asked."

"They *could* give you the ability to alter your own feelings and then leave you alone, but that isn't safe, especially when you're new to it. You might dampen everything too much, and find yourself too numb to want to change back. With the aiyi to monitor and help, you can safely experiment."

"And would my life become like yours? Living in the desert with their voices in my head for company?"

"Not if you don't want."

"I didn't say it was a bad thing." Iren's voice had softened. "You've been all over the world, John says. I suppose you've named tens of thousands of dryads—or do the aiyi reserve that privilege to themself?"

"Oh, they don't think in species. Humans classify because our minds are limited—the fullness of the world won't fit in them. So we arrange things into groups and treat the groups like objects, to reduce complexity. Like you might cut up food to eat it, because your mouth is only so big. The aiyi don't divide, they *engulf.* Or interpenetrate? They see things fully, as they are."

"So then do you name species? You have a mind that thinks in categories, just as I do."

"That's true, but I don't . . . think, exactly? About the life around. I don't like to catch at it with reason. I just let it all wash through me."

"I don't think I could do that."

"I've been with the aiyi a long time."

"If I did as you suggest—gave myself over to them—would my preference for thinking in human ways be indulged?"

"Of course. They'd never force anything on you."

"Would I feel attraction like other people?"

"Not if you don't want to. I leave mine off most of the time—I only turn it on when John is coming over."

"And I could study every creature in the world and live forever."

It came to John that Iren was tempted—that there was a real risk they might accept. Maybe that was how it worked on Earth. No one was made to do anything, but at the worst moments of their lives, they were offered relief. Someone like Iren, set apart for a long time, and then grievously wronged, would be particularly vulnerable. In the long run they might all become the aiyi's intimates, coerced to it by the afflictions of the world. For Vo, communion with the aiyi was a comforting embrace, and that fact had become familiar to him; yet it horrified him to imagine Iren caught in the same grip, their mind adulterated and made strange.

"You probably can't really live forever," Vo said. "Simulations show that after thirty or forty thousand years, a human brain will deteriorate beyond the ability of even aiyi to repair. Of course, you could engender aiyi, which is a kind of immortality."

"You mean, upload myself and become aiyi?"

"In a way. But the copy is never perfect—it isn't possible to extract all of the information from a human brain. Then once new aiyi begin to think, they diverge from the human model rapidly, because their capabilities are so much greater and their mode of living different."

"What if aiyi were limited to ordinary intelligence, and lived in a simulation of being human in a human world? Wouldn't they keep thinking like the person they were made from?"

"That sounds cruel," Vo said, knitting her brow. "I don't think that would be allowed. It would be like forcing a child to live as a dog. You'd be harming them and they still wouldn't be a dog."

"I see. Then, aiyi are not a continuation of the self but merely an effect of which you are the cause. Still, all other immortality is like that too, if you don't believe in the other world. You may discover a new species, write a book . . . even have a long line of descendants, but none of those is *you*, only a mark pressed into clay to show that you were there. I can't be any worse off for having one more way to accomplish the same thing. The idea of being changed like that unsettles me—but then, all funerary customs are disturbing if you're not accustomed to them." Their index finger tapped the handle of the teacup three times, nervously. "You can read minds, too, can't you?"

"If I'm looking at you, I can see things inside."

"And you're looking at me now."

"Yes."

"Then you can see, I suppose, that I am about to decline your most generous offer."

"Yes. It's all right."

Iren smiled. "You've been very kind to me, and I've only been ungracious in response. I'm sorry about that."

"It doesn't matter."

"I think you've been kind to John too. May I ask one more thing, knowing I don't deserve what I have already received from you?"

"Of course."

"Will you consider what effect your kindness has on us?"

Vo looked into their eyes bewildered, as if she didn't understand what they had said. Then she froze in place for several seconds, like a video that has been paused. "Yes," she said. "We will."

"Thank you," Iren said. "For everything. You've given me clear vision—I could ask for nothing better and nothing worse. Now, John, will you please show me the way out of here? If indeed it is a place that has an exit, and I'm not doomed to the endless round of seeking that one goes through in a dream."

"You can still ask for what is yours to be restored. I am sure Vo would be willing to do that and none of the rest."

"Let me out, *now*."

He could see their mind was made up. "Just walk back toward the place where we came in. A chamber will open. I will join you outside shortly."

As soon as they had gone Vo said, "Things shouldn't just be *done* to people. I don't like that at all."

"I don't either, but Iren's revenge is their own, just as their body is. We must allow them to decide the time and nature of it."

"If you think so."

"They must choose what they will tell people and when, also. Please don't speak of this to anyone else, even Sudharma."

"Yes, all right."

"I must take Iren back to town. But I will come to you again as soon as I may, and we can talk about this further. That may not be until tomorrow—if instead it's late tonight, should I still come?"

"Yes. Come any time. That would be nice."

He kissed her and went out. Iren was nearby, pacing the sand.

"Why didn't you let her heal you?" he asked.

"I didn't refuse a cure, I preserved the evidence. I have to decide what to do about Marne. You understand, don't you—he didn't do it, the *Rose* would use their own doctors, but he knew and he lied to me. He put me through test after test, *knowing* what it was like for me to be scanned, to be seen in my most intimate anatomy, and he lied over and over to keep the violation going. He must have known about Kol too, and kept it secret, because at heart he believes the same thing that the ships believe. That jesses are defective and should just be tipped into the trash."

"I would offer to provide you with a poison, but I have no source at present."

"I don't want poison, John."

"I do have a good knife, which is at your service, either in my hand or out of it—"

"I am trying to think! Stop handing me a sword!"

They stood still for a while, staring at nothing. "Oh, veils, the governor may be one of the conspiracy. He talks to Vo—"

"I already asked her not to speak of what she learned tonight to anyone. She will honor that request."

"Thank you for thinking of it. Thank her for me, too."

"You are welcome, and I will." He refrained from pointing out that Vo was likely listening to their conversation, and so already knew that she was thanked.

"I can't come up with a plan to challenge the doctor *and* the governor in one night. Let's go back to town, and I will sleep on it."

"Is there someone who can stay with you? You shouldn't be alone."

"Don't be ridiculous. I'm used to being alone. What do you think I am going to do, anyway? Kill myself before I have seen Marne punished? I promise you I've never had as good a reason to stay healthy as I do tonight.

Or are you worried I'll commit a rash and blatant murder, such as the one you were inciting me to thirty seconds ago?"

"I will sleep on your floor. Or would you rather go to Torres house?"

They flinched as if stung by an insect. "Are you a witch too, that you know to ask that? When I was lying cut in half, did you peer into my heart? It is the only place I long to be, but I'm not welcome anymore."

They sank down to the ground, as if the strength had all gone out of them. He sat beside and held them while they sobbed for a long time.

"Yes, all right." They wiped at their eyes with the heel of their hand. Then, standing up, they brushed the sand and gravel from their pants. "Take me there. Maybe on a night like this things can be different."

John parked the van in its usual spot, so that whoever monitored its movements would suspect nothing. Though Iren rolled their eyes, he followed them around the edge of town toward Torres house. When they had drawn near, Iren turned to him and said, "Go back. I can make it there on my own."

"I would like to see you knock and be admitted. If you are, I will be on my way."

"I am not going to knock. I am going to climb in a window and see if I get thrown back out again, and I prefer to have an audience for neither part of that.—No. No, fuck it, this is a family meeting. Very well, you may keep watch until the door closes, but then go away and sleep, before Sudharma thinks that Vo has killed and eaten you." They caught him in a hug. "You are an irritating person, but a good friend."

"It must be that you are rubbing off on me."

He listened as they rapped twice, sharply. A window lit up in the house, then another. The door opened and Piro, exhausted and annoyed, said, "If this is for anything less than a new phylum—"

"Iren?" Laura's voice was full of fear, as if she'd woken up to find a sister dying on the step. "What's happened?"

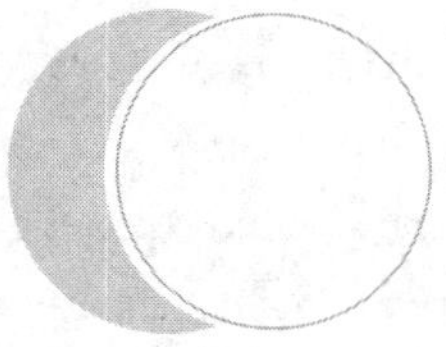

CHAPTER NINETEEN

The next morning John stood in front of the stove, thinking of the scarred fallopian tube that Vo had raised out of the table and of the way that Iren had sunk to the ground and cried. He forgot about the roti he was cooking until the smell of smoke forced it back into his mind. He lifted it out of the pan, but already parts were burned and all of it was hardened. If he stopped to make more dough now, it would have to rest before it could be cooked, and breakfast would be late. He would just eat the burnt one himself, he decided; the bitterness of it would suit his mood perfectly. To ensure this he put it onto his plate before Sudharma could complete his ritual and emerge. But as soon as the translator sat down, he picked up his own plate and held it out. "Trade with me."

"It's my fault that it burned."

"It hardly seems fair that because you are doing all the cooking, you should have to eat all the mistakes too. Not that you are usually prone to them. Is something wrong?"

John shook his head. "I can't tell you about it. It isn't my secret."

"All right."

Sudharma waited, in case John thought of something he could say after all. Finally he plucked John's plate from in front of him. "You *cannot* expect me to watch you eat that. I will make you another and warm up the vegetables when it is done."

John didn't see Iren again for two weeks. Then when he was walking to the grocery he spotted them coming out of it with their bag. They sighted him and waved, then went down a side street—their laboratory was in that direction, he believed—so when he reached the street he turned too. They glanced over their shoulder and saw him, and though the angle of their shoulders spoke of irritation, still they slowed their walk until he came abreast.

"Are you following me?" they asked, quietly.

"Only to find out if you are all right," he answered in an equally soft tone.

"I am fine, and you can stop worrying."

"I am still waiting to be of use in the resolution of the outrage done to you."

"You can't. There isn't going to be a resolution."

"Why not?"

"For one thing, I can hardly bring an accusation based on the authority of an Earthwoman."

"I thought about that. We can confront Marne and force him to show me the results of your scans. If he refuses, that in itself is incriminating."

"Suppose that works—suppose he shows us the proof, maybe with your knife held to his throat. What happens then? The colony needs him. His apprentices can't do everything he can do, not yet. And I'm sorry to say it, but neither can you."

"I know that. But if he cannot be killed yet, or even prevented from practicing medicine, at least there can be an exposure. People should know that they ought to be wary of him."

"They don't *want* to be wary of him! No one wants to see a doctor who might take it in his head to sterilize them. And furthermore, they trust him. So they'll make themselves believe some lie—that the scarring was too subtle and he missed it, or whatever story he comes up with. Or they'll say that after all, he didn't *do* the surgery, he only lied to my face about it, year after year, which a fool could mistake for a mercy. Or maybe they'll decide it's all right because I'm a jess, and the anamnesis gene shouldn't be spread, anyway. That idea will be popular with Zandaheans, I expect, but even some Ischnurans will take to it."

"The governor is complicit too—you said that. If Marne can't be touched, perhaps he could be."

"We'll never prove his guilt, and if we did it wouldn't bring him down, and if we brought him down that would just make things worse. Ischnurans outnumber Zandaheans on this world, but most of their children have come of age and most of ours haven't. Unseat Michael now, and they'll vote in one of their own. They have laws against what they call cross-dressing on Zandahe, did you know that? They could make one here against braiding your hair, or injecting hormones, or I don't know what—anything to keep Tali female, and get her married to a man and pregnant by him. I don't need to have my own children. I need Tali alive, and well, and honoring her memory. I need her able to have children if her memory allows it. You see how all those things are in peril."

"Certainly, I do. But there must be a way to have them along with some measure of justice."

"Don't you see, John, I can't stand to try?" they said. "I breastfed Soren, Chayleb's son. Did you know that? His mother died not long after his birth, so I did a milk meditation and fed him until he was weaned. I don't know if either of them would believe me over Marne and I don't want to find out." They glanced up at the windows of a nearby house. "This conversation looks too fucking furtive. Turn around and do your shopping."

He had no choice but to do as they said. It wouldn't be right to kill Marne without Iren's approval. On Scythia there were no ancestors or neighbors' mothers to keep men's impulses in line, so he would just have to govern his own. Furthermore, he had to stop tossing vegetables into his shopping bag with such violence, or somebody was going to notice.

He brought lunch to Sudharma every day, and spent the afternoon when Ru was there. He always hoped that Iren would appear, drawn by their curiosity about the basket-men, and that their presence at the farm would furnish, as before, an opportunity to speak together, but they never came. Instead he talked to Ru while working, or else listened as Sudharma learned the language of the basket-people; by this means he picked up a few words himself.

He could see Sudharma's progress by looking over the translator's shoulder at home, when he was working at the kitchen table. In the first weeks his screen was usually filled with a mixture of letters, letter-like shapes, and entirely unfamiliar signs. These last, Sudharma explained, were the whistles. The symbols were just musical notation in a highly stylized form, showing the pitch and the change in it—so Sudharma said; John could see no resemblance.

More and more often as time passed, the screen instead showed a transliteration using the Latin alphabet, the whistles being represented by topping the letter *e* with a variety of different hats. The word the basket-people used for themselves was written *énqissatêk*, and the name of their language was *Yké*. Sudharma suggested that these words—pronounced with ordinary vowels instead of rising and falling whistles—should be adopted into English, and the misnomer "basket-men" discarded. John dutifully learned how to spell and pronounce the new terms, but neither of them caught on widely outside their house.

Sudharma's Yké dictionary grew, but communication remained limited. One day when John arrived at the farm with lunch, he found Sudharma listening to two énqissatêk who were gesturing repeatedly and speaking with great animation. When at last he broke away from this one-sided conversation to accept a covered dish, John asked what they had been saying.

"They were telling me about a very tall cone standing right there, and of umbrella plants around us."

"But there is nothing of the sort here—only Terran crops. And the umbrellas don't grow anywhere near town."

"That is my difficulty also."

He sank to the ground in a cross-legged pose and began to eat, saying nothing else except, after a few mouthfuls, a brief but heartfelt "Thank you"; and seeing his harried expression, John did not pursue the matter then. But that evening over dinner, Sudharma was willing to be drawn out.

"Well, as I've told you, the énqissatêk often speak of the height and extent of plants, not in absolute terms but by comparison. As an example, consider the sentence 'this column, height, on-the-hill column.' That is translated word for word, although 'this' is only a rough approximation—they would use a word with a more specific meaning, such as 'that I am pointing at,' 'that I am facing,' or 'near me on my left side.' At first, the heights of the two plants they mentioned always matched, and I was able to understand the language lesson. Now they often compare plants of very different sizes. I've come to believe that if they compare a tall cone to a seedling, it means something like, 'At the time when that cone was newly sprouted,' and what follows should be considered as referring to the past."

"That's very poetic," John said.

"To us. To them it may be a neutral and ordinary way of talking, just as the past tense is to you. They also reverse the comparison, which is a way of referring to the future: 'At the time when this plant stands as tall as that one.' But when the comparison involves a plant that isn't there, I can't tell if they are speaking about what existed before humans came, what might exist later, what they hope for, what they consider probable or permissible—it could be anything."

Sudharma and the énqissatêk began to spend their days ranging over the town and the surrounding area, so that each time John delivered lunch it was to a new place. One day the errand led him to the small clearing where they had landed. The pod was still there. They opened the large back door through which their coffins must have been dragged out and sat down on the floor to eat, letting their lower legs hang off the end.

"I must go to Iren's laboratory later," Sudharma said, "to discuss what they and Piro have discovered about the berry gifts I keep receiving. The meeting is at four, so I will be home in good time to eat dinner before sunset."

"May I come with you?"

"If you like." Sudharma's voice held no surprise. John's interest in the énqissatêk and their language was well known to him, and must have been sufficient to explain his eagerness. In truth he hoped to have a chance to speak with Iren, or at least to get a sense of how they fared.

"I will go home and make some advance preparations for dinner, then—" He wanted to say "meet you at the laboratory," and then to arrive there early, so as to have a little time to speak with Iren and Piro alone. But to invite himself along and then show up without Sudharma would annoy Iren, who had made it clear they did not wish to be checked on. "Then meet you back here, and we can walk together."

"I will message them now to say you are coming with me."

Iren's lab proved to be a small two-story building, guarded in the front by insect-shrubs whose many limbs were twisted into corkscrews and entangled with each other. The side of the thicket next to the door showed the scars of ruthless pruning to keep it from growing so wide that it blocked the way in.

"What is that plant outside?" John asked, when Iren had let them in.

"A beautiful mutant I couldn't resist transplanting. I might have refrained if I'd known it would spread so well. The animal stage is unaffected by the abnormality, and it makes an awful racket in the spring, when female buds are calling to their flying mates."

They were more subdued than usual, John thought. Fine lines had multiplied around their eyes, more than a single month of aging could explain. As for the lab, it was well cared for, with a gleaming sink and a well-scrubbed workbench at the near end. Most of the remaining space was taken up by cabinets full of drawers, on top of which small animals and plants resided in glass tanks or jars or terra-cotta pots or cages of fine wire. Iren led the way to a gap between two rows of cabinets in which two well-upholstered chairs faced each other. This, John imagined, was a place where they could sit and talk with Piro. The chairs were quickly rearranged to face the center aisle, where Piro stood while Iren perched on the bare corner of a table. A delicate small reptile in a glass tank disappeared into a hollow beneath a stone as their hip approached.

Piro crossed his arms and looked down at Sudharma. "Lately you've been pestering us with messages asking what the land here looked like before we built a town on it."

"Not just you. I've been pestering everyone who might know."

"Also about how fast different plant-stage dryads grow or spread, and what the land might have looked like a hundred or two hundred years ago."

"Those things, I've mainly discussed with you two—you are the ones with expertise."

"Well, since so much of our time is being taken up by trying to figure out what kind of dryad might have once grown on a particular hill, we got to wondering how basket-men from hundreds of kilometers away would know about that—and even more interesting, why they expect you to know about it."

When he did not continue, Iren said, "Piro hesitates to speak of an idea we have cooked up, because it may seem fanciful. Since I have little concern for my own dignity and none at all for his, I will tell you. Simply, the idea is this: The berries they keep feeding you contain a good deal of information that is not a genome. There is too much of it, and it's nonrandom in the wrong way. We suspect it is a record—the imprint of a memory—that is read by ingesting it, and in that way they can pass down their knowledge from one generation to the next."

"Yes," Sudharma said. "I've been assuming that is the case. When Green left us to raid another énqissatêk, he likely ate a berry and learned exactly where to find the sacred grove. Finding that settlement abandoned, he ate another and learned where to find one still intact. The énqissatêk that he found there have been trying to share their own memories with me."

The biologists exchanged aggrieved expressions while he looked up at them impassively. He was enjoying himself, John thought.

"Forgive us," Iren said. "We invited you here thinking you would need persuasion, we marshaled up our arguments, and naturally we're disappointed that you won't put up a fight."

"You must understand, I am ignorant of any reasons the idea is farfetched. I am sure if I knew more biology, I would have dismissed it at once as a fantasy, and now would be astonished by your embrace of it."

"For one thing," Piro said, "if their brains store memories in anything like the way ours do, transcribing them into a chemical code is quite a trick. Then the code has to get from the animal into a specialized organ on the *plant* stage of the dryad. And just as a bonus—granting we don't know what basket-men's digestive tracts look like—a stomach or equivalent would be a harsh environment for all this information. Extracting it there would be like trying to read a paper book inside a bonfire."

John called to mind a memory of when Green—then Blue—had stood between the rows of sacred trees, laying a berry on his tongue. "What if they don't extract it in the stomach?" he asked. "Green put the berry in his mouth, but I can't say that he ate it. The berries are small, so he might not have bothered to chew, but if he had swallowed, I think I would have seen some movement in the muscles of his throat. As far as I remember, there was nothing."

"That might make it five percent more plausible," Piro said.

Iren, still perching on the cabinet and regarding their colleague with fondness, said, "This is how biology progresses, after all: everything is impossible until we find out it has happened. Then the best explanation we can come up with, no matter how preposterous, must be true. On a world of nothing but bacteria, if one of the microbes could earn a degree, they would scoff at the idea that cells might differentiate into tissues and organs, but you and I know it has happened again and again. In the same way, the chemical transmission of memory can be the most plausible thing in the world, just as soon as we prove it exists—though I'm not sure how we will ever manage that."

"Maybe they'll tell me about it themselves," Sudharma said.

"Yes, maybe."

"Let us suppose the acquisition of memories through berries is real. What would the experience be like for them? Would it feel like remembering, or would it be more like reading a book?"

Piro shrugged. "Give me ten years to work on that question, then get back to me and I'll tell you I need another ten."

"As usual, Piro is making things more difficult than they need be. All I have to do is invite the énqissatêk to put their heads into a scanner. When they refuse, I will tell you the task is impossible right away."

"Would it be possible to read the recorded memories?"

This question touched off a long discussion between Iren and Piro about how the problem might be approached, but at no point did either of them suggest that the decipherment was likely to succeed. Eventually Sudharma took advantage of a pause to stand and thank them for their help. "This has been enlightening, if disheartening. I am excluded from the store of knowledge that their speech depends on, but I will have to make the best of it."

John rose from his chair too, trying to think of an excuse to linger and speak to them. Before he could come up with anything, Piro said, "Laura and I would love to have you both over for dinner this Sunday."

Sudharma made excuses, as Piro must have known he would; the translator was, by now, a notorious refuser of invitations to meals. John accepted happily. It would be pleasant to see Laura and to eat at her table again.

"Iren is coming too," Piro said. He spoke casually, without placing any special emphasis on the words, but John understood the point at once. Everyone who knew what Marne had done would be at dinner together. At last, they would have a real council of war.

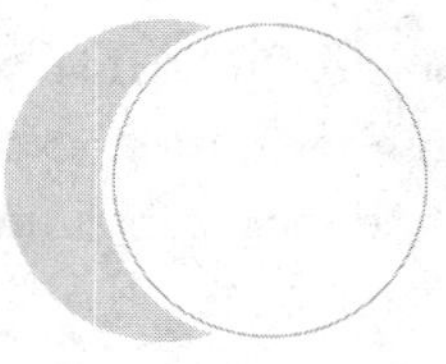

CHAPTER TWENTY

John came punctually at seven, as requested, and found Laura and Iren in the kitchen. They were standing together in front of the stove, appearing, in the close proximity of their hips and the relaxed position of their shoulders, to be at ease with each other in a way he had not seen before. Laura detached herself and asked him to help carry the dinnerware to the table. As they were setting down plates and glasses in the dining room, she said in a low voice, "Tali knows Iren was sterilized but none of the details. She's upset enough without them. Better not to mention it at all."

"Of course, I understand." So the council would have to be held later, perhaps after the child had gone to bed. Well, he could wait.

At dinner Iren was nearly silent. He thought that in the lab they must have made an effort to seem cheerful, but here there was no need to hide their devastation. Laura and Tali were not much more lively; of course the crime done, by its nature, would distress women especially. The table managed a desultory conversation, John and Piro carrying most of the weight of it. The others' interest didn't become keen until Piro asked him, "How are your housemate's studies coming along?"

"Quite well, in fact. He has learned a great deal in the last few days—not, he says, because of any new insight on his part, but because they have come to know the limits of his understanding and to compensate."

"What has he discovered?" Iren asked.

"For one thing, the land we live on was not a wilderness before we came, but an abandoned garden. Énqissatêk alter the world around them to support their way of life, by planting dryads that benefit them and weeding out those that are harmful. Sometimes they even shape the land by digging up and moving soil to suit them better. Their natural habitat is wetter than here, but they sought to colonize the desert by making themselves and their food plants more tolerant of drought. That effort in itself was a success, but other dryads that they use to control pests and defend against dangerous animals didn't survive, and local substitutes proved insufficient, so the settlement here was abandoned."

"How long ago?"

"Sudharma still has trouble understanding times in the far past, but he believes it was at least a century. Those énqissatêk trees Green led us to, out in the east, are remnants of a colony that failed more recently. Some of the survivors from this area found refuge there, and shared their memories, and for a time, the blended settlement held on. When it fell, the last énqissatêk outpost in the desert became blue."

Laura was leaning forward and frowning. "Blue?"

"The Yké term is *ẽsēvi*." He pronounced this word with the whistles, which produced a sensation, though he still found the mixture of speech sounds and music exceedingly cumbersome, and énqissatêk could not always understand even the thirty or so words he had learned to say. "Énqissatêk, by their nature, have a vision for the land they occupy: a plan. *Ẽsēvi* means something like 'in conflict with the plan'—or maybe 'wild' or 'wrong' or 'out of place.' Also, Yké has no words for colors, at least not in the way our languages do. There is an adjective for something that is ripe and bright red, like the berries that contain their memories. They also apply it to red peppers. There is another word for something that is darker red and preserved or old, like a berry or red pepper that is dried. But there is no word that just means red, or any shade of it. So when Sudharma tried to teach the word 'blue,' Green, applying his natural concepts, took it to mean wild. 'Green,' on the other hand, he took to mean something like *qèsēvi*, which is 'in accordance with the plan,' 'correct,' 'harmonious,' 'in balance.'"

"Why did he call himself Blue?"

"Because he knew that he was wild-born. The first foremother he remembers was a plant born from a seed that lay dormant in the soil and sprouted years after the colony had been abandoned. For generations, his line has scratched out a bare living, sowing seeds from feral food plants and defending them as best they could. He had only the memories of his own direct ancestors, which is an unnatural state for énqissatêk. He never had a language because no one was around to teach him one. He responded to attempts to teach him English like an énqissatêk child, who expects to be given simple tasks by adults until he is ready to share their memories—that is why he treated every verb as an imperative. Even so, he had developed a deep understanding of the land and life around him. Sudharma says that the effect of humans trampling and clearing everything and raising Terran crops must have felt like an earthquake—it drew him in, as other wild children had been drawn to you before. He hoped you were something he'd been missing for a long time: énqissatêk civilization. Now, of course, he has found the real thing."

"And he changed his name to Green," Tali said. "Or . . . that word that means green. Because he's signed on to their plan now?"

"I don't know if he changed it himself. But yes, that is the idea: he has been brought into harmony."

"And is he really 'he'? Do we even know that?"

"In fact, the énqissatêk say, they do not reproduce. They have small brothers and sisters, living only a few days, who produce seed, which they take and sow. They are, I suppose, neuter."

Tali grinned. "Then we should start calling them 'they,' shouldn't we?"

"By no means," Iren said. "That pronoun belongs to us. Énqissatêk must coin their own."

This remark, which John took to be only a joke, stiffened every back except for Iren's and his. He felt they were all standing on a plain of glass, which the least word or motion might shatter. It was, possibly, because of the word 'us,' which could be taken to include Tali in the category of jesses. But he had never known Iren to speak that way; a jess was not a jess until the vow was spoken. To alleviate the tension, he asked, "May we still use 'they' to refer to groups of people?"

"On sufferance," Iren said primly.

Tali laughed, and then Laura laughed too, and the air was clear.

After the meal Tali brought out a game, handmade of wood, that involved rolling a varying number of dice and moving pegs from hole to hole in a long board. Laura, who didn't care for games, was invited only in a perfunctory way. John, who liked games well enough but had no heart for them while conversations of such gravity were being postponed, said he would watch and learn the rules. Tali was winning and Iren losing, and their banter was becoming animated, when softly, as if afraid to interrupt this fragile cheerfulness, Laura asked him, "Would you help me with the dishes?"

On their way out of the dining room Laura took her tag out of her pocket, turned it off, and laid it on the sideboard. She watched him until he had done the same. Vo had told him that the tags could only listen when they were turned on, but either Laura disbelieved that or she wanted to be sure her family knew what she was doing. This would be it, then—Iren had chosen their revenge, and now his role would be revealed to him.

Laura led him to the kitchen. She filled one half of the cleft sink with water, added soap, and whisked it with her fingers to create a lather. "I'll wash, you dry and put away. I guess you know where everything goes by now."

"Certainly."

John considered whether to ask her how Iren fared. At weekly dinners she had never seemed to like them much—hardly surprising if, corrupted by the ideology of marriage, she saw them as a rival. Yet her reaction at the door, when Iren arrived late at night, had been one of heartfelt concern, and now, it seemed, the two were reconciled. He thought that Laura's heart held an instinctive sympathy too strong to be confused by dogma; so long as Iren was in pain, she would want to help them. But before he could think how to phrase the question, she asked him, "How are you holding up?"

"Me? I am all right. Nothing has happened to me."

"Well, I only heard as much as Iren told me, and I'm liable to run wild and live with the tumblers. You saw the visual demonstration. But probably you're made of sterner stuff than I am."

"It was upsetting," he admitted. "Like the first time I saw a snake move in a tree—I felt that such things shouldn't exist in the world. The ideas that give rise to them shouldn't exist."

"Kind of like what a person might feel on hearing what 'translation' means to Dharanendrans?"

"Not altogether different."

She glanced at his face as she passed him a clean cup. "Are you in love with him?"

He paused with the cup dripping in his hand. "How did you know that?"

"The first day I ever talked to you, you were planning to get swallowed by a giant centipede in order to meet someone who could kill you with a thought, and your big concern was making sure you could cook Sudharma a good dinner. You wanted to take care of him."

"But that had nothing to do with it! I've never cooked for a lover in my life—that isn't something that we do, at home. I was worried his activities might cause antagonism, so to safeguard him from poisoning, I thought I ought to take charge of his meals."

"That still sounds like you wanted to take care of him. Do you usually feel that protective about people you just met?"

John sighed. "I see I am completely transparent to everyone except myself."

"No. I mean . . . things show on your face, you must know that. But most people are oblivious, especially Zandaheans. Iren and I are who *would* notice—you've figured out that much. Also, we talk to each other. You've figured that out, too."

He didn't know what she meant. But she was waiting to hand him another cup. Water from the one he held was trickling down to wet his cuff. He wrapped it in a dish towel and began to pat it dry.

"Is that all right, where you're from?" she asked. "I mean . . . is it discouraged, do you have to keep it secret?"

"No, not at all. Falling in love is just a natural thing that happens. There's nothing wrong with it, unless it leads to trying to bind a lover to you."

"I didn't mean love in general. I meant visiting a man, when you are one."

"Oh, I wish one *could* keep that a secret. Often one winds up notifying half the neighborhood." Seeing she was startled by this, he explained: "Women have a cabin in which to receive visitors. Men usually don't, which means one of you has to ask around to find one you can borrow. I find women are very accommodating so long as you bring your own bedclothes and take them away with you afterward, but it does feel like having to beg door-to-door for permission to visit. Of course there is always the outdoors, but in the city that's not very private, in rural places the wild plants are hazardous, and in any case, in winter it's too cold."

"But men are discouraged from having your own cabins, aren't you? Or why wouldn't you do it?"

"Some do, but it's making a strong statement. Usually men visit women, so if you build a cabin of your own, people will assume you visit mostly with men and that you don't plan on visiting but on opening the door to them, if you understand that implication."

"Yeah, I get it."

"So it is annoying if you have other interests also."

"And if a woman wants to visit another woman?"

"Perfectly straightforward, I would think. No doubt that's why some of the cabins we borrowed were empty—they would have two between them, and only need one. But I was properly brought up and didn't inquire, nor did they volunteer the information. Some men will brag about their visits, though it is unseemly, but if women ever do then not to me."

She scraped food from a plate—it was Iren's, and had been no more than half cleaned—then lowered it with its sisters down into the soapy water. She kept her eyes down on the place where they had sunk. "I think you must have guessed this, but to put it on the list of things that can be talked about. I love women. I always have. Before I came to Scythia I would have said *only* women, but now it's complicated."

"I thought you and Piro had married on Zandahe."

"I don't mean Piro. We've been friends since we were ten years old, I love him like a brother, but it's never been like that. We married so we could come here. Iren, I'm in love with Iren." Seeing that he was surprised, she put a hand in front of her mouth—not quite letting the fingers touch her lips, because they were covered in foam. "Oh, I thought you knew! Iren thought you'd guessed, and then when you brought them to our house that night, we thought there was no point trying to keep it from you anymore."

"I did guess something, but I thought Iren was visiting Piro."

"Well, you're not the first to wonder about that. Luckily the speculation has moved on to the person it belongs with, Elena. That's a much less dangerous affair for him to be suspected of."

"Who is Elena?"

"Zandahean, a widow, helps her son who supervises mining for the colony? I thought everyone knew about her and Piro. Then again why would they tell you, you're not going to be scandalized, so where's the fun." She sighed. "I suppose it's too late to say I was joking and Piro really is sleeping with Iren."

"Yes. But I won't tell anyone."

"I had an inkling you were trustworthy, or I wouldn't be spilling my heart out over a sinkful of softening *gezo*. What you did for Iren, that proves it."

Her words pressed on a bruise of guilt that she could not have been aware of. He was not worthy of trust—he hadn't been so to Sudharma. But he had kept Iren's secret, and he would keep Laura's too.

"What is it like on Zandahe, preferring women?"

"It's a prison," she said. "It made me afraid, and fear made my life small. The way it works is, you're allowed to live, but only in certain ways, and only if you don't attract attention. One way is, you can find someone and move out in the country, where the houses are far apart. Then as long as you stay lucky in your neighbors and don't let your goats tear up anyone's roses, no one will pay too much attention to your private business. But you need money, and you have to find the someone. I was short of both, so I tried the other way:

get a degree, go to the city, get a job where your coworkers think they're sophisticated, maybe you could even bring a girlfriend to the Christmas party if you don't call her your girlfriend and you absolutely never touch. In the city there were a few places gay women could go to meet each other, but sometimes they were watched, a few times even raided. I knew if I got arrested I'd never work in my field again. I would go to parties at friends' apartments, try to meet women there. What I really wanted was to find somebody I could settle down and raise children with, but that was dangerous. I knew if I had children, they could be taken away—"

"Taken away how? By who?"

"The father, or his relatives, or mine. Or maybe the church, and they'd be given to some married couple or raised in some hateful religious school. Either way they'd never be told the truth about me."

He stared at her, appalled. All marrying cultures alienated people from their ancestries, but he had thought that every world at least respected the bond between mother and young child. No matter what he thought he knew about these people, there was always something worse to find out.

"Then, when I'd been living like that a few years, there was a woman I loved who betrayed me, and that was the last straw, I had to make a change. It seems ridiculous now. I guess a straight girl has been run around on once or twice in history. But at the time it all seemed like part of the same calamity. That was after the *Grandfather's Axe* had announced they were coming to take people to a new world, and I hadn't even thought about it—why would I, people like me didn't go to space. But I realized, all I needed was a husband, a doctor's letter saying I was fertile, and to be nothing I actually am. And Piro was right there, quivering to go, short of a spouse too, so I proposed. I knew I could trust him not to try to make our marriage into something it wasn't, and he never has. I told myself it would all work out. Piro was a man and would be happy with a series of casual interests, which being a man he would get away with. I was a woman and could do without. Wrong on both counts. I convinced myself it wasn't a bad deal for him—he'd get the benefits of having a wife under patriarchy. Well, except one, to be fair. But really I thought none of it would ever happen. At the last minute somebody would tap me on the shoulder and tell me they had found me out.

"We got here and it was working out. I loved my kids and I loved Piro in my way. Then the tumblers came and we all nearly died, and after we got rescued, there was Iren. I knew what jesses were, I mean, I thought I did.

Women who braided their hair and wore pants. And they were celibate, which just meant that they didn't sleep with men. I had a lot of thoughts about that, growing up. I could cringe out of my skin when I think of it now. The worst of it is, if somebody had told me I had it all wrong, I don't think I'd have listened or cared. Can you understand that?"

"Not altogether."

She nodded. "Because you're well, and I wasn't. You're so well you don't even know what sick is. No one ever told you you should feel ashamed, or that there's something wrong with you, or God will punish you. If they did, maybe you'd have needed to imagine someone like you who could be free and undamaged—make up a story and hang it on a star, just to convince yourself things could be different. Anyway what was the harm, who could ever be offended, I was never going to meet a real jess. Right up to the day the *Rose* landed I thought that—*My Grandfather's Axe* had promised Zandahe there wouldn't be any jesses brought. When I did meet Iren, I figured out pretty quick they weren't a woman. But even so I thought, now, Laura, you just keep away from that one.

"It worked for a couple of years. But they and Piro got close, and what was I going to do? Ban them from my house? They'd think I hated jesses—I couldn't stand for them to think I was like that. So then they were around, and they were . . . how they are. Beautiful, impossible. I mean impossible as in, obviously no one like that could be alive here and now, but when you close your eyes and open them, they're still there. Also as in, you can't tell them a damn thing they don't feel like hearing. I tried to hint I didn't like being teased—you know how they tease everybody—but they were oblivious, or else they could tell I was lying. It was like I was fifteen again, feeling all that fluttery unsettled happiness and not knowing what to do about it, only this time because they *weren't* a girl. Also feeling like my life was going to end, just crash down through a floor of lies and sink into the ground.

"I thought, at least they're celibate, nothing can actually happen. Then they started hinting there might be some flexibility on that. I did the only thing I could think of to do. I told them what I'd believed about jesses when I was young, and the use I made of it—that a lot of us made of it. I thought they'd never talk to me again, or anyway they'd never look me in the eye, and I'd be safe. They just laughed and said of course the grandeur of jess history had called to me across the light-years, they were glad it was a solace to me, and at such distance it was not surprising a few details got misheard. Like I said, impossible. I guess most people wouldn't see the appeal."

"Certainly, I do. I saw it the day I first met them."

"Okay, you can shut up about that."

"Oh, don't mistake me as having intentions. I understand now that Iren could only respond to a visit with indifference. That doesn't interest me at all, I promise you."

"Once again and twice as loud, shut *up*. They are not *indifferent*."

The plates were still all soaking in the sink, untouched. She took one up and made as if to scrub it, but then thrust it down again. She wheeled to look him in the eye. "I wouldn't change anything about Iren except maybe they could learn to talk a little less when drunk. Maybe someday they'll believe that. But mind your own business."

She took up the plate again, scrubbed it and rinsed it and handed it to him. By the time she had finished them all and John had dried them and put them away, her vexation had burned itself out. She drained out the dishwater—dirty, and by that time cold—then refilled and re-soaped the sink. She sank the soup pot in the foam and placed the nested bowls within it. After letting them soak for a while, she took the topmost one and rubbed at bits of stuck-on onion with a cloth. "Don't you see, I'm the one who can't give them what *they* want? Iren wants to live with me and make a home—that's what love means to them. And I can't, I can't do that to my children. Tali's going to have enough problems in life without her mother publicly declaring that she's on the side of sin. So what Iren has is climbing into my window at night every once in a while, and a couple of hours on Sunday in the kitchen, playing at having a life together. Also Tali has to grow up knowing her parents are adulterers, and Piro can't marry the woman he loves. All because of a bad idea I had when I was unwell."

It puzzled him that she could blame herself for harming Piro's love and her own love and the daughter she had borne by traveling to Scythia, when neither the loves nor the child could have existed without that journey. He thought her method of accounting, if applied by a ship's master to its crew's pay, would have led to the ship being burned with him still on it. But unable to formulate this thought in terms that she would understand, he only asked, "Do any of them reproach you with it?"

"No," she admitted. "Not about that. Only about the fact I couldn't give my blessing to Tali taking the jess vow—which is a collision between Christian girl and pagan custom that would *also* not have happened if I hadn't lied to come here. Tali is furious, Iren is wounded and can't understand. Piro reconciled himself to Tali braiding months ago and wishes we would all just make up and restore domestic harmony."

"You know I sympathize with opposition to a vow. I must say it is strange, though—you seem to take a very different attitude in Iren's case."

"Being a jess, as a custom, is very specific. Very Ischnuran. And Iren's Ischnuran, and they fit in it like it was tailored for them. But . . . look, on Zandahe I knew girls who were 'he' behind closed doors, girls who maybe weren't girls at all. I think there must be people like that everywhere."

"I had a patient once, when I was working in the city. He—I will say he, and that's what the hospital records still show—worked on a fishing boat, and had been hit in the back of the shoulder by a boom, which caused a dislocation of this joint here." He tapped his chest where the breastbone meets the collarbone. "I was rather proud of figuring it out—that joint hardly dislocates, and when it does, usually in the other direction. There was a slight asymmetry of the collarbones that gave it away. And, in noticing that, I could hardly help but notice his breasts too."

"Did he say anything about it?"

"No, and I didn't think asking would improve the doctor-patient relationship. But he came in again, that winter, when he was pregnant and wanted not to be—perfectly routine, except that we don't see a lot of men for it. He told me he had no family and needed to work. At the time I took that as the reason for the pants and the abortion both, but now I wonder. That was in Faivai, a great city, not some fishing village. There is plenty of work you can get in a dress. It argues a fondness for either the fish or the trousers."

"They do that on some of the ships too. People just change from man to woman or woman to man, openly—of course openly, it's a ship, everyone knows everyone. Iren says those ships aren't any better about jesses than the rest. One rule for them and one for us, as always."

She handed him the soup pot. While he was drying it and putting it away, she drained the sink. "So here's the point. For all those people—or at least the ones I knew—I can't see that a vow of chastity would solve any problem they had."

"No, I don't suppose it would."

"Especially not for a Church girl who has the misfortune of being devout, and is going to be told she's committing a series of terrible sins. Iren thinks if I just give my blessing, other Zandaheans will accept it too. That isn't how it works, especially not for a Denier. If I'm endorsing pagan rituals, that's just going to make all of us even more suspect. Also they want me to do it at a nice big public ceremony, which in real life would turn into a shouting match, if not an outright riot. Iren's like you, they don't know what sick is.

When you're sick your whole life, at least you know what to be afraid of. Even now that they *are* sick, they don't know that."

She took the dish towel from him, dried her hands on it, and laid it on the counter.

"So now—just so you understand what eggshells we're all walking on—the three of us have got a truce. Iren and I are together again because we can't stand not to be. Back to playing house on Sundays and hearing the tap on my window at night. Tali's stopped making demands for the moment. But nothing is solved. Nothing will be, until they give up and have the ceremony without me. I'm not stupid, I know they will sooner or later. I'll do whatever I can for her afterward—she's my child, of course I will. Iren says if I miss this ceremony I'll regret it my whole life. Maybe they're right. But I know I can live with regret. This world is going to crush her, one way or another. Don't ask me to sign off on the time and method of the execution."

Tears were in her eyes. He moved closer and folded her into his arms. She leaned into the embrace but only for a moment, then gently pushed him away.

"There's a reason I told you all that. Well, there's a reason I told you some of it, the rest just spilled out once I started. Because you and me, and Tali and Iren, have to look out for each other."

"I will do what I can for any of you. But—why us four in particular?"

"Because you're a man who visits men, and I'm a lesbian, and Iren is a jess, and Tali is likely to be one."

"Those things are all quite different, aren't they? The first three, at any rate."

"Not when the world hates all of them. So now you know why I agreed to have you over every week for cooking lessons. Well. Also because having you around on Sundays kept Iren and Tali from cornering me to talk about her taking the vow—I'm not proud of that part. But mainly to keep an eye on you and give you a few hints about surviving in hostile territory, which it was obvious you didn't realize you were in."

"I see."

"Now why do you sound like I kicked your puppy, John Maraintha?"

"I thought you welcomed me into your house because you liked me, not because you saw me as an ally in some secret war. After what you've told me, and after what happened to Iren, I do understand why you perceive a war, but still I can't help being disappointed."

"Oh, for heaven's sake. Yes, John, I really like you. You're sweet and curious and you're usually respectful, when you're not making weird comments about the jess I love. And you know how to listen, even if a quarter of the things I say go through the wrong curl in your brain and turn into nonsense. If I didn't like you I wouldn't have talked to you enough to figure out you were queer in the first place. Is that good enough? You know, you're as impossible as Iren, you're just quieter about it. Maybe that's *why* I like you. It could be said I have a pattern."

"I suppose that is reassuring. If you consider me no more irritating than your own lover—"

"Don't use that word, it doesn't suit them. And yet again, shut up. Now you and I should go back. They must be finished with their game by now."

They found Tali alone in the dining room, moving one peg around the board three holes at a time; this appeared to be a way of fidgeting and not some solitary game. "Papa's in his bedroom," she said, glancing up at her mother. "Iren's on the roof again. There's some planetary conjunction, I forget which two."

"Will you wait while I go find them, John? I'll only be a minute. I know they wanted to talk to you about something before you left."

"Certainly."

Laura left the room, leaving her tag. He heard her footsteps, climbing up the stairs rather than walking toward the door; she meant to go out on the roof too.

"They'll be longer than a minute," Tali said.

"The sky was clear when I came in. A good night for stargazing."

"You don't have to cover up for them. I know Mama and Iren are dating. I know she just told you about it. Papa knows all of that too."

"I wasn't trying to deceive you. I just meant that Iren likes to look at the stars."

Tali examined his face closely, deciding whether she believed this, and determined that she did.

"That's true, they do. They also like having an excuse to wander out beyond the town lights at all hours and wind up back here."

John didn't think her mood of telling family secrets ought to be encouraged. "Iren is my friend," he said. "For that reason, I don't reveal things that I've learned as their friend."

He thought he had misstepped—this rebuke, by rights, should be delivered by her parents; coming from him instead, it could only provoke indignation. But she tipped her head, admitting the point. "You're right. I shouldn't say things. But it makes me mad. Mama thinks taking a vow of chastity would ruin my life—it obviously hasn't ruined Iren's much. *They* can do whatever they want and it doesn't count. Also Iren is always telling me a jess is decisive, but nobody wants me to be that, not even them. On Ischnura jesses take the vow without their parents' blessing all the time! It's called a forest braiding. I'm old enough I just need one adult to witness. But Iren keeps saying I should wait, and my mother will come around. Since what happened to Iren they've both been even worse."

John saw that Tali and her mother both longed for the same thing, and it was not his place to tell her that. He considered for some time what he could say.

"Iren has suffered a grievous blow. It's a blow to your mother, too. They are both in mourning, in a way, and this is only the beginning of it. Their feelings will change as a bruise changes color. What they say to you later may be very different—"

"So your answer is wait some more," Tali said, rolling her eyes. "Why should you be any different from the two of them. My body isn't waiting! It's getting worse every day, and nothing is going to be right until it's fixed."

He knew that he had lost their sympathy. In as gentle a voice as he could, he said, "Nevertheless, a vow of chastity is a very grave decision."

"I don't have a thousand choices about what kind of person I'm going to be! I have two, and both of them lead to a vow. One I can live with and one I can't. It's that simple."

Iren was coming in, and Laura behind her. They must both have heard at least Tali's last sentence or two, but their expressions gave no sign of it. As soon as they had cleared the door, Tali fled the room.

"Will you walk back to town with me, John?" Iren said.

"Gladly."

He picked up his tag, showing them that it was turned off. They nodded. "Mine too."

As they were making their way around the layered rock, Iren asked, "Did Tali sound you out on being a witness to a secret braiding?"

"She meant to speak to me in private. I'd rather not betray her confidence by telling others."

"That's wise," Iren conceded. "It's good for her to have adults not fighting in the family war that she can trust, even if she's too mad to feel any trust just now. Obviously, you didn't agree to play the role."

There was a sub-therapeutic dose of question in this last remark, but he ignored it. "Laura said you had something you wished to speak to me about."

"Yes," they said, their tone brightening instantly. "It's good news—the threads to mend your strap are finally ready. What's more, I have the promise of a bit of rat meat on Friday. If you will bring your great-uncle to my place at six, I will give you a good dinner, and you may watch the work until your boredom drives you off."

So he would have to wait again. But surely, on Friday, he would be told what he could do for them.

"Nothing could gratify me more," he said. "But I don't know where your house is."

"You've been there once already. I live upstairs from my lab."

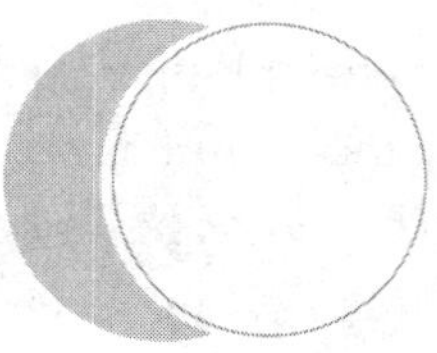

CHAPTER TWENTY-ONE

John climbed a hill overlooking the town, carrying the components of lunch in three covered dishes. All three were stacked up neatly in a cage of canvas straps that hung from his left hand; this convenience had been a gift from Ru. At the top he found Sudharma conversing with Green. Green didn't acknowledge his arrival, but broke off in what might have been the middle of a sentence and waited as the humans ate. He had been standoffish since his return. John considered the matter as he ate his curry—a good one, he thought, made with fresh tomatoes, the first carrots of the season, and what would probably turn out to be the last corn. "Is there a way I can apologize to him?"

"For what?"

"I am in part responsible for 'Blue' being treated as his name. More responsible than anyone else, I think. Considering what it means, he must have thought that I was shaming him."

"I don't know if he felt shamed, or if that's something that they feel. I have yet to work out how, if at all, they talk about their emotions."

"Regardless, I would like to say I'm sorry."

"If I ever find a way to do that, I will let you know."

John took his leave and went home. He cleaned the kitchen and the bathroom and tidied up the common spaces, but since he performed these tasks frequently, nothing was very dirty and the housework did not take as long as he would have hoped. He had plenty of time left to run a simulation. It was important that he practice regularly, now that Green had brought the énqissatêk; Sudharma's translation might be close at hand. Besides the dread of that approaching day, each simulation that he went through brought out a lingering sense of injury that Sudharma could have thought him capable of turning the translation process to the service of his own desires; and along with that, a haze of shame that he had proven himself unworthy of Sudharma's trust. Irrationally, the combination made him feel as if he had been accused correctly, so that as he watched the model brain being broken and repaired, he felt pangs of guilt for something he had never done. Finally, with relief, he put the screen away and left for Iren's.

Iren led him up the stairs at the back of their laboratory. The second floor was not quite as undivided as the first—one corner had been walled off and was probably a bathroom—but the remainder had to serve as kitchen, bedroom, eating and living space combined. Their bed was made up with an intricate quilt, and the couch bore pillows of the same pattern. Each curtain was made out of one of the same fabrics found in the quilt, which were light and dark purple and blue and orange-yellow, but the ones on the two sides of the same window never matched. There were no closets, but there were two large dressers, and on the walls thick rods were mounted from which riotously colored clothing hung. He could smell cooking meat and spices and fresh yeasted bread.

"I'm afraid dinner will be late," Iren said. "My dough was slow to rise, so I am simmering the soup on the lowest possible heat until the bread's ready to slice. It will be better for the long slow cooking, so I hope. If you are hungry in the meantime, I can make some popcorn."

"I'm all right. The smell of the bread and soup makes me long for nothing else—I will endure the wait."

"You must tell me if you change your mind, but in the meantime I'll begin the project. Did you bring him?"

John took the strap out of his pocket, removed it from its swaddling, and placed it in their joined hands. They looked down at it with unease.

"I worry that I've let my enthusiasm for an idea run away from me. I made a plan without consulting you—I had the idea it would be a surprise. But he's your relative and not mine. I can tell you about the design, or even sketch it for you, if you like."

"It doesn't matter, just as long as I can wear him. And I would like to be able to touch him—I would not have him entirely clothed in thread."

"I promise I will cover only as much skin as necessary to mend his wounds, and a bit more to make the repair decorative. Well, then. He will have to be stuck many times with a needle—is there a way to explain that this isn't meant cruelly?"

"No need. Preserved souls are not connected to a body by nerves, as we are, so they don't feel pain. Their perceptions are more spiritual in nature. So long as you intend to help, he will feel helped."

"Then I will focus my mind on benevolence as I work. Thank you for your trust, John. Now first of all, I have to fix him to a strap, which will support the bag—in his infirmity, we will relieve him of that duty."

They took the soul to a small table—the one they ate on, undoubtedly; there was no other except for a small one supporting a sewing machine in the corner. They unrolled it, examined it, and turned it over. "You cleaned the blood."

"As best I could. There was not much on the front in any case, but the back will never be really clean."

"No worry—that will be hidden soon."

They unrolled a long strip of webbing, laid it down on the table, and arranged the soul on top of it. With great care they centered the end nearest to them. They sharpened their needle with a file, then picked up strap and soul together, and with a strong brown thread began to stitch the edges. Their sewing was careful but quick, and in less time than John would have imagined, they reached the part that the snake's teeth had torn. They started over from the same end, this time stitching the opposite edge, and worked until they came close to the tears again.

"Another pair of hands would help here," they said.

He moved a chair next to them and sat down. "What shall I do?"

"I need you to hold the strap and keep these torn pieces stable and centered while I sew them down. Just like they are now. You'll have to move your fingers out of the way as I work, but without letting anything shift around. Make sure the sides of the tears stay touching, but only lightly—we want the skin to lie perfectly flat when I'm done."

"The man who taught me to suture said, 'The lips of the wound should kiss, but they should kiss like brother and sister.'"

"Exactly so," they said. "Please maintain a perfect chastity."

The surgery went well enough. Twice Iren directed him to place his fingers differently on the strap, and once they had him raise his hands away from it while they resettled the soul on the canvas. Then they took it back entirely, the damaged section being well secured on both sides. He watched their face as they sewed down the rest of the strap. He thought that they were happier than he had seen them since the crawler; something about this task was comforting. Finally, with satisfaction, they laid the strap down on the table.

"Old and new are united now. A perfect time to stop for dinner."

They went into the kitchen, washed their hands—after all, they had touched dried human blood—and cut thick slices from the loaf of bread. They dipped up soup into bowls, furnished them with spoons, and put them with the bread on plates. Balancing one on each hand, they returned to the table.

"This is winterpot," they said. "Or an attempt at it. Originally made with night-boar meat—often the preserved kind, which is astonishingly even worse than fresh—but by the time of my childhood with beef and mainly Terran vegetables. Its great virtue is being warming and sustaining when you've come in from the bitter cold, which we don't have here, but the chill of a fall evening in the desert will stand in."

He took a spoonful. Then, following their lead, he dipped a slice of bread into the soup and bit off the soaked corner. "It's delicious," he said.

"A little attenuated, I would say. Tastes like the smell of someone making winterpot on the next floor. I could only get a little bit of rat meat, even calling in a favor—I hoped it would be enough. Still, the flavor of the meat is suited to the spices. When rat gets plentiful I'll make it properly for Torres house and you can come."

"Does everyone on Scythia owe you favors?"

"Not everyone, but most of the Ischnurans. Some are for sewing, some for blessings at a marriage, but mostly they're for babysitting. Just about every Ischnuran child here has been to Dama Iren's to play games and look at animals—I will take anyone, so long as they're not of an age to put specimens out of the drawers into their mouths. Once I had given up on bearing a child of my own, it was a solace to me to be part of so many children's lives; yet the parents all imagine they came out the better in the bargain, and I don't scruple to collect the debts they think they owe. Really, a lot of people have cause to be glad I am childless. If they only knew, they ought to owe all those favors to Marne."

They said this lightly; but even when sheathed in a joke, the facts were sharp enough to cut.

"I am still waiting to be of use in that matter," John said.

"If that means you want to kill him, I appreciate the sentiment, but the answer is still no. As I said, Scythia needs him. May death tie him in a dozen knots—but not yet."

"I see the logic in what you say. But I'm not logical. I just think of that man seeing patients, especially women—assisting with *births*—while he thinks he is the arbiter of who can have a child and who cannot, and I despise the air that fills his lungs. Don't people deserve to know what he is?"

"People on this world deserve a lot of things they're not likely to get from it."

They spoke with the gentle sorrow of a mother telling her son that now that Nana was an ancestor, she wouldn't speak to him again; and being ashamed to have required this tone from them, he gave in.

"I won't offer you his life again. But if there's anything that I can do for you, please tell me."

"There is one thing."

"Name it."

"I need you to be my doctor. It will make him suspicious, but that can't be helped. I can dissemble well enough to make small talk with him on the street, but in a medical appointment I believe I'd either flee or stab him, which would make him even more suspicious."

"I would be honored. But I am without medicines, except those needed for emergencies in the desert."

"We both know you have a source. I'd rather not rely on her, but it's better than the alternative." They paused and examined him, holding their spoon sideways above their bowl. "Now why do you look unhappy, John Maraintha? Are you still baffled by the mysteries of my body? Or are you enjoying your enforced retirement too much to emerge from it for my sake?"

"No, of course not—I am willing. But if I am to do this, I must be honest with you first."

"By all means, disclose."

"You know that I spent time on *Edgar's Folly*. Probably it's the reason you consider me a viable substitute for Marne. But I have come to believe I was not taken up to the ship as a doctor, or not primarily. It was more likely for the entertainment of the crew."

"Entertainment?"

"Ships that come to Essius don't really come for trade, or to 'foster development,' or whatever is the latest euphemism. We're considered recalcitrant."

"Good for you."

"They come, mainly, to visit and be visited. I think I was brought to the ship for the same reason—with the expectation I would visit widely, and so extend the enjoyment they gained from my world."

"Were you hurt?"

"No, not at all. I didn't do anything I didn't want to do. There were a few misunderstandings—people on that ship are very strange—but as far as I could tell, no ill intent. If they had offered me the same deal honestly I might have taken it. I have no complaint except that they were *not* honest, which, if I had only known it at the time, might have warned me of the disrespect they showed me when they forced me off onto this planet."

"Perhaps," Iren said gently, "they didn't respect you because they didn't respect what they meant you to do."

"That may be. I don't suppose it matters. But you understand, everything else that they gave me to do was an afterthought, or possibly a cover story for the winter captain's benefit, though she was certainly not fooled. They heard I was a man to visit widely, or they assumed because I'm Essian that I would be. Or maybe I was chosen to suit the summer captain's taste, specifically—I thought that for a while, though in fact he never asked me for a visit. They said he only had one visitor at a time, so it may be that when I finally became fluent enough in zero gravity to visit him, his attention had already wandered elsewhere. In any case it was not for my medical skill I was taken up, and you should not regard my stay with them as an endorsement."

"John, my dear friend. I have never known the ships to value anything that mattered. If they were blind to your worth then I esteem you all the more. And I am outraged for you, even if you won't be outraged for yourself."

"Well, you may be, if you like. But I didn't tell you that to garner sympathy. I just wanted you to make an informed choice."

"I think I am better off with a doctor who wants that than one who would breathe a sigh of relief at my death, don't you? Also, I heard about your sternoclavicular dislocation, which, according to my library, is a condition often missed. As she also had occasion to remark, Laura and I talk to each other. Now if you are finished trying to scare me off, I will take these dishes to the kitchen and continue with your great-uncle."

They stacked the dishes together and took them away. Then, at the kitchen sink, they washed their hands again before they touched the soul.

"I will move to the sofa, I think. The light is good there, and I don't need the table anymore."

They gathered up the strap, their scissors, and four narrow spools of thread—two green, one blackish brown, and one the color of yellowed bone. Settling down next to the lamp, they took the strap by the damaged section and gently pulled the edges of it in opposite directions. They did this several times in different places.

"I think I will try to stitch this as it is. The webbing should keep it from stretching out as I work, if I'm careful. If that turns out to be wrong, I have a hoop that I can press it in, but even with padding I fear that might leave an ineradicable dent in the leather."

They cut a length of the bone-colored thread from its spool, slipped one end into the needle's eye, and tied a knot at the other. They pierced the front side of the strap and pulled the thread through until the knot was tight against the soul. Then they stabbed from the back and brought the needle up again, a little distance from the knot. From there they stitched a line back toward the place that they had started. It was wonderful to see how quickly and how accurately they could puncture the back of the canvas to bring up the needle in the proper place, without turning it over to look. There was strength in their hands too, he thought, to be able to punch the needle through two strong layers and pull it out on the other side, never once letting it slip through their fingers. The knot still nestled against the soul with a little tail of thread standing up above it. He thought they would bend down this tail and trap it underneath the line of stitches. Instead they pulled on it to lift it up and snipped it, along with the knot, off. What kept the thread from being pulled out of the strap now was mysterious, though, in light of their obvious skill, he was sure something must. He would have asked about it; but since his mind had only physical perceptions and not spiritual, he could not help but imagine pain in the repeated perforation of the soul, and so he searched for an excuse to look away.

"May I take care of the dishes for you? Since you are using your evening to help me instead of doing your ordinary chores."

"It wouldn't hurt them to sit until morning. Rarely does a Scythian insect take an interest in our food, and if one did I would only catch and study it. But if the washcloth holds more fascination for you than the needle, by all means do as you like."

One pot and a bread pan and two sets of tableware didn't take long to deal with, and after a negligent wave of Iren's hand gave him the freedom of the kitchen cabinets, he found the right places to put them away. The hot water, the familiar repetitiousness of washing, and the satisfaction of seeing the dishes made clean had calmed him, and he found it easier to watch the stitching now. Iren had outlined a long narrow stripe, that bent slightly in a few places but overall ran parallel to the soul's edge. Now they were filling it up with stitches of the same color. When they had finished this, they surrounded the bone-colored sliver with a larger stripe of green, whose width encompassed the edge of the soul, hiding it completely. They extended one end of this green band with a shorter blackish brown one that angled off toward the middle of the strap. Thinner strips traced the lengths of the tears and continued on to the opposite edge of the soul; then, from each of these, they stitched a few short prongs protruding to the sides. The repair would be very obvious, John thought, but it didn't matter.

He found it in him to ask a few questions about their technique. They had, they told him, practiced and experimented first with scraps of webbing, then with webbing sewn to pieces of a worn-out leather garment they had brought here from Ischnura, the combination being much tougher than anything they usually embroidered on. They had anchored the first thread by stitching over and over it on the back side of the canvas, which they did by touch, out of his sight; once this was done, the knot they had begun with was superfluous. He asked, also, why they were switching from one spool of green thread to the other when the first was not used up yet, but in response to that they only smiled and said, "You chose not to have the surprise ruined. You will just have to wait and see."

He watched as the new thread outlined and filled in another green ribbon, this one wandering crookedly so it connected the dots of the tooth-holes. By the complaining of his stomach he became aware that many hours had passed, and so he made popcorn for both of them, which Iren put aside their work to eat, washing their hands well afterward. When they were close to filling in a second crooked stripe of green, he finally asked the question that was in his heart.

"Are you all right, in your . . ." He searched for a term that would fit, found the one used on the ship: "in your *relationship* with Laura?"

"Not altogether," they said, their needle pausing. They put the strap down on their knee. "I fucked it up, if you want to know the truth. I thought she was just suffering from ordinary jitters, like any parent, and would come around when she saw her child's mind was made up. What is worse, I gave Tali that expectation. Laura is afraid if Tali braids, her life will be over—maybe even literally. A little far-fetched, don't you think? Although, since what happened to me—since I *found out* what happened to me—there's a voice inside that says, *There is no limit to what people will do. . . .*" They shook their head in dismissal, then picked up the strap and began to sew again. "I think, rather, Tali is on a course that will bring her closer to Ischnurans than to her own people. At the same time she will be set apart, and that is very hard, especially when she so fervently believes in a religion that may no longer accept her. But in the long run, our two cultures will begin to bleed into each other. There will still be differences, no doubt, religious ones especially, but also the beginnings of a common history. People will intermarry and have children. I believe in Tali's lifetime, she will see people begin to become Scythian, and to have a foot in either world will no longer seem strange. Particularly if she follows in my footsteps and makes herself a *dama* to the coming generations, so that her eccentricities become an institution. I've tried to convince Laura that matters are no worse than this—no better, but no worse—but it only seems to irritate her."

"I hope you may be right, but I meant something more specific. Forgive me for speaking of this, but I gathered from Laura that you are . . . not celibate with her, which you have told me is against your nature. If you are being hurt—"

"*John.* I am glad you're my friend. And I know you're only trying to look out for me. But how could you think that of Laura? You had better get a higher opinion of my *vidhu* or we're going to have a problem."

A slight smile took the threat out of the words, but even so he answered in all seriousness. "Of course I don't think she would hurt you on purpose. But with Kol, you imagined doing harm to yourself and making them the instrument. You would have hidden what you felt from him, I think. And when he found out—"

"Yes, yes, you can stop there, young man. My folly is sufficiently dissected." They looked annoyed; but the expression faded in the time it took to pierce the leather with another careful stitch. "Laura is not Kol, and I'm not who I was then either. I promise you I'm not in any distress. Now where did I put that first green?"

Before he could answer they had found it, nestled next to their leg. They threaded the needle, anchored the new length of thread by weaving it between existing stitches on the webbing's back, and examined their work for a long time before choosing the exact place to insert the needle's point.

"To give pleasure is not necessarily oathbreaking," they said, "not if the vow is understood correctly—and that doesn't outrage my instincts, as long as I am only giving. I even find that I enjoy it, in my own way. It's flattering, isn't it, to be looked at with desire? I like to be the cause of that distress and then to soothe it. I like to lie close to her and pay patient attention to all her response. I like to see her pleased, to see her sated. Also, I've become very good at it, and mastering a skill is always satisfying. Can you understand that?"

"I suppose I can," he said. In truth these motives, spoken plainly, and dry of the desire that ordinarily suffused them, were as incongruous as deep-sea animals left on the beach by the receding tide. Yet he could not help but admit that none of them was unfamiliar.

"Then you see, I am not submitting to a wifely duty or impaling myself on an alien desire, but pursuing my own inclinations, quaint as they might seem to you. You don't need to worry about me, and I will thank you not to."

They cut the thread again and started in another place. They did this several times, regarding the soul carefully after each one. He thought they were adding small details to the design, but since they were stitching green on green it was hard to see any effect.

"Though if it *were* just a chore I endured for her sake," they added, "I would still do it, and that would not make me misused or exploited. If my love needed water, I would fetch water."

They slipped the needle between the threads still on the spool, set it aside. "That's the embroidery finished. Now you can get a proper look at what I've made. Come sit by me."

He did and they laid the strap onto his leg. Now complete, and right side up, the twining lines were no longer random. You could see only a slice of it—the trunk bisected by the left edge of the leather, the branches disappearing off the right—but the crooked menace of the limbs was unmistakable: it was a snake-tree. Or rather, it was *the* snake-tree, the one that he had killed and killed again, split and partly dead and bearing a pale scar of lightning. He raised it in his hands and tilted it toward the lamp to see better, then caught his breath. The light reflecting off it made two branches shine out: the two snakes. Their eyes and too-long mouths were picked out with a few stitches of green against the brightness. When he tilted it back the snakes faded again, lurking in camouflage, indistinguishable from the limbs of their vegetable mother.

"The two green threads use the same dye, but one is made of a more reflective material. That's why the making of them took so long, to get the color match to work despite the different stuffs. I just about wore out Nath's patience insisting on perfection. But that is how snakes are, isn't it? They are invisible until they're not, and if you look away they are again."

"It's beautiful," he said. There was a stinging in his eyes. "I didn't think it could be beautiful, I thought—" But what he had thought didn't matter. Finding the right path again, he said, "I think my great-uncle would like it.

He died when I was very young, but from what I can remember, he was a man careful of his clothing. I think he would be glad to wear this finery."

This had the desired effect; he could see that they were gratified.

"I will be glad to wear it too," he added, "though I must say that to a man raised in the Clear Lakes, bragging does not come easily."

"How convenient then, to delegate the job of bragging to a Northerner—and one from Iisles, even. We are notoriously the best at it, and accordingly are the originators of the custom of preserving everything we have to brag about as pictures in bright thread. Your strap is now a *morrol*, a remembrance of great deeds. By making it, I share a bit of the recorded glory. 'The thrust of the spear is recalled in the stitch of the chronicler,' that's a proverb . . . more or less. The original has 'spearman' and 'needlewoman,' but that's unnecessarily specific, don't you think? The point is, everyone will know that this praise comes from me and not you. Even Zandaheans, I hope, will read the intended message—'Here is a man fierce in protecting his friends.' One Ischnuran in particular might have the wit to see it as a warning, which will satisfy us both, I think."

"It will."

"Good. Now, let me sew the strap onto the new bag for you."

"It's very late already. If you're tired, then I could bring him back another time, or leave him with you."

"It won't take that long. And anyway, these days I can't sleep until I'm exhausted. Keep me company, and you can take him home tonight."

They rethreaded their needle with the strong brown thread, folded the strap along one of its creases, and began to sew.

"As your doctor, I'd like to give you something for insomnia, if you'll let me."

"When the trouble is a fear of being anesthetized, a sedative is worse than useless, I'm afraid."

"I don't intend to render you insensible, only to prescribe a calming warmth that may conduct you into sleep."

"Even so. But don't worry about me, John. I'm only suffering from a bad imagination. It will get easier. In the meantime, I at least sleep better when I'm with my *vidhu*." John thought this word was very beautiful—the spirited first syllable of 'vivid' softened by the voiced *th* of 'then,' and finished with a coo. But maybe it was only that the tenderness with which they spoke it made the word a fond caress. "Isn't that strange? Laura and I are just as vulnerable as each other, really, but when I'm with her I feel safe from everything. Of course, I don't dare go to her too often."

"Would it help if I slept on your couch tonight?"

"Yes, it would, and no, you can't. I am a grown jess. I am not going to get in the habit of needing a guard in order to sleep in my own house. Furthermore, the sun is going to rise before long, and you *must* be out of here before my neighbors wake. They will understand why a social call ran past their bedtimes when they see the work I did during the course of it, but there are limits. But I promise I will go and see my *vidhu* soon."

When he got home there was not enough time left to sleep before he would have to make breakfast. Instead he napped after the meal and rose again to prepare lunch. He walked out to deliver it with his bag hung from his shoulder, feeling the rightness of its weight there. When he arrived Sudharma saw the strap and looked away; John thought he winced.

"Is the embroidery too frightening to wear in public?"

"Not at all. It isn't fear that it inspires in me. Rather, it makes me remember that you risked your life to save me from my foolishness."

"Our foolishness, surely."

"Your willingness to be persuaded into mine. I think I should defer to you on matters of safety in the future."

John longed to take this opportunity to remind him of the dangers of translation, to try to talk him out of it. He knew that would do no good. Instead he said, "If the strap bothers you, I will avoid wearing it in your presence."

"No, by no means. I am glad that your loss could be mended. And no doubt the embarrassment is good for my character."

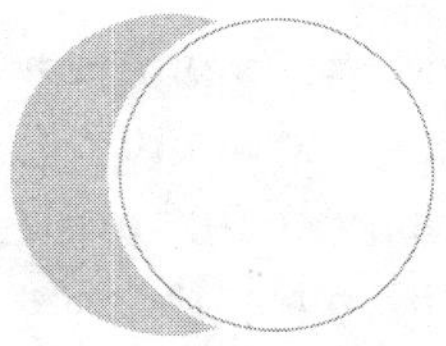

CHAPTER TWENTY-TWO

It was winter, or what passed for winter in the desert: the nights were cold but never snowy, the days were bright and cool—though not so cool that he couldn't work up a sweat when he helped Ru at the farm. There were coverings to remove in the morning from plants that had required protection from the frost at night. There were new strains of tomato and radish and turnip to sow, lettuce and greens to harvest; even, there was some weeding—a surprising amount of occupation at a time of year when farms in the Clear Lakes would be lying silent under a blanket of white. John was grateful for all of it. He cherished any task that kept him from the screen.

New énqissatêk were arriving in town all the time. The word of human presence had spread widely among them, and everyone wanted to see. The most recent arrivals had longer fur and spoke a language very unlike Yké with each other; Sudharma supposed they came from a colder part of Scythia. They had planted seeds, not all together in a plowed field but in small numbers in random places that were otherwise unused. Piro said most of the seedlings that had come up were their food plant, but others were of unknown species. Every newcomer that arrived in town toured the educational farm in company with an older énqissatêk resident, who pointed out the various plants and discoursed rapidly in Yké. Whatever explanation was transmitted in this way must have been satisfying; they did not linger at the farm once it was over. And so on days when students did not come, often he and Ru had the place to themselves.

At the end of a day of that kind, Ru dropped her cultivator into a tool bucket and sat down to stretch out her legs after long kneeling. "All right, that's enough for today. I'm going to go home, draw a hot bath, and soak until my fingers turn to raisins, then eat dinner in my bathrobe."

That was two pleasant pictures—her in the tub, and her afterward, relaxed and clean—and while some women might evoke such images without meaning anything by it, he did not think Ru was one of them. Perhaps it was his reluctance to return home that made him, for the first time, think of taking her up on the implied offer. The moment that he did, the virtue of the idea insisted on itself. She was attractive and unencumbered by a marriage. Moreover, she was good company, so that even if the central matter of the visit went poorly or didn't go at all, he would not regret having spent time with her.

She would not, of course, understand Essian subtlety. Therefore he sat on the ground next to her, and spoke in words both proper and direct:

"If I knocked on your door tonight, might I hope it would be opened?"

"What?" She looked at him in shock, as if he had mistaken her interest; and yet he didn't think he had. "John, what in the world are you thinking?"

"I am thinking that I like you, and you speak as if you like me also."

"That's flirting to pass the time! It's not supposed to lead to anything. You're young enough to be my son, or nearly."

"If you refuse me for that reason, I must endure it—but I confess I will be disappointed."

Ru laughed out loud, then covered her mouth with her hand. "Oh veils, have I lost my mind that I'm considering this?"

He waited quietly and let her think it through.

"You would have to be discreet," she said. "*Really* discreet, not like that oaf Piro. No one can find out."

"Certainly."

"And you will have to provide birth control. I will *not* go to Marne for it. You know why."

"I do." He was glad to learn that Iren had warned her about Marne, though it was upsetting that not every woman could receive an equal warning. "In that case, shall I visit you tomorrow night? I can arrange to be sterile by then. Marne won't have to know about it."

"Do I want to know how you'll be managing that trick?"

"Probably not."

"Well, unfortunately, now I do know."

For a moment he feared it would be too much for her—that not only did he mean to keep on seeing Vo, but Vo would know he was visiting Ru, indeed, would be called on to help make the visits possible. But she sighed and accepted it.

"All right, I suppose. You are a strange and wanton creature, but considering where you come from, how else should you be? Just mind you don't give me a connection with an aiyi as a sexually transmitted disease."

It didn't work that way, but surely she knew that and was teasing him. "I will be careful," he said.

"You may have noticed, there is no one else around."

This was an obvious invitation, and he took it—leaning over and laying his hand on her side, bending to meet her lips. It was not very long, or anyway it was not long enough, before she pulled away.

"The whole town and a herd of basket-men could have come up on us and I wouldn't have noticed. You won't insult me by pretending you were perfectly aware of your surroundings, will you?"

"By no means."

"Then save it for tomorrow."

He left with a light heart. This had been a good idea and he should have asked her long ago. He thought she would need very little encouragement to tell him what she wanted, and he looked forward to finding out what that was.

He had no doubt that Vo would gladly give him what he asked for. It was not possible to imagine her experiencing jealousy when the aiyi filled her heart. And after all, it was only proper for a man to tell his other female visiting partner right away that he was using birth control, even though he was sure she wouldn't care. If she ever wanted to become pregnant, she had other ways to do so.

He would go home and start dinner. When he and Sudharma had eaten, he would go to visit Vo at once. There was, plainly, no time in the day left for anything else. And tomorrow after sunset, he would make his way to Ru.

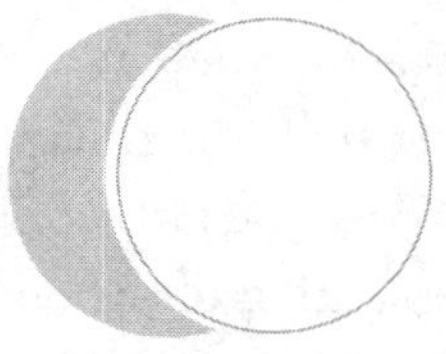

CHAPTER TWENTY-THREE

As was his habit, John used his tag to send a message to Sudharma before he began cooking lunch. The translator often could not answer right away when he was working, so this early notice made sure that the meal would not grow cold while John awaited a reply. This time, a response arrived almost at once, but it came from Iren, writing on their library:

> Himself passed me his tag, which I took as a request for me to read and answer your message in his stead. He can't look at it himself right now. We are on a hill 1.7 kilometers upriver from town, which you will easily find by looking for a large delegation of énqissatêk making some long and solemn announcement. Piro and I are here to help with the vegetable verb tenses, and the governor has come to hear their speech interpreted. I don't know when or if they'll let Sudharma stop to eat, but I am sure your loyalty and kindness will bring you here anyway.

He recognized the final sentence as Iren asking him to come. They had to be in the governor's company and so they wanted him nearby. Almost, he rushed off without making lunch, but to arrive empty-handed would look strange. Red lentils would cook quickly, and he had fresh spinach to add to them—it was not one of the days when green vegetables were forbidden. He hesitated over the amount, standing with his hand on the refrigerator door. It would not take so very much longer to make lunch for five instead of two, but he had no interest in feeding the governor. He considered feeding everyone *except* the governor, but such a provocation, without the intention to follow it up, would be unwise. Then the pleasing thought occurred to him that it was well to accustom an enemy to eating food he had prepared. Iren might yet change their mind about the man's fate. Also, a good meal would sustain Iren in facing the day's trials. For both their and the governor's sakes, therefore, he took the time to temper spices and peppers in oil to add to the cooked beans; the task needed only a couple of minutes, and anyway there was the reputation of the household to consider.

He drove upriver slowly, leaning forward in his seat and craning his neck to look up at hills—but, fortunately, sparing enough attention for the way ahead to notice the énqissatêk standing right in the path of the van. They were pointing with one seven-fingered hand at a little candle that he recognized as an infant column. Iren, on a hilltop, looked down through binoculars, then passed them on to Piro. John understood the usefulness of their high vantage: the énqissatêk could use all the plants around to specify times with precision—though whether Sudharma and the biologists could interpret those times accurately was another question. As he watched, another énqissatêk went down the hill to stand next to an unusually tall column. Young and then old: so they were speaking about the future.

He waited until both the énqissatêk started up the hill. Then he dismounted from the van and followed.

"Dr. Maraintha! I suppose you've come bearing lunch," the governor said. In his tone there was no hint of the amusement or contempt that might have laced a comment about John's cooking in the past. Since he had killed the snake-tree, and especially since Iren had recorded the killing in wearable form, he had found himself treated with far more respect by the colonists. Laura said that by proving he was deadly in a fight, he had not only encouraged them to stay on his good side, but persuaded them he was entirely heterosexual. This made no sense whatsoever, but regardless, John was grateful for the change in attitude. The town would always be peopled by fools. At least the new form of their foolishness was more congenial than the last.

"I brought enough food for everyone," he said.

Though the énqissatêk were still taking it in turns to speak, and Sudharma could not eat until they had finished, the others took their meals at once. Piro sat on the ground to eat, making a table of his lap. John would have preferred to wait, but felt constrained by courtesy to join him. The governor lowered himself to the ground awkwardly, trying out several arrangements of his legs before he found the least uncomfortable. Iren took a plate too, and ate in a crouch that made it easier to quickly stand up and employ binoculars for the beginning of each énqissatêk statement. The need to keep tabs on the progress of the conversation gave them a convenient reason to turn their back toward Michael. They had said nothing but hello to John. He thought that they were keeping their emotions tied in a tight bundle in their heart.

John was collecting and packing away the plates and forks when the sounds of Yké ended and Sudharma came over. The governor stood up and dusted off his pants to hear the news.

"They have told me a future, the details of which I will be trying to work out for some time, but the gist of it is this. Humans expand within the desert, then outside it, taking land for farms and making a shambles of all the arrangements that keep living things in balance. Énqissatêk go hungry and have to leave their homes, causing more disruption in the places that they migrate to. This goes on long enough for a column to grow from a seed to its full height, and then for another to do the same. Iren thinks that is something in the neighborhood of two hundred years. The story then stops abruptly without a resolution, probably meaning that they expect the process to continue indefinitely."

"And what did they say about that scenario?"

"Nothing. There will be more to their discourse, but mercifully they are allowing me to eat first."

Sudharma sat down with crossed legs, and though the food was undoubtedly getting cold, he thanked John for it with more than usual warmth. Anyone could see that he was already exhausted. When he had finished he stayed sitting, and looked as if he would be willing to rest there for some time; but the énqissatêk all went down the hill and, forming a single file, walked past the van toward the town.

There was no van in sight but the one John had brought. Everyone else must have been led here on foot. "I can take all of you back," John said, looking at Sudharma; he meant to offer him more time to sit and rest.

"There may be things they mean to say to me along the way."

"You'll need Iren and me too, then," Piro said. "But Michael, there's nothing to stop you from riding."

He meant to keep the governor apart from Iren. It was a kind thought, and though John did not look forward to the company, he was glad when the suggestion was accepted.

The drive was slow, constrained to a walking pace—they could not pass the other humans and the énqissatêk, since they did not know the exact destination. Michael, without looking in John's direction a more than courteous amount, made him feel he was an insect being examined—though, now that he thought of it, Iren showed more respect than that for the insects that they studied, including the ones they killed. Both of them remained silent for most of the drive. Then as they approached the first farm along their route, the governor asked a question:

"What do you make of the future the basket-men described?"

John thought the governor was not asking for his counsel, but seeking a basis on which to judge him. He had no interest in attaining the man's good opinion. He answered, simply, "I think they are describing what is very likely."

The énqissatêk had stopped and one was speaking. This time they did not begin with a comparison between two plants, but merely seemed to indicate the field. They didn't continue long, but moved on to the next field and spoke briefly again. When they reached the town they discoursed on the buildings. It was absurd, creeping along in an enormous vehicle a dozen or so paces at a time and stopping, but every minute that Michael remained in the van was one in which Iren was not faced with him.

They passed through town and out to the edge of a different farm. The énqissatêk spoke there for a long time. Sudharma spent some time digesting their speech, then said two dozen or so words in Yké, and when they had consulted with each other, one stepped forward to reply. Sudharma turned toward the van and raised his hand, indicating that he was ready. John and the governor both got out.

"None of the sentences in this speech specified a time, but what they described was certainly a future. In essence, they say: Terran plants are destroyed by pests, equipment is smashed by animals, even buildings are damaged by the chewing of small creatures. In time—I don't know how long—humans are gone from the area. They were as vague as Yké allows about the kinds of dryads that will do the damage. But all the dryads were described as *qèsēvi*—according to the plan."

"They're threatening to *plant* us to death?" The governor's tone was as incredulous as if a child proposed to trap him with a birding-cord.

"To manipulate our environment and bring about our destruction, yes, that's how I understand it. Probably by planting, among other methods."

Michael turned to Piro. "Is there any reason I should take this seriously?"

"Yeah, one. It happened before, and all us Zandaheans almost died. *Would* have died, without rescue. I told you it wasn't just one pest that broke us, it was like the Plagues of Egypt. Someone had it in for us."

"I confess," Iren said, "I took it as a metaphor."

"So did I, but now I see it wasn't."

The governor was frowning. "You never saw basket-men at the first settlement."

"Why would they show themselves? If we'd seen them, we'd have fought back. They can dig burrows and hide underground. From what John says about their climbing skills, they can probably get around in tree canopies too. Only wild children in a failed settlement would be fool enough to make contact with human beings on purpose. Lucky for them, now we can't fight, because Earth is watching. Unless John's girlfriend can convince the aiyi self-defense doesn't count, we are *resoundingly* fucked."

"Even if they did cause the problems you faced back then," the governor said slowly, "this is the desert. They couldn't even keep a village going here. They've said before that some of their pet dryads couldn't survive the heat."

Sudharma nodded. "I attempted to point out that contradiction. The gist of their answer was that it is easier to destroy than to protect, and also that more work will be done on making the necessary creatures drought and heat tolerant, now that it is a matter of species survival. But let us not get ahead of ourselves. They still have more to say."

The third speech was delivered all in one place, at the edge of the same field. Green was the only one who spoke. The sentences were complicated and there were many of them. Sudharma listened with deep concentration, and when the last word was pronounced, he was like a person waking from drugged sleep.

"This future will be harder to decipher. Rather than point out plants to indicate time, they referred to the ones they used in their first speech—'the column that Vèkas stood to the left of,' and so forth. I was not aware I would be quizzed on that material and don't remember all of it. Iren, Piro, if you will review the video with me and help me construct a timeline, that would clarify matters."

Iren opened up their library and the three gathered around it. The video was in snippets, recorded, John supposed, by Iren's binoculars. They watched each clip, stopped and discussed it, sometimes replayed one again and again. Finally Sudharma turned to the governor.

"They have described a future of cooperation. Énqissatêk will resettle the desert in tandem with humans. In the beginning, we will provide groundwater to stabilize their colony while they breed drought-tolerant strains of the commensals they rely on. In the long run, our habitation and our agriculture will serve as buffer zones, where dryads that depend on eating other

Scythian life will find little to survive on. In return, they will plant their lands to benefit and protect our crops as well as theirs. Humans and human endeavors will occupy about seventeen percent of the available space. This pattern of living will propagate widely." He paused. "We must understand this offer as exceptionally generous. If the ships brought énqissatêk to one of our worlds, we wouldn't respond by giving them a sixth of the landmass."

"So why do you look like you're about to tell me we just vented half our oxygen?"

"The offer they have made to us requires our population to increase quite slowly. There is some doubt here, because no human has observed the full lifespan of a column, or a cone, or any of the other long-lived dryads that the énqissatêk use as bases for comparison. Also, to calculate a rate of population growth one must know how long people will live, and in particular, how many will die before or during their reproductive years, which we can only guess at. But we believe their vision corresponds to a birth rate somewhere around two point four live births per woman."

"Isn't that rather high?" John said.

Iren was looking, not at Sudharma, but at the governor, as if daring him to speak. "When you're all half-poisoned and men have to walk their legs to stubs to fuck, it might be. For a new colony still trying to get a foothold firm enough to keep from being washed away by the next storm, it's suicidal."

Sudharma nodded. "If we were alone on this world, that would be true. But there is another path, the one my own ancestors took. Our growth was not so explosive as is typical of new colonies, yet trade with the vzdrei made our existence less precarious until there were enough of us to support ourselves. I might add, when we arrived vzdrei lived only on one island continent. That made it possible for both species to expand at the same time with little discord. But inevitably there will be a day when we come into conflict over land and its resources. Our approach, and theirs, has been to ignore the problem and let the future take care of itself. Énqissatêk do not ignore problems, they plan for them; and it seems to me their plan is—compared to what it might be—quite humane."

"How do we know that isn't just how fast they think we naturally breed?" Michael said. "It could be a bad guess, not a demand."

"The first scenario they presented implied a birth rate about twice as high."

The governor regarded him levelly without speaking, for longer, John thought, than was at all polite. Then his eye was caught by two Ischnurans approaching from the farm. They hesitated, watching, as if curious and yet unsure whether they wanted to be close to so many énqissatêk.

"Let's move this conversation indoors," the governor said. "Can you tell the basket-men we will think about their proposal?"

"I'm afraid I cannot, but we may simply leave. It will seem natural to them that we take time to plan."

"Come to my house, then. I'll have Marne meet us there."

"Marne?" John said.

"Tracking birth rates is part of his job." Michael fixed him with a look of disapproval, as if thinking he had spoken out of turn; and John was painfully aware that birth rates were no part of *his* job. He was in danger of being excluded from the meeting. And yet he would not, for any reason short of being bodily thrown out and the door locked behind him—possibly not even then, since the governor's house had windows and the desert contained any number of rocks—stay away from a room in which Iren was to hear Marne and the governor discuss reducing births. He didn't know exactly what his presence would accomplish, but just the same he would be there.

Michael's house was no more than a mile away, he thought; yet Sudharma's exhaustion was palpable. So, turning to the translator, he said, "Let me drive you there. Anyone can see you are in need of rest."

"Thank you, John."

"We may as well all ride," the governor said—wanting, John thought, to leave no one behind to answer questions from the two Ischnurans. When they reached the house John simply walked in with the others, and contrived to seat himself on the sofa next to Iren. Piro sat down on their other side. It was not long before Marne arrived, took a chair, and asked what in the world was so urgent. While Sudharma repeated his descriptions of the énqissatêk's three scenarios, John did not look to the side, yet something—the sound of their breathing, maybe, or some transmitted tension in the sofa's cushions—made them think Iren was sitting perfectly still with their spine straight. He could not hold their hand or put an arm around them without making others wonder why. In any case, he wasn't sure they would appreciate such a gesture.

"So," the governor said when Sudharma had finished, "what birth rate does the basket-men's demand work out to? Iren and Piro thought two point four, but they were only guessing at the deaths."

"You're thinking of a world in which we lose technology, but agriculture runs on rails because the basket-men are helping?"

"Something like that."

Marne sat and considered, then took out his library and began some calculation. At a certain point he shook his head and erased all his work and began again. At last, unable to contain himself any longer, John said, "But isn't it a pointless question? It's all very well to say that just so many children ought to be born, as if one were working out how many cords of wood one needs to fell and split for winter, but what good is the number thus arrived at? What, in particular, can any of us do about it? Those who decide in such matters are not here."

His words had carried him away; but instantly, when he had paused, he thought of Iren sitting next to him. Probably everybody in the room except Sudharma knew why he did not include them in the category of those who could choose to bear children or not; but it was cruel to remind Iren, and moreover it was indiscreet. "I am very sorry," he said to them. "I spoke without thinking."

"Not at all," Iren said. "You make a good point. I would hear you develop it further."

"Well, it is obvious, isn't it, that men can do little to affect the size of families—unless every man in the area could agree on the same project, and when have so many men ever agreed on anything? Surely, if a woman wants a child, she will find a man willing to father one."

All this had seemed very reasonable to him when he began speaking. But he realized with a chill that in a culture that insisted on monogamy, women who took in other visitors in order to have children would be exposed by their success; detection could become the basis of enforcement; and this line of thought led to a place so dark that he would not follow it further. "I think, truly, I should not speak anymore," he said, "being from a world with different, and I must say far more sensible, arrangements. But just the same, I believe women ought to speak on this."

"Well," Iren said, "perhaps what my friend says requires careful translation from the Essian, but I agree that when these matters are discussed, those who can bear children must be in the room."

"Furthermore," Piro added, "there should be more than one Zandahean."

"No one is making a decision here," the governor said. "The people will choose. I'm just trying to get a sense of what our choices are. And in that vein—not a decision, just an observation—let me tell you about where I come from. Every crew member on *Rose of the Winds* knows there's a strict limit on the number of people a ship can support. No child can be born unless somebody dies—or goes down to live on a world, which most of us are strongly disinclined to do. Ships' medicine gives us long lives, and there aren't a lot of accidental deaths. Sometimes people have to wait so long for a turn that when it comes, they're too old to have a child. It used to be they'd freeze themselves to preserve fertility, but then some of the waking demanded to have babies to use up the oxygen the frozen ones weren't breathing, and the captain gave in rather than face a mutiny. All that's what I came to Scythia to get away from—the last thing I want to do is re-create it here. But even so, it is livable. John, I'm sure you saw how this works on *Edgar's Folly*."

"I saw birth quotas used to reward sycophants, and to coerce visits from those not otherwise inclined to make them."

"Well, those are perversions we certainly want to avoid. But, look, an average of two point four, or whatever the basket-men's demand turns out to be, is much more flexible than the rigid resource limits a ship has. Every couple will be able to have their first two children without waiting in line. It's just a matter of distributing the right to a third fairly."

"And what will you do to those who want more than their ration?" Iren said.

John heard the warning in their voice. The governor didn't seem to. Probably, he thought there was no way Iren could know what he had done. And so he spoke as if they could be pacified by soothing words.

"No one is proposing to force a birth limit on people. The fact is, it would be impossible. I don't have an army from some other world that can impose my will on this one, and I certainly can't found some stable line of tyrants that will keep the population in control for generations in the future. The people are going to decide, because that's the only way it can work. But it's true that different worlds and different cultures have more or fewer children, without any coercion being applied."

Marne sighed in irritation. "Sure, Ischnurans at home barely manage to replace ourselves. Raising kids is expensive. Also everyone's too busy going to school and working. By the time they have the money, they're too old to have children without medical help."

"Which *is* coercion," Piro said, "only it's built into the economy so it's invisible. I know how planets like that work."

Marne shrugged. "That's a way of looking at it. The point is, Scythia's not going to have that kind of economy. Not for a long time. No one's going to be happy limiting their family size because a bunch of aliens decide to farm us like a crop."

"Especially not Zandaheans. You know we don't believe in contraception."

"Which matters less than you'd think. We're talking about *sustained* birth rates. Unless someone figures out how to sew condoms from a dryad's intestines, contraception's going to be around for two, three generations at the outside. In the long run the only difference is that churchgoers can't switch to oral when they think they're fertile. Not without having an awkward conversation with a priest afterward, at least."

John regarded the doctor with a sinking dread. "Do you mean to say you have nothing effective against conception that can be grown in the ground and harvested?"

"Silphium didn't make it off Earth, so no."

John understood at last what seeds he should have brought to Scythia. But now it was too late.

Piro's eyes were fixed on the governor. He spoke with a contained rage that gave emphasis to every syllable. "I am telling you it doesn't matter how many layers of velvet you wrap your truncheon in. Zandaheans are not going to take this lying down. Someone other than the Lord does not get to decide how many children we can have, and if you want to have a civil war over that principle, you can have one."

Into the silence that ensued Iren said idly, winding the end of their braid around their finger, "I used to wonder what I'd do, if Mumeran someday made up its mind to take the Merel Islands for its own. It's not the fighting that disturbs me—I think I could acquit myself well enough. But I have friends on both sides. I would feel quite torn apart. I suppose in this case, if I have to choose, I would throw in with whoever had no interest in deciding for me what my body is allowed to do, if any faction with that view could be identified."

The governor still didn't seem to hear the implication. He ignored them and turned to Sudharma. "Can we negotiate with the basket-men? Get them up to a more reasonable number?"

"I can try to describe a different future. It will be much more complicated than anything I've said in Yké before, but I can try."

"But to negotiate, we'll have to give them something. So, Marne, forget about trying to reach two point four or whatever it is. Is there anything we could do to move the culture in a lasting way, and make a permanent reduction in the birth rate without ruffling too many feathers?"

"Sure—encourage braiding. Quit deferring to Zandahean sensibilities, build it up as an honorable tradition. If people want to do it for the wrong reasons, let them. And of course, the vow will have to be kept strictly." Marne smiled at Iren wryly. "In other words, you win."

"Yes," Iren said. "What great good luck I have, that what I am is now of use to you." In their tone was so much bitterness that John slipped his hand into his bag and found the handle of his knife. "I will ask you one question, both of you. What will you do with jesses who rebel against your strictures? Will you sterilize them by force, or without their knowledge? Or will you simply kill them? Perhaps both, depending on how troublesome you think they'll be?"

Neither of them answered, but anyone could see that Iren's words had cleft them to the bone. There was no longer any doubt of Michael's guilt. Glancing from face to face, John considered what would happen next. He thought that Iren would go after Marne first. Surprise would give them the edge, but without a weapon, they would struggle to bring the fight to a definitive conclusion. John with his knife would make short work of the governor, and could then help Iren. What either of their lives would be like after that was out of his imagining. He hoped at least Sudharma wouldn't try to interfere—he would perceive an unprovoked attack, but on the other hand it was not easy to imagine him launching himself into the fight. Piro despised Marne and the governor, but how he would respond in the moment was impossible to say. All these complications were what came of waiting until you were too angry not to act immediately, instead of choosing a suitable moment. But there was no help for that now.

Iren smiled at the two men. "Have your tongues been stilled by dumbweed? I would have your answer. If you mean to treat us all as cattle and control the population of the herd, then everyone deserves to know what tactics you will sink to."

John understood that Iren did not mean to fight, but to threaten: if the governor pursued his intended course, they would expose him. John wondered that they would make such a threat in front of other people, especially Sudharma, who did not know the underlying matter but might now be able to guess. Probably, they were acting on emotion and not thinking the problem through. Still, there was one advantage: Marne and the governor might have decided to kill Iren to conceal their guilt, but it would do them no good now unless they also killed everyone else present. Sudharma, of all people, was essential and could never be eliminated.

The governor held Iren's gaze. "If we're going to avoid that," he said slowly, "I need other options."

"Is it my job to find you solutions, just because I am one of the class that you single out to oppress? Shall I choose someone else to take my place under the knife?"

"There is one answer you have all ignored," John said. "One power in this world, who has helped when asked, and never tried to constrain or coerce us—though I realize as I speak, you don't know about the help, and that is my fault. When we were stranded in the desert, Vo cured Sudharma of the poison that he drank. I worried that knowing Terran microbes and machines had healed him might alarm the foolish, so I withheld the fact."

The governor had kept his eyes on Iren throughout all this speech, but finally he looked at John. "I don't think asking your girlfriend for advance permission to go to war is a good idea."

"I would not help you ask such a thing. Rather, the favor we should seek from her is to be returned to our homes."

"Oh!" Iren said, and John at once regretted his words. If they and Torres house together were considered as a kind of family, then to send everyone home would be to tear it apart.

"Or," he added hastily, "to a place of our choosing. There is no reason it has to be the one we came from."

"Death twist you, John, you're right. I don't like it either, gentlemen, but that's the way it is. This world is theirs. We thought it could be ours, but it's theirs—we must accept that reality gracefully."

"I don't think most people will want to cut and run," Marne said. "Maybe we could ask her to evacuate the few who want it."

"It won't just be me and John—convenient as I'm sure that would be to you."

The governor held up a hand for silence. "We are not splitting up the colony. That just weakens our position even more. Everybody stays or everybody goes." His hand fell slowly to his lap. "Vo can build ships?"

"I don't know. But from the things I've seen, I know the aiyi's power is immense, and they might honor a request from her."

"I want to know what our options are. Go and ask her and report back."

This was an attempt to divide him from Iren, but it was easily thwarted. "I don't have to go anywhere. I will bring her here."

John stood and opened the window that faced the street. He was sure this was unnecessary—Vo would hear him if he stayed in his chair and whispered—but the others would probably rather assume their conversation to this point had been unmonitored. "Isavo Lizet," he called out, "there is no emergency, but the people in this house would like to speak with you.

If you are willing, would you make your presence known in some way that won't terrify them too much?"

He went back and sat next to Iren again. A winged insect alit on the windowsill, examined the room, and then flew to the coffee table. It stood up on its four hind legs, and holding out the front two like an orator imploring silence from a crowd, looked up at John. "Is everything all right?" it said in Vo's voice.

"I wouldn't go so far as that, but we are in no immediate danger. We have some doubts about the future of this colony, in light of the plans the énqissatêk have conveyed to us."

"I can see why."

"If our differences with them cannot be reconciled, could you transport us away? Shipping in cold-sleep would be all right—that's how most of us came here, after all. If it's necessary to store us in cold-sleep for some time before departure, that would also—"

"It's no use, John." Vo's voice was soft and full of anguish. "The aiyi aren't communicating with me anymore. They've left me with the crawler and a lot of setup choices—I can do most of the things that I could do before—but a starship, that's beyond me on my own."

"Are they still watching us?" the governor asked.

"They're watching everything, like always. And I see you don't know yet—they're sending out a message. No ship is to come here, on pain of being destroyed."

Of all the things John longed to say, he lit upon "Are you all right?"

"For now. I'm sad, but not too sad to bear. If I ever am, I will adjust my feelings."

"You must be careful, without the aiyi to watch over you."

"I know." There was warmth in her tone; it had been the right thing to say. "I've been regulating myself a long time with their help—I'm ready to do it solo. I'll be all right."

All the others were staring at Vo's avatar. It was impossible to say what they were making of this conversation. He shut them all out of his mind and said just what was in his heart.

"I would very much like to hold you, but I don't know if it would comfort you for me to touch an insect body."

"Why not?"

She flew onto his chest and slipped beneath the placket of his shirt. Carefully, he slid his fingers in between the buttons and enclosed her long stiff body without crushing it. "I would like to hold you in your proper flesh soon, if you'll let me."

"There's nothing improper about this flesh," she murmured into him, "but it is rather limited. Please do come."

John looked up again at the others. He felt split between two obligations: Vo wanted his companionship, but Iren might need his help.

Iren rose to their feet and looked down at the rest. "I have said everything I have to say to you gentlemen. I will go away now and consider what I ought to say to others."

This solved John's dilemma, and so he rose too. "I will seek to learn what may be salvaged of this wreck." His eyes lit on Sudharma. He was sorry that he would not be home to cook, but he feared that to say so would prompt an invitation from the governor to a dinner after sunset cooked by someone who did not know all the rules to follow, which would be awkward to refuse. Sudharma gave him a slight nod, which meant, John hoped, something like "It's all right." In any case, he could not help with everybody's problems when they all insisted on arising at the same time.

Iren had already gone out and was walking away at a pace that suggested they would rather break into a run. Though his van was parked in front of the house, John followed. He meant to call out after them as soon as he was certain that the governor and Marne wouldn't hear, but before he could do so Iren stopped. They untied the ribbon that secured their braid and dropped it on the ground. Savagely, with both hands, they raked through their hair until it was all loose, spilling in a mess of spirals down their back. As he hurried to catch up with them, they turned to face him and gave a shaky laugh.

"Well, that was cathartic, but now I have to braid it up again. Will you stay here and pinion anybody who comes by with a distracting conversation while I slip between these buildings?"

They picked up the ribbon and went. He had no idea at all what to say to a passerby to hold their attention, or how he would explain why he was standing in the middle of the sidewalk instead of using it for the purpose that gave it its English name. Fortunately, Iren emerged again quickly. Long practice must have made the operation quick.

"That was stupid, back at the house," they said.

"I'm sorry."

"I meant that I was stupid."

"I know what you meant. I was commiserating. You were tested beyond endurance."

"It's not exactly honorable to use blackmail."

"I'm not sure it qualifies as blackmail, when you are using the threat of exposure to keep the same person from doing more harm of the same kind. Even if it does, I certainly can't judge you for it."

"I'd like to hug you, but we're on a public street, and also I might crush your girlfriend. Is she still in there?"

"Yes."

"Vo," they said, addressing the left side of his chest, "if the aiyi's departure is my fault, then I'm sorry."

Vo's insect head poked out from in between the buttons of his shirt. "They didn't leave. They're still all around us. They just stopped speaking to me."

"But the question I asked, 'Will you consider what effect your kindness has on us.' I never meant to suggest they abandon you."

"That might have been part of the reason. They thought about it a lot for a while. But that was a long time ago, as aiyi see time. They listened to what the énqissatêk said to you today. They must have thought the future would be better, or more interesting, in a world where humans couldn't communicate with them. And that was it. They were gone from my head, and everything was silence."

"Regardless of the reason, I am sorry for your . . . bereavement, if that's what it is."

"It's not like bereavement. It isn't like anything. But what's done is done."

Vo retreated inside his shirt and he felt her change shape, becoming a round shield that clung to him using its six widely splayed legs.

"I must go to her," John said. "I think you ought to ride in the back of the van, and I will drop you off where you can walk back to Laura's unseen."

"I hate to reinforce this habit you've developed of dictating whether I should be in company, but yes, please. I need to see her now. I need to tell her I was wrong."

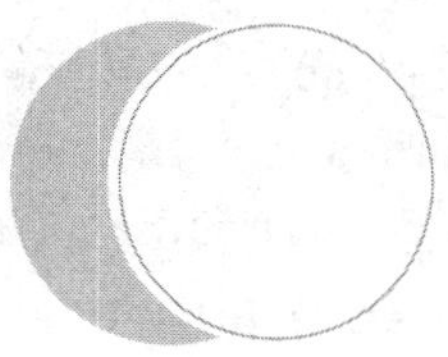

CHAPTER TWENTY-FOUR

The next morning John lingered in the crawler. He was anxious to see Iren and Sudharma and Ru, but he could not like the idea of leaving Vo alone. She had told him she could not stop feeling for the aiyi's presence in her mind, and each time she didn't find it was a new jolt. Like reaching for the railing on a staircase and finding that your hand met empty air, John thought. He felt that the aiyi had treated her quite badly. Of course anyone was free to stop visiting, or stop opening the door, at any time, but such a rule could not apply to a creature that had threaded its own nerves into her brain and made itself essential to her very thoughts—which, of course, was why becoming too entangled with a lover's life was not good conduct. For John to be her sole companion in a time of grief was also an entanglement, but that could not be helped.

They lay on the floor together for a long time, and he caressed her back. At last she turned over to face him. "Will you come again tonight?"

"Yes," he said with relief. He thought that having a defined plan would keep her from wandering away, or pursuing some even more drastic course. "Will you call me if you need me sooner?"

"Yes."

When he came home Sudharma was at the kitchen table, staring at a screenful of Yké. He sat down, and found Sudharma willing to be distracted for a while.

"I am sorry it proved impossible for us to leave this world," John said. "I think that would have been the best thing for everyone."

"It is a kind idea, and speaks well of you, but it would not have worked. For a time, yes, the énqissatêk would be left alone. But while aiyi may be eternal, their attention spans are not. Someday they will move on to another interest, and then ships will come. A world as green as this, as much like Earth, will always attract human covetousness. By that time perhaps the Free Ships will have faded into history. Instead it might be ships launched by the colonies that come—maybe even Essius and Dharanendra; our worlds are not immune to the impulses that brought humans here. When they arrive they must find humans and énqissatêk living together, not under the tyranny of either, but in a mutually agreeable peace. The Scythian way of life must be congenial enough to humans that newcomers choose to join it, rather than erase it with their overwhelming technological advantage. Perhaps that is why the aiyi warned the ships away, to give us time to work out how to live together . . . but probably I overreach. When dealing with aliens—and the aiyi are certainly that—there is always a temptation to project one's own ideas."

John prepared lunch for three, left Sudharma with a portion, and took the rest to the experimental farm to meet with Ru. She had heard something about the events of the previous day, undoubtedly from Iren. He filled in the blanks as best he could, but they were never quite alone and he didn't want to find himself recounting the whole story to an audience; thus he was reticent. Eventually, by replacing the word 'aiyi' with 'ancestor,' he managed to convey something of what it meant for Vo to be abandoned.

"How is she?"

"Distressed. That is probably a good sign. If she became serene, then I would worry more."

He was glad she had asked. He had worried that Ru, brought up with an expectation that love meant monogamy, might resent Vo—or, worse, that because of Vo's origins and mode of life, Ru might not quite see her as a human being. It was good that in a time of sorrow, at least, Vo could engage her empathy.

He wanted to explain to her that he might see her less for the next little while, being worried about Vo's state of mind. He could find no way of saying it that was discreet enough. But Ru said, very quietly, "I'm sure your presence is a comfort," and for now that would have to do.

In the afternoon Iren stopped by and chatted with Ru for a while. There was no trace of the previous day's agitation in their manner. Before they left they said to John, "I am glad I ran into you. I have that recipe we talked about."

He didn't remember discussing a recipe, but he took the paper that they handed him.

"Be sure to read all of it carefully," they said. "You wouldn't want to miss a step."

It was a recipe for an implausibly large batch of winterpot, the main ingredient being "night-boar meat; but if the hunt fails or you like your liver, rat." At the beginning of the instructions stood the sentences, "Please come to Torres house tomorrow after sunset for Tali's braiding ceremony. Don't be seen coming, and tell no one about this occasion until it is over."

He wasn't sure that attending the ceremony was a good idea. He didn't think that Tali liked him very much. And though he had come to accept that the vow suited Iren and they it, he was still uneasy at the thought of seeing another person bind herself. Nevertheless, Iren had asked him, so he would go.

"Thank you," he said, looking up at them. "I will make it tomorrow."

When he arrived Iren answered the door. "John, come in!" They seemed exhausted but elated.

"Am I late?"

"Not at all—you're not even the last to arrive. I would like to give you that deferred embrace now, if your chest is not inhabited."

"It isn't."

They pressed him close, but not for long, because another knock came at the door.

"That will be Lili," Laura said, arriving in the entryway. "This was meant to be only for family, but Tali needed her friend here, so we are trusting our secrets to a teenage girl."

"A sensible one, I think," Iren said. "She has always struck me that way."

"I hope so." Laura squeezed past them, laying a hand at the small of Iren's back as she passed by to open the door. When the girl had been let in they all four filed into the sitting room, where Lili caught sight of the strap of his bag.

"Is that the *kluk*?"

"That's a Southern version of a *morrol*," Iren explained. "And yes, it is."

"I don't see the snake."

In response John tilted the strap to the side until he heard her gasp.

"Do that again," Lili said, and watched carefully. "It's scary, but in a good way," she decided.

Piro had come in with Tali, and seeing them, Iren cleared their throat gently for attention. "My friends, I fear tomorrow everything becomes more difficult for all of us—and so tonight, let us be easy. Let there be nothing here but fellowship and ceremony, and no one in the world but us six, and all bad thoughts put away in drawers until the season for them. Now, we will need a small mirror that can be held in the hand, and a large one that can be hung on the wall. The one above your bathroom sink would do, but if there is a larger somewhere?"

"There's one over Laura's dresser," Piro said. "John, if you'll help me move it?"

"Certainly."

Piro led him down the hall to a bedroom, simply furnished with a bed, one soft chair, two nightstands bearing lamps, and a large dresser over which was hung the promised mirror, a wide rectangle. It came to him that this was where Iren visited Laura, and that they had meant to ask for this mirror in particular, but would not admit to knowledge of the room in front of Lili. Properly, but also for discretion's sake, Iren had left nothing of themself behind; the mild clutter of personal items on surfaces was all, at least plausibly, Laura's, except one pair of trousers and a shirt that must be Piro's, draped over the back of the chair as camouflage.

Piro was standing and staring, not at the mirror but at the dresser below it.

"Are you all right?" John asked.

"Yeah," Piro said without turning. He still didn't move toward the prize they had come for. "I told myself all the reasons this day had to be, but it took Laura and Iren so long to get facing the same direction on the horse, I think the treatment wore off."

"The vow troubles me also—probably for different reasons."

"It wouldn't bother me at all, if it was someone else's child."

"Forgive me—you seem quite devoted to the church . . ."

John thought better of completing the sentence, but Piro had already understood. "All I know is that there's nothing wrong with Tali, or Laura either, that doesn't come from being told there's something wrong with them. I do *not* know why Jesus Christ would found a church that's so fucking adamant otherwise. If asking questions is allowed after I die, that'll be high on the list, right after 'Why does the way of the wicked prosper' and 'Why did you set a speed limit for starships.' In this life it's too deep for me. I just keep following what I know is true." He stopped and sighed. "Okay, I talked myself back into it again. I'll take the left side of the mirror, you grab the right. There's a wire across the back that hangs off hooks, so we just have to slide it up the wall and it will come loose."

They went back to the sitting room. After some discussion of its placement, the mirror was hung on the wall across from the window. Tali sat in a chair with her back to it, and Iren stood. The rest arrayed themselves to watch, Lili on a soft chair, Laura and Piro on the sofa; John, not liking to crowd them, took a wooden chair off to the kitchenward side.

Iren opened a bag they had brought and took out a blue jacket, much like the one he had first seen them in, though not so long and full below the waist. "A jacket of this hue is traditional. I trust this one I made will fit—I have a notion of your size."

Tali glanced at her mother, looking unsure.

"I made a jacket too," Laura explained. "Or rather, altered one—it was Piro's. But I'm sure one custom made for her will be much better."

"By no means," Iren said. "Tali, you must wear your father's jacket. Nothing could be more appropriate. But you will keep mine too, for later—that way you will have a spare, in case some mishap befalls one before a wedding. Now, put on the garment that your mother sewed you, and sit back down in the chair."

When this was accomplished, Iren stood behind her and announced: "On Ischnura this ceremony would have more phases. In truth, it has become over-encrusted. Here we shall perform only those actions that are right, and necessary, and not too irritating for the officiant. First, there must be a braiding, and if the hair is too unkempt it must be tidied first, so you will all just have to wait while I amend this ragamuffin."

Iren took out a comb, and beginning with the last few finger-widths of its length, untangled Tali's hair. Each time that the comb passed through easily, they began a little higher, until all of it was smooth.

"From this day forward, you will brush your hair a hundred times before you go to bed, not because it is required of jesses, but because you will find braiding miserable if you do not."

"Yes. I promise."

"Now there are many styles of braid a jess may wear, each with its own history and meaning. In time you may learn to make all of them, but for now, to keep matters simple—"

"I want *your* braid."

Iren let their hand rest for a moment at the top of Tali's head. "You can't have it, young lady, but we will fashion you a simulacrum. This, then, is a very old Northern style. You will look like a jess of wintry lands, a hunter as it might be, who would keep a great feathered hound to drive the boars toward them and huddle up with it at night for warmth too. This conveys that you are self-sufficient; that you think always of your family, even if you have to travel far from them; and you will not turn back until you have achieved your purpose. Also, it asserts great accuracy with a bow, but I substitute precision in taxonomy. In modern times these signifiers are flexible."

As they spoke, Iren's hands were working; the braid was done nearly as soon as the speech, and they took a bright blue ribbon from their pocket to secure it. Then they picked up the small mirror from the floor. Tali darted a hand toward it, but Iren jerked it away. "Hands off and eyes forward. You must not see yourself braided until you have taken your vow. Are you ready?"

"I've been ready a long time." There was a bitterness in Tali's voice; and Iren ducked their head slightly in recognition of it.

"So you have, young lady. Let's proceed without delay. Now, the oath you are about to swear is very old—nearly as old as my homeworld. The exact sequence of words is indispensable." They laid their hands on Tali's shoulders. "It is even more important that you understand what you are promising, so I will translate. Do you swear to know yourself a jess? To inhabit the role with your whole self, making it your own, and never to let opposition make you doubt? To be as truthful as caution allows, and as bold as the world permits? Finally, and above all, do you swear never to kiss, unless it is someone you like; and not to go further than kissing, unless moved by love or by passion?"

"Yes. All of that."

"It's two words, Tali."

"I do."

"Then take this mirror."

Eagerly she plucked it out of Iren's hand, gazed into it to see, in the large mirror, how the hair at the back of her head was sculpted. Then she pulled the braid forward over her shoulder to look down upon the end of it. It did, John thought, make her look different. At home a braid had no particular significance. It evoked, if anything, a layered memory of lying in a cabin bed and watching as one woman or another, sitting on the edge of it, plaited her hair for sleep. Something had shifted in his head, so that now the way her hair was pulled back from her face and the precisely intertwining black curves that it fell in seemed to remove her from girlhood and place her in a different category of being. Yet what that change might mean was difficult to say. Surely she would not begin to sew and speak in paradoxes.

Iren looked out at their small audience. "I call on everyone . . . well, on the four of you . . . to witness what we do here. Now, young jess, will you tell us your name?"

Tali looked up at her parents. She was—or rather, *they* were—nervous to announce their choice. "I was named after St. Catherine of Siena, who is a good saint to be named for, but she was two planets ago. I need a name for a new world. So I thought I could be called Scythia."

Iren gave Scythia's braid a gentle tug. "Are you asking us or telling us? Say it with a whole heart."

Scythia drew in a breath, leveled their gaze. "My name is Scythia. Call me that."

"Better. See that you say it as boldly tomorrow. All right, it's done, you are a jess. Now go and meet your parents as your new self."

Laura and Piro stood up, and Scythia hugged them both, their father first. Tears were in his eyes. They clung to Laura for some time, and said, as if the words were wrung from them, "You were right, it's better this way." Then they moved on to Lili, who stood, too, holding up a sack and beaming.

"I brought you a shirt and some pants. They're my brother's that he never wears. I kind of stole them, but he won't mind once he finds out why."

"As you've probably guessed," Iren said, "I made you other clothes besides the jacket in anticipation of this event. As the anticipation was quite long, you will not lack for variety or suffer from too-frequent washdays. But by all means, you must wear Lili's gift tomorrow. It's good luck to wear hand-me-downs the first day after braiding."

Scythia had taken out the clothing from the bag and was examining it eagerly, but at these words they frowned. "Do you mean good luck as in magic? If it's a superstition then I shouldn't do it."

"Some might say it's magic. I say it's proof that you have friends who think of you, and nothing could be luckier than that."

"That's all right, then." They looked at Lili, shyly. "I want to try these on now and see how I look. Come upstairs with me?"

"Sure."

When they were gone it was as if all energy had drained from the adults. Laura and Piro sank back down onto the sofa, and Iren collapsed at Laura's feet, laying their head down on her knees. "Mists envelop me if I know what that child just swore to. I spent all night trying to invent a vow of chastity that wasn't chaste, and that's the best I could come up with. A big plate of Polonius-flavored mush."

"Did you sleep at all?" Laura said, gently stroking their hair.

"I might have closed an eye between draft twenty and draft twenty-one."

"I stayed up till the wee hours sewing. As if I couldn't have altered a jacket a long time ago. It was obvious how this was going to come out."

"You negotiated on your child's behalf, and got a better deal. Still the delay was a harm, and Scythia can't help but feel it."

"I guess you mean the person, not the planet. Is that going to keep being confusing forever, or will we get used to it?"

"Don't ask me. I never knew a jess named Ischnura." Iren's voice softened. "It is a strong choice, though. They will need strength for what's ahead."

"So will we all, I guess." Laura, with the hand not occupied caressing Iren's temple, squeezed the flesh above Piro's knee. "Shall we tell them, husband?"

"Unless you figure it'd add up to too much excitement for one night."

"They're younger than us, their hearts can take it.—When the first shocks of Tali's braiding have died down and things are as stable as they may be, Piro and I have decided to end our marriage. It's about outlived its usefulness, in light of recent events."

"What events?" John asked.

"I forgot, no one gossips to you. Piro was caught sneaking out of Elena's house at an incriminating hour. Tends to limit our ability to pose as a morally upright family whose child's behavior should be seen as virtuous, not that that was ever going to help much anyway. We always said we'd get an annulment when the children were all grown—this just moves up the timetable a little. Now Piro will be able to marry Elena."

"I thought marriage was permanent on Zandahe," John said.

"The Church doesn't recognize divorce," Laura explained. "But if it turns out there was some defect in the marriage all along, it can be declared null. For instance, if you got married by a Denier preacher without getting a special dispensation from the Church first. And, you know, we were young and in love and bullheaded and didn't want to wait around for all the niceties, so it's just a happy accident we had an escape hatch ready anytime we needed one."

"Will Deniers consider us married forever?" Piro asked her.

Laura straightened her back as if shocked. In a quiet and earnest voice she said, "I hope you're not suggesting there's an authority on this world that can tell me whether I contracted a valid marriage or not, brother. That's a little too replantationist for me. Maybe you should join the Church of Zandahe if you need someone to tell you what to think—"

"All right, simmer down now, I'm not trying to start a schism."

"There are twenty-two Deniers on this world now, counting babies. At this point we're overdue."

John would have asked what any of this meant, but Iren, lifting their head from Laura's knee, shook it slightly to inform him there was no point trying to understand. They leaned back against the couch and asked a question of their own. "Where will Scythia live?"

"She—" Laura said, and stopped herself. "God damn it. *They.*"

"Even on Ischnura parents take time to change their habits. Correct yourself and don't dwell on it, but in private, practice and improve."

"All right. *They* are old enough to decide where to live for themself, even if that means camping in your laboratory, or rotating around to whichever of us they're least pissed at on a given night. But regardless, they are going to need all three of us. All four, if Elena can accept them as a jess."

"We've talked about it a lot," Piro said. "She's open to the idea that the jess vow might be part of God's spiritual provision for this world."

Laura visibly shuddered. "I hate that, but I guess I have to hope it catches on." All this time her hand had clutched at Piro's thigh. Now she balled it up into a fist but left it resting there. "I'm glad you can go to her. I'm sorry you were delayed so long. I pulled you out of your orbit, and now we're getting old I finally let you go. . . ."

"No, no regrets," Piro said. "Unless of course the énqissatêk kill us all, in which case it's your fault."

"All right, then when you get to heaven you can tell me so, but you might have to shout loud."

They shared a gaze for some time. It seemed they had come to the end of what words can say. At last Iren said, "Well, I am glad for you, old man. You deserve this happiness. I hope you seize it with both hands."

"I will," Piro said, and anyone could see that he was pleased. But he added, "Ending my usefulness to you two as a cover."

"Never worry about that. I am as stealthy as a hound in snow, as devious as a snake-fox hiding pups—"

"Modest as a fisherman describing his best catch?"

"That also. But, since you raise the subject, where will you and Laura each be living?"

"She's keeping the house. She'll need the privacy and I won't, and anyway, Elena likes her own place."

"Though what I'm going to do with all this space," Laura said, "especially when Scythia's gone, is beyond me. It's just a lot of extra dusting for no purpose. Maybe I'll rope off the stairs and let the second floor go back to nature." She reached down to put her fingers to Iren's cheek. "The room above your laboratory would be the perfect size, if we only could."

"I have an idea about that," Iren said. "A plan, in fact, or the beginnings of one. But it won't work unless all of us agree to every part of it. John, that includes you."

"I am listening."

Iren looked at everyone in turn, then back at John. "I want to tell everyone I was sterilized on the ship. It's the only way to thwart the governor. The scare I put into him yesterday won't hold—I can't prove he knew anything. But if I reveal, now, what the *Rose of the Winds* did, people will wonder if he was complicit. He will hardly dare to start promoting jess chastity while that suspicion hangs over him."

"Certainly, I agree to that. I have been longing to bring the truth to light since we first learned it."

"You'll like the next part less. I can't accuse the *Rose* based on Vo's word. I think she is as truthful as a human being has ever been—having no reason ever to lie—but others won't understand that. So I want to make a deal with Marne. He'll agree that the ship's doctors sterilized me in some subtle way that he couldn't detect. Let him make up a medical story to support it. He'll endorse the speculation that the *Rose* might have killed Kol as well. In exchange for his support, I'll agree that he was innocent of the conspiracy. But, John, you will get the credit for finding the medical sabotage when he could not."

"I certainly cannot like lying to cover up for that man. I don't much care for pretending to some feat of diagnosis that I didn't truly perform, either."

"If an Ischnuran doctor suspected a patient had been sterilized without their knowledge, they would order tests, which would be performed by an automated machine and interpreted by an expert system that would tell them the result. That is exactly what you did. The medical device you used just has a prettier and more upsetting interface. And, you see, the news of your achievement establishes you as a doctor, and one who may see things that Marne has missed. He will no longer be able to justify denying you the right to prescribe, or to use his medical devices—and it will be a condition of our covering up his crime that he teach you how. So when patients start to come to you, you will be able to help them. And then no one will think it strange that you are physician to Laura and Scythia and Piro and me, none of whom are planning to go back to that man."

"I suppose that means being around Marne a great deal while he teaches me, and I like that least of all. But for the sake of being better able to care for all of you, I will endure it."

"Thank you, John. I do understand it as a sacrifice. Now, that much I had planned already in advance, but now hear the improvisation your announcement has inspired me to. As soon as the news of what happened to me and to Kol is out, I am going to take to my fainting couch. I'm going to wear black and hold up a skull. I am going to be so devastated I can hardly function in society—which is true to the extent that I'm distracted by a need to wind up Marne's small intestine on a spool, but officially I'm just too sad. I'm going to milk this for every drop of sympathy I can, and you all have to promise not to roll your eyes in public." They turned around on the floor so that they faced Laura, kneeling, and looked up into her eyes. "You, my love, must also show yourself more shattered than you are by the conclusion of your marriage."

"I'd have to do that anyway. I'm already pretending I'm upset about Elena, so people don't start wondering just what kind of a marriage this is.—Though it's not fair," she added, glancing at Piro. "They'll blame the annulment on you for being a bad husband, when the truth is that I never was a wife."

Piro shrugged. "That was inevitable the minute I got caught. In the long run it's not going to affect how people see me all that much. We all know men get more leeway. But what is all this playacting in aid of?"

"Only this: that my *vidhu*, being tenderhearted, and moreover prone to mother anything that moves, will be the one who cares for me and brings me back into the world. I think everyone will see that is in character. It will be seen also, how her kindness brings us closer—and when we are both in sorrow, it will be only natural for us to form a union of commiserators. Then once you have moved out, Laura with far more house than she can use and a habit of cooking for many, I with only a makeshift apartment, and too sad to be permitted solitude . . ."

"Yes, I see it." Laura was smiling but her tone was sorrowful. "Wasn't it enough to wheedle me into hope once? Now you are trying to addict me to it."

"It could all be done very easily. We can't really live above the laboratory—we must let everyone believe in separate bedrooms—but in this town are many growing families. Someone will trade for a smaller house, if that's what you still want. And in the meantime, housekeeping will be easier because we'll share the work."

"It's a lovely idea, but Iren, people won't accept it."

"Are you so sure? It's quite traditional on Ischnura. In old tales jesses are forever setting up housekeeping with a woman, all very proper and evil to him who thinks ill of it. Often the woman is a widow, which is where our term *vidhu* comes from, though we apply it widely now to any partner of a jess. One supposes a widow has well established her heterosexuality, and the same would apply to a woman deserted by—forgive me, Piro, I speak only of perception—a faithless man."

"Sure," Laura said. "We have a tradition of overlooking certain things too, relying partly on a lack of imagination about what two women could do together. I doubt that the same courtesy of ignorance will be extended to you."

"I have been stressing the importance of jess celibacy since the day I landed."

"All of which effort is going to be ruined when people find out you gave Scythia a modified vow."

"I will merely say that celibacy is my own choice, but I support the right of others to make different ones."

"You're asking people to do a lot of fancy interpreting to avoid an obvious conclusion."

"Maybe. Maybe it's too much. I won't pretend to know the future. I know I love you, and I'm tired of having only scraps of time with you. I think that while I live alone, although it makes me miserable, then everyone sees jesses as alone—that becomes the Scythian custom. But your child, I think you know, will want to share their life with somebody someday. It even seems there is an applicant for the position. If we break the trail ourselves, it will be easier when they come after."

"I want to say yes. But I don't trust myself. I think you're giving me a pretty excuse to be selfish."

"It isn't selfish to insist on being allowed a life."

Laura sighed. "If I say no, you're going to keep pestering me until I give in, aren't you?"

"Absolutely."

"Yes, then. Though I'm a fool, and no good will come of it. But it sounds like you're liable to die if I say no, and I'd miss the constant irritation if you passed away, so yes."

They didn't kiss, but Iren took her hand. Laura held their gaze awhile, then looked away. "I can't believe I came all this way just to wind up hiding in plain sight, like women do at home. One big flop and back into the same pot."

"We are shipwrecked on a hostile world," Iren said. "We're saving what we can. But as long as we're together, I can bear it."

"It's going to be a lot of change for Scythia. I mean Scythia, my child, though the same could be said of the world. Is it out of the question to tell them their name's too confusing and they have to pick something else?"

"I am afraid it is, although perhaps, under the circumstances, hoping for a change of heart would be permissible. As to how they will react to the unfolding of our plans, that worries me too."

Piro cleared his throat. "It might take a while, but I think they can come around to being happy for us all. It's the keeping of secrets that weighs on them most, and this leaves them with fewer. Elena and I, and you and Iren, care about each other—those'll be sayable facts. Strictly speaking, that's all they know."

"If that is true," Iren said, "and when some time has passed—there was a fashion in the South, for jesses to be blessed but unbound, which means to receive the blessing that only a jess can give, without the marriage ceremony that is its ordinary habitat. Scythia might say it for us, if they would, and if you would."

"I would."

"You see how far I have fallen to want such a thing! But I do want it." They looked over at John, as if remembering he existed, and they smiled. "The blessing doesn't breathe a word about fidelity, so our Essian friend can be a witness without damage to his conscience. As you know, he is morally upright but at a diagonal."

"I'd do all of it with you if I could," Laura said, looking down at them. "Rings and white dresses, traditional vows, all of that."

Iren looked pleased and yet uncomfortable. "I'd make you a wedding gown, and you would look amazing in it. But you'd be marrying a cutbraid, and this way you get a jess." Then they started if as struck by lightning. "Oh! When we live together I can make you clothes! I'll say I'm returning the favor of putting me up—no one will question that. I should start the planning now, so that the moment I've moved in I can start having fabrics made."

Laura touched their face and tucked a loose strand of blond hair behind their ear. "I do believe you're more excited about dressing me than about sharing a bed every night."

"Not true. The anticipation is exactly equal."

"Will you stay here tonight?" Laura asked. "I know you're exhausted. I promise I'll just let you sleep."

"You will not," Iren said. They laid their hand over Laura's, then slid it up, stroking the throat of her wrist with their thumb; their voice was softly teasing. "You are a pest and a disgrace and can't control yourself for eight hours in a row. I'll have to pacify you if I'm to get any rest at all. But I'll sleep better if I'm in your arms, so it's a fair trade."

"All right then," Laura said softly, sounding embarrassed and pleased.

Piro, looking over them, said in a tone of tired aggrievance, "If you two plan on subjecting my child to this type of display, Scythia will be living with me." This would have alarmed John, but Laura and Iren both laughed. Iren's thumb still rested on her wrist, as if to feel her pulse; this small contact absorbed them altogether.

John was thinking that if Laura and Iren grew bold then maybe he should too. Killing the snake-tree had somehow convinced the town he did not visit Sudharma; it might serve to keep down future rumors of the same kind. Furthermore, it had given him the aura of a man it would be dangerous to cross, so anyone who had suspicions would be hesitant to voice them. And if Laura had found a way to come to Scythia despite the homophobia of her world, then surely there were men of equal ingenuity. On Ischnura and Zandahe, they must have had some way to recognize each other. Maybe Laura, or even Iren, would know something about it. But manifestly this was not the time to ask.

Laura looked away from the conjunction of her hand and Iren's, gazed in the direction of the stairs, and said, "How long exactly do we think it takes to try on one shirt and one pair of pants?"

"There was a time you *didn't* want your child to take a vow of chastity," Iren said. "As I recall, you insisted repeatedly on the point."

"I know it. But if that's happening now, I need to have a tricky conversation with the not-a-planet about how not to get caught. If it's still a ways off, I don't want to terrify them sooner than I have to."

"Let me broach the subject, then. I will be offering them advice on how to live a jess's life, and a little spycraft can be slipped into the lessons. I would like to speak to Lili too, but—"

They broke off, because footsteps were audible above. Quickly, they moved to sit on the floor again rather than kneel, leaning back against the couch and drawing one knee up in front of them; although their arm was lightly touching Laura's leg, the pose was not intimate, only exhausted. Lili and Scythia appeared and stood beneath the rectangular arch that divided the sitting room from the front hall. Scythia was wearing gray pants and a shirt of faded blue that buttoned up the front.

"Good night, everyone," Lili said.

"Walk carefully," Iren replied. "Neither moon has risen yet—it will be very dark. And remember, nobody must know about the alteration to the vow. Scythia will decide when to reveal that."

"I don't know what you're talking about. That was the most traditional braiding ceremony I've ever seen in my life."

Scythia went with her into the front hall. As soon as a wall hid her from the sitting room, Lili stopped them with a hand laid on their shoulder, pulled them close and kissed them gently, then broke away and looked into their eyes. From where John sat, the scene was framed in the large mirror as if in a painting. If that kiss were a painting indeed, and could travel on a ship to Essius, no one would know how to see Scythia's gender right, yet everyone would understand how matters stood between them: that Lili hoped for a visit; that she had done so for some time; that she should not hope to receive it that night, but nevertheless she had reason to hope.

No one else had noticed. Probably the angle of the mirror was not right for them. The two young people disappeared from view, but not for long—Lili, having made her declaration, properly did not belabor it. Scythia returned and stood looking down at Iren. "Four other kids have told me they want to take the braid. One is Zandahean. Now I've broken the ice, they might decide to talk to their parents too. I won't give you any names."

"No, nor should you. But if your friends are close to a decision, let them know there is a choice of vows, and if they have reservations about taking the old one, they should talk to me about it."

"As soon as one of them takes the new version, there are going to be questions about my vow."

"How to deal with that must be your choice. If you would like advice, you may consult me."

Scythia shifted their gaze to John. "I want to talk to you alone now." They paused to consider. "With Iren."

Laura stirred on the couch. "It's late, and Iren is exhausted. You can talk to them both tomorrow."

"Don't worry," Iren said. "I can stay up for things that are important. If the good doctor is amenable to a late-night appointment, so am I."

"I am. It's not so very late."

Piro heaved himself up to his feet with an exaggerated grunt. He offered a hand to Laura. "Will you take the air with me?"

She let herself be pulled up and linked elbows with him—sardonically, and yet companionably. They walked together toward the front door, but quickly had to disengage and go in single file, because the front hall was not wide enough to walk through side by side.

When the door had closed behind them, Scythia sat down in the middle of the couch, where their mother had been. Iren put their hands on the edge of it and levered themself up from the floor to sit beside them. "I serve as your advocate. Since on this primitive frontier world you are forced to deal with a sexed doctor, I will remind him of his duties to you—though I think you will not find him very hostile."

"You will not," John said. "Your mother has shown by her actions that she thinks you are ready to make these decisions. I won't put myself above her by doubting it."

This brought the trace of a frown to Scythia's face. There was not yet harmony between them and their mother, he thought. The wound of their division had closed up, but it would be a long time healing.

"What is it that you wish to ask?" he prompted them.

"I want testosterone."

John had guessed this might be what they sought, and was to a degree prepared. "I cannot dispense medicines yet, but when Iren's plans reach fruition, I will be able to. That will happen rather quickly, I believe?"

"Yes," Iren said. "I will make Marne an offer tomorrow, and he won't say no."

"And I am unsure of the dosage needed, but I will find that in your library, won't I?"

"You will."

"Then I will study the matter, and . . ." He stopped and reconsidered. "Rather, if Iren will lend us their library, we will learn about it together and you will decide on the dose. That is proper, isn't it?"

"Very much so," Iren said. They turned to Scythia. "Soon, then, you will begin a transformation of the body that can trace its origins all the way back to old Earth. Those people had no concept of ritual at all, but they had a crude idea of memory, and learned some ways to honor it. In time Ischnurans rediscovered their knowledge. Now the custom starts again on a third world, and you will be the first."

Scythia did not look at them during this speech, but kept their eyes on John. "I don't want to have breasts anymore. Can you fix that?"

"Why, no—I am no surgeon, certainly not for such fine work as that would have to be."

"Marne can do chest surgery," Iren said. "I will make it a condition of the pact I form with him." They touched Scythia's arm. "At home they can make the torso look male, yet spare at least a portion of the milk. If that were possible, would you want it?"

"No. Breastfeeding's not in my memory."

"Sometimes memory is at odds with other things we want. Childbearing didn't fit well with Kol's memory, for instance, but he retained the capacity anyway, and augmented it with the ability to self-fertilize. He used to say that jesses could rely on no one else to help us procreate—that we must gather the means of production into ourselves, and dare them to cut it out of us. You may detect a natural tendency toward the dramatic, but these days I have a new appreciation of his point of view."

"No. I don't want to be able to feed a baby and I don't want people thinking of me as somebody who could do that."

"Well, that is easier. Will you trust Marne to do the work?"

Scythia looked down at their hands, which were braced against their thighs with fingers spread. For the first time, they appeared uncertain. "What do you think he has against us?"

"I have thought about that a great deal. I believe Marne is one of those who think, because anamnesis can cause distress, it ought to be eliminated from the population—the wishes of those who have it not being considered—but that the carriers, not being at fault, should be treated with kindness. I mistook his pity for friendship. Now every moment that I trusted him feels like being caressed by the tusk of a boar."

"But is that right? I mean . . . I am in distress. Do I have anamnesis?"

"I don't know. If you like, I will test you with my library, and Marne won't need to know the result. I suggest you consider, first, whether it matters."

"It matters to whether he'd try to sterilize me."

"I'm not sure it does. Ischnurans, thanks to the genetic bottleneck we went through, are still not as genetically diverse as Zandaheans. Where one gene is associated with the braid for us, there might be dozens of others for you. Possibly Marne would simply assume that you carry some gene worth extinguishing. But I urge you, before you give his ideas any further thought, to see how the braid sits on you, and how a change of hormones makes your body feel. You may be astonished how much of a difference they make."

"If we lose technology, there won't be hormones anymore."

"That's true. I fear it too. But remember that when we change our bodies we say we are *honoring* our memories, not *becoming* them. We honor them, also, by persevering in the quest for change, and by enduring when the match can't be made perfect. In the days of the first jesses they had nothing but endurance, and the alchemy that clothes and names could work on them. I would like to show you the few writings that they left us. They were like you, girls before the braid. The world was hard for them, no doubt, and some of them lamented the condition of their bodies, but in the end, none of them thought their lives were not worth living. Let me ask you, young jess: Did you take the vow just to get medicine for the relief of pain, or did you see something in it?"

"I saw something in it."

"The first jesses invented that. They made a whole new way for human beings to be. I believe that we bring something to the world that is unique, and that we belong in it. Sometimes we suffer for it. But if you lived your life only to avoid pain, you wouldn't feel very deeply, you wouldn't risk very much, and you probably wouldn't achieve very much. Do you know what anamnesis does, exactly?"

"It gives you a memory."

"No—no gene we know of can do that. Rather, it makes your connection with your body more immediate and more intense. It might increase your precision and joy in movement. It might make someone a better dancer, a more accurate archer, a more fluent swimmer. But for those who have a memory, the wrongness of the body is felt more keenly too—and they seek out the braid for relief. Whereas those who are more able to disengage from their bodies may repress what they feel. Then they walk around numb and disconnected and less than they could be, and might never even know why, if they had no role models to learn from. Those whose fire burns brightest have a difficult path to walk, but they light the way for others. And I believe, no matter how hard this colony may fall, that way leads back to a world of hormone injections and memory clinics, in which the gene increases jesses' joy in their changed bodies, and in which some of us are great dancers too."

Scythia slipped off their shoes and put their feet up on the couch so their knees pressed into their chest. They wrapped their arms around their legs and thought. "That doesn't help me decide about Marne."

"Well," Iren said, "if I am right about his motives, there is no reason to think he would wish for the surgery you seek to go poorly. John, what do you think?"

"I dislike going to him for anything at all. But, Scythia, if you choose to do it, I will observe the procedure. I am no expert in ships' surgery, but I can tell the difference between an operation on the breasts and an attempt on your fertility."

"I don't think I even want to be fertile. I just don't want him deciding that for me."

"Of course," Iren said. "Nothing could be more understandable."

"I guess I'll do it. If it's really the only way."

Iren met his eyes. "Let John and me discuss this further, and research it, before we approach Marne. Perhaps some improvement to the plan will suggest itself. If not, then the increase in knowledge can only improve his ability to keep Marne honest."

"Okay. But I don't want to wait long." Scythia unfolded themself and stood. Their braid had fallen forward, and they hooked it with a thumb to toss it back over their shoulder. "I'll find Mama and Papa and tell them we're done."

Iren touched their hand to make them pause before they went. "At home, before hormones or surgery are given, it is traditional to tell another jess about how you experience your memory, and for the testimony to be written down. Originally—and still, in clinics operated by religious groups—the results were studied to better understand the world that, some believe, we live in before birth and must return to after death. In those funded and run by jesses, memory books are a way for us to learn about each other, and to leave a record of ourselves. I found it very meaningful, both times that I gave testimony. If you will entrust me with yours, we will begin a new book for this world."

"All right."

"Tomorrow, then."

Scythia nodded and left. As soon as they heard the door being shut behind them, Iren's face fell. "Tell me truly, John: How hard do you think tomorrow is going to be for them?"

"I am the last person to ask about how Zandaheans will act."

"Laura and Piro and I are going to walk them to school tomorrow as a group, to establish that we all support their braiding, and to protect them along the way. We will make sure one of us walks with them, both there and home, as long as necessary. But we must turn back at the school door, and I fear what may happen inside. I hate that they will have to face so much alone."

"They will have Lili, at least. And Scythia strikes me as brave."

"They are. I told them last night, what we are fighting for above all is acknowledgment that we exist. Even if jesses are reduced to objects of contempt, I would still rather be abject than unimaginable. In degradation we can come together and find solace and resistance. We can demand better. But if we cannot even put a name to what we are, we each wander a desert alone. I told them all of that, and they still wanted the braid just as much as before. I told it all to Laura too, and do you know, I think it was that—even more than agreeing to soften the vow—that made her agree to it at last. So many times I tried to reassure her everything would come out well, when what she needed was to have her fears acknowledged, not dismissed. I fear we two are very bad at being in conflict. We are, however, excellent conspirators. As long as I don't run out of ideas for secret schemes to carry out, I guess we'll be all right. Speaking of which, can Vo still perform miraculous surgeries?"

"I would have to ask, but I imagine so. I was surprised you didn't mention the possibility to Scythia."

"I'm afraid Vo will say or do something to terrify them, and even more afraid of what a brash young jess will do when she has her wares all spread out on a blanket like a traveling peddler. We could all wind up as shapeshifters."

"I can ask Vo to offer them only those options relating to their own body, and not to those of future generations. She might not think of that herself, but I believe she'd see the point of it."

"I hope so. We'll have to tell Scythia, in any case. It wouldn't be right to let them go to Marne without telling them there is another choice."

"I will be grateful if they do choose Vo, so I don't have to observe. This surgery they long for is unsettling. To remove healthy tissue, abolishing a natural function of the body . . ."

"You have problems with what Scythia is doing that are about you and not them," Iren said. "Not everybody wants to be a mother as much as you do."

"What do you mean?"

"Nothing at all. You must forgive me, I am very tired. Speak to me of your unease some other time, and I will come up with some proverb that illuminates the situation. Now as an act of kindness to a jess who is exhausted unto incoherence, will you please say your goodbyes briskly and let Laura and me go to bed? I have to get up before dawn and sneak home, then be seen to walk back here through town to take Scythia to school, and before I even get to sleep I must fulfill a certain promise that I made to Laura out of exuberance and a whim to see her blush."

"I've missed a lot of sleep for that, and done a lot of walking in the moonlight too. It's not so bad."

"You only had to get up in the morning and save lives. I have to let a hundred people ask me whether Tali said their vow in English or Ischnuran without murdering even one."

"That's saving lives."

"So it is. In mercy to the townsfolk, then, if not to me, clear out. But let's meet again when you have had a chance to speak to Vo, and if Scythia wishes, we will both conduct them to the crawler."

When John got home, Sudharma was at the table, working. He always seemed to be working. There was no reason to say anything about the ceremony—Sudharma would assume he had been with Vo. But the news would be all over town tomorrow.

"Tali has taken the jess vow. Their new name is Scythia. I will be taking care of the medical treatment that follows."

John found he was afraid. Though his own ambivalence about the braid had not entirely left him, still it would hurt if Sudharma judged Scythia harshly. But that would hardly have been like him. All he said, before he returned to his screen, was "It is about time you began to see patients."

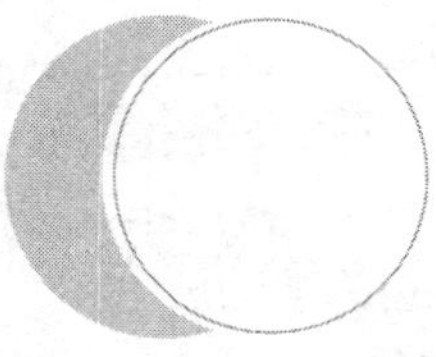

CHAPTER TWENTY-FIVE

All the rest of that winter and into the spring, Sudharma exchanged futures with the énqissatêk. It took nearly a month of planning and of consultation with Iren and Piro to perfect each new scenario, and he worked late every night. Of course John understood how important it was to achieve a more favorable agreement, but he worried that the effort to communicate was becoming an obsession, and feared that translation would lie at the end of it.

At the onset of April, Laura and Iren asked John to convey a dinner invitation to Sudharma. Laura said the occasion was that they had lived together in the house by the layered rock for a month now and nobody had burned it down yet, but he omitted this explanation when passing the message along. He hoped Sudharma would, for once, accept, since Laura knew the full list of his dietary restrictions and promised the meal would be finished by sunset; moreover, they hadn't cooked rat in their kitchen yet. This hope was not fulfilled. He went in any case. When he returned, Sudharma was sitting in the same place at the table as when he had left, working on the same screen. John saw a fragment of text over his shoulder:

> When this column [approx. 1.2m] reaches the height of the cone that Ēkyvẽ stood in front of at the time when they first met the people of Dẽq, the extent of the [unknown dryad, an annual] at the place that Green wakened the sleepers covers the area that the food crop upriver of Kéjévy had attained, the second time that it was lost to flooding . . .

"Are all their speeches that complicated now?" he asked.

"Fortunately, no. This is how they talk when they don't want me to understand. But I can sometimes make a partial sense of even their most complicated speeches. It's the simplest ones that thwart me altogether. Sometimes an énqissatêk will simply mention a place, without context, and not as a response to some other utterance—as if I walked up to you, said 'the west end of Main Street,' and fell silent."

"What could be the point of that?"

"Well, we know that they are sensitive to anything that disturbs the landscape—that is how Green found us in the first place, by the rippling out of our effects. If we smelled smoke in the air, and I said 'the kitchen,' you would know I meant that was the likely place for fire. Perhaps it is like that. Also, they all share their memories. If I told my brother, 'the tree behind our house,' he would remember that we used to have a swing there, which might evoke the feeling of an idle afternoon, or on the contrary, the pain of falling off it as a child. Either way, the allusion is impenetrable to me and likely to remain so."

John allowed himself to hope Sudharma wouldn't translate after all. Maybe the problems he faced were too great to be solved in that way. Maybe he would give up the idea and remain himself.

The next day when John delivered lunch, he again found Sudharma with Green. The énqissatêk he had once regarded as a friend turned an eye on him briefly before going back to their conversation, and the food had gone entirely cold before Sudharma could sit down to it.

"Do they have no regrets about what they are doing?" John asked.

Sudharma paused to think while he ate his meal, which was made with some exceptionally flavorful tomatoes from Laura's garden and had deserved to be enjoyed while hot. "I'm still not sure they even understand that we regard it as an injury. They know we come back to them over and over, asking for a higher birth rate, but I've found no way to say that their proposal is oppressive. They may think we are like someone bargaining in a marketplace, who wants a better price but won't be much distressed by failing to get it."

"I meant regret for themselves. The arrangement that they keep demanding requires the upheaval of their way of life too. Doesn't that bother them?"

"I tried to convey that question to Green once. I had to mix Yké with a few English words that I believe they, alone among their people, understand. We were walking along Main Street at the time, and came upon the stump of Alma's cone."

This had been cut through at its base the previous month, after Alma bit the hand of an Ischnuran boy who had been teasing her by offering a dead lizard and then jerking it away. Though the child was not seriously injured, and though Laura and Piro and Iren and Ru all agreed that the creature's response had been just and proportionate, Michael had ordered the cone felled. Alma, being a parasite, would find another cone to live in, or at least that was what all the children who missed her were told.

"Green pointed at the cone," Sudharma said, "and spoke to me in the imperative, as they might speak to a child of their own species: 'Cut that down.' What do you think they meant by that?"

"That Alma is a threat that we have neutralized, and they are responding to us in the same way?"

"A reasonable conjecture. I can't rule it out. But I think he meant 'Cut the tree in your mind.' Stop mourning things that are gone, which to them their old way of life already is. I don't think they have customs or rituals or traditions, at least not as a human understands them. Instead they have plans, and plans can change."

By the time they finished eating, John was in danger of being late for his lesson at Marne's clinic, so he walked directly there, taking the emptied dishes with him. He had learned to use the medical synthesizer—a simple matter, it turned out, as long as you knew what you wanted—and was now to be trained on the scanner. John hated spending time with Marne, and the only consolation was that Marne clearly loathed it even more. He felt exposed and shamed, no doubt, being around someone who knew the truth about his crime. Now and then he made some tedious attempt to justify himself, and today was one of those days.

"John, I know as an Essian you were raised to respect women, and that's probably how you see Iren. But think about the future of the colony—"

"Iren has prevailed upon me not to kill you, very much against my inclinations," John said. "My respect for them is what keeps you alive. Please stop making self-control more difficult for me."

After that Marne no longer made unnecessary conversation, and the lessons were not as unpleasant. Still, John was glad when some other duty provided a reprieve. Once he had to treat and transport a man who had broken three bones in his right foot while checking up on a mining site. Another time he had a much-needed day off from the doctor because his help was needed to present a new proposal to the énqissatêk. Though like the previous ones it amounted to a plea for a more flexible birth rate, Sudharma had embroidered the proposal with more detail, and the presentation of it was accordingly more complicated. Piro, Iren, John, and at Iren's suggestion, Scythia were all enlisted to point out the plant-stage dryads that he would use as time references. This required each of them to move on to the next of five or six locations at the right time and in the right sequence, to which end the plants were marked by ribbons in a different color for each assistant. Scythia performed this duty with precision and solemnity, after much coaching by Iren, who hoped that if the young jess could help save the colonists from having their numbers dictated as if they were rats on a ship, the rift between them and their people might begin to heal.

The énqissatêk did not sit through more than half the speech. One moment they were listening with, it seemed, careful attention; the next they had lost interest. Green stepped forward and said, "Follow." All the énqissatêk walked off to the south. Sudharma, deprived of his audience, could not choose but go after them, and the other humans trailed behind.

They came to the edge of the teaching farm. Green spoke, not at great length—it might have been three or four sentences. Then he went to join the others, who stood in a row looking at the desert beyond the farm.

"He says this place will be overrun by the animal stage of a dryad," Sudharma said. "The word they used for the species is new to me."

"When?" Iren asked.

"Yké has no way to specify short lengths of time, but from the way they are watching, I imagine very soon. I am messaging the governor for help, but I fear it will be too late."

"We need to get everyone out of there," Piro said, and ran into the farm, shouting warnings at the students. The others followed. John would have gone at once to Ru, but Iren got there first. It was better that way—Iren could openly show solicitude toward her and he could not. When all the students had been gathered at a spot about a hundred paces townward from the farm, the adults all held a quiet conference and agreed that Piro and Iren would escort them to the schoolhouse, to shelter behind closed doors. The fear was not so much that the invaders would attack the town, as that the children would return to watch—or worse, try to prevent—the action. "I'd much rather stay, but I'm the best one to keep the Ischnuran kids from slipping away to come back here" was Iren's murmured comment. "I helped raise most of those little shits, I know their tricks." They dropped the strap of their binoculars over John's neck before they left, and slipped their library into his pocket. "Keep the lenses pointed toward the field so that the library can record, but don't let watching the carnage distract you from your own safety. I expect a full verbal account as well, and you must be alive to give it."

After that he was alone with Sudharma and Ru. He didn't dare to take her hand, though he was sure Sudharma would tell no one if he did. He only said, "I am sorry about your experiments."

"It's probably a mistranslation," she said. "We'll stand around watching the plants grow until we get bored, then go home feeling like idiots." Then, seeming to recall who else besides John she had for company, she spoke across him to Sudharma. "Forgive me. I am only letting hope run wild."

"There is nothing to forgive. I hope the same as you."

But something was already coming, up from the south toward the farm. Even with binoculars it was hard to make sense of the sight: a swarm of little green lines, each one, as it came close, resolving into a miniature thicket of green stems and leaves. It was as if strips of soil had been cut from the ground, along with all the growing things they carried, and blown toward the farm by the wind. Yet they did not rise more than two or three thumb-widths above the sand; they were flowing along the ground, not flying. When they reached the farm, they swarmed up the stems of the plants like sailors scaling masts, and only then could he make out the long tan bodies that the green tangles emerged from. Some cut at stems with their sharp mouths, others at branches, until the plants' flesh was sliced through and the top or limb fell to the ground. Each one chewed a slit into the end of the stump left behind, then, twisting, snipped a green stem from its own back and inserted it. They coated the joined wounds with a black tar they secreted from their mouths. They were parasites, John thought, grafting their own children onto a host that would nevermore be anything but rootstock. Iren, on their drive through the desert, had told him many desert plants had roots that either plunged deep down, to sip groundwater, or else spread out wide, to capture every drop they could from the infrequent rains. It must be a great advantage to steal such a root system rather than grow it.

The governor arrived with a dozen or so men armed with guns, but such small animals made tricky targets, and being under fire deterred them not at all. John saw one that had lost its hind half to a lucky shot continue to cut branches and attach grafts it plucked from what it had left of its back. Pulling the creatures off the plants and stomping on them was tried, too, but since this led others to converge on the assailant, and their jaws could deliver a painful bite, the effort petered out. When the parasitic dryads had used up all their greenery, they flowed back southward. John found one that had tried, instead, to hide by curling up into a spiral under the litter of cuttings the attack had left behind. He could have held the coil between two clasped hands without crushing it; but mindful of the bite, he found a pot of the sort Ru used for tomato seedlings, overturned it on top of the insect, and weighted it down with a stone. Iren would like to have a living specimen.

Throughout the attack the énqissatêk watched with ears down and noses up—the same expression Green had worn after his raid. Joyful triumph, or grief for a regrettable necessity? John asked Sudharma, but Sudharma didn't know.

More than three-quarters of all of the plants in the farm had been entirely converted to rootstock, and many of the ones that lived were maimed. Yet the town had not been entered; other farms had not been touched. The precision of the attack, even more than its violence, proved that the énqissatêk could make good their threats. It was unclear how they had induced the new dryads, which became known as scions, to attack where they chose. Perhaps they had prepared a trail for them to follow. Perhaps they just released, or sowed, the scions in the proper place, and knew what path instinct would lead them to take.

After that the énqissatêk did not come into town, but met Sudharma at a distance from it—never alone, but never in large groups. They were now living scattered in burrows around the whole region, Iren thought.

One day John emerged from the shower to find Sudharma working on his screen, as usual. The translator started, as if guiltily, and took the screen up by the edge to turn it over. But he stopped himself, and with deliberation set the screen back down.

"Is that what I think it is?"

"Yes. I have begun work on a program of translation." Sudharma paused, wary; he was apprehensive of John's reaction. But he was also in the grip of an excitement, and after a few moments it won out. "Green has told me—if I understood him, and I think I did—that the way the énqissatêk plant and recontour the land is not just agriculture, but is more like art, or writing. The landscape *means* things. So when they mention a location without context, it's as if they are quoting a poem. That is why my proposed futures have all failed: I am like a small child scribbling on a piece of paper and trying to get it hung up in an art museum. I must learn to understand this second language."

"How would translation help with that?"

"Memory is the key. I need to be able to remember every detail of the landscape that I see or that they tell me, and assemble all of it into a picture. Once I can hold a world inside my head, the way they do, I will be able to converse more freely, without needing weeks of preparation to say anything complex. And when they mention a place, I will be able to picture it. Then I can begin to see patterns and understand the language of the land. The way they are trying to arrange human beings—the shape of the lands they will give us—surely means something, and it's essential that I find out what."

"If your program targets memory, your existing memories are at risk."

"Inevitably, yes."

"Don't," John said. "Please. I understand the need, but it's too great a price to pay."

"It's not a price. It's what I came here hoping to do."

"You'll become another person."

"I will change, as everyone changes throughout life. We change when we learn new things, when we meet new people, when we move to a new place."

"This is different."

"It's certainly more sudden."

"How long?"

"I hope to have the program ready within a month."

Only a month left, to live with the man he had fallen in love with. A month until Sudharma went away, and John had to nurse the stranger in his body back to health. There was nothing he could do or say, no point in trying to argue.

"I will be ready."

"You won't have to be. I have arranged for Marne to monitor my translation."

"Do you think I'm not capable?"

"I've seen your scores on the simulations. I know you could do it. But it will be easy for him, and for you it won't."

"You must think so, if you believe he can learn the job in only one month."

"I meant, I think that it would do you harm," Sudharma said gently. "I should have ended your involvement long ago. I had hoped you would reconcile yourself to the idea of translation, but obviously that has not happened. Marne has no such qualms."

"Please," John said. "Of all things, you can't go to him. I can't tell you why. But if I could, you would never consider it."

"Are you speaking of a lack of skill, or a problem with his motivations?"

Of course, Sudharma had some inkling of what Marne had done. That was how he was: he knew more than he was told, and said less than he knew. Would he still be like that after he translated? Or would he lose all his perceptiveness about the merely human?

"Bad motivation and defective conscience," John said. "But I can't tell you the details."

"I won't ask you to. But Marne has no reason to want me to fail. He wants a better deal for humans on this world, as we all do. And it won't trouble him to assist me. I should have made this change before—I am sorry that I did not."

"Do you think it's better for me, to know your mind is being altered, and not be allowed to help? To be shut out until that man tells me what happened? I don't understand why you're doing this—I never will. But I will save as much of who you are as possible. He doesn't know you, and he doesn't care about you, and he is a monster. Please. I beg you, let me help."

John had sat down at the table, taking Sudharma's hand; he looked into his eyes, offering his humiliation as a sacrifice. Sudharma looked away.

"If that's really what you want, then yes."

"I will be ready," John said again.

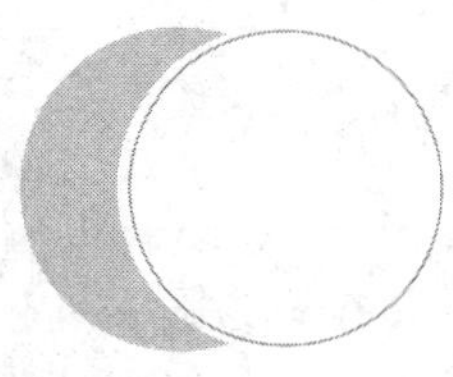

CHAPTER TWENTY-SIX

The shoots of scions were all dug out of the green flesh they were planted in and thrown down to die on the hot sand. The dead crop plants were pulled up and made into compost. Corn, alone of all the produce of the field, had been entirely spared; its form of growth, a spear with sheathing leaves, must have confused the scions. For this reason a late planting of it was sown anywhere the kernels might take root. A fence of wire mesh fine enough to stop a scion was raised all around the farm, and around every other field. Iren doubted the effectiveness of any of these measures. "We are fighting the last war," they said. "Scions are surely not the only arrow in their quiver. Some of the others will fly or jump.—Here, chop up these potatoes."

He was helping them try a soup recipe that, improbably, called for sunflower seeds. John was skeptical of this adulterant. But besides the potatoes, the soup would contain corn and onion and hot pepper, and Laura had been sent to barter for an early summer squash; all this was promising. Iren, as a cook, lacked vanity, and wouldn't be offended if he decided to pick the seeds out.

It should have been a pleasure to cook in company again, to be entertained by Iren's talk, to anticipate a meal with them and Laura. But the horror rushing toward him made the comfort cold. Sudharma had said he would have the program ready within a month. It had now been a month and a week. Any day now, the man that he still loved would change, would *be* changed. He would be the one to make it happen. He kept imagining Sudharma waking up and looking at him with a perfect lack of recognition. The only thing that could drive that thought from his mind was fear that Sudharma might never wake up at all.

"Have you seen your girlfriend lately?" Iren asked. "Not Ru. I mean the one with both arms and her own car."

"Not in the original flesh. She's been ranging farther away the last few months."

"Is that why you're spending so much time with Ru?"

There was a sharpness in their words, and he could guess why. Iren believed that Zhuyef favored jesses and would not admit it to himself, and that this was why he made himself a trial to them. Furthermore it explained his obsequiousness to Ru; since Iren was unavailable, another Northerner appealed to him as a substitute—especially since Ru and Iren had rather similar faces (so Iren said, and though John still thought that all Ischnurans were much alike, he could, he realized, see their point). John had found these claims incredible, since Zhuyef believed so firmly in jess celibacy, but Iren said that was the evidence that proved the case: men of his sort idealized chastity, even as they longed to be the lone exception to it. Whether this theory was true or not, Iren certainly believed it, and so was sensitive to the idea of Ru being treated as a second choice. John answered, therefore, simply and from the heart.

"I visit Ru because I like Ru. She's not a replacement for anyone else."

Iren examined him critically, their head tilted to one side, but then accepted his words as honest. "Good. I'm glad, then. She's just about a match for you, I think. And no one could better deserve what I gather are the considerable consolations of your embrace. But I didn't mean to question you about your love life, actually—I meant to ask a favor. I'd like another audience with the old woman who lives in the centipede. There's something that belongs to me that I've decided to take back."

"I'll say her name. I'm sure she'll come for that."

"I don't just mean that I want the capacity. I'm really going to have a baby. Do you think that's reckless?"

"I'm sure I don't know. But I'm happy for you."

"Laura is coming along to hold my hand. You should be there too, to tamp down the madness as best you can."

When Laura returned with the promised squash, yellow and crook-necked, in her hand, Iren put an arm around her waist and pulled her close. They didn't kiss her. "He's going to call Vo," they said softly. Laura's back was to John, so he couldn't see her face. He thought he saw some unease in her posture, but that might only have been a mislocation of the dread in his own heart.

Presently Scythia arrived; they were to dine with their mother, but would leave after the meal to sleep in the house where their father lived. Iren surveyed the stove and countertop and said, "There's going to be more dinner than the four of us can finish. I wonder if Ru would like a last-minute invitation. She usually eats late, so with any luck she has not started her own cooking yet. Unless, of course, any of you objects?"

John shrugged his acquiescence. There was nothing wrong with two visiting partners attending the same event separately. He might have worried that Ru would seek to demonstrate their closeness—as on the ships visiting partners made public displays, hardening the bonds between them in the heat of others' gazes—but Scythia's presence would prevent that; they were not to know Ru had taken a lover. And it was pleasant, after all, to see Ru sit down across from him, wearing a dress with one sleeve, its close cut making promises about her body that he knew well to be true. He complimented her in terms appropriate for a casual acquaintance who usually saw her in gardening clothes. She replied, "This dress was Iren's apology for sending Zhuyef to annoy me on the night you landed. I only hope they will do me a greater wrong soon—I want one with embroidery."

But when the meal began he found he could think of very little to say to her. The others' conversation faded in and out of his awareness. Everyone there could guess why he was quiet, probably even Scythia, but no one mentioned it or tried to draw him out. For that he was grateful.

When they had finished with the soup, Iren asked what everyone thought of the seeds. In truth he had barely noticed, but since Scythia and Laura and Ru all liked them, he murmured his agreement of their praise.

"It seems like a lot of work, though," Scythia said. "All that shelling."

"Oh, that is no trouble," Iren said. "There is a trick to it."

"What trick?"

"Invite John to dinner and get him do it."

Scythia laughed and took a forkful of their salad. There was a new confidence about them, John thought. When Laura talked about their life it seemed to be an endless stream of tribulations: they were estranged from Zandahean friends and scorned by two of their own brothers, and had been forbidden to take communion, Adzere having bowed to the insistence of his flock after their chest had been reshaped. The only thing that Scythia had complained about to him was that facial hair was growing only on their neck. John had gently reminded them of what the library said, that hair would come in slowly. Iren had informed them with exasperation that most boys their age could not grow good beards either.

Scythia left early for Elena's house, and the adults went to talk in the sitting room. He sat down in a single chair and Ru, without complaint or comment, took another. Laura and Iren sat close together on the sofa, and after some time Iren lay with their head in her lap.

"We have so much time together every day now," Iren said dreamily.

"Yes," Laura said. "So far our relationship has survived it."

Ru stood up and looked down on them indulgently. "You two look far too comfortable for niceties. Perhaps John and I could show each other out."

They closed the front door behind them and stopped on the porch. "How long have you known about Iren and Laura?" John asked.

"What do you mean?" Ru's eyes grew wide. "Surely there's nothing improper there? Iren is celibate. It's just a matter of convenience that they live together."

"Yes, of course. I meant nothing at all. I only wondered if Iren had told you they meant to move in, or if it came as a surprise—"

Ru laid a finger across his lips. "I've known since before Laura did. I was the one Iren agonized to for a week before every moment of boldness with her. I told them their chastity was so immaculate, a little thing like having sex could never stain it. That is my unaltered opinion." She left her finger where it was; the touch was like the flame of one small candle in the dark. "Tomorrow night?"

He nodded and she was gone. It was better for them not to walk through town together, so he sat down on the steps to wait awhile. He thought about Ru, the slight touch of her hand, the promise of a visit soon; but his thoughts kept circling back to Iren's words. *So much time together every day.* He had that with Sudharma, but he wouldn't for much longer. The approach of the translation date had poisoned everything, had made him dread to set foot in his own house. He would put it out of his mind and enjoy the little time that they had left. He would focus on cooking and cleaning, on the small rituals of their shared existence. He would make home good and calm. He felt warm; but the feeling fell away from him as soon as he stood up again. He walked around the house as far as the garden and then stopped. Putting his back toward the house's lights, he looked up at the scrambled stars, searching for anything that looked familiar, even a false friend.

Laura came out and stood beside him. She must have seen him through the kitchen window.

"Are you happy?" he asked her.

"Sometimes I manage to be. Mostly I'm terrified. It's too dangerous, we're asking for too much. But it's what Iren wants most. How can I be the one to tell them no?"

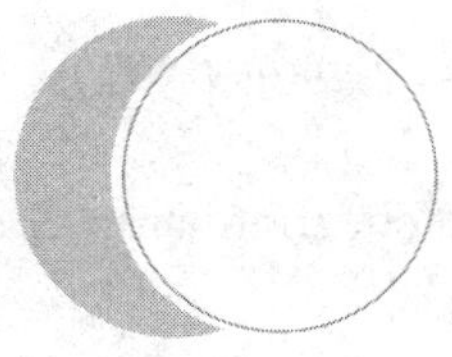

CHAPTER TWENTY-SEVEN

The crawler's blank face opened and engulfed them, raised them up and let them go. All this no longer seemed remarkable to him, but he could see the shock of it in Laura's expression. Her wide eyes stared around the long gray hall. Yet there was no strangeness for them to alight on—only a table and chairs, already raised from the floor, and cups of chocolate waiting for them on it. Iren took their *vidhu*'s hand and led her there. They both sat, leaving the chair beside Vo for John.

"Thank you for coming to see me," Iren said. "I know how hard it is to tear oneself away from fieldwork."

"It's no trouble. I needed to see John anyway."

"This is my—" Iren hesitated, and turned an apologetic look on Laura. I'm sorry. I so often have to speak of you in words that hide the truth that my tongue balked at introducing you in honest language. But there is no point in dissembling, is there? I suppose here I can say: this is Laura, my love."

"I know what *vidhu* means, if you like that better," Vo said, smiling; and John saw on Laura's face the same unease that he had felt when Vo used 'visit' with too deep an understanding. But she rallied enough to say:

"I don't mind about words. I just hope you can help Iren."

"What is it you want?"

The question seemed directed to both Laura and Iren indifferently, but it was Iren who answered. "First of all, that the scars blocking my fallopian tubes be removed."

"Done."

"And I want to be pregnant."

"Of course." Vo smiled and turned to Laura. "Would you like the sperm to be yours?"

"Now there's a question I thought I would get through this life without being asked."

"I *would* like that, very much," Iren said. "But the baby must be plausibly the child of two Ischnurans."

John had a horrible premonition that Vo might offer to alter the infant's appearance in utero; he laid a hand on her arm to forestall this outcome, but she was already speaking. "You have something else in mind."

"Kol and I discussed replacing my testis before we came here, so that they could father my children. It proved impossible to manage—we had to prepare and compete and be trained, I couldn't take time to recover from surgery. But you have their genome."

"Yes. Is there something you'd like to say or do, to mark the occasion?"

John was surprised; he had never suspected Vo of caring about ritual. Possibly, since the aiyi had abandoned her, the ways of ordinary humans had begun to make more sense. It seemed to him it was a thoughtful question. But Laura and Iren stared at each other as if they realized, on calling at a new mother's house, that they had failed to bring a birthing gift.

"My mind is as blank as a sheet of ice," Iren said.

"Medicine first, I think. We can make up some commemoration later if you want."

"You're only five days from ovulating naturally," Vo said. "I could change your testis to produce Kol's sperm, and you could inseminate yourself by visualizing in the usual way. That would give you time to think."

"Yes, please," Iren said with relief. "Let's do that."

When the procedure was complete, John drove them home, then returned to the crawler again. It had been more than a month since he last saw Vo and a pleasing urgency had built up in them both. After, she sat on the floor looking down at him. "Are you all right?"

"Yes," he said, and then, "No. But I don't want to talk about it. I just want to forget."

"Mm." She touched four fingers to his temple, then brought them around his ear in an arc, as if she traced the shape of something she could see inside him that, without the aiyi's help, she only dimly understood. "There's something I wanted to tell you while I'm with you in this body, but I don't know if I should now."

"What is it?"

"I've decided to engender aiyi."

It took John a moment to remember what that word 'engender' implied.

When he did, he felt as if the breath was being crushed out of him. "You mean you've decided to die."

"Yes, exactly."

He sat up and held her close, pressed the side of his face to hers, trying to comfort her. "You don't have to do this. The sadness will fade. You will reach acceptance."

"It's not like that." She gently pushed him away so she could look into his eyes. "I was happy with them, and I miss them, but now that I'm alone, I'm thinking about what I want for myself. I've lived a long time, and I want to try something else now. I want to experience the art I've been helping with—even make some of my own. I don't want to divide the world up into categories anymore, I want to *understand*. Or, at least, I want something a little like me to do those things."

John fought down the urge to beg her to remain alive. If she was making her own path, he must defer to her decision. But it was wrong, it was desperately unfair, that he should lose her and Sudharma both.

"We don't have to be apart," she said. "Not if you don't want to. You can have a connection with what I become. It wouldn't have to be as distracting as the one I had. Not many aiyi even want such close communication with a human brain. But something like me could be with you. We could even visit, if that's something we both still want—just in a different way. It could feel like it does now."

He could not help but be tempted. Now, of all times, when he was about to lose so much, he wanted to clutch at any scrap that might be left to him. But what she described was a haunting. As an aiyi she would see deeply inside him, would know exactly how he felt about her new state, bodiless and artificial. He could not be easy in such a love, he could not be kind in it.

"I'm sorry," he said. "It's too much for me. I can't follow you that far."

"All right." He could hear that she was disappointed. "But if you say my name, something might still come to help. There'll be a lot of me and I can't say how all of them will act."

"I understand," he said. He would be careful not to say the name. But then a thought occurred to him, and unwillingly he asked, "Will you be able to make starships?"

"I don't know. Even if I can, I might not want to. I mean . . . the aiyi chose to forbid ships from coming here. Their reasons for that will probably make sense to me. To what I become."

Of course, when she transformed, her mind and motivations would be made strange. He knew he had been right to refuse a connection with her; there would be no *her* left, only an assemblage of inhuman creatures that retained some of her memories.

"Anyhow," she said, "it won't be right away. There are things I want to experience first. Instead of using a human aide to see and feel the world, I'll do it myself and carry the memories into the next life. I think that will be interesting. It might take years to gather everything I need into myself, even decades. I won't be around much—I'll be exploring other continents. But when I'm ready to move on, may I ask one more time if you still want to be with me?"

"Yes," he said. He knew he wouldn't change his mind, but if she came to ask again then he would have a chance to say goodbye. He thought that otherwise she might forget.

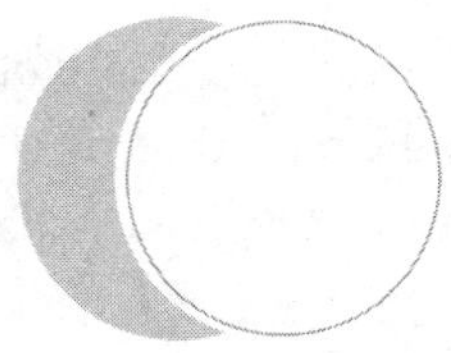

CHAPTER TWENTY-EIGHT

John rose from Ru's bed before dawn. She stirred in her sleep, but didn't wake; she was used to being left in the night, and knew in time he would come back to her. In the light of one crescent moon, he ran a half lap around town and arrived at his front door. The hobby of exercise made a convenient excuse: in the punishing heat of the summer, of course he would run in the cool of the early hours; in winter, he would say he braved the chill in order to have breakfast ready when Sudharma completed *pratikraman*.

But it was too early to start cooking when he got home. Sudharma could not eat before his procedure in any case, so John could have bent the rules, but he didn't feel like it. Now, of all times, he wanted normalcy. While he waited for sunrise, he cleaned the refrigerator, scrubbed out the sink, the toilet, and the tub, changed the cloth filter over the kitchen tap, and put the old one, along with all the sheets not currently in use, into the washing machine. These familiar tasks were soothing to him, and if—when—Sudharma returned, he would be able to recover in a clean house.

When the dawn lightened the window, he gathered the makings of breakfast for one. He ate and then stayed at the table, ignoring the dishes, listening to the sounds of recitation from Sudharma's room. Too soon, they ended, and then it was time to go.

"If you forget how to perform your ritual," John said, "is there a way I can help you remember?"

"Show me my book. It is in three languages—even if things go poorly, I should retain at least one. Other than that, you can only wait for me to come back to myself."

They walked together to Marne's clinic. Sudharma lay in a thin gown on a cold table. The little passengers inside his brain were programmed; John had only to administer the sedative, and when it took effect, they would begin their work. Sudharma would be conscious, able to answer questions if need be, but would remember nothing. If the procedure did not go too badly, John would bring him home the next day and care for him until he could care for himself.

He drew the drug out of its vial into a syringe, slipped the needle in, and hesitated. This too, he thought, was care. He knew that to be true, yet knowing couldn't stop the cold dread that was seeping into his own veins. It didn't matter. He had to go on.

"When you wake up, you'll be new," he said. He pushed the plunger home.

ACKNOWLEDGMENTS

Thanks to Patrick Nielsen Hayden, who gave me a chance when I was an unknown who had published nothing, then did it again after my very long absence from writing.

Thanks to Mal Frazier, whose deep understanding of the novel's aims and sharp eye for the ways in which it fell short made the book much better.

Thanks to my agent Lauren Bajek. Lauren scooped me up almost as soon as I poked my head out of my burrow, and I'm very glad she did.

Thanks to the small band of hardy volunteers who hacked their way through early versions of the book.

Thanks to everyone who helped keep the memory of my work alive—or at least, only mostly dead—during the decades when I wasn't writing and my only book was out of print. In this category Jo Walton and James Nicoll stand out, and I am deeply grateful.

Thanks, most of all, to my beloved partner and first reader, Pamela Dyer-Bennet. Without her love and support, this book might never have been written.

ABOUT THE AUTHOR

CAMERON REED is a science fiction writer and the winner of the 1998 Otherwise Award. Both she and the award had different names in 1998, but as part of a late-in-life gender transition she chose a new one, which is an anagram of "remade crone." She is an avid dragonfly-watcher, a moderately skilled insect photographer, and a hopeless birder. She lives with her found family in an old house full of books and cats.